The Savage On‹

CW00422034

A Brutal Tale Of Violent And
Bloody Revenge Set In The
Very Wild West Of The Late
1860s and Early Seventies.

This Book Is Dedicated
To The Memory Of
JOHN WAYNE.

This book is a work of fiction.
Names, characters, places and
incidents are products of the
author's imagination or are used in
a fictitious context.

The Copyright Belongs To The
Author.

Anthony John Copyright © 2022.

All Rights Reserved

anthonyjohn-thesavageones@outlook.com

Contents.

The Protagonists:

Johnny Hawkeye	Warrior / Scout / Adventurer
Clay Milton	Rancher / Government Agent / Adventurer
Shannon	Bounty Hunter
James Blue	Government Agent / Scout / Adventurer
Fernando Lopez	Mexican Bandit Chief
Rattlesnake Joe	Comanche Half Breed Outlaw
Clay McCandless	U.S. Marshall
General Antonio Gomez	Mexican Revolutionary Leader
Roberto Aguilar	Gunslinger For Hire
Rodrigo Lamas	Pistolero
Barton Lee	Town Sheriff
Virgo Séptimo	Mexican Bandit / Explosives Expert
Zachariah Smith	Mountain Man
Juan Lopez	Psychopathic Mexican Bandit
Colonel Jack Steele	Presidential Security Chief
Sally Kinross	Wife Of Cavalry Officer
Captain Bradley Kinross	U.S. Cavalry Officer
Colonel Jefferson Stard	U.S. Cavalry Officer
Jack Wilson	Outlaw
Major Kurt Schmidt	Ex-German Army Officer / Tactician
Black Eagle	Cheyenne Warrior
Josh Milton	Rancher
Jonas Gordon	Whisky Pedlar
Pete Nicholson	Stagecoach Driver
Strong Lance	Cheyenne Chief
Frank Lawson	Outlaw
Wild Bear	Comanche War Chief
Red Knife	Comanche Warrior
Sofia	Captured Mexican Girl

Chapter One:

He Who Sees As The Hawk.

The wagon train had ceased its seemingly endless snake like traversing of the vast prairie an hour earlier for the funeral. The frail young Dutch immigrant woman had finally succumbed to the fever that had ravaged her for the last four days.

A preacher said a prayer and uttered a few kind words over the hastily dug grave, meant to somewhat alleviate the pain and suffering of her now orphaned son. Her husband, the boy's stepfather looked on showing no sign of emotion. He was a cold callous man who regularly beat her and the boy. She had realised quite soon her mistake in marrying him but was fearful of his temper and violent ways and hadn't possessed the financial means or the courage to leave him. In contrast to the stony faced widower, Jan Van Holt, the young Dutch boy displayed a tearful countenance, sobbing uncontrollably until the grip of his stepfather on his shoulder made him wince in pain as he dragged the boy back to their wagon.

"We have to go, you can drive the wagon, and I'm going to get a drink and some sleep." Not a request or suggestion, a growled order. Jan did not respond verbally. He climbed into the back of the wagon, located her travelling bag, and took out a picture of his mother and his deceased father together in the city of their birth, Amsterdam. It was battered, fading, and tattered around the edges but it was the only one he had. The neanderthal like brute that was his stepfather entered behind him and tore it out of his grasp, tearing the fragile object in half and then half again.

"I told you to get up front and drive the wagon." He bellowed. Then he threw the remnants of the picture out of the rear flaps of the wagon and they fluttered speedily away in the wind.

All traces of fear and grief suddenly left the young face of Jan Van Holt, his eyes seemed to change, to darken. He grasped the barrel of the nearby rifle and slammed the weapon as hard as he could butt first into the face of his tormentor. He turned and climbed out of the wagon as blood jetted out of the almost flattened nose of the now facially damaged man, taking the gun with him. All thoughts and hopes of a prosperous future and a good life in sunny California, the land of opportunity planned by his adoring parents left Jan Van Holt that second.

Chief Strong Lance of the Cheyenne was a peace loving man at heart but after a particularly savage and brutal attack by the Cavalry on his village left his family and tribe decimated he reluctantly donned the war paint and gathered a war party together. The few survivors told of the atrocities committed by the merciless soldiers, of the rape and torture of women and girls. Some were too young to know what was happening to them before they were ruthlessly shot or bayonetted to death. Assuming the role of vengeful savage was necessary and the need for vengeance meant any white settlement or Cavalry troop was fair game. The wagon train below him was perfect for attack and he would not hesitate to give the order.

Jan was walking aimlessly away from his stepfather's wagon when the angry, brutal, wounded man almost fell out of the back, still pouring with blood from his lacerated face and waving an axe at the young boy in a most threatening fashion.

The first arrow hit the lumbering hulk in the chest, he hardly seemed to notice, the second one took him in the throat. He tried to cough, failed as death overwhelmed him and collapsed in a heap.

"Indians!" Someone shouted in alarm. "Take cover." The attacking Cheyenne warriors were suddenly all around them. Jan dived under the nearest wagon and held the rifle to his shoulder. Struggling to control his fear and his shaking limbs he aimed carefully and locking on to his target he squeezed the trigger. The warrior fell dead from his horse.

The young Dutch boy, Jan Van Holt, was ten years old and he'd killed his first man. He wounded or killed three more before the battle was over. The battle lasted only until the wagons were set on fire by flaming arrows and the travellers were easily picked off by the marauding Cheyenne avengers as they ran in panic to escape the flames.

The fighting had soon finished and unbelievably, Jan could see that he was somehow the only survivor. He thought he would surely be killed as he stood alone and walked defiantly towards the warriors, pointing his gun at the man he'd assumed was the chief. Six of the victorious braves aimed their bows or stolen rifles at him.

He pulled the trigger, and nothing happened. He was out of ammunition. The braves laughed at him as he turned the weapon around and prepared to use it as a club.

The chief waved at his men to lower their weapons and put his own bow down on the ground. He signalled to Jan to do the same. He spoke calmly to the frightened boy and smiled. Jan knew he had no choice but to do what he thought he was being told to. He did so, not for one moment taking his eye off the man in front of him. The chief said something quietly to him which he couldn't understand and patted his own chest. He repeated the action and spoke in English.

"Strong Lance!" He was telling Jan his name.

"Jan!" The boy replied, his voice shaking.

"John!" Strong lance mimicked what he thought he had heard, and John it was. The Cheyenne chief admired the young white boy's courage and let him live.

Strong Lance adopted the young survivor as his own child, his real son having been one of the victims of the slaughter for which the wagon train was wiped out in the retaliatory attack.

At first John was appalled by the perceived primitive life of an Indian tribe and tried to break away on several occasions from the camps. He never got far, Strong Lance or his braves always found him and brought him back.

With patience and understanding on the part of the Cheyenne chief the young white boy gradually found not only acceptance within the tribe, but also acceptance of them. He learned from his new father figure of the cruelty and the aggressive wars waged against his peoples by the invasive white man. He began to realise that regrettable though the attack on the wagon train was, the massacre was a tragic but inevitable consequence of the barbaric aggressions of the U.S. Cavalry. An additional, unescapable factor was the never ending flow of settlers into the once free and unclaimed lands.

The Cheyenne and other tribes did not understand the concept of owning land. How could a man own the land, it was here for all, a man would die, the earth would be forever. John learned to ride, fish, hunt and fight. He became fluent in the red man's languages, not only Cheyenne but Sioux with the dialect variations and others which would stand him in good stead for his future adventures. He was recognised as an excellent marksman with both rifle and bow, aided by his remarkable vision. He could see further and clearer than the best of Strong Lance's braves and earned the Indian name "He Who Sees As The Hawk."

Soon he was taking part in violent skirmishes, defending the tribe against the U.S. Cavalry when they attacked the Cheyenne camp. He always acquitted himself with honour and now that they accepted him, he was free, he could have escaped with ease if he had a mind to. He didn't.

One day, three years after his capture, Strong Lance and He Who Sees As The Hawk rode out of the camp. Thirteen years old now, and thinking like an Indian brave, the young boy wondered why he was not helping prepare to pack up the tepees and prepare for the tribe's move to new pastures the next day. Strong Lance took him to the brow of a hill and told him to look. In the distance he could see a white man's fort.

Strong Lance ordered him off his horse and removed the Cheyenne head dress and decorative beads and feathers from young John's neck. He tipped water over his head and wiped off the paint of a warrior from his face, arms and chest. He pointed to the fort.

"You are a man now, you are John, or you are He Who Sees As The Hawk. You cannot be both. You will decide for yourself, what is to be your destiny." Strong Lance stepped back away from the suddenly confused young man he'd grown to love as a father loves a son.

"They are your people, the whites. Go to them, I will not try and stop you." He added after a minute's silence. John still hadn't spoken a word.

Strong Lance turned and mounted his pony. Without a backward glance he rode slowly away, back towards the camp. He rode at a leisurely pace and spent

14

the time thinking about his life, his depleted family, the endless erosion of the Indian lands. And the desperation of his nation in the face of insurmountable odds, the unrelenting, invasive, unstoppable force of the white man. His meditations were interrupted after a while by the sound of an unshod horse galloping behind him, drawing closer. He turned to face the rider, rifle in hand. He relaxed at once and lowered his weapon. Once more resplendent in headdress, beaded necklace, and speeding towards him was his son, He Who Sees As The Hawk.

"Maybe one day Father. Not today." Was all the young brave said to Strong Lance.

By the time John was fifteen he had taken a wife. He'd fallen in love with Morning Cloud, the daughter of Strong Lance's cousin, Red Elk. Red Elk had wanted to kill the young Jan at the time of the attack on the wagon train but had grown to respect and eventually to accept He Who Sees As The Hawk as a worthy addition to the tribe. He welcomed him with genuine love as his daughter's husband and she adored the handsome young warrior. Black Eagle her brother treated He Who Sees As The Hawk as his own brother and they would go hunting together.

At eighteen years of age, and with a devoted wife and two young sons the young Cheyenne warrior was content. Peace was never assured with the white man but a recently signed treaty had not been broken as yet. Life was good.

It was while out hunting for deer with Black Eagle one morning that the two young braves heard the sound of gunfire in the distance, coming from the direction of the Indian village. Armed only with bows, arrows and hunting knives they set off to investigate as fast as their mounts could carry them. They had no expectation of an attack by the Cavalry, a kind of uneasy peace was maintained at present between the white and red man because of the treaty. The Cheyenne scouts kept the fort under constant surveillance and had not reported any current or imminent threat for several months.

As they drew closer to the village the shooting subsided, and plumes of black smoke could be seen rising up into the sky. Fearing the worst the two warriors urged their mounts to go even faster. Eventually they reached the top of a hill where they could look down and see what was happening.

The tepees were all on fire bar one, six white men were busy bending over the twenty or so bodies of Cheyenne women, children and old men. The young men, as He Who Sees As The Hawk and Black Eagle had been, were out hunting or scouting. The scouts posted to the very hill where they stood were laying at the foot of it. Not only had they been killed, the bloody tops of both heads told all that their hair had been taken.

"Scalp hunters!" Black Eagle exclaimed and prompted his horse to begin the descent towards the desecrated scene in front of him.

"Morning Cloud! My sons!" He Who Sees As The Hawk cried in anguish and followed, reaching for his bow and his arrows as he did so. They managed to get just within range and shoot before they were spotted. Two of the raiders fell, an arrow sticking out of each chest. The four other men raised their rifles and fired at the vengeful warriors, diving for cover as they did so. Black Eagle fell holding his shoulder, blood pouring from it. He Who Sees As The Hawk could see one of the men closing in on his wounded friend, knife drawn. He drew his own knife from his belt and threw it, the man dropped to the ground, clutching at his neck. It didn't do him any good, the blood spurted violently out of the red gash and within a few seconds stopped as did the man's heart.

Turning his attention to the other killers he loosed off another arrow, this one hit a very tall assailant in his stomach. The man writhed in agony on the ground where he fell. That left two, no, wait, there was another man coming out of the only tepee still standing. The man stood holding three blood soaked clumps of jet black hair. He was not quite white, not quite red, a half breed. His head was shaved at the sides leaving a dark strip of hair down the centre and growing into a pony tail at the back, Comanche style. A vivid red scar ran from the outer corner of his left eye to the side of his mouth. Fear gripped the young warrior for the first time since the wagon train massacre. The tepee was that of He Who Sees As The Hawk. This time the fear was not for himself but for his cherished family. He knew if he stood up he would be a target but his rage was overwhelming. The desire for vengeance proved too strong and he rose up swiftly, fired off an arrow at the scalp holding killer and leapt sideways, trying to dodge the inevitable bullets from the man's cohorts.

Two shots rang out, one caught him in his left arm, just below the shoulder and the other screamed by his left ear. He could feel the heat but was grateful to still be alive. He needed to live until the Comanche half breed was dead.

Whooping and hollering could suddenly be heard in the distance and realising other hunters were returning to investigate the smoke and gunfire, the three remaining raiders ran to their tethered horses. They would have to escape the retribution that they would surely face if caught. One of them didn't make it as He Who Sees As The Hawk struggling against the pain in his arm managed to shoot one last arrow striking his target fatally in the middle of his back. The other two didn't even look back at their fallen comrade and whipped their mounts until they were speeding away from the scene of the carnage.

He noticed the man who'd been in his marital home had part of an arrow sticking out of his right lower leg and had been limping quite badly, he hadn't missed completely in his anger. He rushed into his tepee and was immediately confronted by a sight he would never ever be able to forget.

Morning Cloud lay dead, she was naked and covered in blood. He knew at a glance she'd been sexually violated, beaten savagely and had her throat cut before being scalped. His two young sons lay beside their mother, butchered and scalped by the murderous scar faced half breed. He walked out of his tepee for what was to be the last time.

The other returning hunters had arrived and were in the process of finding the mutilated bodies of their own wives and children. The old men who'd remained in the village had also met gruesome deaths, slaughtered and scalped. Their hair would soon decorate the white man's homes, saloons and forts, after earning the vicious scalp hunters a generous payment.

Among the victims of the atrocities were Strong Lance and his cousin Red Elk. Black Eagle was beside himself with grief and anger. He was not alone in his mourning, or his thirst for vengeance. Ignoring the pain of their wounds He Who Sees As The Hawk and Black Eagle set off with the others to chase the escaping murderers. Two warriors stayed to prepare the funeral scaffolds.

On the way to reclaim his horse He Who Sees As The Hawk passed the tall man with an arrow in his stomach, he was still alive, plainly not for long, but still squirming in his suffering. The bereaved young warrior stared coldly into the pleading eyes, roughly removed the barbed projectile causing more excruciating agony for the fallen scalp hunter and blood to flow freely from the wound. He held on to the arrow, moving the point a few inches to one side and then ferociously stabbed it back into the stricken man. He used so much force it pinned the dying body to the ground.

"You will die, but slowly and in pain." He spoke in English for the first time in years.

It took the braves four hours to be within sight of the two fugitives. Safety could only be found for them in the white man's fort and that was plainly the destination they had in mind.

An open space surrounded the fortified battlements and the scalp hunters raced as fast as their horses would carry them towards the gates. Six of the braves were gaining on them, including He Who Sees As The Hawk and Black Eagle. The latter painfully raising his bow before the soldiers could see a group of Indians chasing what looked like two white men and open fire on them. The Comanche half breed now hid his Indian style hair and pony tail under a bowler hat as he always tended to do when moving in the white man's world.

Black Eagle had time to shoot one arrow as the troopers started firing at them. The nearest of the scalp hunters fell, the arrow sticking out of the back of his neck. The leading man, the scarred man with an arrow in his leg made it to the now open gates and vanished inside the sanctity of the fort. He Who Sees As The Hawk, Black Eagle and the others retreated out of range. Leaving two scouts to keep watch, the remainder of the Cheyenne hunters made their way back to the remnants of the village.

Sitting while having his wound tended by another of the braves Black Eagle voiced his question.

"How could white men surprise Cheyenne scouts, and kill two of us without being seen or heard?"

"They were not all white men. The leader, the one who hides in the white man's fort is of two bloods." He Who Sees As The Hawk told them all quietly. "He has shaved his head but he is part red man, he has the look of Comanche. He has a face I will remember. A scar here." He drew a finger down the left hand side of his face. "He will move in the white man's world but he will not fit, they will call him half breed. He will never be one of them just as he is not one of us."

"You are a white man but you are one of us." Black Eagle reminded him.

"Yes, I have thought of nothing else on the journey from the fort." He Who Sees As The Hawk continued. "My father, Strong Lance took me to see the white man's fort forty moons past and told me I could be John, or I could be He Who Sees As The Hawk. I was not John anymore."

"We will hunt the half breed down, he cannot run further than we can follow him." Black Eagle was as determined as his murdered sister's husband to inflict a terrible revenge on the savage scalp hunter. The others wanted to meet up with other branches of the tribe to try and assemble a large number of warriors for the pursuit. He Who Sees As The Hawk and Black eagle

21

decided two warriors on their own would stand a better chance of success and made plans accordingly.

The next morning, early, the two of them slipped away from the others and set out back to the fort. The scouts met them on the trail to report the man with the limp was gone.

He'd left in the company of a troop of cavalry soldiers heading south east. Silently, filled with the numbing sense of grief, desperation and the irresistible desire for revenge the two braves followed after the troop until a small stream attracted the attention of He Who Sees As The Hawk.

He beckoned his brother to join him as he dismounted nearby. Removing his head dress he immersed himself in the water and washed off all his Cheyenne markings. He emerged looking every inch a suntanned white man. He pulled his long hair together at the back of his head and hacked off a substantial length of the dark mane with his knife, leaving it hanging loose at his shoulders.

"My brother. It is time for me to be John again. I will find the half breed and I will take our revenge. Go back to our people. See that Morning Cloud and my sons are prepared for the afterlife for me. Live as a proud Cheyenne warrior, they are in need of a chief, a great leader." The look of shock and astonishment on Black Eagle's face was another vision that would remain with John for the rest of his life. Silence filled the whole area for what seemed like an hour but was actually less than a minute. Black Eagle eventually nodded, he could not hope to move freely in the white man's town and John could. He himself would be more of a burden than a help.

"I will wait with our people." He said at length. "You will return?" He took a large Eagle's feather from his head dress and handed it to He Who Sees As The Hawk, John, his brother. "Keep this with you, bring it back to me when you have fulfilled your task. You will always be my brother.

"I will not return until the killer of our people is dead." And he added with a humourless laugh. "Or if I am killed in the hunt."

"Goodbye He Who Sees As The Hawk." Said Black eagle as he turned to his horse.

"Keep this for me until I return." Said John passing him his beaded necklace.

"Goodbye Black Eagle, my brother."

Chapter Two:

The Battle Of Santo Juanita.

The old Mountain Man had travelled a long way from the northern Rockies to the rough and rowdy border town of Santo Juanita. The town was named after the favourite daughter of a long forgotten Mexican land owner who had founded the original settlement.

Zachariah Smith would never have left his beloved mountains by choice but vengeance is a strong force, it propels men to do extraordinary things in order to achieve it. He was searching for a man he knew as Rattlesnake Joe, a half breed Comanche renegade, a gun runner, scalp hunter, whisky pedlar and a myriad of other unsavoury appellations. There were many such men throughout the west, indeed, throughout the whole world. But not all of them had killed, raped and scalped his Dakota Sioux wife and daughter. Zachariah had been appointed as a Deputy Marshall in earlier times but he had not journeyed all this way, all those thousands of miles, to arrest the man.

Two long years the old man had been trailing Rattlesnake Joe. His age was sixty nine as close as he could guess, ancient for a man in his profession. The Sheriff in the last town he'd visited had pointed him to Santo Juanita. The description of the hunted killer fitted a man who'd been involved in a bar brawl only days before Zachariah got there. The Sheriff had run him out of town.

The Mountain Man selected the noisiest, busiest saloon he could find, the choice was limited to three so it didn't take him too long to decide. He bought a beer, chose a table in the corner and prepared himself to wait for as long as it took.

Rattlesnake Joe was a man for whom the word evil could have been coined. Born of the forced union between a Comanche warrior and an unwilling captive white woman, he fitted nowhere but managed to find a way to co-exist with both white and red men. He operated beyond the perimeters of civilised society. He would sell scalps from murdered Indians to the white man, stolen guns and liquor to the red man. He had no regular gang, picking up gun hands and strong arm men whenever he needed them. There was always someone he could treat as a dispensable commodity, down on their luck drifters who would agree to work outside the law for money. Four such men were with him now, as he entered the roisterous saloon at the end of the street. Three white men, two still wearing grey jackets from the rebel army of the defeated south two years on, a third in a ragged leather coat and dirty black jeans, and a Mexican, looking like the caricature of the bandit he probably was, sombrero, crossed ammunition belts and all. This quartet of very hard men made up Rattlesnake Joe's current gang.

Zachariah Smith watched his prey strolling casually to the bar with his associates. A few miles further north he thought Rattlesnake Joe wouldn't even be allowed in a saloon let alone get served. Be that as it may, the population of border towns harboured such a vast range of races, creeds and colours, but cash didn't discriminate and nor did Santo Juanita. His eyes weren't as good as they had once been but he would never be able to forget the face of such a man, even in the hazy, smoke filled atmosphere of a small town saloon. He swallowed the remnants of his fifth beer in one gulp. He was prepared to accept it may have been his last. He was liable to be killed in his attempt to execute the monster who'd slaughtered and defiled his family. Rattlesnake Joe had to die, whatever the price Zachariah Smith had to pay. The old man's hand slowly reached for his gun.

The cavalry and the scalp hunter had gone their separate ways after half a day. The tracks told John that an unshod horse had broken away from the main party of riders and headed towards Texas. The warrior continued to track his quarry for days which soon stretched into weeks, without a clear view of anything but dust in the distance.

His journey was interrupted five days into Texas when he came across a wagon, broken down on the trail he was following. The family consisted of a man, his extremely pregnant wife and a young toddler. Unable, because of her condition, to help her husband lift the wagon and replace a wheel which had come off, the woman could only watch helplessly as the man tried in

26

vain to get the job done. John could remember again, another wagon, another lifetime. He rode down to help, it wouldn't take too long and he could see they needed to get to a town soon, before the imminent birth. At first they were frightened of the strange young newcomer in Indian leggings and riding an unshod pony. The husband understandably reached for his rifle and stood protectively in front of his family as John approached.

"I can help." John said. "I mean you no harm." The man hesitated, he needed help but who was the rider on the Indian pony? Could he trust him?

"If I meant you harm I could have killed you before you knew I existed." John smiled and patted his rifle. Something in the manner of the young man reassured the husband and he lowered his weapon.

The husband's name was Perry Howard, his wife was Emily June. He was a Doctor and he and his family were travelling to a town called Stoney Valley where he would take up the position of town Doctor upon the forthcoming retirement of the current holder of the job.

Within two hours the wagon was ready to continue towards the nearest town and John, the grateful recipient of a freshly cooked breakfast prepared to leave

"Wait, John, take these." Emily June handed him a pair of jeans, a blue shirt and a pair of boots. "If you go into a town or meet people on the trail, these will make things easier for you." They were her husband's clothes, he was tall, around the same size as John.

"I cannot pay you." The warrior told her.

"You already have, thank you for your help John, and wherever you're going, good luck." Her husband added. The clothes although not perfect were an adequate fit and thanking them again he bid them goodbye. He was now to all intents and purposes, a white man.

Three miles outside the little town of Santo Juanita his tracking skills informed him that the scalp hunter's pony was traveling towards the town. It had taken much hard traveling and many long weeks but he could sense retribution was at last within his reach. He didn't realise it at the time but he would be nineteen years old the next day.

John came unnoticed, under the cover of darkness, into the little settlement that was Santo Juanita. He tied his horse to a rail outside the first store front he passed and progressed on foot. The only two streets crossed at one point, the crossroads serving as the centre of town. He wandered unobtrusively down the busiest of the four options and stopped outside a busy, booming, clamorous saloon. The unshod pony tethered out front was all he needed to see. The scar faced, murderous half breed was inside. He'd finally tracked him down. What to do next? The only weapons he had brought into the town centre were his knife and his rifle, he didn't as yet possess a pistol. He held his rifle ready for instant action if required, and peered through the window.

Zachariah Smith stood up, aimed his pistol at the chest of Rattlesnake Joe and pulled the trigger. The noise of his chair legs being scraped on the floor only attracted the attention of one man, his intended target. The natural instincts for self-preservation were inbuilt and in less than a second the renegade scalp hunter recognised the old man and understood his intent. In the time it took to think about it he'd pulled the nearest of his recently hired gunmen, one of the grey coats, in front of him as cover. The bullet hit the man in the chest, killing him instantly.

Zachariah could not believe what had happened and before he could collect his beer befuddled thoughts the Mexican fired at him. The front of his leg suddenly turned red and he began to fall. Rattlesnake Joe's fast following second shot missed by a fraction of an inch as the old man hit the floor and rolled agonisingly behind his now fallen table trying to focus well enough to aim at the scar faced target of his mission. The three hired guns advanced on the wounded Mountain Man before he could bring his weapon to bear on any of them. The Mexican grinned evilly at him, exposing a mouthful of blackened teeth and he kicked Zachariah's gun out of his hand.

"Kill the old fool." Rattlesnake Joe rasped angrily at his subordinates, and that is what would have happened but…

Zachariah Smith prepared to die and closed his eyes as the Mexican moved closer and pointed his pistol at the old man's head. The gunman didn't feel the disturbance in the cloudy, unventilated atmosphere as the knife flew viciously from John's hand to embed itself deep into the back of his skull. Two shots were fired almost together and Rattlesnake Joe's remaining entourage perished without even having enough time to turn and see their killer. The first Zachariah knew of his salvation was the heavy crashing of the dead Mexican onto his wounded body. The man's final foul smelling breath penetrated his nostrils causing him to retch in disgust. It pleasantly surprised him that he was still in a position to be able to do so.

Rattlesnake Joe had no inkling of who or what John was. He had many, many enemies, but he could tell at once that the young killer was a formidable opponent and might not be alone. He fired his gun randomly in the general direction of the new arrival and threw himself through the nearest window during the ensuing confusion. His reflex action shattering the frame and glass alike and leaving two more wounded and several diving anywhere for cover. John found he could not get past the panicking human obstructions to chase the fleeing renegade. He changed direction and rushed out of the front entrance just in time to see Rattlesnake Joe, on a stolen horse, disappearing on the east road out of town. He took note of an unusual, conspicuous hoof print left by the speeding animal.

John returned to check on the injured Mountain Man, standing aside as people streamed out of the door to let them pass. He wanted to see if the old man was going to be okay. He might be able to get some useful information out of him and find out why they were hunting the same man. Zachariah was unconscious by the time he reached him.

"The Doctor's on his way, young feller. Your pa will be okay. It's just a flesh wound." A middle aged man holding a case of whisky samples was crouched over the wounded Mountain Man.

"We saw what happened. What the hell was he thinking? Going up against Rattlesnake Joe." The bartender had joined them, the bar was emptying fast as the Sheriff had been informed of the incident and would be on his way to investigate.

"Rattlesnake Joe?" John asked.

"The man with the scar, the one who smashed my window. He's a bad one." Now the young hunter had a name for his enemy. Rattlesnake Joe. He would not forget it.

The Doctor duly arrived and bound the wounded leg of Zachariah Smith who was now wide awake. The Sheriff entered the room ten minutes later, having forced himself to leave the bed of his favourite prostitute to attend.

Sheriff Bert Jackson was a strong personality and upheld his own version of the law with an iron fist. Santo Juanita harboured many fugitives from the law, bandits, killers, rustlers, he didn't care as long as he was well rewarded for turning a blind eye. Rattlesnake Joe was among the people who paid Jackson a tariff for being allowed to stay undisturbed in his town. The events were reported to the Sheriff by the barman and the grey haired, middle aged man, embellished somewhat to show John and Zachariah in a good light.

Rattlesnake Joe was well known and well despised in equal measures. Jackson possessed a wanted poster of the renegade scalp hunter in his office, it had been around for several years but the reward offered for his capture, dead or alive could still be seen quite clearly even if out of date. $4,000. A huge amount of money in the west of the late 1860s. Jackson never put himself at risk by trying to collect the bounties offered on his posters. His regular and substantial income would be under threat if sanctuary from the law was not guaranteed, not to mention his life. The town was certainly rambunctious but most of the citizens were safe most of the time and a kind of reciprocal order was maintained.

With no grounds he could be bothered to invent casting doubts on the words of many witnesses, to arrest and charge the old man and his young saviour, Jackson ordered them both out of town. The young man had no money on him and the old man had less than five dollars, not worth the effort of even a fine. They had until noon the next day. The Doctor arranged for them to share a room at the town's only hotel and Zachariah happily paid for the both of them, depleting his purse substantially to stable the two horses at the same time.

The strange young man who'd saved his life helped the injured Mountain Man across the road and up the hotel's creaky staircase. They slept the sleep of the weary and awoke early, they would hunt Rattlesnake Joe together.

By the time the sun had completely banished the moon from the sky Santo Juanita could only be seen by looking backwards. Something neither of the traveling companions had an inclination to do.

Chapter Three:

The "L" Shaped Saloon.

The "Double Dollar Saloon was "L" shaped with a well-stocked bar occupying the whole length of one side. At the wide end of the room was a small stage, fronted by an out of tune piano. An old man without a hair on his head sat playing a barely recognisable version of "Clementine" hoping someone would reward him with whisky. Occasionally a visiting cowboy would take pity on the old man and buy him a drink on condition that he'd stop making such an unpleasant noise.

Callahan was at a table playing poker with three other men. All of them had seen better days. Time and prison had battered their minds and bodies into an acceptance of their lot. Being infamous outlaws brought as many dangers as it did riches. The banks, stage coach companies and latterly the railroads had hired their own well-armed agents to fortify themselves against bandits such as Callahan and his small band of cohorts. Forced to run and hide from the law they moved from the cities to the smaller, less protected towns where pickings were easier and less likely to attract the attention of any posse or bounty hunter. Most perhaps, but not all.

Callahan was a big man, six feet four inches tall and weighed two hundred and ninety pounds, a fair amount of his bulk was muscle. His barrel chest sported tuffs of thick black hair matching the straggly unwashed rat tails that hung greasily from his massive head. Staring out through week old stubble were whisky painted red rimmed eyes, glowering disappointedly at the cards in his hand. The only clean thing about the man was the well-used sixgun in the worn holster strapped to his right leg. Sitting between the discordant pianist and the bar Callahan could see both the stage to one side of him and the large double swing doors to the other.

The saloon was filling up as the evening closed in on the town. The incompetent pianist began attempting to play a dancing tune as three dancing girls appeared on the stage to kick their legs high in the air to a less than rhythmic, and even less melodic rendition of a song they couldn't recognise from its current rendition. It didn't matter too much to the attendant trail weary cowboys and itinerant drifters who frequented the "Double Dollar", they came to see the dancers not the dance. Callahan was no exception, he threw his cards down signalling the end of the game and concentrated on the stage. He stared with ill-concealed lust as more female flesh became exposed.

"Senor Callahan." The young Mexican boy repeated, Callahan had not heard him the first time, he was so engrossed in his lecherous imaginings. He did hear him the second time, turning swiftly, hand reaching for his gun until he saw the young boy.

"What is it, Boy? What do you want?" He growled.

"Senor." The boy looked nervous as he handed the outlaw a piece of rolled up newspaper. "The man said you would give me a dollar."

"What man? What is this?" He squinted at the newsprint, Callahan couldn't read.

"He said you would give me a dollar." The boy reminded him. The big man looked angry, he was missing the show. He scowled an obscenity at the young Mexican and ungraciously threw him a dime.

"Here. That's all you're getting." The disappointed boy walked sullenly away. Callahan unrolled the sheet of newspaper, curious to see what it contained. A look of confusion spread all over his grimy features as he found himself looking at a "Wanted" poster, the face on view bore a reasonable artist's likeness to the man now holding it. The name printed underneath it was unmistakable, "Michael Callahan." At the bottom he could make out the faded legendary promise of reward. "$2,000. Dead or Alive." Illiterate or not Callahan understood the meaning.

"Who gave you this, Boy?" He bellowed, but the boy had gone. The reply came from elsewhere. The voice was cold, detached from any emotion, and as sharp as a well-honed Bowie knife.

"I did." It said. Behind the voice, Callahan saw a man, he was standing just in front of the still swinging doors. The new arrival stood around six feet tall, slim, and dressed from the Stetson on his head to the boots on his feet, completely in black. His hair, reaching to his shoulders matched the colour of his clothes. The stranger's piercing stare penetrated deep into Callahan. He found it impossible to return such a glare, the man's eyes, black as coals appeared to be inviting him to hell. Women would have found the man in black attractive, not pretty or handsome, not ugly, but dangerous. Callahan did not find him attractive at all. He was not a coward but fear gripped him now, he noticed the pistol low on the black clad hip in front of him.

"What do you want Mister?" He didn't mean to sound so timid. The piano player at last took pity on his long suffering audience and stopped torturing everyone's ears. The dancing girls, sensing violence was to come, ran off the stage and the saloon's clientele moved away from the immediate vicinity of the outlaw to seek cover. The stranger positioned himself with his back to a wall, allowing the doors to swing again as people chose to leave. Callahan and his three poker playing gang members remained seated.

"I said, what do you want Mister? I don't know you." Callahan sounded stronger now.

"I know you, Callahan." The voice was colder than before. "Dead or alive the poster says. I'm easy whichever. Your choice."

"Dead or alive?" The wanted man regained some of his bluster. "There are four of us, I only see one of you."

"I've got six bullets, Callahan. I won't need them all." The icy response. Not a boast, a fact.

"Get him!" Callahan spat the words to his cohorts in the same movement as upending the table, his hand lunging for his pistol.

Even as he shouted he knew he was going to die. Indeed, that very fact entered his mind at the same second a bullet entered his heart. His hand changed direction from his gun to the hole in his chest and made a vain effort to stem the blood pumping vigorously through his splayed fingers. Before his last breath had faded into the smoky atmosphere he was joined on the floor by his lawless companions. They had all reached for their guns, only one of them made it. He died first. Two shots later all four of them were dead, tangled up with fallen, broken, tables and chairs, and blood, lots of blood, their own. The stranger had used four bullets.

The man in black walked casually over to his fallen prey and examined their faces, a look of disgust formed on his face as he realised only Callahan was worth a reward. He picked up the table and some of the cash that had comprised the poker pot. He called to the barman who reappeared from under the bar, he threw the money onto the table.

"For the damage." He said, then he hoisted the corpse of the huge Callahan onto his shoulder and walked out of the saloon. The local Sheriff was on the point of entering to investigate the shootings.

"You owe me $2,000 Sheriff." He told him and briefly explained the events that had taken place, the barman nodded in agreement.

"We don't have that sort of money in the Sheriff's office, you'll have to come back tomorrow morning." The Sheriff answered in a distinctly unfriendly manner.

"Fine with me, Sheriff." The bounty hunter was unfazed. "I'm staying in the hotel tonight, I'll drop by in the morning."

"Hey Mister." The voice was female. The stranger turned to see one of the dancing girls, she was smiling at him. "Do you want to by a girl a drink?" she laughed. She was a very pretty girl and he'd been a long time on the trail. Was that the hint of a smile on his face, she wondered?

"I'll be back in a minute." He answered her and left the saloon carrying the corpse of Michael Callahan to the Sheriff's office, keenly relinquishing custody to a distinctly unappreciative custodian.

The young Mexican Boy was loitering outside the saloon wondering whether he had the courage to approach the man in black and complain that Callahan had only given him a dime. The bounty hunter didn't need to be told, as he passed by on his way to the sheriff's office he tossed a coin for the boy to catch.

"Here's the dollar I promised you." The voice was a little lighter now.

"Gracias Senór. The boy, happy now, ran home to show his mother the fruits of his labour.

The man in black counted the $2,000 and signed the receipt. The unfriendly Sheriff took note of the name.

"We don't like your kind, bounty killers, in this town, Shannon." He told him bluntly.

"Well if you did your job, Sheriff, you wouldn't have my kind in your town." An equally frank retort. The stranger walked to the rail, pausing only to remove another poster from the "Wanted" board. He unhitched his pure white stallion and rode steadily out of town.

Chapter Four:

The Road To Hawksville.

The trail left by Rattlesnake Joe was not an easy one to follow, the mount he'd stolen had been shod as had most of the horses he could have chosen. Had he ridden the unshod pony John had tracked for weeks it would have been simpler. The only identifying mark was a slightly uneven nail pattern in the front right horseshoe which would sometimes leave a faint trace depending on the surface of the terrain over which the fugitive was traveling.

Zachariah Smith was first to speak after a lengthy silence.

"I never thanked you properly for saving my life son. What made you help me?"

"I was hunting the half breed, the one called Rattlesnake Joe."

"So was I Boy." Zachariah told him bitterly remembering why. He related his reasons for wanting to kill the renegade and then asked the younger man. "Why do you want him? What is he to you?"

"I am going to find him and kill him slowly. He and his men attacked my people, he slaughtered my wife, my children, my father, my village. The men who were with him are dead, he is the only one left and I will not stop until he is no more." John explained.

"I knew you were an Indian, Cheyenne?" the old man had been around the Indian tribes for most of his life and knew instinctively that John was at one with their ways. The white Indian nodded in affirmation.

"I lived with Strong Lance and our people for eight summers. Strong Lance made me his son and I will honour his spirit with vengeance, Rattlesnake Joe will pay for his evil ways."

"What is your name, Boy? John what?" The old man wanted to know.

"Just John, my given name means nothing to me now, I cannot be that person."

"What is your Cheyenne name?"

"Strong Lance named me "He Who Sees As The Hawk." John would never be that person again either.

"Hell Boy, that's one hell of a mouthful. You can't use that in the white man's world. I know, I'm gonna call you Johnny, Johnny Hawkeye. That suits you, yeah?" The old man had just named one of the west's most revered heroes although he didn't know it yet.

Johnny Hawkeye and Zachariah Smith stayed riding together searching for signs of the elusive Rattlesnake Joe for months. The Mountain Man's leg healed but still gave him aches and pains, he put it down to the price of being allowed to grow old. Moving from town to town following tracks when they could, hunches when they couldn't, the hunt went on. With every day and every town Johnny became more used to and immersed in the white man's ways and culture. He listened to the old man's tales of life in the Rockies and his adventures, real and imagined, as a young man in the early days of the west, when it was truly wild and untamed in the purest sense of the word.

Endless miles they travelled, town after town after town they visited. Occasionally they would meet trouble and have to deal with it, violence and danger had always been a part of their lives and was met with whatever action was required to survive and move on.

Each escapade served to enlarge the embryonic legend of the young adventurer as his exploits became more widely known and exaggerated. Zachariah Smith was guilty of such overstatements concerning his young companion's heroic achievements on occasion, usually whilst partaking of a glass or two too many of the local whiskies. Johnny Hawkeye was becoming a name spoken of in the same context as the famous heroes of the west, Wild Bill Hickok, Buffalo Bill, Kit Carson, Davy Crocket, and Jesse James to name but a few.

Mason looked to the two man hunters just like Santo Juanita or any other of the dozens of scattered ramshackle tiny settlements of their acquaintance since they joined together in the search for Rattlesnake Joe. It was named as were many places in the West, after the man who founded the town. Jake Mason was an old man nowadays and spent his time drinking whisky and playing cards in his own saloon. The population were accepting of their subjugation in the past as Jake had always ensured peace and affluence for everyone.

Things had changed recently however, the prosperity was only distributed away from them under a new dictatorship. Jake Mason's son, Bubba ran the town now, he had assumed the roles of Sheriff, Mayor, and Judge and in most cases Jury. Sometimes if he was so inclined, he would be the Hangman as well. He ruled through fear, with the help of a band of tough brawling men, handy with guns, knives and fists. Order was strongly enforced according to the whims and dictates of the brutal, bullying Bubba.

Johnny Hawkeye and Zachariah Smith rode unknowingly into the centre of town under watchful eyes, not many strangers entered willingly into Mason these days. There had been only one in the last week. They stopped outside the saloon and walked in. Johnny had seen the tell-tale sign of the unique hoof print on the trail and it pointed them to town. He spotted it again outside the saloon, it belonged to a grey mare tethered to the rail. Johnny was gambling that Rattlesnake Joe would react to seeing the old man and that would give him a second's advantage. That would be all he needed to end the long arduous quest for revenge. There was no sign of their quarry, just two men at the bar and a few playing poker at one of the tables. It was early in the day for a full house, except perhaps in a game of five card stud.

"The grey mare, who's is it?" Johnny asked quite loudly and attracted everyone's attention.

"Who wants to know?" A surly response from a tall fat man who turned from the bar to face the young inquisitor.

"I do." Johnny was unfazed at the aggressive attitude and stepped forward, deliberately invading the man's personal space. "I asked you a question." He spoke quietly this time.

"You'd best tell him." Zachariah spoke up. "He asked you politely."

"A wet behind the ears kid and an old man." The big man uttered trying to supress a laugh. "Do you know who owns this town?" He would've said more but the sudden pressure of a knife blade at his throat changed his mind.

"I don't care who owns the town Fat Man, I want to know who owns the horse." Johnny's voice was harder now.

"I own the horse son, let him go. I own the town as well. My name is Jake Mason." The voice sounded old but firm and came from one of the occupied tables. "Let him go and come and sit with me." The town's patriarch ushered his companions away and motioned Johnny and Zachariah to sit. Johnny lowered the knife and watched warily as the big man scuttled as fast as his now shaking legs would carry him, out of the swing doors. The old Mountain Man and the young hunter did as Mason had told them, Johnny making sure his back was against a wall and he could see if anyone came into the saloon.

"Where did you get it?" Zachariah asked the town boss.

"I won it at poker, from a Comanche half breed."

"Rattlesnake Joe." Zachariah stated.

"Where is he now?" Johnny asked him.

"I don't know, we've got men out looking for him, he stole my son's horse, his prize black stallion and rode off to the south in a hurry, probably in Mexico by now. But Bubba will get him."

"Bubba?"

"My son, the Sheriff." Jake Mason explained. "He runs this town for me."

"That's me, Kid, now drop your weapons and stand up." The booming voice belonged to the tall man with a rifle aimed at the table. Johnny had seen him enter and was prepared.

"Your father would be dead before you could pull the trigger, and if your first shot didn't kill me you would be dead also." Johnny Hawkeye looked the Sheriff in the eye and told him calmly. Bubba believed him.

"And if he didn't kill you I would." Zachariah waded in.

"Put the gun down, Bubba." The senior Mason told his son. "They want the breed." The doors swung open again, this time faster than before as the fat man rushed in followed by three other men. All of them were brandishing weapons and all of them stopped still immediately on seeing Bubba and the stand-off occurring in front of them.

"That's them Bubba, they're trouble." The fat man blustered.

"More than you can handle Fat Man." Johnny Hawkeye didn't like the situation but knew if he could intimidate the other man it would give him the edge if and when it came to a fight.

"Quiet! All of you." Jake Mason was shouting now, he could sense the matter was at the point of unravelling, he was not used to not being in control.

"We've got what we came for, a lead on the Rattlesnake." Johnny would happily leave without further conflict. "We'll be leaving now." He looked carefully at the six townspeople to consider their attitude. Bubba and the fat man, he deduced would be the ones to watch.

"We could have a problem there Kid." Bubba's thundering voice took on a substantially menacing tone. "You see I can't have you, two saddle tramps coming into my town like you're something special and threatening my men, I'm the law here and I'm gonna have to arrest you."

"You can try but I've already warned you what will happen." Johnny reminded the angry Sheriff, Mayor, Judge, Hangman etc. Bubba found himself in a position he didn't like, he would not be able to take on the two strangers without loss of life and one them might be his own. He couldn't back down in front of his men and any of the general population of Mason. His rule of fear would crumble if he showed any sign of it on his own part or exhibited weakness in the face of a boy and an old man. The older of the two looked as though he would be too slow to pose much of a threat so the younger one would have to be the primary target.

"Let them go, Bubba. It's not worth the trouble." Jake Mason interrupted his son's thought processes with a vocal plea for common sense. The moment of possibility for reaching a peaceful outcome to the predicament passed the next second as the barman, forgotten after being dismissed as an irrelevant consideration by both parties, made a foolish move.

He stood up from his hiding place beneath the counter brandishing a pistol, and haphazardly fired a shot at the nearest of the two out of towners, Zachariah Smith. The shot smacked harmlessly into the wall above the Mountain Man's head but it gave Bubba his chance to act. The Sheriff raised his rifle in one easy motion and fired, diving for the floor as he did so. In his haste he missed Johnny Hawkeye but Zachariah fell, clutching his chest and dropping his weapon.

Johnny reacted with the incredible speed of a battle hardened Cheyenne warrior. He fired at the barman who'd stupidly waited, standing, to see if he'd hit his target. His curiosity killed him, Johnny's first shot finished him instantly. The second shot from the young hunter hit the fat man in his hard to miss gut. He screamed as he fell and he and carried on doing so until energy and breath deserted him a few seconds later. Bubba fired again at the same time as Johnny's third shot flew towards him. Bubba died wondering if he'd hit

48

Johnny Hawkeye with his life's final action. He had, but only just.

A bullet grazed the young hunter's arm an inch away from his previous injury. Painful indeed but not serious enough to be concerning. The three men who'd entered the saloon with the fat man had rapidly taken cover behind two adjacent swiftly upturned tables at the front of the room and fired at the wounded Zachariah, hitting him in his gun hand as he too, barely conscious managed to crawl for cover, behind the large, static figure of the town's founder.

Johnny Hawkeye fired his rifle furiously towards the three men, grouped closely behind two adjacent tables. They cowered lower to escape the fusillade of death and this brief respite allowed Johnny to break from his own cover and move silently and quickly to the staircase at the side of the bar. He collected the barman's fallen pistol as he ran. He didn't normally carry a hand gun, but he knew how to use one. Before it dawned on the men that he'd moved he was shooting them. Two fell dead at once, the third stared unbelievingly at the blood on his chest and tried to lift his gun to fire. Johnny fired again, the hammer clicked ominously on an empty chamber, he was out of bullets.

Again memories of a similar occasion, years earlier flooded his brain for an instant and were gone. The man in front of him didn't take advantage, he couldn't, he was already falling, a dead man, to the floor.

"Did you really think you could come into my town, the town I built from nothing, kill my boy and get away with it?" Jake Mason's voice was as loud in his grief driven anger as his dead son's had been. He stood over the still form of Zachariah aiming the Mountain Man's gun at Johnny Hawkeye.

"Now you are going to pay." He spat out in his grief driven rage. His finger tightened on the trigger. His intentions were never realised, the knife that severed his carotid artery put paid to any and all ambitions of Jake Mason. Blood soaked the dying man's shirt front as he sagged to the floor, gurgling pathetically in his final attempts to breathe and stave off the inevitable.

"Did you not hear my words of warning you foolish old man?" The victorious Johnny Hawkeye muttered to himself as he retrieved and wiped clean his lethal blade on the dead man's sleeve.

A tall man in a suit entered carrying a black bag. Johnny, having retrieved and reloaded his rifle, swung it round to cover the unknown quantity.

"I'm a Doctor." The man said, unafraid in the face of such bloodshed. "One of the poker players came to get me. He said I might be needed."

"An Undertaker would have more business." The young man told him and lowered his weapon. He pointed to Zachariah. "My friend has been wounded."

Several people now came into the saloon, curiosity overcoming their fear. Who was this young stranger who'd single-handedly unburdened the town of the tyrannical Mason family?

"What's your name young feller?" A grey haired man, a whisky salesman, asked him politely.

"My name? It's Johnny." He said. "Johnny Hawkeye."

"I think, No, I know. I have seen you before, in the saloon at Santo Juanita. You saved the old man's life then, you killed four outlaws. Must be a year ago by now. I didn't know who you were. So you're Johnny Hawkeye." He nodded to himself. He'd heard of Johnny Hawkeye on his travels, Johnny Hawkeye the hero, and he was talking to him, a pal. Wait 'til he got home, he'd demand a few drinks for retelling the stories of his friend, the famous Johnny Hawkeye. The word was beginning to spread. He would spread it further, a legend was being born.

Zachariah Smith was seriously wounded, not fatally, but recovery would take months, not weeks. The remnants of the Mason entourage dissipated and left town in the face of a powerful resurgence of the townspeople, encouraged by the deeds of the old man and especially their new hero Johnny Hawkeye.

A week later the town was renamed Hawksville in his honour and he was feted as if he were Royalty. His room at the hotel was donated free of charge by a grateful town, the storekeeper supplied him with his first ever new outfit. He accepted with bewildered appreciation and grace, a pair of jeans along with a couple of shirts, greatcoat, boots and another first, a saddle. He was presented with a hat, in the band of which he placed Black Eagle's long treasured gift of a feather. A reward was authorised to be paid by the newly installed town council such was their gratitude for the liberation of the people, which Johnny insisted went mainly towards caring for the gravely ill Zachariah. He kept just enough for himself to pay his way when he resumed his hunt for Rattlesnake Joe.

The newly appointed Mayor tried to persuade Johnny to take the vacant position of Sheriff, a proposition he politely declined. His mission was not yet complete. The adulation and sycophantic fawning did not sit well with the young recipient. He thought how strange life can be, a year or two ago he would probably have been shot at on sight by the very people who now placed him on such a high pedestal.

Another week on from the renaming of the town, Johnny Hawkeye took his leave. Zachariah was unlikely to be able to continue the pursuit of the fugitive scalp hunter for the foreseeable future and Johnny did not want to let the trail get even colder than it already was. Promising the old man he would take revenge for both of them and return to let him know when it was done, Johnny set off alone to recommence the hunt.

He began by heading south, towards the Mexican border. The Rio Grande would not be a barrier to blunt or deflect the determination of the young man on his quest, his need for retribution was absolute.

Chapter Five:

The Raid.

Clay McCandless had been a U.S. Marshall for many more years than he would care to remember. The once tall and straight lawman now displayed a gently stooping figure with greying hair, showing more than slight signs of thinning and receding. The lines on his weather battered face grew more pronounced every year and had been likened to a relief map of the Rockies. He felt and looked every minute and more of his close to fifty years on the planet. He studied the empty plate in front of him on a table in the largest cantina that Indian Buttes had to offer and wondered whether or not to order a further plate of bacon and eggs. He decided against such an extravagance and settled for another coffee.

He'd travelled halfway across the county to warn the local Sheriff of a possible impending bank raid on his town. He had obtained the information from one of his regular Deputies with contacts in low but advantageous places. The Sheriff, an immensely overweight giant of a man had deployed extra guards inside the bank, the biggest and most secure in the area this side of Apache Bend, and set a few lookouts on roofs at either end of the main street. Otherwise he'd dismissed the idea as saloon gossip inspired by alcohol. Needing time to rest McCandless had booked a room at the only hotel in town and gone out for something to eat. A week on the road was beginning to seem like a month these days. He'd brought one Deputy with him, a man named Jud Evans, who'd gone to the saloon for a drink and would keep his ears open for any chatter that may lead the lawmen to identify potential bank robbers.

The obese Sheriff sat in his office, barely able to squeeze behind his desk. He was dealing cards to himself and two of his Deputies, they were enjoying a game of poker, untroubled by McCandless's warning. They should have taken more notice of the veteran Marshall.

The door burst open with no warning and a lone, tall figure wearing a sombrero stood facing the three transfixed poker players. The Mexican laughed and emptied his double barrelled shotgun at the table. The Sheriff, facing him tried to stand but was slammed against the wall behind him as the full blast hit him in the chest which promptly became a scarlet and white mess of blood and bone. The two Deputies were caught with shotgun pellets but not fatally. Their deaths came via the speedily drawn and discharged pistols as the shotgun fell to the floor and was replaced by the smaller firearms. The killer walked through to the cells and finding no one else present left the way he'd come in, stopping only to retrieve the shotgun. Fernando Lopez smiled, now for the bank.

The explosion seemed to rock the whole town. The bank, a once solid building was seen to disintegrate into a pile of rubble. Interspersed with the remains of the guards and the twisted remnants of the metal vault fortifications were two dead Mexicans. They could not have been identified easily by looking at what was left of them but Fernando Lopez knew he'd lost two men. He cursed the incompetence of one of the deceased. The explosives man had only been instructed to take out one wall of the building, not demolish it and risk destroying the cash and the safe.

McCandless rushed to the window of the cantina to see the tall figure of a man he knew to be the Mexican bandit supreme, Fernando Lopez, striding towards the ruins dragging a small man in a suit by the neck. The safe had miraculously survived the destruction unscathed and Lopez almost threw the terrified man to the ground in front of it. Another Mexican of similar but younger appearance, to the bandit chief, joined them in front of the safe. He held a woman and a teenage boy at gunpoint and called to the suited, shaking, man, cowering in his fear. McCandless guessed he would be Juan Lopez, brother of Fernando, a vicious man who killed for the fun of it. The Marshall could count about thirty bandits on the street but guessed there would be many more close by and ready to shoot anyone foolish enough to intervene in the proceedings. He didn't even wonder why none of the Deputies posted on the roof had taken action, he knew they would all be dead.

For a brief second he contemplated taking a shot at the bank robbers but instantly thought better of it, pointless suicide did not appeal to the aging Marshall.

"Open the safe." Fernando Lopez ordered the kneeling, suited bank manager.

"I....I can't." The man was petrified and where he found the words to refuse no one would ever know. Juan Lopez squeezed the trigger and the woman fell dead, a bullet passed through her temple and buried itself somewhere in her lifeless brain.

"Open the safe." Lopez repeated. "I shall not ask again."

Still shaking uncontrollably the quaking man, fearful for the life of himself and his son was numb with shock but struggled to comply. He removed a key from the chain connected to his waistcoat and fumbled to insert it into the lock of the amazingly still upright safe. A few seconds later the door swung open. Lopez bent down to look inside and grinned, the stacks of $100 were undamaged. Tens of thousands of Dollars were on view. As the only bank for many miles all the local businesses and ranchers used the facilities offered thinking their riches would be secure. Lopez waved at two of his men.

"Take this, put it in my saddlebags." He ordered them, pointing to the cash. Then he drew his gun and shot the bank manager. Juan laughed and drawing his own pistol again, killed the teenage boy without a thought. Fifteen minutes later the Mexican horde rode out of Indian Buttes taking with them the financial lifelines of many of the local citizenry and businesses.

Fernando Lopez was last to leave. Three of the town's braver souls stood up from behind a horse trough where they'd been biding their time and wildly opened fire on the departing bandidos, hitting no one. A flashily dressed Mexican stood off to the side watching, he did not appear to be part of the gang. His hand hardly seemed to move and the three shots sounded almost as one. The three men fell dead. The few other brave townspeople who'd foolishly tried to prevent the robbery lay dead in the streets along with the guards, deputies, the bank manager and his family. Fernando Lopez had seen the man's intervention as he rode after his men. He wheeled his mount round and rode over to the man, it looked to the watching McCandless as if they were strangers to one another.

The Marshall continued to be puzzled as the newcomer turned to walk away but after the exchange of a few inaudible words changed his mind and direction to join with Lopez and his men as they left the battered town of Indian Buttes.

McCandless and his Deputy, Jud Evans let the bandits get out of sight and then set off the follow them. They knew it would be a long job, and they were not quite sure what they would do when they caught up with Lopez and his bunch of killers.

The third day of the following week, around noon, McCandless and Evans discovered signs indicating that three riders had broken away from the main party of the bank robbers and were riding towards Casas Blancas, yet another of the hundreds of small towns to be found in the area. They decided to follow the breakaways and see if they could detain and question whoever they might be.

The two desperados sat laughing at the table, swigging tequila, a young saloon girl on each lap, giggling insincerely along with them, tolerating the groping, the bad breath and the rancid body odour, and shutting out the thoughts of what was almost certainly going to happen before the night was much older. The saloon owner would beat them if the girls did not submit to the whims of his customers and so probably would the men who'd paid him extra for them. The third member of the trio had taken his girl up to a room as soon as they had arrived an hour ago. His gang mates assumed he was sleeping off his exertions at this very moment. The tequila was raw and strong, inebriation consumed the men at the table and their female acquaintances within a short time. One of the men climbed unsteadily to his feet, he needed to visit the outhouse.

Jud Evans who was about to enter through the back entrance was taken by surprise as the bandit came out of the door, he already had his hand on the handle, about to open it. With the advantage of sobriety on his side Evans drew first and hit the man hard on the head with his pistol. The drunken desperado collapsed. Robbed of his consciousness the man couldn't control his bladder and wet himself where he lay. Clay McCandless casually walked into the bar area via the front door, making sure his Marshall's badge was on prominent view. The seated bandit took one look, forced his befuddled brain to process what his eyes were seeing and reached for his gun.

"Don't do it, son." McCandless told him. The man ignored him, he pushed the sleeping form of the saloon girl roughly onto the floor and continued his reactive movement towards his weapon. The girl hit the floor only a second or two before the man she'd just been sitting on. The Marshall fired and the target of the man's chest, made bigger by the unseating of the girl, took the bullet squarely in the centre. Jud Evans rushed in, gun drawn and ready to fire. He didn't see the man he'd knocked down staggering in behind him, blood running down his face, the front of his jeans showing moist as a result of his recent leakage.

Evans had not hit him as hard as he thought or else the man had an extremely hard head. It didn't matter which, the shovel he was aiming at the Deputy's head was of more and pressing import. Before the makeshift weapon could connect, McCandless fired for the second time, a second man fell dead. The girl scrambled away to her companion and they ran out of the room. The third bandit, disturbed by the sound of shooting appeared at the top of the stairs. He was using his nearly naked, erstwhile bed mate to hide behind, she looked to be about fifteen years old and terrified. Marshall Clay McCandless recognised his adversary at once and stood at the bottom of the stairs glaring at him.

"Give it up Juan. You've got nowhere to go. He said in a voice that sounded way calmer than he felt.

"Drop your gun, now." Ordered Jud Evans from the side of the stairs, he had a slightly better chance of a shot without hitting the girl. Juan Lopez was not a stupid man, he realised this and shook his head.

"Okay, Senors, Okay." He said and begun to lower his pistol. Jud Evans stepped forward to collect it and that's when the bandit took his chance.

As soon as Evans moved into an easily targeted position Juan Lopez raised his gun again and fired, simultaneously shoving the now screaming girl down the stairs at the Marshall. Seeing Evans fall and blood staining the front of his shirt the bank robber turned his attention back to McCandless. He fired twice, the first shot killing the girl, the second missing the Marshall's head by inches as the weight of the dead girl knocked him to the floor. Clay McCandless returned fire and was thankful to see the robber clutch at his arm and lose balance, causing him to fall down and land in a heap at the foot of the stairs. Juan Lopez struggled to roll out of the way and aim his weapon again but the Marshall was on his feet by now and viciously kicked the gun out of his reach.

"Get up Lopez." He spat the words out, and glanced over to confirm what he already knew. Jud Evans was dead. "I really want to shoot you again, you murdering bastard, but I'll see you hang instead. Apache Bend has a good strong gallows." McCandless, still fighting the urge to put a bullet in the outlaw's head bound and gagged the wounded Juan Lopez and the two of them left for the return journey to Indian Buttes.

There they would board the stagecoach for the larger town of Apache Bend where the jail would be more secure and well-guarded than most in the area.

Chapter Six:

The Revolutionary.

The Rio Grande was two days behind Johnny Hawkeye when he came upon the black stallion. The little village was called Paredes De Adobe, Adobe Walls. The name would be applicable to every dwelling place he'd travelled through since entering Mexico. It had been an uneventful ride for which Johnny was grateful, he wanted no unnecessary trouble to further hinder his quest to track down Rattlesnake Joe. The sun was beginning its slow descent towards the west as he studied the horse tied to the rail outside an ancient cantina. It was the only one there until he tied his own right next to it. He felt the handle of the pistol he now wore on his right hip, the holster tied to his leg. Reassured he walked into the building. Two old men sat at a battered table playing cards. A younger man in a huge sombrero sat at the bar attempting to seduce the girl serving him with his third tequila of the afternoon.

"Buenos Dias, Senor." Johnny greeted the sombrero in a friendly manner. "I couldn't help but notice you have a lovely horse outside, would you consider selling it to me?" He asked him. The Mexican would be about the same age as he himself Johnny calculated, around twenty, twenty one.

"Ah, Senor, I cannot sell you the horse. It does not belong to me. It belongs to a man who works for the General. I am here to guard it, under pain of death." The Mexican answered.

"Oh well, we can't have you being shot for letting a horse go. Who is the man it belongs to, maybe I could ask him, is he here?"

"No, he has gone with the General, to his camp in the hills, he went in the General's carriage, with the General himself. General Gomez. He will be back to collect his horse when the General has given him his orders."

"Perhaps I will wait with you until he returns and ask him myself. Tequila?"

"You are most generous Senor. My name is Luis, Luis Hernández." The Mexican tilted his sombrero to the back of his head, smiled and held his glass for the girl to fill.

"I'll have the same, Senorita." He said to the pretty young bar maid. "And my name is Johnny, Johnny Hawkeye." Johnny told her ardent young suitor, and waited for any sign of recognition, there was none. "Tell me Luis, what is the man's name? The man who owns the horse."

"He is known in Mexico as El Serpiente De Cascabel, as you Gringos would say The Rattlesnake."

General Antonio Gomez was the leader of his own revolutionary army. He was a man of large girth, not very tall but impressive in the manner with which he presented himself. A preening peacock with a Napoleonic complex. His ambition to rule Mexico was not motivated by a love of democracy or freedom for the masses, but a fanatical desire to impose his own dictatorial doctrine on the long suffering people of his native country. The General had assembled a huge armed militia and trained them in the art of warfare. To this end he employed people he was familiar with from his own distant past in the armies of General Santa Anna, whose disgrace at the Battle of San Jacinto he was pleased not to have been involved with. He not only wanted to be the Emperor of Mexico, he had designs on reclaiming Texas from the Americans, the Gringos. He would become the most famous of all his race, the man who humbled the United States.

His soldiers were drawn from the ranks of deserters, mercenaries, bandits, political activists and young, impressionable idealists such as the tequila drinking young man guarding the black horse. General Gomez employed a simple method to raise funding for his ambitions. He would simply steal it. His men would occupy a town, eliminating any resistance by force or fear, and sometimes both. Then he would assume control of the banks and requisition all funds and valuables stored within the vaults.

He would have everything transferred to his own personal war chest, a huge bank safe loaded onto a wagon and guarded twenty four hours a day, every day, by eight of his most loyal men, true believers in the revolution. The wagon needed eight horses to pull it. It went everywhere that Gomez went.

He was camped in the hills above the village of Paredes De Adobe to allow a day's training for his troops on the way to the next town. His current need was for heavy armaments, field guns, cannons and Gatling guns. He knew just the man to supply them for him, and where from. He looked at the man beside him, he did not see a man to be trusted. The head, shaved at the sides was showing signs of stubble, the pony tail had been hidden under a bowler hat. The livid scarlet of an ugly scar showed almost luminously in the shadows of the evening when caught in the flickering of the camp fire. The man's eyes showed no emotion except bitterness and hatred for everything they beheld. It didn't matter to Gomez, El Serpiente could do the job he had for him and that was all he cared about.

"El Serpiente, I will pay you $5,000 Dollars in gold. I want you to hire a certain man to steal some heavy artillery from the Americano soldiers and bring them to me here. If you can find this man and persuade him to carry out the mission I will pay you a further $5,000 on delivery of the weapons. I believe you know the man I speak of. Fernando Lopez." He watched his guest for a reaction. Hardly an acknowledgement showed on the battle scarred face.

"Why don't you ask him yourself, you don't need me?"

"Ah, but I do, El Serpiente." Gomez explained. "I don't know Lopez, I don't know where he is, I don't have men who can move around on the other side of the border as well as you, and you will know how to find him, you are part Comanche, no?"

"Why Lopez, he is a bandit?" Rattlesnake Joe blurted out the question. "I haven't seen him in years." Rattlesnake Joe told him in a voice that resembled a cross between a hiss and a growl, the result of a throat wound from his childhood. Gomez had anticipated such a query.

"Because I know he has done this kind of thing before, he has a band of loyal men and he hates gringos." Came the answer. "Yes, he is a bandit. But he is a clever bandit who organises big robberies, he organises many men and he is successful. The reward on his head is the largest offered so far to my knowledge, more than the James brothers, more than John Wesley Hardin and more than your own $5000. $10,000 Dollars is offered for the capture of Fernando Lopez, he worked hard and well to be so sought after. You are a renegade, a scalp hunter, a gunrunner, a whisky pedlar and very accomplished at your chosen professions. These are not a handful of rifles or Indian hair I am talking about. These are big field weapons, Lopez knows what he's doing with them. They need to be taken from the Fort Boone, it is very well fortified. Lopez could do this, he is a planner. Your job is to contact him and work with him.

Should he not wish to take part in such an operation, your job will be to kill him. Then the reward can be yours." He calculated that Rattlesnake Joe would contact the legendary bandit and the appropriation of the required weaponry would go ahead. Rattlesnake Joe was a cunning, crafty, evil man who would undoubtedly be adept at seizing the moment if it presented itself. But he was smart enough to know his own limitations, some like Fernando Lopez, and he himself, could plan ahead and employ tactics that would ensure that the moment did indeed present itself. It didn't matter to Gomez if the combination of Lopez and the half breed was amicable or if one of them killed the other after the delivery of the arms to his army.

"I'll need my horse." Rattlesnake Joe growled at the General.

"Take one of mine from the coral, I'll send someone to collect yours from the cantina and you can swap it back when you return." Gomez told him. The scalp hunter nodded and left to choose another mount. He wasn't the sentimental type, a horse was a horse.

Johnny Hawkeye was sitting down at a table in the cantina when the young Mexican recruit was joined by an older, uniformed man. The young man had consumed far too much tequila to stay awake and Johnny was pretending to be as drunk, sleeping off an evening's over indulgence. The new arrival grunted something incoherent at the sleeping Mexican and gave him a kick to wake him, the drunken youth stirred, struggling to gather his senses.

"The General sent me to fetch you, and El Serpiente's horse." The newcomer grunted.

"Oh, give me a minute, where is El Serpiente, this man wants to buy his horse?" The slurred response.

"Well he won't be buying it today, El Serpiente has gone. The General has sent him to Texas. To find Lopez." Johnny Hawkeye stirred at this revelation.

"Where will I find him?" He asked the man in the uniform.

"What's it to you Gringo? Go and find another horse." The reply was less than helpful.

"Adios my friend." Johnny said pleasantly to the recovering young man, Luis Hernández, and he took his leave. The older man looked as though he might start something for a second but he changed his mind, ensuring that he lived to be unpleasant to someone else. Johnny left the black stallion where it was and rode out of Paredes De Adobe to begin the journey back into Texas, across the Rio Grande. The search would continue.

Chapter Seven:

Dead Or Alive.

"Dude" Wallis was a gambler, he was also wanted for the murder of a prominent banker in Denver who'd accused him, quite rightly, of cheating at poker and had a $1,000 reward on his head. "Red" Riley and Jed Masters were sitting with Wallis, the three of them playing blackjack in the only saloon of yet another nameless small town along the dusty trails of the Texas / Mexico border. Riley and Masters were likewise wanted by the law, $500 each they were worth for robbery and murder. If Wallis thought the cards were unkind to him that night, he would be appalled to learn things could and were about to get worse, far worse.

Ellen Payne was a saloon girl, a singer and a dancer. Often more was expected of her but she was strong and independent, she could afford to be selective and she was. The tall man at the bar intrigued her, dressed in black and casually sipping at a bourbon on the rocks while watching the three men playing cards at one of the tables. She selected.

"Hey, Stranger. You wouldn't see a girl without a drink would you?" She enquired, confident in her approach.

"Sure." The stranger pointed to the girl and motioned for the bar keeper to pour her a drink. "Whatever the lady wants." He instructed.

"Thanks Mister." She laughed as she accepted. "My name is Ellen. What's yours?"

"People call me Shannon." He replied. "Just Shannon."

"Well just Shannon, what brings you to our little town?"

"I've got some business to do, I'll be gone tomorrow." He nodded towards the table where Wallis and his card playing companions sat. "Perhaps you would help me." He passed her three large rolled up pieces of paper. "Would you take these posters to that table for me while I get you another drink?" Shannon smiled, knowing she would do as he asked. She took them, knowing at once what they were and took them to the table concerned.

"A man asked me to bring you these." She told them and walked back to the bar where Shannon quickly but gently pushed her away from him and stood forward.

"What is this?" Wallis spluttered unrolling the wanted posters to see his own likeness and that of Riley and Masters staring up at him.

"It says Dead or Alive." Shannon cut in sharply. "Your choice." He was ready for the response. He had guessed what it would be. Ellen noted how his voice had suddenly become harsh and flat.

70

Wallis stood up reaching for his gun, Riley launched himself to one side of the table, clawing at his holstered weapon as he did so. Masters threw himself to the floor grabbing desperately at his shotgun which was leaning against his chair. Shannon drew and fired three times before any of them could succeed in raising a weapon against him. Two of them died before the bounty hunter had walked calmly over to the now upturned table and checked on the results of his gun play. He saw a faint flicker in the eyes of Wallis but it was gone immediately as life left him also.

"Take the pot for any damage." He said to the bartender and left to find the Sheriff.

"Hey, Shannon, are you coming back?" Ellen called after him.

"As soon as I cash them in." He pointed to the three dead men. "Order us another drink."

The Sheriff didn't take kindly to being disturbed, the sound of gun shots had brought him running out of his office towards the saloon. Shannon stopped him halfway.

"It's over Sheriff. Wallis, Riley and Masters, you owe me $2,000. They're in the saloon. I'll collect in the morning, give you time to get the money from the bank."

"You? You killed them all?" The Sheriff was surprised.

"They didn't think much to the idea of shooting themselves." Shannon told him with grim humour.

"But Riley was supposed to be the fastest gun in the county."

"That's what he thought too. I'll see you in the morning." Shannon turned and walked back to the saloon, the Sheriff followed. Ellen was waiting at the bar with a bottle of bourbon. He picked up the bottle.

"Have you got a room here?" He asked her with a smile. She nodded. "Lead on." He told her and she did.

The next morning, $2,000 richer, Shannon took a few minutes to examine the notice board on the Sheriff's office wall. It consisted mainly of wanted posters, among them was one for Michael Callahan. Along with several others Shannon tore it down and handed them all to the puzzled lawman.

"Keep up Sheriff." He told him. "These have all been collected."

"All of them. What? You?"

"Me." Shannon studied the remaining posters for a couple of minutes before selecting the three with the highest value rewards printed.

"Are these up to date, $5,000 each?" he asked sharply.

"As far as I know they are." The Sheriff answered him and added. "I heard Hardin got hisself arrested but the half breed, Rattlesnake Joe, he's supposed to be operating somewhere near the border. I don't know where. The other one, Jack Wilson, last I heard he was in Apache Bend, he's got a woman there, or did have." Shannon dropped the poster on John Wesley Hardin

72

and took the one showing a representation of the renegade half breed Rattlesnake Joe with him, along with the one displaying a picture of a man called Jack Wilson. Another poster caught his eye as he was about to leave, he tore it down and looked closely at it.

"This one, Frank Lawson, where would I find him?"
"I have no idea, I do know he sometimes works with Wilson. Why do you want him? He's only worth $500 to you."

"My business." The emphatic reply.

Before he left town Shannon had a final drink in the saloon. Ellen came to say goodbye, she knew they wouldn't meet again.

"I wish I was leaving too." She said, he heard her but she was really just thinking out loud.

"Why don't you? There's a stagecoach through town later today." He told her. "Here, go anywhere you like, you don't belong in a two bit graveyard like this." He handed her $500 and walked out of her life before she could respond.

Chapter Eight:

The Stagecoach.

The dust was choking the stagecoach driver and his shotgun rider companion, even with neckerchiefs pulled up tight covering their faces and their hats tied down low. The staging post would soon be visible in the distance, it had been a very long fifty miles since the last rest. This would be a very welcome overnight stop. The two men looked forward to a hot meal and a chance to sleep for a few hours before continuing the trek to Apache Bend where the journey reached its termination. Good news for the passengers, including a rancher traveling on business with his wife and son, and a U.S. Marshall who'd boarded the stage at Indian Buttes, with a prisoner chained to his wrist at all times.

The prisoner was tall for a man of Mexican ethnicity and appearance, around five eleven, he looked to be in his early to mid-twenties his name was Lopez, Juan Lopez. The Marshall was older, bigger in bulk but a couple of inches shorter due to an inconsequential but noticeable stoop. His lined features betrayed the experiences of many years in his uncompromising profession and he looked way more senior than his actual half century. The Marshall's name was Clay McCandless and he wanted badly to deposit his charge into the custody of the local Sheriff and along with it the responsibility for looking after such a disagreeable human being. The possibility of a rescue attempt by the man's notorious brother, Fernando, was ever present as was the opposite kind of threat. A revenge attack by one of the many people whose lives had been affected by the murderous, rapacious reign of terror imposed on the population for miles around both sides of the Mexican border by the hot headed psychopathic killer, rapist and his infamous brother.

McCandless recounted to the rancher and the driver how he had been hunting Juan Lopez since the violent bank raid in the town of Indian Buttes, tracking him down to a bordello in one of the hundreds of small towns which dotted the banks on both sides of the Rio Grande. He explained how the fugitive had not come quietly, the loss of his Deputy during the confrontation, and the murder of the terrified young whore Lopez was using as a human shield. Shot in the back by Lopez whilst aiming in haste at his pursuer. McCandless explained how resisting an almost overwhelming desire to kill the ruthless bandido he settled for a shoulder shot and took him prisoner. Yes, he would be mightily relieved to part with his prisoner to the Sheriff in Apache Bend.

The Rancher was on his way to Apache Bend to oversee the hiring of enough reliable cowboys to transport a herd of recently purchased beef cattle to his massive ranch just outside Wickenburg, Arizona. His ranch Foreman, appropriately named Ben Foreman, would meet him from the stage and between them the job would probably take a couple of days to complete before the long journey south-west would begin. The rancher's name was Josh Milton, his wife was Margaret, and they had two sons and a daughter. The daughter, Lindsey and the youngest son, Johnnie were being taken care of by their ageing grandmother at home while the eldest, Clayton, shortened against his mother's wishes to Clay, travelled with them. Clay Milton was twenty four years old and had been sent away for an education to a highly prestigious school in Philadelphia. The knowledge he'd accrued was almost as extensive as it was expensive. He was happy for the experience and learning but equally happy to return west, and momentarily south.

There were two other people aboard the stagecoach, one, an unlikely looking preacher who after a careful appraisal of his fellow passengers kept himself very much to himself. Completing the quotient of fare paying travellers was a grey haired liquor salesman who introduced himself as Jonas Gordon, an ironic name for a purveyor of the finest whisky. Quite the opposite of the unforthcoming preacher he couldn't stop talking. He delighted in promoting the benefits of indulging in the pleasures of his wares and as an inducement to purchase offered a minute free sample to all. McCandless refused on behalf of his disappointed prisoner, the preacher declined gracelessly with a grim shake of his head. Margaret Milton also declined and looked disapprovingly on as her husband and son, along with the Marshall accepted with grateful nods and smiles. The alcohol served to loosen Gordon's tongue even more and he was soon regaling a trapped audience with extravagant tales of the adventures of his friend, the hero Johnny Hawkeye.

The stagecoach driver was Pete Nicholson, he'd been doing the job for fifteen years, summer and winter. He'd been attacked by Indians, bandits, confederate soldiers, union soldiers, every type of threat he could imagine, and survived them all. Once he'd even survived a buffalo stampede, although that cost him his horses and one of his passengers and took him three days to make up the lost time. His was a simple philosophy, things are what they are. If you can't change them for the better, learn to live with them or get out. He learned to live with his lot in life.

Riding shotgun on this trip with the experienced driver was an enigmatic, mysterious drifter named James Blue aged around thirty. Since moving West, Bluey, as he was known, had scouted for the army, various wagon trains and cattle drives during his ten years in the Americas. He'd arrived from his native Australia, having some said having been a bush ranger until things got too hot for him. He stood just under six feet tall, at around a hundred and sixty pounds. A faded blue shirt was covered by a buckskin jacket which had seen better days. A black belt over black jeans held a worn holster containing a six gun on his right hip, on his left hung a large leather sheath containing a Bowie knife. Across his lap as he sat beside Pete, he carried the shotgun descriptive of his current employment.

The staging post consisted of a four roomed cabin, two bedrooms, one used by Walt, the host and his wife, an Indian woman he called Rita. They were both old looking forty somethings. The other bedroom was used as a guest room for any women passengers who stayed overnight. The men slept where they could find a space on the floor of the big multi-functional room which served as dining room, dormitory and if necessary, hospital. The remaining room was a kitchen. Behind the building were two more wooden constructions. A barn which was used as a stable for the replacement teams of horses required by any stagecoach that did not need to stay overnight. It also doubled as a store for feed and anything else deemed necessary or convenient. The other, much smaller structure was a particularly uninviting outhouse. Walt had seen the dust in the distance that signalled the imminent arrival of the stagecoach and instructed Rita to boil some coffee for the travellers.

Pete was warmly greeted by Walt as the stagecoach drew to a halt on the trail immediately in front of the staging post. They'd known each other for the best part of ten years and had become friends.

"Walt, good to see you again, how's Rita? I hope she's got the coffee on, I'm spitting trail dust." He responded to the stage post manager.

"Already boiled and waiting for you, Pete. Who's your friend here?" Walt nodded towards James Blue who was unfastening the horses for the night, including his own mount, a chestnut gelding tied loosely to the rear of the coach.

"This here's James Blue, we call him Bluey. He's from Australia."

"Howdy Bluey, welcome to paradise." Walt greeted the other man.

"Nice to meet you Walt." Bluey responded and the two shook hands. By the time Pete and Bluey had fed, watered and settled the horses it was getting late. They hastily unloaded the luggage for the night and deposited it in a pile inside, near the front doors of the building. It would be closer for loading again in the morning. The Stagecoach Company employees chose a vacant table and Rita supplied them with gratefully accepted coffee and a hot meal of steak and beans. Then she retreated to the kitchen, leaving everyone to eat, drink and converse. Walt poured himself a coffee and joined Pete and Bluey. He and Pete had plenty to talk about and Bluey took the time to relax, enjoying the warmth of a huge fire blazing in the dim lighting. He appraised his fellow travellers again, as he had every time a stopover occurred. He knew who would be sitting with who and that the whisky salesman, Gordon would be indulging in his verbal excesses with whoever he could corner. Today it was the turn of the unsociable preacher who blatantly yawned in the whisky drummer's face and picked up his bible. Undeterred Gordon continued his monologue and Bluey did not bother to hide his smile. The Miltons were together as usual, tonight joined by the U.S. Marshall McCandless who had temporarily attached his chained prisoner, Juan Lopez, securely to one of the wooden support pillars adjacent to a nearby table. The prisoner sat alone, sullen and silent, searching, so far in vain, for a means of escape. The shotgun rider finished his third coffee, bid his company goodnight, and taking his blanket settled himself in a corner near the fire before drifting off into a light sleep.

Clay Milton was the last to bed down for the night. His mind wandered back to his times in the east, a young man with a good education and the intelligence to make the most of his knowledge. He'd not fought in the War Between the States but his sympathies were firmly behind Abraham Lincoln's policies of emancipation. He'd been devastated by the murderous actions of John Wilkes Booth, a man he'd admired as an actor of some ability and star quality.

His schooling complete the young Clayton Edward Milton had stayed in the East, moving to Washington and working for a firm of lawyers as an investigative clerk to pay his way while deciding his future. He always intended to return to the ranch but not yet.

A year before his intended return to the West, Clay had met with the President, Ulysses S. Grant, and been mightily impressed with his philosophy of equality for all. He remembered how the war Commander had pulled him aside and spoken to him of a problem he might be able to help with. His old school Principal from Philadelphia was close to the some of the President's confidents and had recommended Clay Milton to a

Colonel Jack Steele, Security Chief, as a patriotic young man with the qualities of courage, conviction and the intelligence to be of assistance. A strong opponent of the rampant Ku Klux Klan, Grant had reason to fear that his life was in danger from southern sympathisers. His spies had eventually traced two possible conspirators to a club in Philadelphia of which Clay had been a member. Infiltration by security forces would take longer than could be allowed in which to expose and prove any existent plot to assassinate the President. Clay Milton, after a thorough vetting by the President's intelligence staff, had been selected and requested to volunteer as an undercover agent for the United States.

The move back to Philadelphia was swiftly achieved and Clay was soon established again in his old social circles. Until his return Clay had been a mainly observant, rarely vocally active member of the debating club, but now, newly re-joined, he became a florid campaigner against racial reforms and freedoms for the black and red man who shared the land with the dominant white race.

His thoughts and memories moved on at a faster pace, soon reaching the point where one of the senior club members had made a clandestine approach to the newly outspoken and radicalised young westerner.

Secretly horrified that such conspiracies existed undetected under his nose until now, Clay had made great show of being suspicious, intimating that the people he was being introduced to were not genuine plotters and maybe trying to trap him. There were six in the group, four men and two women, and additionally Clay, who would be the seventh and youngest recruit. The unidentified mastermind behind the whole operation would not be revealed until later.

The more he displayed his suspicions and doubted the seriousness of their intent the more they revealed of themselves in an effort to convince him. Eventually a meeting was arranged to outline the plan for the assassination of President Ulysses S. Grant. The mysterious leader would be present to address his full complement of fellow conspirators including the newest member, and announce who would be honoured as the one to pull the trigger.

The evening of the meeting arrived. It was to commence at eight P.M. The rendezvous point announced at the last minute was a tavern back room, not far from where Clay Milton had lodgings. He was pleased that the secret service would be trailing him as there was not time to otherwise inform them of the precise location where the gathering would take place. As soon as all were present the agents would wait for twenty minutes and if no one came out, they would come in, fully armed and prepared for whatever action needed to be taken.

The plotters were all present apart from the leader when Clay arrived at the tavern. The backroom table had two spare seats, one at the head, unoccupied as yet and one at the foot in which Clay sat himself down. They waited saying little other than greetings for a few minutes until the final seat was taken.

The leader was revealed to be the Vice Principal of Clay's old school. The young man was shocked that the slight, almost effeminate middle aged man opposite him would be capable of controlling a band of conspirators and would-be assassins. Before the identity of the person chosen to be the actual killer could be disclosed the security forces struck.

The door to the room was kicked in and twenty armed men stormed in. Clay and the others raised their hands and were led out to a waiting carriage and taken to an empty warehouse close by. They were to be questioned separately by experienced interrogators, they would soon tell all they knew. Clay was released as soon as he was removed from the group. He sat with Colonel Jack Steele, whose previously slight English accent seemed more prominent on this occasion.

"You were supposed to give me twenty minutes, I didn't have time to find out who was going to pull the trigger, or what the complete plan was." He complained.

"I know, but you had to look as surprised as they did. The triggerman is not one of you, it is one of us, a professional. Someone will tell us who." As if on cue a shot rang out, it came from the next room. The chief agent, Steele, and Clay rushed in to see what had happened. One of the security men was bending over the dead body of the effeminate looking vice principal.

"He tried to take my gun." The shooter explained.

"Now I'll take it." His boss told him. The man looked surprised at Steele's harsh tone.

"We knew the triggerman was one of us, Grey." The security chief said to the man. "You just told me who it was. You killed the only one who could betray you." The man, Grey changed. His face twisted into an expression of anger and fear. He lunged at Jack Steele, standing in front of him, who fired once before he was knocked to the floor, gun spinning out of his hand. The shot somehow missed Grey who raised his own weapon and pointed it straight at his fallen superior's head. Clay Milton who'd moved speedily to pick up the fallen pistol now pointed it at the traitorous Grey.

"Drop it, now." He shouted. The desperate man began to swing round to attack the young inexperienced undercover man. Clay Milton pulled the trigger, Grey died instantly. Jack Steele climbed back up to his feet and took the gun from Clay.

"I'll take that. You did well Son. You saved my life." He said quietly.

"How did you know he wasn't telling the truth about what just happened? Clay asked.

"I didn't know it, I had to push him, and it worked." Was the answer.

Clay Milton was twenty one years old when he killed Grey. He declined the offer of a permanent position in the security forces but had subsequently carried out occasional missions for the chief when requested. He'd had to kill once more, in self defence against a drunken gun runner in Boston. He became well practised in hand to hand combat. It was preferable to obtain information from live bodies than to bury dead ones. Clay Milton rarely spoke of his work for the security forces, preferring to respect the need for secrecy. His father had only found out about some of his exploits because Colonel Jack Steele had been present when Josh had visited his son. Clay was working on an undercover case in Washington D.C. at the time and a sketchy outline of the young agent's involvement was deemed necessary to alleviate parental concerns.

Clay Milton dragged his thoughts back to the present. He had been restless and unable to settle since they'd picked up Marshall McCandless and his prisoner. He was well read and whenever possible would scour the available news sheets for anything of interest or that might prove useful to the running of his father's ranch. An article published recently focused on the increasing threat of violent incursions by bandits from the other side of the Mexican border. The raiders would target trains, banks, and stagecoaches, robbing and killing without conscience or reason. They would then disappear across the border back into Mexico where the American lawmen could not follow or apprehend them.

Most prominent and feared amongst the influx of brutal bandit leaders was a man named Fernando Lopez who led a gang of fifty or more loyal desperados. He was suspected of being responsible for hundreds of murders and hundreds of thousands of dollars' worth of robberies. Juan Lopez, McCandless's prisoner was his brother, and Fernando would want to rescue him, no matter the cost to human life. He'd spoken to the Marshall about his concerns and found that McCandless had the same point of view. His plan was to get to Apache Bend before Fernando Lopez found out his brother had been apprehended, and where deputies could be appointed to deal with any threats that might be forthcoming.

If they were attacked on the journey who amongst the travellers could be counted on to help mount a credible defence, Clay pondered? Apart from the Marshall, a proven campaigner, his father, Josh? He could handle a gun and did not lack courage or strength of character. Pete, the stagecoach driver, also a long time survivor of the west's tough life? The shotgun, Bluey, an unknown quantity but looked as though he could handle himself? He discounted the others, the preacher, the loud whisky salesman, although they could certainly use his "friend" Johnny Hawkeye, Clay reasoned. He also discounted his mother, Rita the hostess, the prisoner for obvious reasons and probably Walt, he wasn't sure. Clay finally drifted off to a fitful sleep.

Chapter Nine:

The Pistolero.

Rodrigo Lamas had been ten years old when they came to his village, the bandidos. They'd wiped out the whole village with the exception of his older sister and most of the other young girls. They were spared only to be taken away, and would be forced to pleasure the plundering desperados and keep them warm at night.

The raiding party had erupted into the excess violence because there was no grain left, or bread to give them the supplies that they were used to being able to steal from the terrified farmers. Another roving band of marauding robbers, the Rurales, had visited the area only two days before, and stolen everything there was to steal.

His own survival could be attributed to the perversity of luck, he'd been unwell with a fever and confined to his bed. The sound of shooting and screaming had woken the young boy from his hallucinatory dreaming and something in his mind had told him to hide, which he did, under his bedroll. A perfunctory glance by one of the killers into his home and seeing no one to kill or anything to steal resulted in him being ignored as the slaughter took place outside.

From that moment on Rodrigo Lamas had two missions. The first was to find and rescue his Sister. The second to find the murderous collection of plundering brigands who'd perpetrated such an atrocity on his family and friends. He'd dedicated the next several years of his life to joining up with outlaw bands across the country, learning how to draw fast, shoot straight and track a man or men across any terrain. He knew who he was looking for, Lopez. Not Fernando who was a feared leader of many men throughout Mexico and the southern parts of the United States. No, he wanted Juan, Fernando's younger, sadistic, psychopathic brother, who'd led the gang responsible for the killing spree. To this end the young pistolero had joined Fernando Lopez and his men, hoping to get the chance to take his revenge. He was eighteen years old by now, around the same age that Juan Lopez had been at the time of the massacre. Juan Lopez or any of his men would not be able to remember, let alone recognise the vengeful Rodrigo after this length of time.

Juan Lopez did not always ride with his brother, he could not adhere to the discipline or follow orders closely enough to be of much use. If not for the fact that he was family, Fernando would most certainly have killed him years ago. He'd joined up with his brother for the bank raid after a clash with the Rurales had eliminated all his men bar the two who'd accompanied him to Casas Blancas. Rodrigo had been left on guard at the outlaws' hideout while the bank raid had taken place, he'd feigned a sickness, not wanting to have to kill innocent people, and Lopez didn't think he'd be any use to him that day. He had been disappointed when

Juan Lopez did not return with his brother but was subsequently relieved to find out his quarry hadn't been killed, just gone his own way.

Breaking away at night, unnoticed from the bandidos, Rodrigo had tracked Juan and his two remaining gang members to the town of Casas Blancas but didn't make it there in time. Marshall Clay McCandless had left for Indian Buttes with the hated Juan Lopez as his prisoner.

The saloon owner had relayed the facts of the incident as Rodrigo stood at the bar with a whisky, it had been a long trip and he needed a rest. He paid for a room and the man called out to one of the two young women who'd been present at the killings.

"Maria, get a room ready for the Senor." He ordered one of them, the girl came through from the back and obediently began to climb the stairs. "For a dollar she will stay with you all night." He said to Rodrigo.

"She is a pretty girl Senor but I do not pay for my women." The young pistolero told him. The older man showed surprise and did not seem pleased to hear such talk from a traveling gunman. Most would have accepted his offer with a grin of anticipation. Ten minutes later Maria came back down the stairs.

"Maria, can I buy you a drink?" Rodrigo asked her. She looked fearfully at her boss who nodded, and thinking Rodrigo had changed his mind smiled, as he reached for the bottle of tequila.

"Thank you Senor." She said and went to sit beside him. This was a different kind of man than she was used to. He was young, handsome, and clean, he didn't smell bad at all. There was something about him... She summoned her practised saloon girl smile and moved closer to him.

"Where do you come from Maria?" The pistolero asked her. The smile left her face to be replaced with a wistful look of longing and sadness. She couldn't speak for a minute.

"The man asked you a question. Answer him Bitch." The saloon keeper raised his voice and his hand at the same time. Before he could leave the bar and get close enough to make contact with the girl's face he found himself staring down the barrel of Rodrigo's pistol.

"If I ever see you raise your hand to my sister again I will kill you." The pistolero informed him quietly as he replaced the gun in his holster.

"Sister......? Oh Dios mio! Rodrigo it can't be....." She sobbed compulsively and collapsed in her brother's arms. There was something about him...

"I have been searching for you since the bandidos took you, I never gave up. People told me you would be dead but I never gave up." He was struggling to hold back the tears himself now.

Realising he could be about to lose one of his money making assets and possibly face retribution from the young man in front of him the saloon owner reached under the bar and brought up a shotgun, pulling back the hammer as he did so. Rodrigo Lamas did not bother turning to face his assailant, he drew and fired in the blink of an eye. It was not only the fastest draw the foolish man had ever seen, it was also the last. He was dead before the pistolero had replaced his pistol in its holster for a second time. The saloon keeper took a few seconds to fall, the shotgun fell first and then he collapsed on top of it causing it to fire and his insides then became his outsides. He didn't feel a thing.

Rodrigo escorted his sister and her friend away from Casas Blancas the next morning. He took them to another town, a hundred miles back into Mexico, away from anyone who might know them. A man he held in high esteem, Father Michael would take very good care of them until he could return, if he could return. Rodrigo made a healthy donation to Father Michael's church and local wine supplier, and left to resume his hunt for Juan Lopez. He knew he wouldn't get to Indian Buttes in time to catch up with the Marshall and his prisoner. He would head for Apache Bend and hope to catch up with them on the trail.

Chapter Ten:

Stratagems.

The stagecoach left early, the passengers were rested and fed, ready to embark on the next part of the journey to Apache Bend. There would be one more overnight stop on the way, another staging post, and then a day later they would hopefully arrive at their destination. Juan Lopez did not share the desire to complete the voyage which would not end well for him if Marshall Clay McCandless had his way.

The party had said their goodbyes to Walt and Rita three hours previous when James Blue nudged Pete in the ribs.

"There's dust rising up a couple of miles back, we're being followed." He told him. The stage driver turned to look and his eyes confirmed what his partner had seen.

"Folks, there's some people coming up the trail after us, I'm gonna speed up a little." He shouted and cracked his whip over the team of horses with the desired effect, they doubled their pace at once.

Inside the coach, Clay McCandless felt helpless, he couldn't release his prisoner and so he couldn't climb out to see what was going on. The man who shared his first name, Clay Milton, could sense the frustration in the Marshall and checking his gun, stood up.

"I'll go and see what's going on Marshall, I'll let you know." McCandless nodded.

"Be careful, Son, There's some rough people out there. Tell Pete if it looks dangerous to find some cover and we'll pull over and wait."

The trail ran through flat, open land now, no cover to be had other than the stagecoach itself. Bluey and Clay could see the mounted party in the distance, gaining steadily on them with every second. Soon the watching men could count ten riders. Within very few minutes they could see the weapons of their pursuers being raised and shots followed. They were still too far away to be accurate as yet but the warning was stark. They were not friendly.

"Here, take this." Bluey said to Clay Milton and handed him the shotgun. "Do you know how to use it?" Clay nodded and the Australian handed him a bag of cartridges.

"What are you going to do?" Clay asked him. James Blue reached out to his case which was tied along with the passengers' luggage on top of the stagecoach roof and pulled out at long barrelled rifle with a telescopic sight bolted along the top.

"I'm going to reduce the odds, maybe scare them off some." He sprawled himself as low as he could on the roof and raised himself on his elbows. Using a pile of cases to steady the rifle against the frenetic rocking of the speeding stagecoach, he took careful aim and squeezed the trigger. Clay thought the chasing pack was still too far away and Bluey should have waited, but a couple of seconds later the sight of the lead horseman falling backwards off his mount and the sound of a scream led to a change of mind.

"That was one hell of a shot." He exclaimed. Bluey took aim again, a second man was hit. The following band then decided to pull back a little and spread out making things more difficult for the sniper.

"They'll think about things for a while now, that should give us until dark to find somewhere to make a stand." James Blue went forward to sit with Pete. "If they get any closer let me know." He called out to Clay as he went. It was going to be a long day.

It had been a very long day before Pete sighted the staging post ahead. The eight riders chasing them had remained just outside the range of Bluey's rifle but followed them doggedly all day. Dusk was announcing its forthcoming presence as they reigned the exhausted horses in close to the doors of the largest of the three buildings, as at Walt's place, the other two were a barn and an outhouse. Bluey and Clay stood on guard while the passengers dismounted and went inside, Clay McCandless leading the way with his unappreciatively close companion. Pete and Josh Milton disconnected the team and took the horses into the barn for the night and while Pete took care of the feed and rub downs Josh and the whisky salesman unloaded the passengers' baggage.

The Marshall found the bodies.

The stage post had been run by a man and wife team. They laid where they fell, cowering behind the still warm stove in the kitchen. It had been used since the killings, by the killer, or killers McCandless presumed as the couple's remains displayed severe burns. The bullet holes were several days old surrounded by blood, the deceased pair did not smell good. McCandless found a huge solid oak table, too heavy for one man to move without help. He fastened Juan Lopez to one of the support struts and calling on the reluctant preacher to help him, they moved the bodies outside and covered them with blankets.

The kitchen had been ransacked but was still quite well stocked with the basics. Margaret Milton set about making the weary travellers hot meals of eggs and beans. Clay Milton found himself a vantage point on the roof of the barn and kept watch through the increasing gloom while Bluey took a break to eat and freshen up. He sat next to the Marshall who asked him.

"Pete told me about what you did. Where did you learn to shoot like that?"

"I've been around a bit Marshall, I used to work for the British Police in Australia. We needed to be able to fight and shoot."

"What made you leave and come here?"

"Not all the Police were good guys, I fell out with a Sergeant and a Captain when they tried to beat up on a couple of families who were just trying to make a living without paying extra taxes for protection from the people who were supposed to be looking after them."

"What did you do?" The Marshall was curious.

"Well I persuaded them to stop but they didn't take kindly to my interference and pulled their guns on me." Bluey looked directly into the face of Clay McCandless and carried on. "I had no choice but to shoot them, they both died and the rest of their squad branded me as a bush ranger. They chased me for months until I got fed up with their games and let them catch me."

"What happened, did you kill them all?"

"No, not all of them, the farmers I'd helped got together with some of their people and helped me out. After that I'd had enough and left to travel around. I ended up in Washington, then I drifted west, and here I am, still getting shot at." He laughed wearily.

"What do you think happened here?" McCandless changed the subject to the present problems.

"I think what happened is there to see." Bluey pointed outside in the direction of the covered corpses. "Who did it and why I haven't a clue. What's your take on it?" Pete Nicholson joined them.

"What have you got in the cash box Pete?" The Marshall asked the driver. "How much are we sitting on?"

"One consignment of cash, from the makeshift replacement bank at Indian Buttes to the main bank at Apache Bend, $5,000."

"Take it outside and bury it somewhere." McCandless ordered. "Whatever happens they won't get it."

"Travis and Millie were good people." Pete explained to the two men as he got up to do the Marshall's bidding. "They wouldn't hurt anyone. I reckon they were killed so that they couldn't warn us about whoever that is chasing us."

"But that has served to warn us that something's wrong, maybe not what or who." The Marshall commented. "But $5,000 is a good enough reason why."

"Senor Marshall." Juan Lopez intruded into the conversation, an evil grin across his leering face. "It is to let you know what will happen to you when my brother finds you."

"I wouldn't get too excited Lopez, if I think I'm going to get killed, I'll make sure you die first, then you'll be there to welcome me to Hell." McCandless snarled, nobody present had cause to doubt him. Juan Lopez became silent once more.

James Blue grabbed a couple of hours sleep and then silently left the room to relieve Clay Milton from his watchful appraisal of the surrounding area. Nothing to report but a faint glow in the distance. Probably where the following band of men were bedding down for the night he supposed.

"Can you give me a couple of hours before you go and get some rest?" Bluey asked the younger man.

"Sure what have you got in mind?" Clay voiced his curiosity.

"Just a little sightseeing." Came the answer, and then the Australian was gone from his sight. Clay continued to peer into the darkness, he thought he saw

Bluey's shadow as it disappeared into the night. A second later he saw something else, a similar movement, it materialised for a split second and like the ghostly figure before it, it vanished. As quickly and silently as he could Clay descended from the roof and went inside, he spoke to the Marshall and Pete.

"Bluey's gone to find the people who followed us, but I think there's someone else out there, maybe one of them, I'm not sure. Pete can you take the watch, I'm going after him?" Pete looked concerned and checked with the Marshall who nodded.

"Yeah, I'll make sure we block the windows here and if you need to just holler." He told the stage driver.

"Okay, Clay, let me have that scatter gun, anyone who gets too close is gonna get a hole where their guts oughta be."

"Be careful Son." Ordered Josh Milton, his son was already on his way.

"Is he gonna be okay?" Clay McCandless asked of the rancher.

"He's a tough kid, and clever. He doesn't talk about it much but he's worked undercover for the government back East a few times. He helped save President Grant's life some years ago, and managed to prevent the head of his secret service being killed. The man himself told me Clay shot a traitor who was about to kill him. He's done things most young fellers haven't even dreamt about. He'll be fine."

"Well, him and the Aussie should make a good team then." The Marshall felt a little easier at the revelations.

Bluey had not been the earlier of the two figures to leave the staging post as Clay had imagined. He had seen another shadowy form first, the second man had been the Australian.

The man in front was as silent as the shadow he resembled. He drew closer to the camp fire of the group of men who'd pursued the stagecoach travellers earlier. Bluey equally as furtive and noiseless followed at a safe distance. The Australian thought he might have detected a hint of a limp in the shadow's gait, but he wasn't sure. He watched as the perimeter was effortlessly breached by the wraithlike shape in front of him and decided to hang back.

A tree stood ten yards to one side of a barely visible sentry. Bluey crept past the less than alert man as easily as the previous trespasser and without making a humanly audible sound climbed up the tree to a substantial branch fifteen feet above the ground. He would be able to hear any normal conversations taking place from his observation point and hopefully remain undetected.

Bluey scoured the scene under and beyond him, apart from the incompetent guard near where he hid there were two more, strategically placed around the area. Five men slept in blankets scattered round the remains of the fire. He could not at first see the shadowy figure of the person he'd followed. Then he could, a man's figure strode into the centre of the makeshift camp, he exhibited a slight limp. He stopped right next to the fire and raising a rifle fired into the air. The noise of the shot woke the sleeping men with a start and they all automatically reached for their weapons, but they found none to hand. The visitor had stealthily removed every firearm he could find without disturbing anyone's slumber.

"Which one of you is Frank Lawson?" The intruder spoke in a strange, accented voice, not Mexican not American, not quite Indian either, guttural, rustling sound issued from his lips. Bluey watching from his vantage point could make out an unevenly positioned bowler hat exposing just a little of the partly shaven head and Comanche style pony tail of the speaker's hair, the dimming firelight also highlighted a red scar on the left side of the man's face. He'd never met Rattlesnake Joe but he'd been around the West long enough to have heard of him and he knew that he was now looking at the scalp hunting, gun running killer.

"I'm Lawson Mister, what do you want?" One of the men answered just as the armed sentries rushed towards them.

"Put your guns down or I will shoot Lawson." Rattlesnake Joe ordered, not moving his aim from Frank Lawson's chest. The gang leader knew he'd be the first to die if shots were to be fired.

"Put the guns down, boys." He ordered, the sentries complied nervously. "Well? What is it you want?"

"I want to help you, I already have. You are chasing the stagecoach, yes?"

"That's right, but we don't need your help, I've got enough men to do the job."

"You've lost two already and you haven't got close to them yet, I know of the man you're up against, a U.S. Marshall, McCandless, he is tough, clever and he has a sharp shooter with him." Bluey couldn't resist an invisible smile at the description of himself.

"We can handle the sharp shooter, he can't kill anyone he can't see." Lawson was becoming impatient and frustrated as his immediate fear subsided

"I would think the best place for an ambush would be the canyon halfway between here and Apache Bend, yes?" The scalp hunter queried.

"That's right, they won't even see us 'til it's too late." Lawson was almost gloating now.

"That's exactly what the Marshall will figure." The half breed lowered his rifle. "Pick up your weapons." He pointed to a pile of guns just out of reach of the outlaws. The potential stage raiders scrambled to re-arm themselves. Rattlesnake Joe watched closely for any kind of threat, not seeing one he continued. "We surround them at the staging post, now, and attack in morning as soon as it's light enough. I've already dealt with the people who ran it." Lawson thought hard for a minute before agreeing. So that's the who and why of the killings at the staging post. Bluey realised Rattlesnake Joe was a cunning and resourceful adversary.

"Okay, we'll do it your way, and split it between the nine of us." Lawson tried to sound as authoritative as he could. He suddenly didn't feel it.

"The Marshall has a prisoner with him, I want him, and I want him alive." Rattlesnake Joe added. "Alive!"

Bluey had heard enough, he climbed silently down from his hiding place and began to make his way back and report his findings. A faint movement to his left caused him to stop motionless for a minute and listen, nothing. He carried on with his careful journey until out of earshot of the outlaw camp.

"You can show yourself now, Clay." He laughed. "You're very good, just one slight footfall."

"How did you know it was me?" Clay Milton asked him as he appeared from the darkness to take up with the Australian.

"Well, I'm not a bad judge of character. Besides if any of the men in the camp were following me one of us would be dead by now. You're young but this ain't your first rodeo, you've been around, you've seen and probably done things a lot of Eastern educated kids couldn't even imagine. Am I right?"

"Kind of. What are we going to do? I think we've got about an hour on them before they surround us."

"Oh, you got that close?" Bluey's appraisal of the younger man was justified he thought.

"I just followed the guard when he heard the shot. Who is the half breed, why does he want Lopez?"

"His name is Rattlesnake Joe. He is well named, he is wanted in every state he's ever been in, he's a murderer, scalp hunter, gun runner, rustler, you name it, and he's done it. If he's after Lopez it's either to kill him himself or set him free."

Clay and Bluey reported what they'd seen and heard to all as they sat round the largest table at the staging post.

"We don't want to be caught in the open, which we will be if we run." McCandless thought out loud. "We have to make a stand here."

"That's what I figured." Agreed Bluey. "The roof, we need people who can shoot on both of them."

"I'll take the house if you take the barn." Clay suggested to the Australian who nodded in agreement.

"We tie him up and leave him in the kitchen." The Marshall jabbed a finger at his prisoner. "I'll stick a gag in his mouth to shut him up and I'll cover the front window." He turned to Josh Milton. "Can you cover the rear?" Josh picked up his own rifle and checked his pistol.

"Yes, no problem." The rancher said, feeling nowhere near as confident as he tried to sound. "Margaret you stay under cover, if things go wrong hide under the bed, take this. It's loaded." He handed his wife a small single shot derringer. She took it with tears in her eyes. She knew what her husband was telling her.

"I'll be in the barn with the horses, if the worst comes to the worst….." Pete left the sentence unfinished. McCandless looked around at the two unknown quantities. The whisky salesman looked terrified and was busy consuming too many of his promotional samples.

"Can you use a gun, Gordon?" He asked the semi sober quaking little man, now silent for a change. "Never mind. What about you Preacher?" The preacher sighed.

"Thou shalt not kill." The man of few words said in reply to the question. Marshall Clay McCandless shook his head in anger.

"Perhaps you'd better tell that to Rattlesnake Joe and Frank Lawson."

Clay Milton saw them first, he signalled across to the roof of the barn and stuck up three fingers to alert Bluey to the number of attackers he had seen. Bluey replied with one finger pointing to the front followed by two pointing to the rear. Pete had a good view of the outhouse from where he crouched near the open barn door, behind a bale of hay. He spotted a shadow moving as the Sun's early rays began to be noticeable in the eastern sky. He waited until he could get a better view of the armed man approaching the house and pulled the trigger. The noise of the shot served as a signal for Clay and Bluey, both opened fire in the same second. Two men fell, the shape by the outhouse vanished out of sight of the stage driver who swore at his own nervousness, which had caused him to miss the easy shot. Clay and Bluey fired again but their intended targets were on the move and although Bluey succeeded in winging one of them they escaped serious injury taking cover behind nearby bushes.

"Josh Milton fired next, he had a good view of the man who rounded the corner of the building to his right. He pulled the trigger as the intruder aimed his own weapon at the window. The man screamed and fell, two more shots rang out as Marshall McCandless killed another of the bandits who had the drop on Pete, standing in the barn doorway. Realising he could have been killed, Pete dived back into the barn and died. Frank Lawson was standing, waiting to greet him and emptied a double barrelled shotgun into his chest. The Marshall took a shot at Lawson but his vision was blocked as the outlaw retreated deeper into the barn. One of his men took the chance of exposing himself to the Marshall's view trying to get a better aim at the lawman. Clay Milton shot him down and fired a second time to make sure. He climbed down from the roof as a horse and rider speedily left from the rear of the barn.

Frank Lawson had had enough, he abandoned all thought of the $5,000 and put his own survival at the top of his list of priorities. He did not give a thought to leaving his remaining men at the mercy of the Marshall and his helpers. Clay took a shot at him but the escaping outlaw was already beyond the range of his rifle.

"Alright. We've had enough. Don't shoot." The remaining two of Lawson's gang surrendered. They marched slowly into the open space in front of the house and stopped, arms raised and no weapons in sight. Clay McCandless walked out to meet them, gun never wavering from where they stood. Josh Milton moved from the back to the front window to cover him.

Rattlesnake Joe had moved fast, he'd climbed up to the roof on seeing Clay Milton come down, making sure he was out of sight of James Blue on top of the barn. He'd soundlessly opened an upstairs window and climbed in. The second Josh Milton's attention was on the Marshall and the surrendering men at the front he stepped from the stairs into the main room.

The preacher saw him first and started to form a word in his mind. No one ever found out what he might've said as Rattlesnake Joe shot him dead. Josh Milton turned to find the gun now pointing at his heart. He dropped his own gun and raised his hands.

"Marshall!" Rattlesnake Joe shouted in his uniquely unpleasant voice. "If you do not do what I say I will shoot everyone in here." McCandless moved swiftly out of the line of fire. The scalp hunter fired twice in rapid succession, the two remaining outlaws fell dead.

"Cowards!" He spat the word out as he repositioned the bowler hat to cover his hair completely. "If I will shoot my own men, I will not worry if I kill two old men and a woman. Bring me three horses to the front, now." He turned to the whisky salesman Jonas Gordon. "You! Fetch the woman and untie the prisoner." The grey haired drummer, scarcely able to control his bladder hurried off to do as he was told, returning within a minute with Margaret Milton.

"Lopez! Untie him, now." Again the whisky salesman scuttled away to do as instructed. Juan Lopez walked into the room, stretching his limbs and rubbing his wrists and hands to stimulate circulation as he searched for a weapon.

"Juan Lopez, I have come to take you to your brother. I need to find him."

"Ah! Senor, my brother will be most grateful. And I. I thank you. You are the Comanche, Rattlesnake, yes?" The freed killer said to his benefactor.

"Get yourself a gun and tie up the woman, we are going to need insurance. She will come with us." Lopez retrieved Josh Milton's discarded weapon and looked around for some rope.

"I will shoot the Marshall before we go." His malicious intent was more than evident in his voice and likewise in his twisted, venomous expression of unhinged hatred.

"I think not Senors." A new voice.

Rattlesnake Joe and Juan Lopez turned to see a newcomer, a young Mexican, flashily dressed, but that is not what concerned them. The two pistols aiming at them did. Juan Lopez did not recognise the youngster even though he'd spent some time riding with him. Margaret Milton could take no more and fainted, Josh moved towards her, Rattlesnake Joe turned to deal with him and Rodrigo Lamas fired twice.

Juan Lopez staggered backwards, dropping his newly acquired pistol before he could use it and fell. Rattlesnake Joe felt a searing pain in his chest and fired back, hitting the wall behind where the shot had come from. He made his painful exit through the back door, before the gunman could refocus his aim. His horse was tethered right outside in case an emergency escape was required, it was and stifling a cry of pain the wounded half breed mounted swiftly and galloped away. Rodrigo fired after the fleeing man but only succeeded in putting a hole through the top of his bowler.

McCandless could hear the sound of hoof beats receding in the distance as he burst in loudly through the front door and took immediate stock of the situation as he saw it. He raised his gun to point at the pistolero, Josh Milton shook his head.

"He helped us." He explained and the Marshall lowered his gun. Rodrigo Lamas stood over the fallen, gasping Juan Lopez.

"Lopez, you pig, I want you do die slowly and in great pain, I want you to remember what you did to my family, my village." Juan Lopez stared blankly upwards, groaning in his agony, unknowing and uncaring, his sight fading along with his life. He only lasted another minute. At least Rodrigo could be satisfied that his enemy died in great pain.

"You'd better tell us who you are, Son, and what your purpose is." Clay McCandless said to the young Mexican avenger. Rodrigo introduced himself and gave a brief outline of his reason for being there. The whisky

108

salesman went outside to relieve his complaining bladder and to be violently sick.

Clay Milton found a spade in the barn, and he, James Blue and Rodrigo Lamas dug holes to bury the dead, and the grim task took them nearly all day. When they'd finished, and now in the absence of a preacher, Jonas Gordon found his voice again and said a few words from the bible over the graves. The Marshall and Josh Milton had collected the bodies together, they were ten in number. Margaret Milton recovered quite well from her ordeal and prepared food for everyone. Rodrigo Lamas expanded on his earlier revelations during dinner, in response to the curiosity of the others, he recounted his story and his ensuing quest for vengeance in more detail.

It was decided to rest the night and set off for Apache Bend at first Light. Marshall Clay McCandless located the hidden cash box without the need for much searching and they departed. Clay Milton volunteered to drive the stagecoach while Bluey would scout ahead, Rodrigo Lamas would ride shotgun before taking his leave for a return to Mexico.

Chapter Eleven:

Tumbleweed Cross.

Jack Wilson enjoyed being a Sheriff. He was used to being on the other side of the law. A hunted gunslinger, murderer and bank robber with a $5,000 price on his head. But not anymore, the town Mayor had appointed him Sheriff of Tumbleweed Cross. He had no choice, Wilson had killed the previous holder of the office and his solitary Deputy, and held a gun to the heads of the Mayor and his family in order to convince him it was the right thing to do. With his own choice of four Deputies sworn in Jack Wilson took complete control of the town, levying taxes on businesses, commandeering weapons, food, drink, clothing and anything else he and his men desired, all free of charge. Most of his time was spent frequenting the town's only saloon, which as in many places of a similar size and population doubled as a hotel and brothel.

Tumbleweed Cross was so named because it consisted of two streets which crossed, like numerous other small towns, and because being flat and open the wind blew the rolling tumbleweed constantly along all the routes in and out of the place.

Jack Wilson was preoccupied with the attentions of the woman in his bed and missed the arrival of a stranger in black, mounted on a white stallion. Shannon dismounted a hundred yards away from the saloon. For the hundredth time he thought to himself, it's always the saloons, never the churches. He was just about to walk towards the establishment when a voice called him from across the street.

"Hey! Mister! I'll take that gun." The man wore a Deputy Sheriff's badge. Shannon recognised the man's face. He didn't remember his name but he knew his value as a reward. A $300 bonus he calculated. The man wasn't alone and his badge wearing colleague, another $300, Shannon counted, began to walk towards him, hand hovering over his holster.

"You can try and take the gun, but I wouldn't advise it." The bounty hunter told him. "Where's Wilson?"

"Stranger, perhaps you don't hear so good. I told you to hand over your gun." The persistent Deputy raised his voice to emphasise the intended menace.

"Where's Jack Wilson? I won't ask again." Shannon repeated.

"Looks like I will have to take it." The Deputy moved forward and his hand reached towards his holster. It didn't get there. Shannon shot him between the eyes before he even saw the bounty hunter move. His less vocal partner managed to touch his own weapon a split second before he too was dead, a bullet an inch to the left of his blood stained badge. A grunt of pain came from somewhere behind Shannon and he spun round to deal with any threat, throwing himself to the ground as he did so. The body of another of

Wilson's Deputies landed in a crumpled, dead heap five yards in front of him. A movement on the roof of the saloon alerted him and he looked up, he couldn't see anyone but knew the Deputy didn't jump of his own accord or inflict the massive knife wound across his own throat.

"I didn't think you deserved to be shot in the back." Came a voice from the roof.

"I'm obliged to you." Shannon answered the formless voice. "Would you care to show yourself?"

"Sure, just don't shoot me." Shannon watched as a tall athletic young man in his twenties showed himself and descended from the roof with the grace of a cat. The man was dressed in black jeans and boots, a red shirt and a buckskin jacket. His black wide brimmed Stetson sported an eagle's feather in the hatband. All looked relatively new apart from the feather. He wore a pistol low on his right hip, a large knife on his left, and on his back was slung a repeating rifle. He turned to face the bounty hunter with a smile on his handsome face.

"By the look of you, you're Johnny Hawkeye, I've been hearing about you." Shannon told him. "What brings you to these parts?"

"And by the look of you, you must be the bounty hunter, Shannon. Right?" He continued in response to a guarded nod in the affirmative. "Well, I reckon I'm after the same person as you, Wilson. But I'm not after the reward, I only want information. I'd be obliged if you'd let me talk to him before you kill him. When I've found out what I want to know, he's all yours." Johnny watched a faint smile fleetingly appear on Shannon's face and disappear in a rare moment of amusement. They walked towards the saloon together.

"I owe you so I'll give you an hour, he's in the saloon I don't know where his other Deputy is."

"He's not going to cause either of us any trouble, you can check if there's a price on his head in the Sheriff's office, that's where you'll find his body. He didn't give me the information I want." Johnny Hawkeye casually explained. Shannon thought to himself the stories he'd been hearing about this young man were not necessarily all, the fiction he'd suspected.

"Out of interest what is it you think Wilson can tell you?" he asked the hunter.

"I'm searching for a man called Rattlesnake, Rattlesnake Joe. I think Wilson may be able to tell me where to find him, they were together a few months back. And when I do find the son of a bitch I'm going to kill him."

"I'm going to be looking for him myself. I hope we don't have a problem there." Shannon informed Johnny Hawkeye.

"I don't see why we should, I'm going to kill him, and then you can have him. It would be better if we worked together on this. That way we don't have to worry what the other is doing."

"Or I could just kill you." Shannon told him. "Then I wouldn't need to worry about what you are doing." Johnny Hawkeye laughed.

"You could try, but why bother? I'm not a threat or a profit to you. And you've never done anything to make me want to kill you." He laughed again. "I wouldn't have helped you if I thought I'd end up having to fight you."

"It makes sense." The bounty hunter conceded. "What has Rattlesnake Joe done to you?"

"I lived with the Cheyenne when I was younger, he and his men raided my village when the men were out hunting. They slaughtered and scalped everyone, all the women, old men and children. First, they raped all the women and young girls. My wife and my two children were there. The rest of his men are dead, they did not die easy, nor will he, but he will soon join them. I will be the one to kill him. If I have to kill you to get to him I will, but I don't want it to come to that."

"It won't come to that Johnny Hawkeye." Shannon said softly, he was thinking back to his own past. "You've got yourself a partner." He couldn't believe that he'd just said that, a man who always works alone just took on a partner. They drew level with the saloon.

"Here's the saloon." Shannon paused, just a second's hesitation, and then he asked, "When you ask him about the Rattlesnake, can you find out if he knows the whereabouts of a man named Lawson, Frank Lawson?" Johnny Hawkeye nodded to his new colleague and pushed open the swing doors.

The saloon keeper was a large, swarthy, unwashed bulk of a man. Johnny could smell the sweat on him as soon as he entered the bar area. The bar was quite busy for mid-afternoon and many of the tables were occupied. Johnny chose a stool at the quiet end of the bar and immediately wished he hadn't as the odious bartender approached. His breath was as bad as his body odour and Johnny knew the stench would stay with him until he bathed.

"Whisky." The hunter ordered and seeing the filthy hands of the man mountain grab an unclean glass with his thumb inside it added. "Leave the bottle." He paid and the foul smelling hulk wandered off to find him some change. He sat there surveying the clientele whilst swigging sparingly from the freshly wiped neck of the whisky bottle. He knew what Wilson looked like, providing his wanted poster did him justice but he was not present. He could smell the bar keeper's return and as he took his change from the man's grimy paw he asked him.

"Wilson, where's Jack Wilson?"

"I don't know any Jack Wilson." The gust of latrine breath lied.

"Where is he?" Johnny's knife was suddenly nuzzling under the man's sweat drenched throat. "The Sheriff, are you telling me you don't know the Sheriff?"

"Okay, Okay!" It seemed impossible to Johnny Hawkeye but with fear entering into the equation the stink of the saloon keeper intensified. The frightened man nearly retched because of the fright, Johnny from the induced nausea. "He's upstairs, third room along, he's with one of the women." Johnny Hawkeye lowered his weapon.

"Thank you, pass me the cleanest cloth you've got, if there is one." A quizzical look appeared on the bar tender's face as he sighed in relief but he found a semi clean cloth and handed it to Johnny Hawkeye. The hunter wiped his hands and threw the cloth back at him. Then he picked up the bottle of whisky and walked to the stairs, watching in a usefully positioned mirror to check that the shotgun he'd spotted behind the bar stayed there. The terror he'd instilled into the malodorous oaf insured that it did.

Johnny knocked on the door of the third room he came to.

"What is it?" a female voice inquired.

"The fat guy downstairs the one who stinks up the bar, he sent me up with a bottle of whisky for Jack." A man's voice called out.

"Bring it in." Johnny Hawkeye opened the door and walked nonchalantly in carrying the bottle. Jack Wilson was about forty years old, he was sitting up in the bed, and the naked woman next to him had the sheet pulled up to her neck in an attempt to preserve her limited modesty.

"Who are you?" He asked the hunter. He held a gun in his hand, pointing at the younger man.

"I'm just the guy who brought you up a bottle of whisky, Sheriff, the man behind the bar......"

"Silas wouldn't send me up a bottle, what do you want?" Wilson cut him off. "Who are you?"

"Okay." Johnny smiled. "I really came here to warn you. There's a man down in the street waiting for you. A man called Shannon, do you know him?"

"Shannon! The bounty hunter?" The bravado evaporated and Wilson suddenly became fearful. "My men they'll....." It was Johnny's turn to cut in'

"Your men are all dead, he's killed them all, all four of them, and he's waiting for you."
Wilson's face paled noticeably and his gun hand wavered.

"Why did you warn me and who are you?"

"My name is Johnny, and I can't let him kill you until you answer a question for me." He answered frankly. The gun hand began to shake markedly and Johnny, who'd been slowly moving closer to the bed moved to put the bottle on the bedside table. While doing so he quickly grabbed at Wilson's gun and reversed its direction of aim. Wilson's increased fear was evident and uncontrolled, he was one of many bullying tyrants whose courage fades when the guns are pointed at them.

"Now, I've got about an hour before Shannon comes for you. You can tell me what I want to know straight away and I'll be gone. Or you can keep me waiting and I'll cut you many times, I will cause you so much pain you'll wish the hour was up with fifty five minutes still to go." Johnny Hawkeye smiled, exposing his even white teeth, it was not a pleasant smile. The hunter showed Wilson the knife, and it looked huge and very sharp to the cowardly Sheriff of Tumbleweed

Cross. The woman next to him, modesty forgotten crawled hurriedly out of the bed and reached for her clothes.

"You can get dressed, but then you sit quietly on the floor, down there. Where I can see you" Johnny told her and gestured to the side of the bed.

"What is it you want from me?" The wanted man tried to fight his overwhelming cowardice and failing miserably.

"I want Rattlesnake Joe. You rode with him, where can I find him?"

"Rattlesnake Joe? I only rode with him once, that was months ago, he was looking for Fernando Lopez. I don't know where he is now." Hawkeye noted a succinct realisation dawn on his captive.

"What is it Wilson, what do you know?"

"Well I heard that a U.S. Marshall took Lopez's brother, Juan, prisoner and was taking him to Apache Bend. I don't know how to find Rattlesnake, but he didn't know where to find Lopez. Juan will know how to find his brother and if Rattlenake cut him loose...."

"He would use Juan to take him. You just might have saved your life. Oh and Frank Lawson, where's he?"

"Frank Lawson? He's no one, a two bit hold up man, he could be anywhere between Indian Buttes and Apache Bend." Wilson sagged back in the bed. "Are you gonna let me go now?"

"I don't care what you do Wilson, but my friend downstairs might." Johnny told him.

"Your friend, I don't understand." Wilson began to shake again.

"He means the bounty hunter, you idiot." The girl spat at him with spite. "How you ever became worth $5,000 to him I'll never know." Wilson ignored her. She turned to Johnny Hawkeye. "Do you wanna buy a girl a drink?" She asked trying for all the world to look attractive.

"Some other time." The hunter told her. Some other girl, he told himself as he left the room.

Shannon was waiting outside and then took his own turn to scare the terrified man inside.

"You!" gasped Wilson. "He told me I'd got an hour."

"He had an hour. You haven't. $5,000, dead or alive, your choice." For once the bounty hunter would be correct in assuming alive would be the choice of his less than courageous quarry.

They took with them the bodies of the deceased Deputies, draped across the backs of their horses and set off, Johnny Hawkeye, Shannon and Jack Wilson. They were headed for Apache Bend.

Chapter Twelve:

The Gatherings At Apache Bend.

Frank Lawson blessed his luck, he'd escaped from the staging post unhurt and made his way to Apache Bend ahead of any pursuers. He checked into a good quality hotel, using most of his cash to do so, but who would look for a two bit hold up man in such a grand establishment? His plan was to contact an old acquaintance he'd ridden with in the past and make another attempt to rob the stage before the cash could be transferred to the formidable town bank.

The man he was looking for was Jack Wilson. Wilson hadn't been seen in town for months, he and four other men had travelled north to a town called Tumbleweed Cross. He wasn't the only one who wanted to find him, but he didn't know that, or that he himself was the subject of the same predatory hunter. Had Frank Lawson been able to see the future he would have cursed, not blessed his luck.

The Sheriff of Apache Bend was Barton Lee, a tall, gangly man with a mop of dark hair and a walrus moustache. He didn't look for trouble but he and his four deputies, Eric, Bill, Tex and Jed, would handle whatever problems arose with force if necessary. He knew not every visitor was a good person and that some were wanted by the law. But if peace was maintained he would turn a selectively blind eye when it suited him. He reasoned that anonymous lowlifes such as Frank Lawson were not worth the trouble of arresting if they behaved. If they didn't he would deal with them severely. However Barton Lee was no coward, if disruptive, famous, or infamous outlaws came to his town, someone like the James and Younger gang, Fernando Lopez or John Wesley Hardin he would have no choice. He would have to intervene and he would do it bravely and give it everything he'd got.

Rattlesnake Joe arrived in Apache Bend a day later than Lawson. His wounded chest was giving him a lot of pain and slowed him down considerably, the bullet had not penetrated deeply but had been deflected by a rib causing blood to flow but no serious or lasting damage. The renegade Comanche half breed sought refuge in the saloons and whore houses of the town's less reputable areas and finally rested with a saloon girl he'd known for several years whose discretion was assured, if not through care and love, then certainly through fear.

Apache Bend, so named because of its position on the bend of the river. It had been the site of a long abandoned Apache camp and was now the largest settlement in the area by some way, a bustling, busy town surrounded by many ranches. The railway passed through the centre and a train station now served as an arrival and departure point for visitors and residents alike. It co-existed comfortably with the stage line at present although future expansion and the coming of the motor car would eventually annihilate the horse drawn competition. The stores were well supplied and busy. The hotels were always filled close to capacity, and the many saloons were rowdy, noisy and thriving, as were the brothels which often shared the same premises.

It was into this cauldron of activity that the stagecoach and its passengers found themselves materialising late in the afternoon. Josh Milton took it upon himself to book everyone into a large hotel nearest to the centre of the sprawling town, at the convergence of the four main streets. Only the Marshall was reluctant to accept the gift of a comfortable hotel room but Clay Milton persuaded him to endure the comfort offered along with the others in the party. James Blue wanted to pay his own way but eventually accepted Josh's generosity with gratitude. Rodrigo Lamas explained that he had to head back to Mexico and reunite with his sister but again Clay Milton convinced him to at least stay the night and get some rest. The whisky pedlar, Jonas Gordon accepted immediately, and offered a few of his remaining samples as a gesture of appreciation. The influx of so many people in one party meant that they would be two rooms short of being able to accommodate everyone. It was agreed that Clay and James Blue would share, and so would Jonas Gordon, and the short straw went to the young pistolero who would have the dubious pleasure of hearing all about Johnny Hawkeye until the older man fell asleep.

Marshall Clay McCandless had left the stagecoach party to their relaxations and refreshments and gone to see the Sheriff, Barton Lee. He left the cash box from the stage coach with the Sheriff, to arrange its safe passage to the bank, his first task. If anyone was looking out for him or one of the other passengers to carry out the task they would be disappointed. Frank Lawson was discussed along with the renegade Rattlesnake Joe. Lee had not seen Lawson in recent months and had never set eyes on the half breed but would alert his deputies to be on the lookout. Clay McCandless felt an affinity with Barton Lee, he reminded him of himself a few, no, several years ago.

After leaving the Sheriff's office McCandless visited the nearest saloon, and making sure his badge was concealed beneath his jacket, he sat nursing a glass of beer, unwinding from recent stresses and generally studying the comings and goings of the drinkers and revellers. Two hours later he returned to the hotel. Josh and Margaret Milton had retired for the evening, the others occupied a large table and were indulging in discussions and recollective conversations regarding the eventful journey to Apache Bend.

"Pull up a chair, Marshall, join us." Clay Milton invited him.

"Thanks, I will." He answered and did so. Clay poured him a large whisky which was gratefully received with a nod of appreciation. "So what now? Who's doing

123

what next?" He asked and looked around at his companions. As expected Jonas Gordon was the first to answer.

"Well I have to go back East, I need to process my orders and restock my samples. I have an appointment with a friend of mine, a writer, he wants to hear about Johnny Hawkeye." There had to be someone, somewhere, the Marshall thought to himself. He'd heard of Johnny Hawkeye, a lot of people were hearing about him, not just from the sycophantic whisky salesman but from people all over the south and beyond. If he was half as wonderful as Jonas Gordon would have us believe we could have used him along the trail he reflected. Indeed we could use him now.

"He wants to publish books about him." The drummer continued. "He'll be famous." Cynically McCandless said.

"He already is, isn't he?" He changed the subject. "What about you, Young Feller?"

"I will return to Mexico, I will go to my sister and we will journey to our village and rebuild our lives." Rodrigo told him, McCandless thought he saw the hint of a tear in the young man's eye.

"Good luck Son, I wish you well. What about you Bluey? Got any plans?"

"Not really Marshall. Never been too good at plans, something always seems to get in the way of them." Came the truth.

"Well, I could use a deputy, think about it. The pay's not great and you could get your arse shot off, but if you've got nothing better to do. And you get to wear a badge"

"Don't you mean a target? I'll think about it, it's not every day I get such an inviting proposition." Bluey had collected his wages earlier while returning the stagecoach to the company office and was free to consider alternative employment.

"What about you Clay? Won't you find ranching a little tame and even a bit boring after your exploits back East, or even here, in the last week?"

"To tell you the truth Marshall, I don't know. My Pa wants me to be responsible for running the business side of the ranch so he can take it a bit easier, and I owe him that. At least until my younger brother Johnnie can take over, but that's a few years off yet."

"What about your ranch Foreman, Foreman? Josh reckons he's a good man." McCandless inquired. He could sense he was right about Clay Milton. There was more in him than being a rancher.

"Ben's a great Foreman and the men respect him and work hard for him. The ranch would be in really safe hands with him, but he is not a business man, he doesn't know or want to know about finance, wheeling and dealing, paperwork and the like. I can do all that and leave him to do what he's good at, working with the men and the cattle."

The conversation ended abruptly as Jonas Gordon fell off his chair. The whisky salesman was gasping in his surprise and pointing to a man who'd just entered the hotel.

"That man!" He exclaimed. "That man is Johnny Hawkeye."

And indeed it was.

Johnny Hawkeye stood at the reception desk, the man behind the counter looked at him with ill-concealed distaste.

"I'm sorry Sir, all our rooms are taken." He told the hunter not trying too hard to supress an expression of glee.

"I don't want a room, I'm looking for a man named Frank Lawson, is he staying here?"

"I'm sorry Sir." The man repeated and then added. "We are not allowed to give out any information about our guests to...to... anyone who asks."

"I'm sure you could help me if you wanted to." Johnny told him and placed a handful of Dollar coins discreetly on the desk in front of him. He also looked pointedly down at his gun, making sure the clerk followed his line of vision and added menacingly. "Or even if you didn't want to." The obstructive attitude vanished as quickly as the money into the man's pocket.

"Of course Sir, I will check for you." And a minute later after a thorough search of the register. "No, I'm sorry Sir, there is no one of that name staying with us at present."

"Much obliged for your help." Johnny told him and turned to leave the building.

"Johnny! Johnny Hawkeye." Jonas Gordon's shout was heard throughout the foyer and Johnny looked to see the whisky salesman waving frantically from a table in the adjacent restaurant / bar area. He knew if he didn't walk over and speak to the older man he would probably shout again, so he casually walked towards him and nodded to all seated at the table.

"Won't you join us, I'll introduce you to my friends." Jonas Gordon could hardly contain his excitement at being able to prove his friendship with the hero, Johnny Hawkeye.

"Mister Gordon, isn't it?" Johnny said softly and added with more politeness than he felt. "Nice to see you again."

"Sit with us, have a drink." Gordon pulled a chair out for him and poured a whisky.

"I don't want to butt in on your evening." Johnny said, he was mightily embarrassed at the attention his arrival had caused and the others round the table could see this.

"Please, join us." Clay Milton said warmly. "We feel as though we know you already." Johnny smiled and accepted the seat, suddenly realising how much he could use a drink.

"I wouldn't believe everything you hear." He told them. The introductions followed and the atmosphere eased as the modest, friendly character of Johnny Hawkeye became evident during the course of the evening's conversation.

"What brings you to Apache Bend Johnny?" Clay McCandless asked of the young avenger. He gave them all a very brief outline, some of which Jonas Gordon had already revealed in past conversations. They were able to let him know of their unpleasant encounter with Rattlesnake Joe along the trail.

"I'm also looking for a man called Frank Lawson, or rather a friend of mine is. That's why I came in here, we thought he might try and hide in an upmarket hotel to throw us off the trail. Does anyone know where we might find him?"

"Frank Lawson was one of the men that attacked us, he was the one who got away before the half breed." James Blue supplied. "Who's your friend? What does he want him for?"

"He's a bounty hunter, but I don't think this one is for the money, it's personal."

"Lawson's not worth much compared to the Rattlesnake, I think he's posted at about $200," McCandless let them know. "Your bounty hunter friend, what's his name?"

"Shannon." Johnny watched the people round the table for a reaction. He wasn't disappointed or surprised. The whisky drummer gasped again, James Blue and Clay Milton showed by their expressions that the name Shannon meant something to them. The Marshall, whistled.

"Shannon, he's the best, the elite, what does he want with rubbish like Lawson?"

"Like I said, I think it's personal. I didn't press him on it." Johnny told them. "I don't think Lawson's going to want to see him."

"How did you get mixed up with a man like Shannon, he doesn't work well with others?" James Blue was curious, he could remember seeing the bounty hunter in action a few years ago and was impressed by his ruthless ability to carry out his dangerous work without relying on or wanting anyone's help.

"You could say we've got a common interest, I want Rattlesnake Joe for what he did to my people and Shannon wants him for the $5,000 reward. It's better to work together than have to go up against each another."

"Where is he now?" The Marshall wondered.

"He's taking a guy called Wilson and four of his men's bodies to the Sheriff's office, we found him earlier. He told us about Juan Lopez, it's a pity the scalp hunter knows he's dead, he would have come looking for him."

"I had to kill him Senor Hawkeye, like you will kill the Rattlesnake, for what he did to your family. I had waited eight years to find him for what he did to mine." Rodrigo ventured a rare but heartfelt comment.

"He had no choice, he saved my parents from being killed." Clay Milton interjected.

"Oh, I'm not blaming you Rodrigo, I would have done the same in your boots. I've been searching for that scalp hunting bastardo for nearly five years now. And I will find him. You say he's wounded, if he's here he'll be laying low." Johnny Hawkeye stated with a certainty he really did feel. He would catch and kill the renegade Comanche half breed for his family, for his people, for Zachariah Smith and the old man's family and for all the countless victims of the man's evil excesses. But most of all he would kill him for himself.

It was time for Johnny Hawkeye to take his leave. He and Shannon had booked rooms in a less salubrious establishment in the downtown area, hoping that the lively goings on would attract the likes of Lawson and supply the Rattlesnake with somewhere to recuperate. Tomorrow he and Shannon would visit other hotels and boarding houses in their search for the fugitives.

There was yet another visitor to the town that night. Clay Milton and James Blue had just bedded down for the night when there was a gentle knock at the door. Clay threw back his blanket and noiselessly crossed the room to open the door. A tall man in a black great coat brushed past him and pushed the door closed behind him.

"Long time no see, Mister Milton." The man bent to light the lamp and as the light flickered and lit up the room he stood up. He smiled to find both Clay and James Blue, who hadn't moved from his bed, pointing guns at him. "What a stroke of luck, Mister Blue as well." The English voice was unmistakeable.

"Colonel!" Clay exclaimed and was immediately echoed by James Blue.

"I am so glad you two know each other, it saves lengthy introductions." Colonel Jack Steele said to the astonished faces of the room mates. "You can discuss things amongst yourselves when I've gone, but for now I need you to listen. I've travelled a long way to find you both. I was as astonished as you must be at this moment, to find out you were traveling together. Even more delighted, if that is the correct terminology considering what I have to tell you, that you were this far south."

"What is it Colonel, I don't work for you anymore?" Bluey asked his ex-boss.

"I know you don't James and nor does young Clayton here, but I would like you both to consider a very important mission. A threat that needs nipping in the bud so to speak." The English inflection already evident in Colonel Jack Steele's rhetorical presentation became more progressively dominant as he continued. "Have you a drink I could possibly avail myself of?" Clay handed him a half empty bottle of whisky.

"Why us Colonel?" Clay was thinking he might already know the answer. The Colonel swigged from the bottle neck, sat down on the nearest bed and then told them.

"I need people who can think on the move, clever, resourceful men who can exist comfortably in the dangerous circles necessary. Proven operatives who have never let me down in the past. You two would be perfect if you can speak a modicum of Spanish?" Both nodded but wanted him to get to the point. He did.

"Have you ever heard of a Mexican General, a rebel called Gomez, Antonio Gomez?" Clay and Bluey shook their heads. "Or a Mexican bandido called

Fernando Lopez?" This name caused a more positive reaction.

"We've had dealings with his brother, Juan." Bluey explained the happenings on the road to Apache bend including the death of the bandit at the hands of the vengeful Pistolero. Jack Steele listened and digested what they had to say and then carried on with his exposition.

"We have reason to believe that General Gomez has sent someone to find Fernando Lopez and persuade him to steal a lot of big guns from the army. I mean really powerful field weapons, cannons and Gatlings. He thinks he's a Mexican Napoleon, he has ambitions to reclaim the Texas that Santa Anna lost to Houston and he's stolen enough money to try it. It's a delusional fantasy but a lot of people could die if he gets those guns. It could sour an already very fragile relationship with Mexico, we don't want another war. I want you two to stop him." He sat back on the edge of the bed. "From what you've told me I would guess that this Rattlesnake fellow is the messenger, the General's fixer. That's why he wants to find Lopez."

"You want the two of us to stop an army?" Bluey laughed sarcastically. "What next, fly to the moon?"

"But you've got professionals to do this type of work, I don't know about Bluey but I'm a rancher." Clay argued.

"And I'm Australian, I ride shotgun on stagecoaches." Bluey stated. "And like Clay said, you've got professionals."

"I can't use professionals, they can't cross the border and you will have to do that. Another thing, if you get caught you're on your own." The Colonel took another hit from the rapidly depleting whisky.

Clay had been correct in his assumption that he'd known the answer to "Why us?"

"You really are trying to convince us Colonel. What's the pay, a public hanging?" Bluey did actually manage a wry smile at his own comment.

"What, if any is the back up on this?" Clay asked, only slightly more seriously.

"Whatever and whoever you want, as long as nothing and no one can be traced back to the White House. I can let you have a $5,000 war chest, anything more you'll have to earn or steal." He looked directly at Clay Milton and then his eyes caught those of James Blue. "The President sends his regards and his thanks to you both."

"How did you find out about this plot?" Clay asked him.

"One of Gomez's men said too much in a bordello across the border, the wrong person, or right person overheard and passed the information on to one of my men in San Antonio. It cost my man and his source their lives. They were both found with their throats cut a day after he'd sent a letter to me. Gomez probably doesn't realise we know anything."

"What else can you tell us?"

"Absolutely nothing, other than I believe the threat is real."

"There's easier ways to die." Bluey said as the Colonel stood up and reached for the door handle.

"Yes, but you would still be dead. Good luck Boys." Steele opened the door. He threw a package onto the bed. "$5,000." Then the Englishman left the room.

"We haven't said yes." Clay called out to his retreating back.

"But you will." Colonel Jack Steele said, and was gone.

Chapter Thirteen:

An Alliance Of Interests.

Clay Milton and James Blue explained as briefly as they could to each other how they'd come to know Colonel Jack Steele. Clay gave the Australian an outline of the events surrounding the plot against President Grant and a few other of the cases he was involved in.

Bluey told a similar tale of working undercover as a spy for the Union during the savage, bloody civil conflict, and after. Exposing various threats to the fragile peace that laboured to survive in the tumultuous aftermath of The War Between The States.

He'd been recruited by Steele soon after his arrival from Australia. He'd found a job working as a bodyguard for a Washington businessman Walter Johns, who at first unbeknown to Bluey, was deeply involved in extortion rackets, prostitution and bank robberies, an organised crime lord.

Refusing an order from his boss to kill a rival and wipe out the man's family, including his wife and four children, Bluey had succeeded in putting a price on his own head. His disgruntled chief had sent three of his best men to eliminate the Australian upstart.

Steele, who'd been keeping an observation team on Johns sent two of his own men to protect James Blue with a view to turning him, and using him to help supply evidence leading to an arrest and conviction.

Bluey had a room in a boarding house on the second floor. The two agents could see a light on through the window as they crossed from the opposite side of the road. They were hurrying to try and catch up with the three gunmen who were a minute in front of them. The shattering of glass and a man's shout of fear made them look up. They managed to step aside just in time as the body of the man thudded to the street where they'd been standing. There was then a gunshot followed by the sounds of a fight, the smashing of furniture and another shout, more like a scream. The agents rushed upstairs and burst into Bluey's room. The Australian stood looking down at the two men sent to kill him, he was casually lighting a cigarette. One of the men displayed a bullet hole in his throat, he was unmoving, not breathing. The other was struggling to remove a large knife from his chest but ran out of strength and life before he was able to complete the task.

"You're too late officers." James Blue had told the agents as they stood embarrassed by their tardiness. "You've been following me on and off for days. What do you want?"

"I think you'd better come with us, our boss will want to see you." One of them said. The other asked him.

"How did you know who we were, we could've been back up for them?" He gestured to the dead men on the floor.

"You're not the only ones who can follow people, and you're certainly not the best at it. Let's go and see your boss." The Australian reached for his coat.

Colonel Jack Steele had offered him a job within an hour of meeting him. His information helped bring down Walter Johns, and his contacts proved effective in collecting enough evidence to send the criminal chief to prison for a very long time. He'd subsequently worked for Steele on many clandestine missions, but eventually his natural wanderlust instigated in him a desire to move west and so he quit and began his roaming. His initial thoughts had led him to consider California. He was in no hurry and so he was still a long way off, in Apache Bend, in the company of a Marshall, ranchers, a pistolero and a whisky drummer who'd introduced him to a vengeful killer who rode with a merciless bounty hunter.

"I'm going to do it, what about you, Bluey?" Clay asked the Australian.

"Oh Hell! Now I'll have to. You'll only go and get yourself killed if I don't come with you." Bluey answered with a half meant laugh. "The Colonel knew we wouldn't turn him down."

"We're going to need help, and a plan." Clay was muttering to himself, trying to force himself to think.

"Johnny Hawkeye, he would be useful, and Rodrigo, he'll know Mexico better than we do and he speaks the language much better than I can." Bluey suggested.

"Hawkeye's only got one thing on his mind, the half breed."

"But to help us, that would help him. We know the go-between is probably Rattlesnake Joe, find him, find Lopez, then we'll be halfway to finding the mad General."

"Easy." Lied Clay. "Let's talk to them. It's a good job Hawkeye told us where he's staying. What about Hawkeye's friend, the bounty hunter, if he is really the best?"

"I reckon he probably is. Getting Shannon on board will be difficult, we can't pay him, and the man's a mercenary."

"Better with us than against us, he'll be able to collect on the Rattlesnake and Lopez is worth twice as much."

Josh Milton went out early from the hotel to meet with Ben Foreman at the cattle market. Margaret Milton decided to rest in their room for most of the day, recent events had taken quite a toll on her. The Marshall was indulging himself in a huge breakfast when Clay and Bluey joined him at the table, Rodrigo sauntered in a minute later. The four sat together drinking coffee and Clay was the first to broach the subject of the forthcoming mission. He gave a brief outline of what had been asked of them.

"It's not going to be easy." Bluey understated. "And we're going to need some help."

"We need to find the Rattlesnake, he can lead us to Lopez." Clay stated. "That's got to be our first step."

"Not necessarily Senor Clay." Rodrigo spoke out with a broad smile on his face. "I have ridden with Fernando Lopez, I think I can take you to his hideout, a little village high in the hills. It is across the river, the Rio Grande, unless of course he has moved on to somewhere else."

"He'll have you shot on sight if he knows you betrayed him, Rodrigo. But if you could just draw us a map." Clay didn't want the young pistolero to underestimate the risks involved in such a course of action.

"People have been shooting at me all my life, but I am still here. Some of them are not." Rodrigo answered him. "I was never really accepted by Fernando, he thought I was all show because of the way I dress, and it suited me to let him think so until I could find a way to go after his brother. Then, as soon as I could, I left him to hunt down Juan and shoot him like the dog he was. The Bandidos, the Rurales, they are all a curse for my people to fear. I will come with you."

"If I was fifteen years younger, young feller, I'd come with you myself. Why not try the man who was here last night, Johnny Hawkeye, he strikes me as the sort of man you could use?" Clay McCandless had come to the same conclusion as Clay and Bluey, that the hunter had his own mission to accomplish, he wouldn't want to be caught up with anything that could distract him from the relentless pursuit of the object of his all-consuming hate.

"We've thought of him, we'll go and see him later, first let's eat." Bluey ordered a plate of bacon and eggs with more coffee.

"I guess this means I've got to look elsewhere for a Deputy." Clay McCandless told him.

They were nearly finished when Jonas Gordon joined them. He sat down as Clay, Bluey and Rodrigo stood up to go in search of Johnny Hawkeye.

Johnny Hawkeye and Shannon were just leaving their hotel in search of a cantina as Clay Milton, Rodrigo Lamas and James Blue arrived. Greetings and introductions were speedily carried out.

"Can we buy you both breakfast?" Bluey asked. "We have a proposition for you."

"Well for a breakfast we'll give it a listen." Johnny Hawkeye told them.

"Anything more than a listen will cost more, much more." Shannon added seriously.

The five men found a small cantina on the same street they were on and went inside. There was a young family at one table and another was occupied by a couple of Mexicans. Nobody seemed to take any notice as they sat down.

The bounty hunter and his partner listened intently to the outline of the mission as they ate and consumed their coffees.

"Rattlesnake Joe is the one I'm after and I've got no other trail to follow, so until I have, I'll help you." Johnny agreed.

"Let me just get this straight, you want us to work for you to get rid of this General Gomez, who to the best of my knowledge has no price on his head, at least not this side of the river, and you can't pay us?" Shannon needed the deal spelling out in detail.

"We want you to work for yourselves, just with us." Clay explained. "If Johnny can get his revenge on the half breed there's $5,000. Lopez, if you take him is worth $10,000, there are bound to be rewards on several of his men. All we want is to stop a mad man, a war."

"The odds aren't good." Shannon's turn to understate the situation.

"They weren't that good in Wichita two years ago when I saw you walk away from a gunfight against six men without a scratch. You left five of them dead and the other one wishing he was." Bluey told him. "I was with the Sheriff that day and told him we should help. He told me it would be over before we got close enough, he was right. I didn't know anything about you then, but I made a point of finding out. Odds don't frighten you Shannon."

"I made a lot cash that day, they weren't as good as their boasts. Fernando Lopez doesn't boast, and if he did he would be as good as he said he was. The Rattlesnake didn't get to be as old as he is without being dangerous, too many people hate him, not just because he's a half breed, but because he is an evil son of a bitch." Shannon paused to let his words sink in. "If I throw in with you it's going to be money hard earned." Johnny Hawkeye looked at the bounty hunter and then at the three men with them

"Okay, so where do we start?" He asked as the two Mexicans got up to leave.

Before anyone could answer him Marshall Clay McCandless walked in, he spoke directly to Johnny Hawkeye.

"Sheriff Lee came to see me." He began. "One of his Deputies found something out. A man matching the description of Rattlesnake Joe was staying at a place just two streets from here with one of the women who works there." Johnny immediately stood up. "Sit down Son." McCandless continued. "He's gone, left town last night, heading for the border. The other name you asked about, Lawson, he found out about your friend here being around and lit out this morning. He was heading north." He turned to Shannon. "I don't know what it is you want with Frank Lawson, Shannon but he sure looked scared according to the manager of the hotel he was using."

"He has cause to be Marshall." The bounty hunter said coolly and stood up. "I'll catch up with you Hawkeye. Leave enough of the Rattlesnake for me to collect on." He put on his hat and walked out, calling to Bluey as he went. "Thanks for the breakfast."

"Bluey, let's go get our horses and anything we need and we'll meet Johnny back here in half an hour."

142

Clay Milton suggested and received a nod of the head in reply. "Marshall can you tell my folks what's happened and that I don't know how long it's going to take, but to go home and I'll head for the ranch when this is over?"

In the months and years following the scalp hunting raid on the Cheyenne village, Rattlesnake Joe had heard of a man called Johnny Hawkeye, who was hunting him in search of vengeance. He realised the young avenger he'd encountered in Santo Juanita was this nemesis and that one day there would have to be a reckoning. But not now, he was too busy on a quest of his own to waste time on the youthful upstart, he had many enemies and one more did not concern him overmuch. Yet. For the moment he would concentrate on finding Fernando Lopez.

Josh Milton returned with his Foreman, Ben Foreman, to the hotel and found Clay McCandless waiting for him. He quickly explained the reason for Clay's absence and passed on his message. On being informed of the situation, Margaret was upset at her son putting himself in danger but Josh understood. Clay was always going to need more stimulation in his life than being a rancher could offer. Ben Foreman had been close to the young Clay as he grew from boy to young manhood and offered to go after him to help in his mission but Josh and McCandless both advised him against the idea.

"Believe me, that man knows what he's doing, and he's got good people with him. The Australian has been around and lived some. Johnny Hawkeye can more than handle himself I'm sure. The whisky man's stories can't all be made up. If only some of them are half-truths then I wouldn't want to go up against him, and I've seen all sorts come and go."

"The young feller, Rodrigo, the pistolero he's fast and accurate, he'll be a help, anyone who doesn't relate to the life those four have led would be more of a hindrance than a help." Josh added. "You've taken down the odd rustler and had a few bar brawls Ben, trying to match up to them, you'd be out of your depth and I can't get a Foreman as good as you at the drop of a hat." Ben Foreman saw the sense of what was being said and agreed not to pursue the matter.

The next morning Josh Milton, Margaret and Ben Foreman along with the newly hired ranch cowboys and a freshly gathered massive herd of cattle set off for Arizona and home. The whisky pedlar returned eastwards to restock his sample case, place his orders and further expand the stories of his friend the hero to his writer acquaintance.

There was probably only one man in the area apart from Shannon, the bounty hunter and possibly the Sheriff Barton Lee, who possessed the experience and courage to join up with Clay Milton and his party. Marshall Clay McCandless was looking at him right now, wondering if he was correct about the courage part of his thinking. He was looking in the mirror. Clay McCandless paid a visit to the Sheriff's office and after a lengthy conversation with his fellow lawman Barton Lee called in his Deputies.

"Eric, you've been with me for years, I want you to take over. I have a job to do with the Marshall."

"How long for?" Eric inquired. Lee looked at McCandless for guidance. McCandless shook his head.

"I don't know is the truth. I hope it won't take too long, I'm getting too old for all this." He answered.

"Okay. Can you tell us what it is, this job?"

"Don't really know exactly but it could save a lot of American lives if we pull it off. The Sheriff told them.

"We are going after Fernando Lopez and his gang, which I've been doing for some time. But there's others involved now, other things to consider." The Marshall answered.

"Just the two of you, you'd need an army?" Eric showed astonishment, he knew Lee wasn't a coward but he didn't think he was crazy either.

"There's more of us, the others have gone ahead." The Sheriff Looked at McCandless, knowing the next question before it came.

"How many?"

"Counting us, six, maybe seven." Eric scratched his head but remained silent.

"When do you leave?" Bill asked this time.

"Now, in a few minutes." McCandless stated, and then he took off his badge motioning Lee to do the same. "We can't wear badges, we'll have to cross the border." The badges were placed on the Sheriff's desk.

"Keep them 'til we get back." Barton Lee told his Deputies and left with the Marshall to protect the United States from an attempted invasion.

The first thing Barton Lee said To Clay McCandless as they rode out of Apache Bend together was.

"You didn't tell them that we might have to take on a Mexican army, and possibly a bunch of Rurales, along with Fernando Lopez and the worst gang of marauding cutthroats either side of the border."

"It must've slipped my mind." Came the answer.

Chapter Fourteen:

Luck On The Trail.

The pain of his injured rib was intensified by riding a galloping horse so Rattlesnake Joe had to stop often and rest, temporarily easing the pain. He'd taken note of the men who'd forced upon him the circumstances in which he now found himself. The shotgun rider, an excellent shot and a formidable opponent for sure, the Marshall, aging and slower than he used to be but still very dangerous. He remembered the younger man he'd watched climb down from the roof of the staging post, a fearless gunman and a good tactician for one so young. And finally he thought of the pistolero, so fast, so deadly accurate, and who'd robbed him of his prize, his route to finding Fernando Lopez.

He'd ridden with Lopez for a few months, years previously, but was not a natural gang member. He had grown up to be self-sufficient, a loner and they'd parted company after a short tenure. Now he wanted to find his old associate and didn't know exactly where to start, so he rode as fast as his wound would allow towards the border. He knew it was a long border but somewhere along it he would pick up the trail. Maybe the news of a recent raid by a large group of bandidos, or a big scale bank raid, even a train hold up. He was certain he would find something, somewhere. He did, it was sooner and simpler than he could have hoped for.

Miguel Chavez and Ramon Mendoza were tired and weary, in need of food and rest. They'd been riding all day after leaving Apache Bend with urgent news for their boss. They had recognised the pistolero, Rodrigo Lamas, at the cantina and knew of Shannon and Johnny Hawkeye. Their boss was Fernando Lopez and he would not be pleased with what they had to tell him. But he would be far more upset with them if they withheld the information they had overheard. That the pistolero had joined up with the bounty hunter Shannon, Johnny Hawkeye and an Australian, along with a younger man called Clay. And that he, Fernando Lopez was one of the men they were hunting.

Darkness was falling as the two bandidos reached the town of Dos Calles, Two Streets. They tied the horses outside the only saloon and eagerly walked inside. They chose a table and ordered a bottle and two glasses from the man behind the bar who in turn instructed one of the busy saloon girls to attend to the request. The girl accidently knocked Mendoza's glass over and spilt drink down his shirt and jacket. He swore at the unfortunate saloon girl and removed the damp items, ordering her to clean them and bring them back quickly.

A battered looking man approached their table, he had a weather beaten, dark face, lit up by a vivid scar down the left hand side of his face and he wore a bowler hat with a bullet hole through the top.

"Chavez?" The man spoke as though he already knew the answer, which he did. "Do you remember me?" Chavez carefully, but unnecessarily, studied the face of the half breed, and his blood stained shirt front.

"El Serpiente, Rattlesnake. Yes Senor, I remember you. What do you want?" Miguel Chavez recalled that Rattlesnake Joe had ridden with Lopez for a while several years before.

"Do you still ride with Fernando?" The half breed asked him in response.

"Why do you ask?" Ramon Mendoza, who had not been with Lopez long enough to know of Rattlesnake Joe took an aggressive tone towards the raggedly dressed, unkempt stranger with blood on his shirt.

"Ramon, I will deal with this." Chavez warned his younger companion, he answered Rattlesnake Joe. "Yes, we are riding to meet up with him, we need to tell him some bad news. Juan is dead."

"I know, I tried to save him." The renegade Comanche pulled out a chair and joined them, uninvited at the table. "I know who killed him. I need to see Fernando, where is he?"

"We cannot give such information to....to a half br...." Mendoza began but stopped as Rattlesnake Joe's knife stabbed violently through his right hand pinning it to the table top and causing him to scream in agony.

"The next time you insult someone Idiota, know who you are insulting." The half breed hissed at the unfortunate Mexican. He left the knife where it was to immobilise his victim and returned his attention to Chavez. "Where is Fernando? I have a message for him, there is a lot of money involved."

"He is in the hills, just the other side of the river, you can ride with us." Rattlesnake had a fair idea of where Chavez meant.

"I will ride with you." He said and withdrew the knife roughly, giving it a vicious twist as he did so, from the groaning Mendoza whose other hand moved to try and comfort his wounded and now mutilated gun hand. The excruciating pain would leave him in seconds as Rattlesnake Joe slashed the blade across Mendoza's throat, the spurts of blood covered the table top, obliterating any evidence of the previous violent action. "Not with him. But I will take his shirt." He added as the girl brought back the freshly cleaned items of clothing. "And the jacket." Chavez neglected to tell the half breed that he was also a target for the hunting party following behind them.

Shannon was a patient man he'd waited ten years already, a day longer would be okay. He rode at a moderate speed to conserve the energy of his white stallion. The bounty hunter doggedly followed the tracks left by Lawson's mount, easily identifiable because a galloping horse tends to leave a deeper and more distinct hoof print than those traveling at a more sedate pace. A speeding horse also tires more quickly and that would give the bounty hunter his edge. There was a good day and a half's easy ride to the next substantially sized town, Shannon would have his prey well before he could reach any sanctuary.

Frank Lawson's heart was pounding, the adrenalin and the fear of the bounty hunter combined to blunt his powers of reason. He whipped his mount to ever greater speed away from Apache Bend, ignoring the fact that the poor creature's heart was beating faster than his own. Until it gave out that is. Lawson felt his horse suddenly stagger, stop and heard a faint whinny before the exhausted beast collapsed and died. The dead weight of the horse trapped Lawson's left leg underneath it and the outlaw felt his ankle snap, sending a wave of agony shooting through him. He couldn't move and lost consciousness. He awoke later, he didn't know how much later but the sun was beginning to sink in the west and he could see buzzards hovering above, the scent of the dead horse was attracting them. He knew he had to get away somehow or he would join his mount as food for the carrion birds. He drifted in and out of consciousness as darkness and pain enveloped the fugitive outlaw.

The sun was rising when Frank Lawson awoke to his final day. He opened his eyes as water splashed his face. The body of his dead horse was still pinning him down but his left leg had lost all feeling, his circulation cut off by the weight of the animal. He blinked his eyes furiously, trying to focus his vision to find the source of the moisture but the light was too bright and all he could make out was the silhouette of a man standing over him. He didn't need to see to know who it was, he knew he was going to die.

"Shannon." Frank Lawson resigned himself to his fate.

"Lawson, it's been too long, you've wasted a lot of my time."

"Shannon, I didn't mean for Marianne to die, I swear. She just got in the way." Lawson tried to excuse himself for murdering the girl.

"You were the one in the way Lawson, it was her wedding day. She was my sister, my only family." Shannon was cold and decidedly unmoved by the wounded man's protestations. "And now you're going to pay, painfully."

"Shannon, you can't do this." Now he was blubbering with fear. "I only wanted to kill Joel. It was unlucky she tried to stop me."

"Unlucky she tried to stop you murdering her husband?" Shannon cocked back the hammer of his pistol and fired into Lawson's right knee, scaring off the circling buzzards and eliciting a piercing scream from Lawson. "She was unlucky, she didn't try and stop you, she had no idea what was happening. She really was unlucky, choosing a cowardly bastard like him, he pulled her in front of him as a shield and you shot her."

"You see it was him, he moved her in the way, and it wasn't my fault." Shannon wasn't listening he shot Lawson again, this time in his right shoulder. The resulting cry of pain served to deter the birds above from getting too close.

"Shannon, please don't kill me. You should kill Joel. He...."

"I already did, but now it's your turn." He fired once more into Frank Lawson's throat, he watched emotionlessly as the outlaw struggled in vain for a few seconds to retain his frail grip on existence.

"Bon Apettit." The man in black muttered to the buzzards above as he rode off, back in the direction from which he's come.

The reward in this case had been completely irrelevant. He would not speak of Lawson or his reason for hunting him down to anyone else, ever.

Chapter Fifteen:

Fort Boone.

By the time Colonel Jack Steele reached Fort Boone it was early evening and still light. At least he should be able to approach the fortified walls without being shot by over eager sentries he reasoned. He was escorted civilly to the Commandant's office by Captain Bradley Kinross where Colonel Jefferson Stard welcomed him with a handshake and a glass of whisky. The Captain also accepted a drink from his commanding officer and the three of them sat in comfortable chairs in front of a warm fire to discuss the reason for the visit from a high ranking secret service agent.

"I'll get straight down to business if I may Colonel." Steele began. "I believe my preceding letter was vague, I'm afraid it had to be in case it didn't get here and / or fell into the wrong hands."

"You mentioned something about a problem with our big guns, what was that about Colonel Steele?" Stard needed some clarification.

"What I actually stated was that there is the possibility of a problem arising concerning your field weapons, not with them. I assume they are working as they are supposed to, and act as a deterrent against aggressive action and insurgencies by the Indian tribes."

"Colonel, since The War Between The States field weapons are seldom needed. You cannot fight Indians the same way you fight soldiers. You cannot use a cannon on an enemy you can't see or one that moves so quickly and in smaller numbers. The guns are in the storage sheds, converted barns at the back of the fort." Stard explained. "I have been requesting that they are transported away from here. I don't use them since we became less of a strategic outpost, and given that most of the Indian tribes have surrendered. Just one of the Gatling guns would be all we would need."

"We can keep the redskins under control without using cannons." Captain Kinross put in, too enthusiastically for Steele's liking, but he ignored him and carried on.

"How many exactly do you have, I'm informed that there should be eight cannons and three Gatling guns, correct?"

"Yes, although one of the cannons is in need of repair, a cracked barrel, it happened in the war."

"The problem that concerns me could arise because your weapons are amongst the most powerful and advanced in the whole of the southern States. If they were stolen for instance, and used against us, we would be in serious trouble, would we not?"

"Stolen? It would take an army to be able to do that, no Indian war party could succeed in taking them, and they would not know how to use them." Stard was quite indignant at the very thought of such a thing.

"An army or a large, well trained band of men, led by a very clever and resourceful leader." Steele suggested.

"A bunch of bandits you mean?" Kinross again. "They wouldn't dare."

"Have you heard of a man called Fernando Lopez, or a Mexican General, Antonio Gomez? They would dare, and they are not as you refer to them, a bunch of bandits." Steele was already, not a fan of Kinross. "Gomez has his own army and Lopez is the leader of a very big band of bandidos. Even the Rurales are scared of Lopez and his men. Colonel, I would advise you to take special care, if possible keep the weapons somewhere away from prying eyes and make sure they are well protected at all times."

"I'll take on board what you have told me Colonel Steele, I will double the guard and send out more scouts, and more often. Stard looked carefully at the Englishman. "I feel I should know you from somewhere Colonel, have we met before?"

"I was present at West Point when you received your commission." Steele smiled. "I wondered if you would remember."

"Your face seemed familiar, I thought you were there on business from England."

"I was, I was working for Queen Victoria's security services when Mister Lincoln asked if he could borrow me for some complicated business which of course I can't go into here. I have probably outstayed my welcome after all these years. I received a letter from England a month ago, I have to go back, some family issues. I will not be returning to America, it's time to go home. This will be my last mission for your government."

"I wish you well Colonel, please give my regards to Her Majesty. More whisky?" Stard offered.

"Why not?" If he was going to try and get his message across he might as well do it with a fine whisky in his hand. He would give Colonel Stard as many facts as he could and hope he didn't listen to more of the Captain's unfounded derisory comments regarding the forces against them. The discussions continued through dinner and on until late.

The bottle was empty when Jack Steele took his leave of Stard and Kinross to go and find the room allocated to him for the night. Kinross had consumed far more than he could handle and rambled on about himself and his many attributes for most of the evening. Colonel Stard's eyes glazed over after he too had over-indulged. Steele thought to himself that stuck in a fort for months on end would drive him to drink, it was good to be leaving early the next day.

He'd spoken again with Colonel Stard in the morning as the two of them walked together while he collected his horse, he was ready to depart.

"I was thinking last night before I went to sleep. Anyone who knew about your big guns and wanted to steal them would know where to look, wouldn't they?"

"Yes of course, it's well known we have the weapons."

"So, if any aggressor was able by some miracle to overcome your troops they would have them, yes?"

"Well, yes I suppose so. But...?

"But what if they weren't here?" Steele suggested. "What if they were spirited away somewhere unknown to all but a few of your men?"

"I'll give it some thought." Stard promised. Captain Kinross joined them as they reached the gates.

He'd left them with a stark warning.

"Do not under estimate the threat of what I've told you Colonel Stard. I would not have travelled all this way if I did not think there was anything of concern to consider. I have two of my best men working on this but they are up against very dangerous opponents."

"Only two men?" Kinross interjected. "If these greasers are so dangerous why didn't you call for us? I could've led a troop against them, they wouldn't have stood..."

"That's enough Captain!" Stard finally shut the boastful Captain up.

"I will answer you Captain." Steele had reached the limit of his own patience. "The two men I have commissioned have between them prevented four well planned assassination attempts against two different Presidents. They have taken down bands of pirates, murderers, organised crime syndicates, southern spies, and that's before I even teamed them together. They didn't have a troop or even a weapon in some instances. They had brains, courage and resourcefulness, does that answer your question?"

He didn't wait for a response.

Chapter Sixteen:

The Bandido.

The problem as Fernando Lopez saw it was simply one of trust and strong leadership. The man was new to his gang and didn't seem to grasp that when he, Lopez gave an order, obedience was not negotiable. The instruction had been plain enough, he would tolerate no claims between his men of theft from each other. If he did not hear about it there would be no problem but he'd heard of this incident from the aggrieved party whose share of the proceeds from the Indian Buttes bank raid had gone missing. The suspected thief had compounded his guilt by attempting to leave the hideout with the ill-gotten loot hidden upon his person. He stood now in front of the formidable figure of Fernando Lopez, quivering with fear and grovelling apologetically as he begged for forgiveness along with the promise of future complete adherence to the gang leader's rules. Beside the bandit leader stood a smartly dressed man with a fancy double holstered gun belt. He looked ready to draw and fire either or both his weapons at the slightest provocation.

"I told you when you ride with Lopez we do not steal from each other." Lopez reminded the cowering man. "And now I have to kill you. If I let you live people will think I am soft, that I can no longer lead."

"Please Fernando... Please I give you my word....."

"You already gave me your word, this is what it is worth. Not gold, not silver, but lead." The bandit chief drew and fired in the blink of an eye. The man screamed as the bullet shattered his knee, he fell writhing in agony and clutching at the ruined joint. A second shot destroyed his other knee accompanied by a shrieking extension to the first scream. A third time Lopez pulled the trigger and the man's left elbow was rendered useless, then a fourth to the right elbow and the evocative screams became pathetic whimpers.

"You see Pedro, the truth is you have made one very stupid mistake. A very big one. It is not that you stole, we are bandidos, and it is what we do. It is not even that you broke my laws, but that is why I have to kill you. No, the biggest mistake you made was getting caught." A fifth shot ended the suffering and the front of the man's head suddenly sported a third eye, a red one. The flashily dressed gunman lost interest in the proceedings and wandered away.

While reloading his pistol, Fernando Lopez addressed his second in command, a much shorter, battle hardened man with fifteen years loyal service to the head bandido. His name was Pancho Garcia and he was feared nearly as much as his leader. He had a vicious, short temper which he struggled to control in times of stress. What he lacked in intelligence and finesse was more than compensated for by brutality and callousness. He would not have been a good leader and

160

he knew it but he made a good job of being the right hand man for Fernando Lopez.

"Miguel and Ramon, they have been gone too long, send two men to find them. They should have found the pistolero by now. And get someone to move this." His boot was pointing at the body on the ground.

"I'll send Alfredo and Ernesto, Ernesto is quick with his gun. He might need to be if there are problems." Garcia suggested, Lopez nodded.

"Bring Sofía to my room." He added and Pancho called out to the two bandidos mentioned.

Fernando Lopez was relaxed, he sat in a luxurious leather armchair, looted some years ago from a Spanish land owner who didn't need it anymore. A violent death had removed the man's necessity for any kind of seating altogether. He poured himself a fine wine and lit a huge cigar. He was a man at the top of his game. He'd been there for years and intended to stay that way until he felt he was rich enough to retire. Then he would go to Europe, Spain or France, perhaps even England, no need to plan yet. Just one more big haul.

His mind wandered back to his youth as the son of a peasant farmer. He remembered his father, a hardworking man who struggled all his life to provide for his family. Times were hard and taxes were extortionately high, and after a bad harvest there would sometimes be no food on the table for the young Fernando, his mother and his two brothers Raúl, the elder by five years and Juan, younger by eight years. He remembered seeing his father on his deathbed, an utterly exhausted, very old thirty something man who could easily have been mistaken for his own grandfather.

Fernando had promised himself at that moment not to die an impoverished peasant, a victim of the pitiless, fruitless existence that would appear to be his destiny. The sixteen year old knew there were only three options open to him. Stay where he was and live hard, a guaranteed way to stay poor and die young was one. Joining the priesthood was another but the young Fernando did not share his father's belief that a divine being would show them any love or mercy. Besides he was already a favourite with the village girls and did not wish to live a life of celibacy. His elder brother on the other hand embraced what he referred to as his calling and left home to follow his faith. He had warned Fernando not to take the path he suspected was inevitably beckoning to his younger brother.

The third option was to be an outlaw, a bandido, it was in Fernando's eyes the only credible way to go. He'd left the morning after Raúl. A day later he'd killed his first three men, the first of innumerable victims and adversaries. He had taken with him two of the local young men and they had robbed an army supply merchant in his own store. The man had two assistants and one of them foolishly tried to stop the three young raiders. Fernando's long hours of practice with his father's old pistol stood him in good stead. The assistant managed to shoot one of his accomplices but paid for his actions with his life. Fernando had shot him dead.

Before the panicking merchant and his remaining assistant could reach the weapons they frantically scrambled to get to, Fernando had killed them both. He quickly took cash, weapons and supplies from the store and packed them into sacks.

His wounded companion had laid gasping for his breath on the floor and the other had just stood transfixed in a state of shock, watching what was happening but trying not to believe it. They could hear people shouting, Rurales. His village playmates were not coming with him, one was incapable and looked as if he was dying. The other, still stunned by the turn of events raised his hands in surrender as if in a trance. Fernando Lopez took his sack of stolen items and left through the back door alone as armed soldiers entered the front. He selected the finest mount from a rail outside the saloon and rode off into the hills. He would take money to his mother and Juan before he left the area to seek out his destiny. The legend of Fernando Lopez began that day.

He came out of his daydream when Sofía walked in, she was beautiful, around twenty years old and the most desirable of all the women in the hideout. She smiled as he poured and handed her a glass of wine. She'd learned it was very wise to show pleasure at being in his company. Besides, Fernando Lopez was a very handsome man, rich and powerful. He treated her well. Because she was thought of as his property the other bandidos, who were not always so good to their women left her unmolested. Sofía removed her dress, she wore nothing underneath, and knelt down in front of him. He smiled back and placed a hand on the top of her head.

Chapter Seventeen:

The Chase.

The hunting party arrived at the Dos Calles cantina half a day after the departure of Rattlesnake Joe and Miguel Chavez. Clay and Bluey went to buy a few supplies and some more ammunition and then to book a couple of rooms. They found only one place that could accommodate the four of them, a small but sufficient boarding house. Johnny Hawkeye and Rodrigo Lamas had taken the horses to the little town's only livery stable to be looked after for the night. They met in the cantina and the barman was keen to tell stories of previous violent incidents of which there were many considering the size of the town. They listened with interest as he related the exchanges between two of his own countrymen and the Comanche half breed with the scarred face the night before.

"Ramon had a big mouth, full of hot air and not as good as he thought he was, Miguel is an old hand, and trusted by Fernando Lopez. The two we have to look out for most apart from Fernando himself, are Pancho Garcia, his second in command, and Ernesto Moreno. Garcia is as tough as they come, he is a ruthless killer and loyal to Fernando. Moreno is fast with a gun, very fast, he shoots quicker than it takes him to think about it. There is also a new man, very smart and very quiet, I don't know about him." Rodrigo supplied.

"Is Moreno as fast as you?" Clay asked him.

"With his brain, no. With a gun? That I do not know, I would not want to find out if it could be avoided." Rodrigo told them modestly.

Clay McCandless and Barton Lee had been at least a day behind Clay Milton and the others on leaving Apache Bend but had ridden fast. They rode cautiously but confident in the assumption that any trouble would've been encountered by the preceding party and that their passage should be reasonably threat free. By the time they'd reached Dos Calles they'd gained a couple of hours on their colleagues and decided to ride through the night in the hope of catching up with them sooner. Three hours of sleep just off the trail was all they allowed themselves. McCandless found himself ignoring the aches and pains throughout his chest, ribs and back, sacrificing as he'd always done, comfort for speed. The same procedure was followed for the next two nights as they travelled through the more hilly regions of the countryside, and they confidently expected to catch sight of the other four the following day.

Halfway through the morning the silence of the journey was interrupted and their attention drawn to the sounds of gunfire coming from, McCandless estimated, about a mile away, out of their present range of sight. They spurred the horses to go faster and rode towards the crest of the adjacent hill hoping to be able to see what was going on. As the two men looked down from their vantage point Rattlesnake Joe was the first man Clay McCandless recognised. The half breed was taking cover behind a rock on the level below them, he was shooting at a lone man at the bottom of the hill who had only his dead horse for cover but was firing back gamely , if intermittently. Maybe he's low on ammunition considered the Marshall. Fanning out furtively from the half breed, to stay out of the man's sight were three men. They were endeavouring to surround the subject of their attack and negate his meagre protective cover. The men were Mexican in appearance, evidently associates of Rattlesnake Joe and therefore not to be treated as neighbourly.

"We have to help whoever that is, it could be one of your friends." Barton Lee said to McCandless.

"It's not anyone I know, not from up here anyway. But we do have to help him. I'll try the breed and the one nearest to him if you keep the other two busy." Lee nodded to him and stealthily worked his way to the left of McCandless to improve his angle of attack. As soon as he got into a reasonable position he raised his hand and the Marshall opened fire. The Mexican nearest to Rattlesnake Joe staggered and dropped his rifle down the steep slope of the hill. He turned in surprise to see McCandless fire again, and trying to stem the flow of blood from his two chest wounds lost his balance and followed his weapon out of the Marshall's sight.

Barton Lee just fired once, his target dropped like a stone. The other Mexican drew and fired towards him so fast Lee didn't have time to see him move. Fortunately the man didn't use enough time to aim sufficiently and from quite a distance away the bullet merely removed the Sheriff's hat. Rattlesnake Joe moved out of sight as McCandless tried to take aim, he fired a couple of random shots at the Marshall and his companion forcing them to take cover and then he was gone.

The remaining Mexican began shooting at the spaces recently occupied by the two lawmen who now were taking cover out of his line of vision. The man at the base of the slope took a potshot at the gunslinger who decided that discretion was the better part of valour and carefully but hurriedly ran off to find his horse.

Rattlesnake Joe had beaten him to the mounts and already departed the scene. Ernesto Moreno jumped onto the nearest horse and sped after him. He'd only met up with his friend Miguel Chavez and the half breed the day before and already he did not like the scar faced scalp hunter.

Alfredo the man shot by Barton Lee hadn't died from his wound, he'd been lucky, the bullet intended for his heart had hit his bulky gold neck chain. The force had knocked him down, painfully winded but still able to gasp for air. The lawmen had chased fruitlessly after El Serpiente and Ernesto Moreno and had forgotten him by the time he'd recovered enough to try and stand up.

He soon spotted that the man who'd actually started the shooting, the man whose horse they'd killed was struggling up the steep slope towards him. Alfredo finally reached his feet. He drew his pistol and took careful aim, he would kill the man now.

A shot rang out and Alfredo dropped for second time that morning. This time there would be no gasping for breath, there would be no breath at all. He was dead before the man coming towards him realised he wasn't going to die himself, not today anyway.

"I'm always saving your life old man." A voice called out from somewhere, a familiar voice to Zachariah Smith. "I thought I told you to wait at Mason, I would let you know when it's done."

"Son, I couldn't wait forever, I'm too old." The Mountain Man shouted at the hilly countryside. "Are you gonna show yourself or have you gone back to being a Cheyenne Brave?"

Johnny Hawkeye, Clay Milton, James Blue and Rodrigo Lamas emerged from cover and revealed themselves to the old man as McCandless and Lee returned to greet their colleagues, and explain the reasons for their unexpected presence.

"Don't shoot the young feller, he's with us." Johnny could see confusion in the Mountain Man's eyes when he caught sight of Rodrigo. Introductions were swiftly carried out and the subject of Rattlesnake Joe became the main topic of conversation yet again.

It was decided that Zachariah would appropriate one of the remaining horses left by Rattlesnake Joe and

Ernesto Moreno and ride with the hunters in their quest. Bluey and Clay Milton led the way followed by McCandless, Lee and Rodrigo. Johnny and Zachariah made up the rear of the now seven strong posse.

"So, Old Man, tell me how you got here." Johnny was curious how the old man managed to find Rattlesnake Joe before he had for a second time.

"Hell, Boy, it was an accident, I was headed for Apache Bend. I've been trying to catch up with you for months, since I left Hawksville. It ain't called Mason anymore and you know it." Zachariah paused to get his breath. "You know it took me an age to get better, if you hadn't left me some cash..."

"Carry on with how you came to be heading for Apache Bend." Johnny changed the subject back to something he was more comfortable with.

"Well, I was getting ready to leave when there was some talk in the saloon about a shootout in Tumbleweed Cross, a stranger with a feather in his hat and good with a knife teaming up with a bounty hunter. I ain't so smart but I ain't that dumb either, I figured it was you. Took me a long time but eventually I got there, a saloon girl told me about you and the bounty hunter looking for a half breed in Apache Bend. That's where I was aiming for when I came across the murdering son of a bitch and his bandido buddies. If they hadn't seen me at the same time I might have got him, I had my rifle out when they started shooting."

"You're a tough old hombre Zachariah. We were chasing him but my friends here are looking for

Fernando Lopez, I'm riding with them. It gives us the best chance to find the Rattlesnake, he's got business with Lopez and they have to stop it from happening. If you ride along it could be very dangerous, what do you say?"

"Hell Boy, I survived for fifty years in the Rockies, I ain't scared of no bandidos, I need to see the half breed dead." The old man suddenly realised someone was missing." Where's your friend, the bounty hunter, Shannon, I've heard of him?"

"He'll catch us up, he had some personal business to take care of."

"You sure he's coming, I hear tell he don't work so good with other people?"

"He'll be around. We've got a deal, as long as I get to kill Rattlesnake Joe, he can have the body, $5,000 Dollars' worth, and Lopez is worth $10,000. He won't let that go without a fight."

"Do you trust him?" Zachariah was suspicious of anyone motivated purely by the possibility of monetary gain.

"You know Old Man, I reckon I do." Johnny Hawkeye answered, and surprised himself at the same time.

"Then that's good enough for me, Son." They rode on in silence.

Shannon had ridden hard and fast since completing his vendetta against Frank Lawson. He'd taken a different route towards the border from Johnny

Hawkeye and his party. Without realising it he was actually a good half day ahead of his partner when he picked up the trail of a group of horsemen, six horses he counted. He followed them for several hours until he saw the tracks merge with a larger band of riders. Now he estimated he was trailing around thirty to thirty five men, all heading in the same direction, towards Mexico. He gained on the riders steadily until he could see the dust from the horses' hooves in the distance, and then he held back. He left the trail and took to the surrounding hills to give himself cover and a better place to keep them in view.

When night fell the light from the riders' camp fire glowed dully in the darkness and Shannon crept closer to try and listen to any conversations, hoping to hear something that would help him in his quest. The bounty hunter had identified them all as Mexican before he managed to get close enough to hear anything specific being said. The overabundance of sombreros and the aroma of cheroots gave him that knowledge along with the sound of an out of tune Spanish guitar being strummed. A quartet of drunken voices attempted to sing along, under pressure from the more musically discerning among them to desist or face the infliction of grievous pain.

Shannon remained observing and listening for two hours, until the majority of the riders bedded down for the night. He'd managed to confirm his suspicions that the group were riding to meet up with Fernando Lopez at his hideout and would arrive at their destination sometime the following day. Four men were posted to keep watch and the bounty hunter decided to withdraw and find himself somewhere more distant to rest while he pondered his next move.

The sun was already high in the sky and throwing out a substantial heat when Shannon resumed his tracking of the riders. They'd been in no hurry to continue their journey and he needed to remain inconspicuous behind them.

Ernesto Moreno, riding high in the hills was searching for Rattlesnake Joe. The half breed had ridden off at speed from the encounter with Zachariah Smith and the Gringo retinue and had not been seen since. He felt sure he should have come across him by now. He'd followed the tracks of many riders as he rode towards the hideout of Fernando Lopez, including the lone horseman he thought may be the scar faced renegade. He gazed down upon the solitary rider now, it wasn't Rattlesnake Joe. He urged his mount forwards and began to descend the steep slope towards the figure on the white stallion below. One loose piece of tree bark was disturbed by the horse's right front hoof and that was all it took, the noise was slight but enough. Shannon turned to see Moreno clawing for his pistol and did likewise. Fast as the Mexican killer was, Shannon was faster. The bounty hunter fired from the hip and Ernesto Moreno, who'd considered himself the fastest gun alive died with his gun still only halfway out of his holster. Shannon didn't wait to see if the noise had carried to the riders ahead of him, he galloped speedily away in the opposite direction.

Another pair of eyes had been watching from a discreet hiding place five hundred yards away from the fallen pistolero. He pulled his battered bowler down lower on his head and watched as the bounty hunter disappeared from view. He raised his rifle but lowered it swiftly when he realised his target was moving too fast and was too far away to guarantee a hit.

"Shannon!" He recognised him even though he'd never met the man in black, if he had he speculated, one of them would be dead by now.

Johnny Hawkeye heard the shot that killed Moreno from a distance of two miles away and rode towards the sound alone leaving Bluey to follow at a respectful distance and Clay a further length behind, nearer to the rest of the hunting party. He soon recognised the rapidly moving white stallion and showed himself to the rider, waving his distinctive feathered hat in the air to attract Shannon's attention. It worked and the bounty hunter changed his direction of flight to ride towards his partner.

The man watching the two riders from a distance squinted against the sunlight to try and improve his view. He stayed still for a moment and then pulling the bowler hat down even tighter on his head he crept furtively to his mount and when Johnny Hawkeye and Shannon disappeared from sight he rode off to find Fernando Lopez.

"Did you find Lawson?" Johnny asked the bounty hunter as they began riding together.

"I found him." Was all the response he would get on the subject.

Johnny Hawkeye and Shannon rode back to the rest of the now eight strong party of hunters. Each of them had their own reasons for being involved in the mission to defeat any attempt by General Antonio Gomez to obtain the weapons he required. He could not be allowed to launch attacks, not only on his own government, but more importantly the State of Texas.

Clay Milton and James Blue were acting agents for the United States security services. Clay McCandless and Barton Lee as lawmen, considered the mission to be a patriotic duty. Johnny Hawkeye and Zachariah Smith sought a bitter revenge on the Comanche half breed Rattlesnake Joe and were using the mission to hopefully help them get close to their quarry. Rodrigo Lamas was helping them to find the hideout of Fernando Lopez, something he was willing to do as he travelled home to Mexico to meet his sister. He didn't know General Antonio Gomez but he knew if he succeeded in his ambitions there would be more killings and massacres taking place in an already blood soaked nation. One dictator was pretty much like the previous one, and the next one, to most of his fellow countrymen, they certainly didn't need yet another. The young pistolero just wanted to live in peace.

And Shannon? He told himself he was in it for the money, and to a certain extent he was, but beyond that, he didn't even know himself. He would perhaps find out soon, the hunters would find the hideout of Fernando Lopez the next day, but unbeknown to them Rattlesnake Joe would beat them to it.

Chapter Eighteen:

The Hideout.

The skills acquired by Johnny Hawkeye while living with the Cheyenne people and the survival instincts instilled into James Blue from his days living on the run as a bush ranger in the Australian outback made the two of them the natural choices when it came to selecting scouts to make a reconnaissance of the area. Rodrigo had pinpointed the location of the hideout, a secluded valley hidden from view amongst the surrounding mountains. Lookouts would be posted all around to preserve the secrecy of the location from being discovered by any passing traveller's eyes, whether by accident or design.

The cold of the early morning bit into the two men as they surreptitiously climbed around the tallest of the peaks. One hundred yards below a shivering Mexican, hunched beneath the inadequate protection of a large blanket. Killing him would have been a lot easier than avoiding him Johnny and Bluey both knew but discovery would then be assured when his relief found him dead, or didn't find him at all. By the time the sun shone down on them and the chill was gone, the scouts were sweating with the physical exertions of their task, but they had managed to locate the hideout of the notorious outlaw Fernando Lopez.

Under different circumstances the scene before them would have been described as idyllic. Johnny and Bluey gazed down upon a small village consisting of one large cabin and half a dozen other dwellings with a nearby huge barn come stable next to a mountain stream. They decided to split up and investigate further, agreeing to meet back at their current position of concealment. Although neither of them possessed a time piece, they would give each other an hour and then begin the long arduous task of returning to the others with any information they might discover. Johnny would begin at the far end of the settlement, near the bigger cabin and Bluey would aim for the other, nearer the barn.

It was becoming unbearably hot to spend much time in the open as the sun glared relentlessly down into the valley. Most of the residents had the good sense to be indoors as Bluey crept around the huge building that housed the horses and supplies for the whole village. He climbed up carefully to the opening about ten feet up on the side of the barn hoping that, A. There was a platform inside, and B. That the lookouts posted on the surrounding countryside were looking outwards from the village and not inwards towards it. He was fortunate on both counts and he made his way into the relative coolness inside without incident. He stayed still for a couple of minutes, allowing his eyes to adjust to the dimness of his surroundings, and then he began to look around. The platform he stood on was used primarily as a hay loft, a swift perusal revealed evidence of another purpose for which the place was employed as he discovered a few items of female under garments scattered around in the semi darkness. He stealthily descended the rickety ladder, taking great care not to spook the horses. James Blue had a natural affinity with animals and seeing no sign of any humans present he spoke gently to the bandidos' mounts seeking to evoke calm as walked silently among them, counting. Sixty four he counted, that's a lot of guns, he thought to himself. That's a lot of men who need paying and feeding. His heart jumped slightly as he recognised one of the horses.

"Rattlesnake Joe!" He muttered to himself under his breath. He came to the open main entrance and peered carefully outside. He went back inside and left the barn through the less conspicuous rear door, he could scout the smaller buildings with more ease by keeping to the perimeter of the hideout.

Johnny Hawkeye kept to the shadows as much as possible on his way to the larger of the cabins, he correctly assumed it would be the home of Fernando Lopez. Remaining away from the centre of the settlement he arrived at the rear of his destination and peered carefully through the back window. The sight of a large bed greeted the eyes of Johnny Hawkeye, under the covers slept the figure of a young woman, alone. He moved on quickly to the next window, a store room, a few guns, a traveling chest and a few clothes. The hunter scouted carefully around and then moved into the space between the cabin and its neighbour, a smaller dwelling of similar design. The window of the smaller building did not reveal anything other than an empty bed, he returned his attention to his original target.

A tall Mexican stood polishing his pistol as he spoke to two other men. He was an imposing figure of a man, Fernando Lopez, he exuded authority and confidence in equal measure. He smiled, if a mountain lion could smile, Johnny thought that's what it would look like. The bandit leader beckoned one of the men with him to open the door. The man was a foot shorter than his leader but had the tough rugged appearance of a man who'd lived a lifetime in this violent world embraced by the bandidos, Pancho Garcia, Johnny knew it intuitively. The third man sat silently, also cleaning his gun. He looked to Johnny as if he could have been Rodrigo's older brother, a flashily dressed pistolero. Garcia opened the door as commanded and called for someone to enter. Johnny Hawkeye almost shook with a mixture of shock and rage as Rattlesnake Joe entered the room. The avenger in the hunter grasped his pistol and drew it, intending to exact his long awaited revenge right there, right now. His senses intervened and he replaced his gun in his holster. He could kill the half breed there and then, he was sure of that, but he wanted the man to suffer, to know who was killing him and why. If he just shot him now he probably wouldn't even know about it and Johnny himself would be dead before he could escape from the hideout of Fernando

180

Lopez. Better to wait. He could hear what was being said even with the window closed.

"El Serpiente! It has been a long time, a very long time, what leads you to the village of Fernando Lopez? And how did you find us?" The bandido chief asked his visitor, more interested in the answer to the second part of his question.

"Miguel, I rode with him, he was bringing me to you. I bring you a message, an offer of..." Lopez then cut in, his question not answered to his satisfaction.

"I do not see Miguel, or Ramon here, and I sent out two others, Alfredo and Ernesto to find them. What happened to them?"

"They are dead. There is a man, a man known as Johnny Hawkeye, he and his friends killed them. The one you called Ernesto was killed by a bounty hunter, Shannon. He and Hawkeye ride together with others Fernando, and they ride for you." Rattlesnake Joe informed him, and having gained his attention ploughed on. "We were coming to warn you, I have had cause to be wary of these people in the past. I rescued your brother from the U.S. Marshall, McCandless, you may know of him." Lopez nodded, Rattlesnake Joe continued. "But I regret Fernando, that Juan was killed, shot down by a pistolero, I tried to save him but I got this for my trouble." The half breed opened the shirt he'd stolen from Ramon to show the still raw wound on his chest.

"Juan is dead?" Fernando Lopez ignored the half breed's injury, but involuntarily showed a very brief flash of grief in his expression before anger superseded the rarely indicated emotion. "What is the name of this pistolero?"

"I do not know Fernando, but he rides with Hawkeye and the others, and so does McCandless."

"Describe him to me."

Rattlesnake Joe did so, as accurately as he could remember from the short encounters he'd had with Rodrigo.

"Rodrigo, I know Rodrigo, he rode with us. He ran out after we attacked the bank at Indian Buttes. I will take care of the pistolero myself." The bandit leader glanced around at the rest of the people in the room to be met with nods of acceptance and understanding.

"I have known of the bounty hunter, Shannon for years but never had cause to concern myself with him. He must be a very fast gun to take out Ernesto." Lopez speculated.

"He is the fastest I've ever seen." The seated man looked up quizzically and without speaking at this comment. "They were both on horseback, Ernesto did not have time to raise his pistol but he began his draw first. I was too far away to shoot the bounty hunter so I came alone to warn you."

"So tell me El Serpiente, how many are there out there in this, this hunting party who dare to kill my brother and come after me?"

"I counted eight of them, including an old man and the Sheriff from Apache Bend. There are two others, I don't know them, but they travelled with the Marshall when he held your brother prisoner."

"Eight men!" Lopez thought for a moment. "Eight men? I have seventy here and more ride to join me as we speak. How can eight men think to attack so many of the toughest bandidos, even if they find us?" He allowed himself a brief laugh curtailed almost immediately as anger reinstated itself. "Pancho, send out six men to patrol all around us, report back to me as soon as they find any sign of anyone out there." Pancho left to carry out his orders. Lopez turned back to Rattlesnake Joe. "You were about to tell me of a message, what is it, and who is it from?"

"It is from Gomez, Antonio Gomez."

"The mad General, what has he got to say to me?" Lopez allowed himself an inward smile. He'd never met the "Mad General" but he was acutely aware of the man and his far reaching ambitions. He couldn't see that they would have anything in common, certainly not in the field of politics or military conquest. Out of curiosity he bid El Serpiente to proceed with his message from the self-styled General Antonio Gomez. The half breed repeated almost word for word the conversation he'd had with the General, leaving unsaid only the parts that Lopez would not appreciate, but would, with his intelligence and comprehension of the way the human mind functions, easily be able to work out for himself. Fernando Lopez listened and sat down to ponder the offer and the requirements involved. Rattlesnake Joe would not have been surprised if the idea had been rejected on the spot in which case he would have to decide what his own future plan of action would be.

Johnny Hawkeye, watching and listening patiently and unseen outside the window would have to leave soon or Bluey would come looking for him. They'd both agreed not to do so if the one of them was late back to the meeting place, but they both knew the other would not go back to the others alone. He heard Pancho Garcia come back into the room and he began to move away when Lopez spoke again at long last.

"You know what, El Serpiente? I do not know or trust the mad General, I have known you, and your own trustworthiness is only guaranteed if things are working in your favour. But I like the idea, I can make a plan. We will do this thing and take the guns from the Gringos and the money from General Gomez. I want you to work with Roberto here. I have a mission of some importance for you both." Lopez indicated the silent figure of the other man in the room, the gunman who looked up casually and seemingly uninterested at the mention of his name.

"This is Roberto Aguilar, he is known as "El Àguila Del Diablo", "The Devil's Eagle." He is the fastest gun I have ever seen, he will be interested to meet this Shannon." Lopez introduced them as Aguilar looked up again, distinctly unimpressed.

"What is the task you have for us Fernando?" The Devil's Eagle spoke at last, he had a smooth, emotionless, hushed voice.

"I want you to break Barrera out of jail." He looked at the two men he'd chosen for the job, Aguilar was totally unresponsive, Rattlesnake mildly curious.

"Emilio Barrera?" The half breed queried. "He is as unstable as the glycerine he uses."

"Yes, he is as you say, unstable, but he is the best explosives man I know of and he will be necessary to my plan. Because of that fool Carlos blowing himself and half of Indian Buttes up, I have need of him."

"Where is he being held?" Aguilar sounded completely disinterested in hearing an answer.

"There is a big prison four days west of Apache Bend, over the border, it is in the desert, a place called Horquilla Doblé. It is not used so much now, there are not many prisoners kept there anymore. The Gringos call the place Two Forks and that is what it is, two forks in the road, one each end of the street, two trails go into the desert, one to Fort Boone and the other to Apache Bend."

"I know Apache Bend, we can leave at once." Rattlesnake Joe re-entered the conversation.

"I will send some of my men with you." Lopez told him.

The half breed had other ideas.

"I would prefer to use some of the men I know from the area if that's okay, Fernando? They will be expendable." Lopez looked towards Roberto Aguilar for an opinion. The pistolero shrugged his shoulders, totally indifferent as to who he worked with, he was used to working alone, as a hired gun.

185

"Okay, El Serpiente, but do not fail me, I will not be pleased if you do." Rattlesnake Joe knew what the statement meant. Failure to complete the task would result in Lopez sending men after him with orders to shoot on sight.

"Fernando. If the pistolero gets in my way?" Aguilar began, he left the rest of the sentence unsaid. Lopez had moved beyond his initial outburst of anger at Rodrigo's betrayal.

"If he gets in your way kill him, tell him Fernando Lopez sent you." He said. The Devil's Eagle attempted in vain to smile, his face broke into a faint grimace. Lopez turned again to address his second in command. "Pancho, I want you to take four men with you. Go and find Gomez, tell him I will get the weapons and to meet me here." He reached over to his conveniently close by saddlebag and pulled out a map, he spread it on the only table and pointed to a particular area. Aguilar stood up to take a look and the sudden noise of his chair scraping on the floor obliterated the sound of the bandit leader's voice as he spoke the name of the place in question. Pancho Garcia emitted an affirmative grunt and left to recruit four men.

Johnny Hawkeye could wait no longer, Rattlesnake Joe and his new riding companion left the thoughtful figure of Fernando Lopez to himself and his bed mate while the hunter crept away to meet up with Bluey. The Australian was waiting for him and relief showed on his face as Johnny Hawkeye returned. They did not speak until sometime later when the lookout's vantage point was left behind, out of sight and beyond the range of their voices. The two of them took great care to keep their eyes open for signs of the six men Lopez had sent out to look for them, they saw no traces of pursuit or tracks in front of them.

The eight hunters spent the rest of the day traveling, the destination was a return to Apache Bend. It disappointed all of them to leave the Bandidos unscathed but eight versus nearly seventy did not seem like sensible odds to challenge.

By nightfall they'd still seen no signs of the six men from the hideout and calculated that they were beyond a reasonable distance from where the search would be concentrated. They made camp for the night and lit a fire, something not risked while closer to the enemy. Even so they took it in turns to keep watch. The old Mountain Man, Zachariah Smith took first duty while the others discussed plans, such as they were.

"I have to return to Apache Bend." Barton Lee asserted. "I can't leave my men to deal with Rattlesnake and a gunslinger on their own."

"I'll go with him and pick up my badge, then I'll go and see the governor at the Two Forks prison." McCandless added.

"I'll come with you to the prison." Clay Milton said and looked towards James Blue for confirmation that he agreed.

"Good idea, I think Johnny and I ought to leave for Fort Boone as quickly as we can, we have to warn them what might be coming if Lopez has his way." The Australian added.

"I'll go along with that." Johnny Hawkeye said, and then turned to the bounty hunter. "What do you think, Shannon?"

"I'll go to town with the Marshall and take it from there, I want to keep an eye out for the half breed." He answered. "Don't worry Hawkeye, I won't kill him unless I have to."

"What about you Rodrigo, You don't have to come with us, you can stay this side of the border and go find your sister?" Clay Milton spoke to the pistolero.

"Senors, for the first time since I was a kid, I feel as though I am with friends. I would like to help. What do you want me to do?" The young Mexican spoke with an instantly recognisable sincerity. Clay answered him.

"If that's okay with the Sheriff, I think an extra gun would be useful to have on call in Apache Bend, that's where the first sign of trouble may show."

"That's fine with me, I never say no to help. I'll deputize you, Son." Barton Lee told him. "That way I can pay you." Rodrigo smiled, he'd ridden with Fernando Lopez only a few months ago, and now he was being offered a job with a badge. McCandless allowed himself a smile as he shared the same thoughts.

"Who is Roberto Aguilar, Lopez called him The Devil's Eagle?" Johnny Hawkeye remembered the flashily outfitted, menacing presence of the quiet gun man. Nobody had any knowledge of the man.

"What does he look like?" Bluey asked and Johnny Hawkeye described the clothing and the attitude of the unknown man.

"He could be the killer I saw at the raid in Indian Buttes, he is very fast. Three shots fired, three dead, one second taken to do it. I think he might have joined up with Lopez that day." McCandless offered. "We had best be on the lookout for this man, if it is this Aguilar, he is a very dangerous man." The warning was noted by everyone present.

"What about the old man, Zachariah?" Clay Milton asked Johnny Hawkeye.

"He can ride with us, if he wants to." Johnny answered looking towards Bluey for an opinion. The Australian nodded, signifying approval and reached for his rifle.

"I'll go and relieve him, he could use a rest." He said and stood up. Before he walked away he asked. "Who is this guy they want to get out of jail, Emilio Barrera?"

"He's an explosives man, dynamite and nitro glycerine. He got too close too often to his own handiwork and the results are he's gone a bit crazy, it happened a lot in the war, they haven't got a name for it yet but they will." Clay McCandless said. "He's supposed to be the best as long as he's calm, which ain't often enough, not near a whisky bottle anyhow."

Chapter Nineteen:

The Devil's Eagle.

Eric, the acting Sheriff of Apache Bend eagerly returned the badge of office to Barton Lee the minute the tall man walked in the door.

"Good to have you back, Sheriff." The Deputy told him sincerely.

"Good to be back, Eric. We need another badge." He introduced Rodrigo and duly swore the young pistolero in as a Deputy. "We might have trouble coming, get the boys in will you?" Eric disappeared out of the office to find Bill, Tex and Jed. The Sheriff handed the Marshall's badge to Clay McCandless who placed it in the normal position on the front of his shirt.

Barton Lee had regretted that he couldn't offer everyone lodging at the house he shared with his wife and two children, but he hadn't got enough space. However he invited Clay McCandless to stay overnight before the Marshall left on his journey to warn the prison governor of the plot to break Barrera out. Clay Milton had gone to book rooms for himself and Shannon, just for one night. Rodrigo would be housed at a boarding house where the single Deputies lodged. Shannon had accompanied the others to the Sheriff's office and stood idly studying the wanted posters displayed on the notice board while the lawmen conversed. As far as he could tell they were all up to date. Barton Lee ran a tidy, efficient system. Johnny Hawkeye, James Blue and Zachariah Smith had not returned with the rest of the party to Apache Bend but instead set out on the longer trek to Fort Boone.

Barton Lee's wife of ten years was named Nancy, they had two children, boys named George and Denny. Clay McCandless was welcomed into the house like an old friend. In truth he just felt old, the days and nights on the trail took more and more out of him these days and the occasional pains that wracked his chest were more intense than usual tonight. The meal was of a superbly cooked steak and beans washed down with a few generously filled glasses of whisky. The table and after dinner chatter was punctuated by a couple of large, good quality cigars and then it was time to sleep. He was grateful to retire to a comfortable soft bed that night.

Clay Milton and Shannon had few things in common other than mutual respect. Diverse conversation at the bar of the hotel was limited because apart from recent events their life experiences were totally different. The topic discussed was inevitably the situation at hand, and any possible anticipated variations on the previously proposed action each of them would take. All speculation they accepted, but when dealing with people such as The Rattlesnake and Fernando Lopez it would always be wise to consider alternative reactions to any and all actions perpetrated by such formidable enemies. As the evening drew to a close Clay decided to call it a night and headed for the stairs. He left the bounty hunter talking to one of the attractive waitresses. Shannon too, would soon go up to his room but he would not be alone.

Clay and Shannon rose early to take breakfast together. The Marshall was expected and Clay was ready to leave for Two Forks when he arrived. McCandless never came to meet them. Barton Lee arrived instead, a look of grave concern on his face.

"The Marshall, he's sick, the doctor's with him now at my place. He won't be going anywhere today." He told them in haste.

"What happened?" Clay asked him as he stood to leave. Shannon reached for his hat.

"He collapsed this morning, it's his chest. The doctor reckons his heart is on the way out."

"We had better go and see him." Clay said and turned to the bounty hunter. "You coming Shannon?" Shannon threw a few dollars on the table to pay for the meal and stood up.

"Yeah, let's go." He answered. The Sheriff led the way to his house.

The doctor, widely known by all only as Doc, an elderly man whose rarely used name was Frederick Desmond didn't want to let anyone in to visit the ailing Marshall but McCandless had other ideas.

"Let me talk to them Doc." His voice rasped weakly through the pain in his chest. "It's important." Doc threw his hands up in a gesture at the futility of his advice.

"Be quick." He ordered Barton Lee and his companions. "If he don't get his rest here now, he'll get it in the cemetery tomorrow." Marshall Clay McCandless struggled breathlessly to sit up in the bed. Barton Lee and Clay Milton helped him, placing a spare pillow behind his back to try and make him more comfortable.

"Take it easy Marshall, you've got to rest." Clay told him.

"The jail, you've got to warn them Clay." The voice was fading but the urgency was not.

"I'll take care of it." Clay reassured him.

"I'll go with him." Shannon volunteered. "An extra gun may come in handy." McCandless managed to nod in approval before he slipped into unconsciousness.

"He can stay here, Nancy will take good care of him." The Sheriff told them. "You'd best be going, he'll complain if you're still here when he wakes up." He added with a slight smile.

"Right, that's it. Out! All of you." Doc insisted, they filed out of the room.

An hour later, Clay Milton and Shannon left Apache bend travelling westward, towards Two Forks.

Another hour after that Rattlesnake Joe and Roberto Aguilar entered Apache Bend from the East.

The half breed left Aguilar drinking alone in one of the downtown saloons and went searching for men of his acquaintance to recruit for the forthcoming jailbreak.

Roberto Aguilar had not often ventured north from his native Mexico unless business necessitated and he did not have price on his head either side of the border until recently. He had usually made a very substantial living from hiring his gun out as protection and enforcement to wealthy landowners and other businessmen. He would have been content to continue as a hired triggerman but his last employer had welched on his obligations and sent two of his own men to kill him. He sent their heads back to their boss.

The bullet holes dead centre of both foreheads gave the recipient an indication of how they died and how he would meet his own end. The man was a ranch owner who soon regretted his mistake and surrounded himself with his ranch hands and a handful of other hired guns. Twelve men in all, including the rancher rode out to meet Roberto Aguilar with an avowed intent to kill him. Twelve men in all died, including the rancher.

The price on the gunman's head was set at $4,000, American, put up by the rancher's wealthy brother. The Devil's Eagle decided to live up to his name and become an outlaw. He would start at the top by joining up with Fernando Lopez, and contrived, thanks to a temporarily expensive tip off, to conveniently be on hand when the bank at Indian Buttes was raided. The invitation to ride with Fernando Lopez followed and after a feigned initial reticence he joined up with the infamous bandido.

The bandit chief would never know that one of his own men possessed a loose tongue and had been bribed while drunk. The unfortunate informant would never confess, he had suffered a fatal accident on his way back to the hideout from the night on the town. He was found on the trail by two of his colleagues the next day. He'd apparently fallen from his horse and broken his neck, $2 was all the cash he carried on his person.

Aguilar was not a heavy drinker, he let nothing get in the way of making sure his ability to use a gun at speed and with accuracy was always at a peak. Instead of a fourth whisky he bought one of the saloon girls for the afternoon and disappeared upstairs with her. The Rattlesnake would have to wait if he wanted him for anything. Rattlesnake Joe was a man Roberto Aguilar did not warm to, not that he actually made any friends, just acquaintances. But the Comanche half breed oozed untrustworthiness and The Devil's Eagle had a highly developed sense of awareness when it came to a person's character. He would work with the scalp hunter while it suited him as instructed by Lopez, but at the first sign of treachery he would shoot him down with no qualms whatsoever.

Rattlesnake Joe easily contacted the men he had in mind for the job of breaking Emilio Barrera out of jail. Six hardened, down on their luck, tough fighting men, ex-Confederate soldiers. They were not smart enough to be outlaws in their own right and needed someone to take charge, Rattlesnake Joe managed to convince them he was that man, a few dollars up front sealed the deal. He wanted one more person to complete his recruitment. A man who'd spent two years inside the Two Forks prison, a man he'd ridden with many months ago, Jack Wilson. The trouble he could foresee was that Wilson was being held in the jailhouse, here, in Apache Bend pending a trial, and the Sheriff was a tough, smart man with well-trained Deputies. He would undoubtedly object to releasing the prisoner of his own free will. Rattlesnake Joe came to the conclusion that to facilitate one jailbreak another earlier one would be required.

Rattlesnake Joe and his new recruits were sitting around a table in the saloon when Roberto Aguilar came back down the stairs. The half breed carried out speedy introductions, names which the gunfighter promptly forgot as irrelevant and told of his plan to free Jack Wilson, and why he needed him for his plan. He would take three of the men with him to the house of the Sheriff and take his wife and children hostage. The Sheriff would then be forced to release Wilson for fear of losing his family.

"You would send these clowns out against a man you say is good?" Aguilar spoke quietly but the menace and contempt for the plan was unmistakable. "Even if your plan worked, as soon as you let his family go, or even if you kill them, he would come after you with everything he's got."

"Who are you calling a clown, Greaser?" The biggest of the men sitting, began to stand up at the insult from The Devil's Eagle and reached for his gun, rage pushing sense aside. The Mexican's pistol was pressed against his nose before he could even touch his weapon. The man sat back down.

"You see what I mean? Clowns!" He spat out the words with appreciable contempt.

"Whatever you do, you're going to have the Sheriff chasing you, unless he and his men are dead. If we take out some of them he won't have enough people to follow us without leaving the town unprotected, giving us the advantage. Why don't we just walk into the Sheriff's office and take this Wilson?"

"Why not?" Rattlesnake Joe grinned his evil grin in agreement.

"We will strike tomorrow morning. That should give us a full day's ride before anyone gives chase." Aguilar concluded the conversation and returned upstairs to the waiting girl.

Eric had finished his night shift as had Tex when Bill and Jed entered the Sheriff's office to take over their duties.

"The prisoners are fed and watered, there's a message for Barton from the Mayor, he wants to see him tomorrow, and the new Judge is due next week or sometime soon." Eric informed the newcomers, he was still holding the keys to the cells.

"Fine, we'll tell him, where is he?" Bill enquired.

"He's out with the new guy, Rodrigo, showing him 'round the town. He seems okay for a Mex." Tex replied.

They all turned as the door opened and two men walked in, guns drawn and aiming at them.

"Wilson. Fetch him." Aguilar instructed.

"Now!" Rattlesnake Joe added venomously and pointed his gun directly at the man holding the keys, Eric.

Tex saw what he thought was a chance and grabbed at his rifle which was leaning against the wall next to where he stood. And next to where he died. Aguilar fired twice with the gun in his right hand, drawing his second pistol at the same time and firing twice more. Barton Lee's four Deputies died within a second of each other.

"Get Wilson." Aguilar told the Rattlesnake. The half breed took the keys from the dead hand of Eric and vanished into the back of the Sheriff's office returning a few seconds later with a scared looking Jack Wilson.

"What shall we do with the other prisoners, take them with us?" Rattlesnake Joe thought it was a good idea to increase the size of his gang.

"No leave them, the Sheriff isn't here, he won't be able to leave his prisoners unattended which cuts down the number of people he can come after us with." Aguilar was clever, the scalp hunter had to admit.

"Where are we going?" Wilson found the courage to speak.

"To jail." Aguilar told him flatly. He pointed to the dead lawmen. "Get the badges." He instructed Wilson. They left the Sheriff's office less than a minute after they'd walked in and rode quickly out of town, westwards.

Barton Lee and Rodrigo Lamas were at the other end of town when they heard the sound of gunfire coming from the direction of the Sheriff's office and being on foot they had to run to investigate. The few minutes it took them to reach the building meant they were too late to see nine men riding out of town at a rush. Rodrigo waited outside, gun in hand while the Sheriff went inside to investigate. He came out ashen faced and shaking with anger and in deep distress.

"Dead. They're all dead. And Wilson's gone." He leaned against the outer wall of his office for support while Rodrigo ventured in to take a look. The Mexican wasn't long assessing the situation and emerged from the scene of death to find an old man relating what he'd seen of the incident to the Sheriff.

"Nine riders." Barton repeated to his remaining Deputy. "They headed west, by the old man's description one of them was Rattlesnake Joe. Wilson has been inside Two Forks jail. That must be why they want him, information, the layout." He speculated.

Barton Lee had swiftly regained his composure, he was a tough, experienced lawman, but he'd never lost four Deputies in one incident, ever. It hurt and he was determined to make the killer or killers pay. He left Rodrigo in charge of the office and cells while he went home to check on the condition of Clay McCandless and if possible talk things over with the veteran Marshall.

Clay McCandless was sitting up in bed when Barton Lee returned home. Nancy had taken good care of him as Barton had promised she would. The Marshall hadn't eaten anything but a bowl of hot beef broth, but swore he felt a lot better than the previous day, not that he could remember much of it. The Sheriff went through the details of the morning's killings and the rescue of Jack Wilson while McCandless listened patiently.

"They only took Wilson? That means they left the other prisoners for you to look after, to keep you from taking as many men after them as you might otherwise be able to."

"Yeah, I figured that out. They could've got Wilson out without having to shoot them all. We can't let it stop us chasing after them." Barton agreed with sadness in his voice." I've known those boys for years, Clay, I've got to tell their folks. Eric had a wife, three boys, what the hell can I say to make them feel better about it?" The Marshall looked Barton Lee straight in the eye.

"It comes with the job, Bart. You'll think of the words."

Chapter Twenty:

Long Night In Muddy Creek.

Johnny Hawkeye, James Blue and Zachariah Smith were tired, weary and hungry, they decided they would rest overnight at the next place they came to. A hot bath, a hotter meal and a soft bed for the night would be a welcome relief from the sweat of the trail, and Zachariah's burnt beans washed down by his bad coffee. The three of them had endured five scorchingly hot, dry days and after each had followed five extremely disagreeably hard nights in the cold and under the stars. The white man could do a few things right, Johnny Hawkeye had realised a long time ago, and supplying a modicum of comfort to a travelling man was one of them.

The three of them rode into Muddy Creek just after noon. Bluey booked three rooms at the only hotel and was lucky to get them. Two hours later he was taking a bath in his room when he heard a commotion downstairs at the desk. Johnny Hawkeye had finished bathing earlier and Bluey could hear the faint sound of the next room's door opening and closing as Johnny went to check things out. He got out of the bath and dried and dressed himself as quickly as he could to follow. The only sound audible from upstairs was the slow, rhythmic snoring of Zachariah in the room to his other side. Down at the reception desk it was a different matter. An army Captain was arguing that he wanted a room for himself and his wife, and another for three of his troop, a Sergeant and two Corporals.

"I am sorry Sir, we just don't have the vacancies. We don't have any rooms available." The clerk was telling the enraged officer.

"Well that's just not good enough. I need two rooms, I have my wife and three men with me." The Captain's voice was becoming vaguely hysterical and Johnny Hawkeye, watching passively from the landing could see the man's arrogant manner was an enormous embarrassment to his wife. She was a very attractive, although tired looking woman, Johnny guessed she was ten years younger than her husband who he put at around thirty five years old. "I am Captain Bradley Kinross of Fort Boone. I am on important business on behalf of the nation and I demand that you find me two rooms. Can you not make some of your other guests leave and go somewhere else?"

"There is nowhere else in town, only the saloon and their rooms come with......er... how shall I put it...? Sitting tenants, Sir. I mean Captain. To let you have a room here it would mean putting people on the street, if you had booked in advance....." Kinross cut him off with an open hand pushed close to the poor long suffering man's face.

"Do you think my wife should sleep on the street, you oaf, well do you?" Kinross raged on. His pretty wife intervened.

"Bradley, the man's only doing his job....."

"Keep out of this Sally, I'm dealing with it." Kinross glared angrily at his wife.

Johnny Hawkeye took an instant dislike to Captain Bradley Kinross, but felt an immediate attraction combined with sympathy for Sally Kinross.

"Maybe I can help out here." Johnny said to the cowering man behind the desk and finished coming down the stairs into the small foyer.

"You keep out of this matter, we don't need a saddle tramp poking his nose in." Kinross could thank the presence of his wife for the restraint of Johnny Hawkeye who felt a real urge to punch the pompous cavalry man. Sally's eyes met Johnny Hawkeye's for a brief moment, a moment both would remember.

"Bradley....." She started to say and stepped forward. The ungracious Captain cut in again and roughly pushed his wife back.

"I told you to keep out of this, and you, whoever you are, I've told you once." He retorted angrily to Johnny. That did it. Two strides later, before Kinross or anyone else could react Johnny Hawkeye was standing toe to toe with the offensive cavalry man. He tried not to show it but Bradley Kinross felt fear like he'd never felt before as he tried in vain to hold Johnny Hawkeye's cold gaze.

"If I ever see or hear you disrespect the lady again I will make you regret it. Captain or not." He told Kinross, the tone was icy cold, then ignored the man as he turned to Sally. "My apologies Ma'am." His voice altogether more pleasant now. "What I was going to say was that you are more than welcome to my room, I can move in with a friend of mine. We can't have a pretty lady sleeping rough." He smiled at the pretty girl who suddenly looked more like a love struck teenager than an army wife. He addressed the clerk again. "I'll move my stuff out of room five and into seven with the old man."

"Sir, I.... Well, thank you so much. I, we don't even know your name." Sally was stuttering now. The Captain didn't care what the stranger's name was and so of course Johnny took great pleasure in telling her.

"People call me Johnny, Johnny Hawkeye." He said with another smile, she nearly melted. Captain Kinross watched as his benefactor walked back up the stairs to transfer his belongings to Zachariah Smith's room, undisguised disdain mixed with fear could be seen in his eyes.

James Blue holstered his pistol as Johnny passed him on the stairs.

"You sure know how to make friends, Johnny." He laughed.

"Don't worry about Kinross, he just needs some of the wind knocked out of his sails."

"I didn't mean Kinross, I was referring to Mrs. Kinross. She couldn't take her eyes off you. Trouble just waiting to happen." Bluey laughed lightly again. "He's not gonna be pleased when he finds out we're headed his way."

"Don't worry about it, I'm more concerned that Zach hasn't had a bath yet, five days on the road is a long time." Johnny laughed this time.

"I'll see you at the bar, I need a drink." Bluey left him to his change of rooms.

Johnny Hawkeye found Bluey twenty minutes later, sitting at a table with three cavalry men, a Sergeant and two Corporals. The Sergeant's name was Flynn and the two corporals' were Petty and Ryan. Flynn and Ryan, a very short man, around five feet two inches tall, both spoke with discernible Irish accents. Bluey conducted the introductions as he poured a whisky for Johnny and pulled a chair from a nearby table for him to sit with them. There was no sign of Captain Kinross or his lovely wife. A mild source of disappointment for the hero.

"I'll be thanking you for what you did for Mrs. Kinross, giving up your room like you did, she is a fragile young thing. We're used to sleeping outside." Flynn said to him.

"It's okay." Johnny told him. "What are you doing, riding with a woman in this part of the country, just four of you?"

"Well, it's the Captain, he sent for his wife before the trouble started, we had to pick her up from the train station at Jackson Wells, a few days north of here." Flynn answered.

"What trouble?" Bluey wanted to know.

"Well we had reports that a Comanche raiding party is attacking the settlers and the smaller ranches around our way, we're based at Fort Boone. The Colonel wasn't best pleased with the Captain, he reckons there's already too many women in the fort, especially if trouble's on its way. He told the Captain he could only spare three men to go with him. He chose me and I chose Petty and Ryan, they are good men. The Colonel told us to keep our eyes peeled for signs of Mexican bandits, I haven't seen much sign of any Mexicans for a long time. Not anywhere near the fort anyhow. Must be something to do with the Englishman who came to see him."

"Englishman?" Bluey raised an eyebrow.

"Yes, a Colonel Steele I think his name was, he came all the way from Washington to warn us of some plot and only stayed the one night. Some story about a Mexican bandit stealing our field weapons, big guns. The Captain told us it was rubbish and the Colonel was mad to take him seriously. Said we should concentrate on the redskins."

"The Captain's an idiot." Bluey told him. "That visitor was Colonel Jack Steele, the President sent him, and the threat is real, it is happening. The Mexican bandit as you called him is on his way and he's not coming on his own."

"What's he bringing with him that could give us that much trouble?" Flynn had a lot of faith in the cavalry's ability to fend off any aggressor. The problem as Bluey saw it was Lopez, he was not just any aggressor.

"Hell." He replied. "And plenty of it."

"And you are...?" The Captain's voice interrupted. Bluey turned to answer him, Johnny was ready for trouble, almost wishing Kinross would transform his verbal aggression into a physical form. The Captain's wife was nowhere to be seen.

"My name is Blue, James Blue, I work for Colonel Steele."

"Stand up when you address a superior officer." The Captain ordered.

"I will. When I address a superior officer." Bluey said with a sudden steely edge to his voice and remained seated. The Sergeant and the two Corporals struggled mightily but in vain to supress their grins. It was evident that Kinross was not well liked or respected as much as he felt was his due.

"Impudent saddle tramp." He turned to Johnny. "What about you? Are you one of Steele's super agents?"

"Hell no, I'm just along for the ride." Johnny told him. The Captain turned away from the men at the table and marched purposely towards the reception desk.

"Do you have such a thing as a Doctor in this godforsaken place? My wife is not well." He bellowed at the long suffering clerk.

"We do have a Doctor, but he covers a wide area, he's out of town for a few days, won't be back 'til Sunday." The man shook as he answered.

"That's no good, we have to leave in the morning. She's in no state to travel. She's burning up with a fever." The Captain was indignant, his plans might have to be altered.

"When did this fever come on Kinross?" The question came from Johnny Hawkeye.

"I've told you before, keep out of my business Hawkeye, or whatever your name is."

"Listen to me you pompous son of a bitch. There's no Doctor. Your wife is sick. I might be able to help. If it was just you, I'd leave you to die, no problem. But she strikes me as a nice lady, she doesn't deserve to die because you don't like me. Now you can tell me what I ask or I will go and see for myself." Johnny stood up to face the Captain, the burning in his eyes reminded Kinross of the fear he'd experienced a little earlier.

"Well, okay, if you think you can help." A more conciliatory tone evident in the officer's speech now. "The fever came on as soon as we got upstairs, but she'd felt a little unwell on the road this morning. I thought a rest overnight would be sufficient to allow her to recover, until now." The cavalry officer looked genuinely concerned for the first time. Johnny Hawkeye's voice was gentler as he spoke his next words.

"Can you take me to see her, I just need to judge for myself, I've seen and had to treat fevers in the past." Far back in the past, he thought, another life, another wife. Kinross looked at Hawkeye, the suspicion faded a little, he nodded.

"Come on." He said and went up the stairs, Johnny Hawkeye followed.

Sally Kinross tossed and turned in the bed, her face was wet with perspiration and bright pink with the heat of the fever that gripped her. As her husband entered the room with Johnny Hawkeye she threw off the sheet and heavy blankets covering her. The thin nightdress she wore had ridden up to the top of her thighs and clung tightly to the outline of her body. The sweat soaked material displayed in more detail than the Captain would like Johnny to see, the curves and contours of her very shapely figure. Kinross hurriedly pulled the bedclothes back over the writhing woman as Johnny Hawkeye leant over her and placed his hand gently on her forehead. He muttered something gently to her unhearing form and turned to leave the room.

"What did you say to her? I couldn't make it out." The Captain demanded to know.

"It is a Cheyenne saying." Johnny told him. "It means rest easy little one, the earth with mend you. At least that's the best translation I can give you."

"Cheyenne? I don't want you performing medicine man, redskin quack treatment on Sally. She's my wife for God's sake." Kinross moved to stand between Johnny and the door.

"Kinross, I don't like you, and you don't like me, but I won't lie to you. If I don't treat her tonight, with redskin quack treatment, she is going to die, and soon. Now get out of my way." Their eyes met again. "And don't keep her covered up, modesty won't help her, you can't sweat out a fever. Keep her cool, it will help." He added as the Captain stepped aside. Hawkeye exited the room and walked down the stairs. He called to the clerk and asked him a couple of questions and then left the hotel, nodding to the four men still sitting at the table as he went.

"Tell us about your friend." Flynn said to Bluey. "He's a name I know of but I'd never seen him before today. What's his story?"

"I haven't known him myself very long but he's a good man. He's got a bit of a history and done a lot of traveling." Bluey kept it vague, he didn't know that much himself, only the basic outline of the hunter's life to date.

"What about yourself, how come you're a government agent?" The little man, Ryan wanted to know.

"Well, actually I'm not a government agent. I'm just signed up for this job, a one off mission."

"The Captain said there are two of you, if Hawkeye ain't him who's the other one?" Flynn again.

"Oh, he's busy elsewhere at the moment, but he'll show up sooner or later." Bluey answered. Sooner I hope. He thought.

The Captain joined them, he planted himself in the chair vacated by Johnny and helped himself to a drink, he swallowed it in one. He began to pour himself another shot and spoke to Bluey as he did so.

"Your friend, Hawkeye, how does he know about Cheyenne medicine? And how can I trust him?" Blunt and to the point.

"Did you ask him about the medicine?" The answer. "As far as trusting him goes, I would, and I'm sure your wife can." He looked at the Captain squarely. "You? I'm not so sure." The Sergeant and the Corporals laughed out loud at this last comment. If looks could kill Kinross would have been very popular with the undertaker, but probably arrested for the murder of four people. He swallowed the contents of his glass and reached for the bottle again.

"What are you doing here, how can two of you be of any help if this Mexican bandit does find enough courage to attack us? If he's as formidable as your Colonel Steele tells us, you and Hawkeye aren't going to make much difference." Captain Bradley Kinross tried to reassert his damaged authority by attempting to diminish Bluey and Johnny in the eyes of his men.

"All I can say to that is we've both had to face times where things have looked bad for us, but we're both still around to do it again. You'd think we'd learn wouldn't you?" This time the soldiers made a better job of hiding their mirth. The Captain reached for another refill, this time he emptied the bottle. A few minutes later he fell into a drunken slumber, face down on the table. The other four left him alone and continued to talk amongst themselves.

An hour later Johnny Hawkeye returned carrying a small bag and a leafy plant. He took a jug of water from the nearest table and headed for the stairs. He looked over to where Bluey and the others sat and noticing the still unconscious Kinross said to Bluey.

"Can you get someone to send me up some boiling water?" He asked Bluey and then he jerked his thumb at the sleeping Captain. "And keep him off my back, I haven't got time for any interference from a drunken idiot."

"Okay, Johnny. If you need anything else just shout." Bluey and Johnny exchanged nods and the medicine man ascended the staircase to apply his quack treatments.

Sally Kinross had fallen out of bed, still wrapped in the sheet her husband had covered her with. Johnny gently picked her up from the floor and laid her on the bed as soon as he entered the room. The fever was causing the young woman to thrash about in her delirium, calling out as if addressing someone urgently but the words were unintelligible. Johnny soaked his necktie in the cold water and held it gently to her forehead. He kept it in place for a few minutes until the frantic movements ceased and she became calmer. He filled a glass with cold water and held to her lips, holding her delicately to help her sit up as he did so. She managed with his encouragement to drink it down, it would help reduce the fever.

The hot water arrived, brought to him by the clerk's wife who generously offered to help in any way she could. Johnny thanked her and told her he could manage but would call her if he needed to. The woman told him they made a lovely couple and went on her way. Johnny took out a tin from the small bag and shook some of the contents into a cup, then he added a large spoonful of honey from a jar, and a small amount of ground ginger, also taken from the bag and poured the hot water on top. He left the contents to soak while he cut the leaves and roots from the plant he'd brought back from his recent excursion and chopped them into very small pieces with his knife. Placing them in another cup and adding a little cold water he ground the resulting concoction into a paste using the hilt of the knife. He stirred the by now integrated hot mixture and left it for a few minutes longer to let the temperature reduce. He took the cloth from Sally's forehead and using his hand he scooped out some of the cold paste. He spread it thickly in place of the necktie, covering the young woman's forehead and surrounding areas as far back as both ears. Johnny tasted the hot mixture to test the temperature, it was ready. It tasted foul but it was ready. He carefully manoeuvred Sally into a sitting position once more and made sure the thin sheet was maintaining her modesty. Then he put the cup to her mouth and aided her to drink. In her semi-conscious state it was a difficult task but he talked softly to her in a quiet, reassuring tone, she wouldn't have understood a word if fully alert, the Cheyenne language would be unknown to her. He held her nose delicately so that she had to open her mouth to breathe and he poured the warm liquid into her, releasing her nose at the same time. She coughed a little but automatically swallowed his remedial brew. Johnny held the cup to her until it was empty and then pulled her back down into the bed so that she was laying down again. He waited an hour and then repeated the operation with the still warm liquid and replaced the paste with a fresh, cooler application. He waited a further hour and then managed to pour another glass of cold water into her.

Satisfied he'd done all he could for the moment he moved away from the sleeping form of Sally Kinross to sit in the only chair in the room. The young officer's wife was more comfortable now, more relaxed, the delirium noticeably subsiding, and he let her rest. Another hour passed and Johnny himself drifted off into a light sleep.

He was already awake and on his feet when he heard the sound of clumsy footsteps coming up the stairs. It was daylight and he looked over at the sleeping form of Sally Kinross, she looked at peace, settled. Taking care not to wake her Johnny had gently wiped away the pasty substance from her head which was much cooler now, although still warm to touch. He applied another similar quantity but concentrated on just her forehead and temples. He would order some more hot water and create another herbal mixture for her to drink throughout the day.

Bradley Kinross had been alone when he awoke from his drunken stupor, he was still face down on the table where he'd succumbed to the sedative effects of the whisky he'd consumed the night before. His head was pounding and he felt nauseous in the extreme as he clambered in an ungainly, most undisciplined gait up the staircase and along to his hotel room.

"What are you still doing here? If you......." He blurted out on seeing Johnny Hawkeye bending over the bed containing his sleeping wife.

"Kinross, sit down before you fall down, and shut up." Johnny told him in a restrained voice. "Don't wake her, she's sleeping." Kinross didn't want to do as he was told but his physical vulnerability forced him to accede.

"Have you been here all night?" Kinross asked angrily.

"Someone had to be, you were not around." Johnny glared ferociously at the Captain. "She is sick, she'll get better now but she needs to rest."

"What the hell is that stuff on her head, it stinks, get it off her."

"Leave it where it is, that's what's helping her, and this." He showed Kinross the tepid remnants of the brewed concoction he'd made Sally drink.

"What is that mess?" Sally's husband demanded to know.

"It is called the cooling plant or the healing plant, it is echinacea tea with a few herbs, honey and ginger. There is no word for the paste in English, in Cheyenne it is known as many things, the calming of the fire, not quite accurate but a close enough translation."

"I'll have to wake her, we need to leave for Fort Boone today." Kinross told him.

"You're not listening, Kinross. Your wife needs to rest. She needs to regain her strength. You'll have to wait at least two or three days before she's going to be well enough to travel." Johnny was becoming annoyed again with the Captain's attitude.

"We leave this morning." Kinross stated defiantly, momentarily shelving his trepidation where Johnny Hawkeye was concerned. "Sally can stay in the back of the wagon, I'll make sure she has a soft bed."

"If you do this, you put her at risk."

"Thank you for what you've done for her." Johnny could feel the resentment in the reticently offered words of gratitude. "But I will take charge of things now, she looks much better. I don't think I will require your services any longer."

"You aren't getting my services Kinross, but your wife is. My friends and I, we're going to be riding along with you, all the way to Fort Boone." Johnny Hawkeye told the Captain. Before he went out of the room he added. "I will leave the honey and the ginger along with the paste I've made, and the tea. I will get the lady downstairs to bring up some hot water to mix with them. Make sure she drinks it, and plenty of cold water, it will help."

Bluey and Zachariah were mounted and ready to move out before Johnny came out of the hotel. He walked out with Sergeant Flynn and Corporal Ryan. Petty sat poised to drive the wagon, Kinross sat beside him, and their horses were tied behind. Bluey had seen the Captain help his frail wife climb unsteadily into the back of the wagon. Johnny ignored the hostile stares from Kinross as he poked his head through the rear flap of the wagon to check on the condition of the Captain's wife. At least Kinross had listened to some things he'd been told, Sally's forehead showed a sufficient spread of the pasted healing leaves. The party set off on the two day journey to Fort Boone. With Kinross and his men leading the way, Bluey dropped back to ride alongside Johnny and the old Mountain Man.

Chapter Twenty One:

Two Forks Prison.

The Warden of Two Forks Prison was not pleased to see Clay and particularly not Shannon, he had a distaste for the "dubious", as he called it, profession of the bounty hunter and he knew right away who he was looking at from his appearance and manner. He considered that the making of a profit by vigilantes was immoral. He didn't consider the practice of hiring out prisoners as labour for any local mining firms or ranchers in order to line his own pockets fitted into the same category. The Warden's name was Kenneth Franks, a hypocritical man with a blinkered view who in spite of receiving Clay Milton's warning, continued in his belief that his prison was secure against any escape plot or any scheme to rescue one or more of the inmates.

There were not many other dwellings other than the prison in the place known as Two Forks, Dos Horquillas to the Mexicans. A few scattered houses on the opposite fork, a small store which doubled as a saloon in the afternoons and evenings, a livery stable on one of the roads out and a rarely visited church on the other. Half the houses were abandoned these days, nothing to stay for in a desolate dead end trail crossing surrounded by desert. At one time it was expected that the railway would pass through the area and that the place would become a thriving town but many dollars had changed hands and the route planners disregarded Two Forks in favour of more lucrative options.

"Tell us about Barrera, would he be capable of blowing up a specific target?" Clay asked of Franks. The Warden viewed Clay suspiciously. This man had just come to see him, unannounced, with no legal status, claiming to be working for a mysterious government security chief. He was warning him of an impending attempt to engineer the escape of an insane explosives expert. No one had ever escaped from Two Forks in his eight year tenure as Warden. Now he was being asked for information and opinions on and about the prisoner in question.

"What can I tell you Mister Milton? The man is a lunatic, he cannot understand a word anyone says to him. He just makes animal noises and tries to imitate the sounds of an explosion."

"Does he eat, drink, does he wash, speak. Does he communicate with anyone?" Clay was becoming annoyed with the Warden's dismissive non agreeable attitude.

Kenneth Franks sighed deliberately showing his own dissatisfaction with what he considered an infringement of his authority.

"There's only one man who can calm him down long enough to get any sense out of him, his cell mate, another Mexican, his name is Séptimo, Virgo Séptimo. He's only been here a few weeks but Barrera listens to him, he speaks to him. Now if you've got nothing more, I have work to do."

"Can we speak to this Virgo Séptimo?" Shannon asked the uncooperative Warden.

"Oh, come back tomorrow and I'll see. I've got other things to do other than worry about a few Mexican bandits."

"We'll be back tomorrow Warden." Clay assured him, letting him know that awkwardness and delaying tactics would not deter himself or the bounty hunter. Such a strategy would certainly not delay Fernando Lopez or his men from their task.

"I would advise you to listen to us." Clay Milton emphasised his advice. The Warden nodded impatiently.

"Now if you don't mind." Franks gestured towards the door. Shannon was already out of the Warden's office and Clay followed close behind. They were escorted to the gates of the prison which slammed shut as they exited.

The two men on a mission decided to see if the store / saloon could offer them board for as many nights as may be required. No rooms were available but the proprietor recommended that the two travellers pay a visit to one of the remaining occupied houses nearby. A Mrs. Bartholomew would be pleased to offer rooms to let at a very good price along with morning and evening meals. It was as they had been advised and rooms were booked and paid for up to a week ahead.

Clay and Shannon returned to the saloon for a much needed drink.

"What can you tell us about the Warden at the prison?" Clay enquired of the store keeper who doubled as a bar tender. They sat at the small bar which took up the narrow end of the store. He ordered drinks for himself, Shannon and the man serving them.

"Not a lot really, he keeps himself to himself. He doesn't come in here much, he sends his guards in if he wants to buy a drink." The man said.

"What do his men have to say about him?" The bounty hunter wanted to know.

"They say he's a stickler for discipline, he'll stick a man in solitary confinement if he don't work hard enough for the miners or the ranchers he hires out to."

"Do you know anything about any of the prisoners? He surely can't risk hiring out some of the most dangerous ones." Clay was searching for any information he could use.

"I know he won't send some of the worst, I don't know their names but some of them are mass murderers and gang leaders. One of the newer ones is a soldier, a deserter who killed another trooper over a woman. The worst is a Mexican the guards say."

"Emilio Barrera?" Clay expected the bar tender to confirm.

"No, that's not his name, I can't remember exactly, September? Something like that."

"Séptimo?" Shannon suggested.

221

"That's it. Séptimo, first name of Virgin or something, seems a silly name to me."

"Virgo Séptimo." Clay corrected him. He turned to Shannon. "You took notice when you heard his name. Who is he?"

Virgo Séptimo is $5,000 to me. He is a Mexican gun for hire, he works for anyone who pays well, either side of the border. His first name is Manuel or something but he goes by the name of Virgo because he was born in September and a girl he was with said it suited him. He's smart and he's dangerous, I didn't even know he'd been caught."

The following morning after a good night's sleep, Clay and Shannon were refreshed and ready for a day of confrontation with the Warden of Two forks Prison. They were not disappointed. The guard on the gate had been given explicit instructions not to let them in and told them that unless Clay had official papers proving he was who he said he was, the Warden would no longer tolerate his interference. Clay Milton shook his head and said to pass on his response.

"Tell the Warden that we didn't come all this way for our benefit and when one of Lopez's men sticks a gun down his throat remember we tried to warn him." He turned to Shannon. "Let's go, we'll get more joy scouting around for the Rattlesnake's tracks than trying to get that idiot to see sense." The lack of cooperation had been half expected and scouting the area for any signs of the outlaw band was the secondary option for the two frustrated men. Before leaving Two Forks they decided to split up, it would be easier to cover more ground that way. Shannon would head west, circling round to the south and return from the east. Clay would take the reverse route starting in the east and then circling round to the north, returning from the west. They would meet back at the saloon that evening. The day was uneventful for both scouts, no sign of Rattlesnake Joe, Aguilar or the men travelling with them.

They returned within an hour of each other and after a bath and a hot meal, courtesy of Mrs. Bartholomew the agent and the bounty hunter ventured over to the saloon. They spent the evening drinking whisky and listening to the bar tender and the very few locals tell stories they'd heard of the prisoners and their crimes. The man who ran the livery stables where they left their horses overnight entered and they bought him a couple of drinks as a bribe to let them know if any other strangers were to appear. Four of the prison guards came in to socialise but, under instructions from Franks, they kept as far away as the small premises would allow from Clay and Shannon.

The next day they'd planned to continue scouting the surrounding area but as they walked out of Mrs. Bartholomew's front door, about to collect their mounts from the livery stable, they caught sight of a man riding casually towards them in the distance. That man was Rattlesnake Joe, he was alone. He noticed them at the same time and immediately turned his horse around and kicked it into a gallop, speeding as fast as he could back in the direction from which he came. Clay and Shannon looked at each other and broke into a sprint. The two of them saddled up as quickly as they'd ever done and chased after the half breed who was already out of sight. The renegade Comanche half breed was very good at hiding his tracks and secreting himself from the hunters and they could only find intermittent fragments of recognisable, maybe, signs of his recent presence. By midday there was still no sight of their elusive quarry but they carried on the search, wishing that Johnny Hawkeye or James Blue were present with their superior scouting expertise.

Back in Two Forks the storekeeper / saloon keeper saw the men come into his store and went forward to greet them. There were two of them, a flashily dressed Mexican who wore a double gun belt and holsters with two ornately handled pistols on view. The other was a white man. The white man wore a Deputy Sheriff's badge but did not give the impression of being a lawman. He wasn't. Jack Wilson, much braver holding a gun than looking down the barrel of one spoke.

"My friend would like a new outfit." He gestured to a rack of jeans and jackets lining the wall.

"I like this, I'll take it." Roberto Aguilar said as he helped himself to a pair of denim jeans and a buckskin jacket. "And I'll take this as well." He removed a blue shirt from a rail and placed them on a chair. He stood in the centre of the store and removed his boots, then his jeans, jacket and shirt, replacing them with the newly chosen garments. "Just need a hat now." He chose a Stetson from a rack of various designs and handed his sombrero to Wilson to hold." Pack these for me." He pointed to his discarded clothes. The store man began to do what Aguilar had told him to do.

"The pants, the coat, the shirt that comes to...."

"Your life, I think is a fair trade Senor." Aguilar told him and walked out looking every inch a Gringo. "Put these in my saddle bags." He ordered Wilson handing him the freshly wrapped items along with his sombrero. While Jack Wilson did as he was ordered Aguilar pinned a badge on the front of his new shirt.

The guard at the prison gate looked carefully at the two men with badges demanding to see the Warden.

"I'll tell him you're here." He said reluctantly. "What is the name again?"

"Deputy Sheriff Bob Eagle." Roberto Aguilar repeated in a very good American accent. "And these men are also Deputies." He motioned to Jack Wilson next to him, and to the six men mounted across the street from where they stood. "Tell him it is very important that we speak with him, there is a threat to his security." The guard did not notice the spare horse the men had with them. He left The Devil's Eagle and Jack Wilson outside while he went to consult with the Warden. Five minutes they waited until the guard returned.

"Warden Franks says he's very busy but he can spare you ten minutes." He grunted and opened the gates to let them enter. Unlike most of the men Aguilar had found himself working with in recent months this was the first time he'd ever seen the inside of a prison. He was determined to make it his last. One of the internal guards ushered Aguilar and Wilson into the Warden's office and quickly departed.

"Well Deputy." Franks blustered impatiently. "What is this threat you have to tell me about?"

"I am." Aguilar told him and suddenly Kenneth Franks found himself looking at the wrong end of a pistol. He suddenly recognised Jack Wilson.

"Wilson! What are you doing, what is this?" He was flustered now and beads of sweat began to form on his face and brow.

"Barrera. Get one of your men to bring him here." Aguilar ordered flatly.

"I can't do that, the man's a lunatic. It needs at least two men to subdue him." Franks was clearly terrified of Barrera.

"Wilson will go with one of your guards, call someone in." The Devil's Eagle instructed. Franks complied and the guard who'd escorted the outlaws into the office appeared.

"I want you to bring Barrera to the office." The guard noticed the fear in his boss's voice and also the guns in the hands of Aguilar and Wilson. Aguilar disarmed him and stuffed the pistol in his own belt. "Just do it." Franks insisted.

"Any trouble and you and your boss will be dead, do you understand?" Aguilar didn't need to scare the man, he was so frightened already he was struggling to retain his breakfast.

"You know Barrera is mad, don't you?" The man stammered as he led the nervous Jack Wilson through first one and then a second set of locked doors before coming to the cell of Emilio Barrera. Wilson ignored him. Another guard appeared and wanted to know what was going on, and then realised as he spotted the gun. Wilson shot him dead before he could react to what he'd seen and collected the pistol from his holster. The guard's hands were shaking as he opened the cell door.

"Barrera?" Wilson called out and entered the cell. Barrera sat bouncing up and down on his bunk making squealy animal like noises, a maniacal grin covered his face. The explosives expert, come casualty, smelled badly of stale urine and weeks of unwashed bodily grime, the stench was overpowering. He pointed at the gun in Wilson's hand and laughed hysterically. Another man occupied the cell with Barrera, a tall man with jet black hair and a moustache to match leaned over to him.

"Calm yourself, Emilio, these are friends." The man looked at the guard and his armed companion, he spoke smoothly to Jack Wilson. "As you can see Emilio is not as well as he could be. He will be quiet with me. If you've come to kill him I cannot stop you. If you've come to rescue him, you will take me with him or he will be no use to you. I assume you need him to blow something

227

or someone up." The black haired man paused to let Wilson absorb the situation.

"Come on, bring him." Wilson had decided to risk taking the other man along to control the lunatic Barrera and let Aguilar decide whether to take him with them or not.. "Who are you, Amigo?" He asked him.

"I am Virgo Séptimo, I am good with a gun and I can use explosives." Wilson did not respond.

"Let's go." He said and ushered Virgo out of the cell pushing the incohesive, shuffling figure of Emilio Barrera.

"Give me a gun" Virgo said to his rescuer. "Your shot will bring other guards."

"I keep the guns." Wilson grunted emphatically. "Move." He didn't see what happened next. Virgo's right foot tapped Barrera's right ankle causing the gibbering wreck of a man to trip. The Mexican leaned forward as if to catch him but then swirled around to face Wilson. Before the armed man realised it, he was now the unarmed man. Virgo had disarmed him, snatching the pistol from his hand the spare from his belt, now they pointed at him.

"If you want to get out of here you will do as I say." He told the hapless Wilson." Two other guards ran towards them, guns raised, Virgo fired both pistols at once. The two guards fell dead.

"You are fast Virgo." Wilson told the other man.

"There are two types of men, Senor, the quick and the dead." Virgo laughed heartily adding. "So be quick."

The man with them wanted to run but was too scared and led the way back to the Warden's office. Emilio Barrera giggled loudly in staccato bursts, it was a nauseatingly unnerving noise.

"I wondered what happened, I heard the shots." Aguilar said inquisitively at Wilson's reappearance. Then he noticed the guns in Virgo's hands. "Who's this?" he jerked his gun at Virgo Séptimo.

"He is with Barrera, he shot the guards." Wilson muttered, embarrassed and ashamed. "He says he is good with explosives.

"My name is Virgo, Senor. I am at your service. Emilio is not so well, I can talk to him, and sometimes he talks back."

"Give Wilson his gun, you can ride with us." Aguilar didn't want to waste time weighing up the pros and cons of the situation, that could be dealt with later. Virgo handed the weapons back to a disgruntled Jack Wilson

"What about Lopez, or the Rattlesnake, they have the say, remember we've got the fort to take care of?"

"You've got a big mouth Senor Wilson, I would keep it closed more often if I was you." Aguilar was angry at the former inmate's loose tongue and Wilson's innate cowardice began to resurface.

"I... I'm sorry Roberto, I didn't mean..."

"Before I was brought here, I heard whispers about a job, a big job stealing guns," Virgo butted into Wilson's grovelling. "If that's what you want Emilio for I think you should know that in here somewhere there is a soldier, he was at Fort Boone, he would know the layout and the procedures at the fort. I don't know what cell he's in but you might think it useful to take him with us." The information made sense to Aguilar.

"Where is he?" The Devil's Eagle demanded of the Warden.

"Tyrone Black, he's in cell 47, two corridors away." Franks shivered with terror as he answered. Why, oh why hadn't he taken notice of Milton and the bounty hunter?

"Do you know where that is?" Aguilar scowled as he asked Wilson the question. Wilson nodded. "Go and fetch him. You." He looked savagely at the cowering guard. "Go with him." As Wilson and the terrified guard left the room for a second time. Virgo walked over to a locked cupboard and then looked over to the silent, shaking Warden.

"Key." And held out his hand. Franks stared fearfully at Roberto Aguilar who nodded. Virgo had to step closer to the Warden to catch the heavy bunch of keys because the strength had deserted Kenneth Franks and he couldn't reach the outlaw with his weak attempt to throw it. Virgo opened the cupboard and removed a hat a gun belt and a gun, he strapped it on and also took out a rifle.

"Now I feel dressed." He smiled and checked that the weapons were loaded.

Ten minutes and three shots later Wilson came back into the room pushing before him another man, ex-trooper Tyrone Black. The guard was nowhere to be seen.

"What happened to the guard?" Aguilar asked Wilson.

"He's dead, so is the other man who was in the cell, they were no use to us." Wilson told him.

"We heard three shots." Virgo commented.

"Yeah, I thought the guard deserved two." Wilson laughed, his confidence rapidly reasserting itself. He grinned and aimed his weapon at the Warden. "Two years I was in here, now I'm the one with the gun, Warden Franks." Franks put his hands together as if to pray for mercy but his mouth was too dry to speak, even to beg for his life. Wilson shot him and would've stayed to watch the life ebb away from him but Aguilar was ready to go. Wilson led the way back to the gate followed by Virgo, almost having to drag the odorous, babbling figure of Barrera with him. Tyrone Black was next and Aguilar last.

Two more guards tried to stop them reaching the gate, Virgo killed one of them, Wilson wounded the other and Aguilar finished him off with a shot to the head. The man on the gate realised some of what was happening and ran for his life. Aguilar shot him down after three attempts by Wilson had failed to hit their target. The waiting gang members were ready to defend against any possible attack by the remaining guards on the escaping men. There was no sign of any forthcoming aggression, at least not from the prison.

The storekeeper had fretted and cursed himself for being a coward because of his perceived weakness in letting Roberto Aguilar steal from him and came for the Mexican now. He burst forth from the entrance to his building brandishing a shot gun and raised it in the direction of his target. The Devil's Eagle had drawn, fired and replaced his pistol before the man realised he'd been shot through the heart. He died still wondering why the ground was rushing up at him.

"We haven't got enough horses for everybody." Wilson pulled at the sleeve of Roberto Aguilar while telling him. Aguilar drew and fired with the same speed and accuracy displayed only seconds earlier.

"Don't touch me." He hissed. Wilson crumpled to the sidewalk and rolled into the dusty street.

"We have now." Aguilar added. He turned to Virgo and gestured towards the gibbering mess that was Emilio Barrera. "You say you know about explosives, are you as good as him?"

"I'm not as good as he was, he was the very best." Virgo answered carefully. "But I am better than he is now."

"Why do you look after him?"

"When he is calm, he talks, I listen and I learn. Using explosives, glycerine, dynamite, it is a science, and an art, who better to learn from?" Virgo sighed. "Sadly he is too far gone now to be of much use to me, he is too erratic, his brain is no more."

"I agree." Aguilar said and fired his gun for the fourth time in less than two minutes. Emilio Barrera fell dead to join the store keeper and Wilson on the ground.

"And now we have a spare horse and an explosives man. Let's go." He said. "The Rattlesnake will be waiting."

It seemed to Clay and Shannon that Rattlesnake Joe had vanished from the face of the earth. They both lamented again, the fact that the only people of their acquaintance who could probably have tracked the half breed successfully were many hundreds of miles away, Johnny Hawkeye and possibly the Australian, James Blue, both proven scouts. The sun was beginning its descent towards the west as they returned empty handed to Two Forks.

They saw the smoke rising in the fading of the light as they drew closer to the semi deserted settlement. The realisation hit them both hard as they could only watch while the little store / saloon collapsed into the flames. They'd been had. Rattlesnake Joe's appearance had been deliberate ruse, a diversion to get them both out of town while Roberto Aguilar had carried out the operation to break Barrera out of the prison. Franks hadn't been the only idiot that day.

Mrs. Bartholomew stood with her arms around the shoulders of the store keeper's widow to try and comfort the poor woman. Half a dozen others wandered aimlessly about the scene of the devastation. Three bodies were set out as if for inspection against the wall of a neighbouring building. Some of the surviving guards from the prison were busy dragging others to put with them. Someone would need to appoint an undertaker, one with a strong back for digging graves. The man who ran the livery stables was pointlessly throwing buckets of water onto the remaining flames. Clay and Shannon called to him and one of the more approachable guards to tell them what had happened. The store keeper they knew, Jack Wilson, Shannon could identify, and the guard told them the other dead man was Emilio Barrera. That surprised them both.

"Why go to the trouble of rescuing an explosives expert and then killing him before he could be of any use?" Clay put into words what they were both thinking.

"Virgo." Shannon realised why Virgo Séptimo had made a point of befriending a so called mad man. "Virgo will be their explosives man."

"We might as well stay tonight, get some food and sleep, and then leave at first light." Clay proposed.

"Yeah. By the looks of the tracks and from what the livery man tells us, there's nine of them. Plus the Rattlesnake makes ten. We should be able to travel faster than ten men. They'll probably have to meet up with Lopez somewhere between here and Fort Boone." Shannon surmised.

"I wonder if anyone around here's got a map, I don't know this part of the country at all, do You?"

"Not well, I've not been this way for years." Shannon replied.

Only Mrs. Bartholomew, of all the remaining group of people surprisingly, had a map of the whole area, including the location of Fort Boone. It had belonged to her long dead husband and she couldn't bring herself to throw it out. She willingly gave it to Clay and Shannon to help them track down the gang of killers who'd mercilessly murdered her friend and destroyed her small community. She made them a hearty breakfast and watched with tears in her eyes as the two men rode off to hunt their adversarial prey.

Chapter Twenty Two:

The Indian War Party.

There was nothing on the horizon, and then abruptly there was. They materialised as if from nowhere, Johnny Hawkeye counted them. Twenty four Comanche braves, armed and painted for war. The travellers were still half a day from the relative sanctuary of Fort Boone. Johnny reached for his rifle, Bluey did likewise as he too spotted the horsemen in the distance. Petty halted the horses and Captain Kinross ordered his men to dismount and prepare for an attack as the Comanche warriors spread out and began to circle the lone wagon and accompanying riders.

"We're sitting ducks out here Johnny, they've only got to fire the wagon and we've got no cover." Bluey stated the obvious. Johnny nodded.

"I'll try and talk to them." He told the Australian. He took off his gun belt and handed it, along with his rifle to Bluey.

"What are you doing Hawkeye, stay where you are?" The order came from Kinross on seeing Johnny begin to ride towards the nearest circling warrior.

"If they attack us we'll lose. I'm going to try and parley with them." Johnny said without looking back.

"If you go one more yard I'll shoot you down like the deserter you are Hawkeye, now stop we need everyman here."

"If you pull that trigger Kinross we'll be two men down, because you'll be dead one second later." Bluey said bluntly and was pleased to see the irate Captain lower his weapon.

"I'll be thinkin' Hawkeye's right Captain." Sergeant Flynn advised his superior officer. "We'd be cut to ribbons, we've got no cover." Captain Bradley Kinross coughed with embarrassment and finally spoke again.

"Huh! Yes that's why I changed my mind." He asserted. Zachariah Smith who'd tied his horse behind the wagon with the other tethered mounts, crawled out from underneath it where he'd taken what little cover was available.

"What's that young feller doing now? He'll lose his hair if he ain't careful." He hoped his friend hadn't taken on one challenge too many.

Johnny Hawkeye held the reins in his teeth, arms stretched out at his sides to emphasise the fact he was unarmed and rode slowly towards the man he assumed to be the Comanche war chief. He spoke to the warrior in his own language as he drew closer. The other braves stopped circling the wagon and closed ranks around him.

"Tell me, who is the mighty warrior who would attack a sick woman?" He began.

"Who is the white man who dares to address Wild Bear, War Chief of the Comanche in such a tone?" The enraged warrior bellowed at Johnny.

"My name is Johnny Hawkeye, I am called He Who Sees As The Hawk among the Cheyenne." He had not used or heard his Indian name for years. "Truly Wild Bear does not need the scalp of a sick woman to prove his courage?"

"He Who Sees As The Hawk is a great warrior, I have heard the stories. But he is no more. He is a white man who hunts a red man, a Comanche, for five long summers."

"I hunt the Rattlesnake, a taker of scalps from the women, children and old men of my tribe for sale to the white man as trinkets. He is not fit to be known as Comanche." Johnny stared at Wild Bear directly. "And I will find him and I will kill him." The warrior chief thought things through for a full two minutes before continuing.

"I know of this man, the Rattlesnake. He Who Sees As The Hawk is a brave warrior. I will respect his courage and let him travel in peace. Your party will be safe from my warriors today, but the blue coats are my enemy and I will not be merciful should our trails cross again." The War Chief climbed down from his horse, his men and Johnny did likewise.

"Wild Bear is an honourable and wise man." Johnny told him as he dismounted.

"Wild Bear is an old woman. We should kill this white man and all his kind." The hate filled voice belonged to a young painted brave who pushed through the surrounding throng to confront Johnny Hawkeye face to face, eye to eye. Johnny returned the excessively hostile stare in silence and with no outward display of emotion.

"Red Knife!" Wild Bear was angry and impulsively took hold of the younger man's arm. "I have given my word. He Who Sees As The Hawk is to be shown the respect that a great warrior deserves."

"A great warrior? I have seen nothing but two old women gossiping." Red Knife was enraged.

"Red Knife speaks too much, do not……" Wild Bear stopped talking as Red Knife whirled around and savagely sliced into the chief's arm with his knife. Blood gushed out of the wound and Wild Bear drew back, instinctively reaching for his own weapon. Johnny moved fast, his left hand chopped down on Red Knife's wrist causing him to drop his knife. His right fist struck the hot headed young warrior flush on the jaw knocking him down. By the time he regained his senses Johnny was straddled on top of him, the fallen knife was now pressing sharply against his throat.

"Do you really want to see any more bloodshed today, Red Knife?" He asked the dazed warrior. He didn't wait for an answer, he removed the knife and threw it away, and then he stood up. Wild Bear was bleeding quite badly and Johnny took off his necktie to tie it tightly above the cut, as a makeshift tourniquet. He glanced around at the other warriors. He asked if they had bandages or a needle and thread. He was met with blank faces and negative gestures.

"You need to have that wound stitched Wild Bear. If you come with me to the wagon I will get someone to deal with it for you." The wounded warrior chief looked around at the ring of shaking heads. "I give you my word, you will not be attacked, as you gave me yours." Johnny looked to where the wagon waited. He could see the Captain waiting ready to order his men to fire at the least provocation, he could see the ever vigilant figure of James Blue poised to take whatever action he deemed necessary. And he could see that Sally Kinross had emerged unsteadily from the wagon to find out what was happening. Zachariah was standing by her in case she needed any physical support.

Wild Bear barked an order to one of the other braves and two of them took hold of the sullen Red knife and put him on a horse, then they mounted and rode off with him. He sent all his other warriors after them with the exception of the one he'd spoken to first, a brave named Tall Horse, who was as his name implied very tall, around six feet three. Although he was particularly non equine in appearance, possibly one might have observed ungenerously that bovine would be a more appropriate description.

"I will come with you He Who Sees As The Hawk, Tall Horse will ride with us." They mounted and rode at a light canter towards the waiting wagon.

"Tell your men to put down their weapons Captain." Bluey said as Johnny and the riders flanking him drew closer. "They're coming in peace, with Johnny." Flynn and Ryan didn't wait for Kinross to give the order, they lowered their guns and waited. Kinross and Petty followed with some reticence a few seconds later.

"This man is Wild Bear, he has a bad cut on his arm, and he needs stitches." Johnny Hawkeye called out while dismounting. "I gave him my word we'd help."

"I can be doing that for you, bring him to the wagon." Flynn volunteered. Kinross looked as though he might object but dual glances of warning from Johnny and Bluey served to change his mind. Flynn beckoned the Indian chief towards him, Johnny nodded in affirmation that it was okay and Wild Bear went with him. "This is gonna hurt you more than it's going to hurt me." The Sergeant told him, Johnny interpreted for Wild Bear who forced a smile and gratefully accepted the offer of a bottle of whisky. "That was really for me." Flynn let him know.

Zachariah spoke a little Comanche and called to Tall Horse, finding the warrior something to eat while Flynn began cleaning and treating Wild Bear's wound prior to sewing it up. Ryan stood by to help the Sergeant if required and Bluey suspiciously scrutinised every move Kinross or his lackey Petty made.

Johnny Hawkeye was out of sight on the opposite side of the wagon to the others, buckling on his gun belt when the frail figure of Sally Kinross came quietly up to him.

"Johnny?" She spoke so softly even with his sharpened, Cheyenne trained hearing she was almost inaudible. "Mister Blue and Zachariah have told me what you did for me. You saved my life. I want to thank you."

"You're welcome Mrs. Kinross. If there'd been a Doctor..."

"Call me Sally, please. And I'm sorry about Bradley, my husband, he wasn't always like that. He's changed since he came out west. I know you stayed with me all night while he was drunk in the bar. Just... Just thank you." She began to cry gently and moved to go.

"Mrs. Kinross, Sally." Johnny's voice was as soft and gentle as the woman's. "Anything you need, anytime." He smiled. She wanted to throw herself into his arms and stay there for eternity. She returned the smile and dabbed at her wet cheeks as she walked back to the rear of the wagon.

Wild Bear and Tall Horse were ready to depart. The wound was stitched and bandaged but the effects of the whisky were still evident. Tall Horse did the speaking for his chief.

"Wild Bear will tell of the great warrior He Who Sees As The Hawk, a man whose word is good." He told Johnny Hawkeye.

"And I will pass the word, Wild Bear is a great warrior and leader of good men. I hope our peoples can live in peace at some time." Johnny added. "What will become of Red Knife?"

"Red Knife will be banished from our tribe, it will cause Wild Bear great pain. Red Knife is his son."

"I thank you for his life, He Who Sees As The Hawk." Wild Bear managed to say through the pain of his wound and the alcoholic haze that befogged his mind. "I know you could have killed him in one beat of a heart. Goodbye my friend." The Comanche warriors galloped away.

"I should shoot them now, before they get out of range." Kinross blurted out in anger.

"Then Sally would be a widow." Bluey promised him.

The rest of the day and early evening was remarkably uneventful and the stars were beginning to show as dull pin pricks in the grey canopy of the sky when Fort Boone at last loomed in the distance.

Chapter Twenty Three:

Revenge Of The Zodiac.

"Who are they? Where is Barrera?" Rattlesnake
Joe wanted to know. He'd met up with Roberto Aguilar
and the rest of the men as arranged, waiting ten miles
along the trail after luring Clay Milton and Shannon
away from Two Forks to chase him. The wily half
breed's many years of avoiding pursuit had stood him in
good stead. He occasionally watched the two hunters as
they'd wasted the day trying to track him down, they
didn't even get close. That was a mild disappointment
to him as he would have relished the chance to shoot
them down. But, he reasoned there was always another
day. Until there wasn't.

"Barrera is dead, he was of no use. So is Wilson, he
couldn't be trusted. This is Virgo, he will be Fernando's
explosives man." Aguilar informed him. The black
haired man raised his hand in greeting. The Rattlesnake
ignored him.

"Who is the Gringo?"

"He was a soldier, he was at the fort, and he will
know where the guns are, or where they might be
hidden." Tyrone Black nodded, he didn't trust any of his
new companions and could sense hostility from
Rattlesnake Joe as soon as their eyes met.

"I think we need a demonstration of your skills Virgo. Before we meet up with Fernando." The scar faced scalp hunter turned towards the recently freed Mexican, making sure that Aguilar was in earshot. "I have heard your name, but you are a bandido, a gun for hire. I have never heard of Virgo the dynamite man."

"And I my friend, have heard of the Rattlesnake, a scalper of women and children, a runner of whisky and guns." Virgo faced the scar faced Comanche half breed, there was no fear in his voice, and there was the trace of a smile on his lips as he continued. He looked towards Roberto Aguilar, who just shrugged his shoulders in his usual gesture of absolute detachment.

"Of course, proof that I can light a fuse. I know a town, not too far away, a bank that needs to be robbed. I was going to suggest a visit to Mina De Plata later after we have raided the fort but now will be a good time. The Gringos call it Silver Town but the mine is nearly empty now. The bank still exists for the ranchers and traders. And I owe the Sheriff a visit. He is the one who sent me to jail, I will send him to his grave."

"We have dynamite, but no nitro." Aguilar explained to Rattlesnake Joe. We took it from the store at Two Forks before we burned it out."

"Well, Senor Dynamite, let us see how good you are." Rattlesnake Joe said to Virgo Séptimo. The Mexican smiled again.

"Yes Senors. You will see."

The Sheriff of Silver Town was aware the town was dying. The mines had played out, the businesses were moving their cash to bigger, better banks in the more thriving areas. His name was Buck Simpson, he was forty five years old and he'd had enough. His last big arrest had nearly cost him his life. He'd tracked a Mexican gunman, wanted for bank robbery down to a local brothel. He'd kicked in the door to the fugitive's room and disturbed the sleeping man with a jab to the face, using his pistol's barrel. The bank robber awoke with a startled look on his face. Simpson had sent the man's female companion out and his two Deputies helped him to tie the prisoner's hands behind his back. The three of them walked him down the stairs towards the rear exit.

They had nearly made it but their progress was halted by the sudden and unwelcome reappearance of the woman. She carried a pistol and fired twice, hitting the Sheriff in the leg and killing one of the Deputies. The other one shot her and she fell. The prisoner tried to get out of the door but the wounded Simpson had hold of his arm and between him and his remaining Deputy they eventually deposited him in the jail. He would soon be moved to the more secure location of Two Forks prison. The woman was dead. The man in custody was Virgo Séptimo.

The Sheriff's leg still hurt, he knew he wasn't as fast or as strong as he used to be, it was time to go, he was getting out. The last shipment of cash and valuables would be loaded onto the stage the following day and the bank would then close its doors to business for the last time. He would ride along to ensure the safe passage of the goods and passengers to the nearest large town in the area, Apache Bend. This would be his last duty as a lawman, he would not return to Silver Town. That was his plan, but plans do not always work out as intended.

The first Buck Simpson knew of anything being amiss in his town was when the main door of the bank exploded. The noise was not unlike a thunderclap to his ears but there was no sign of a storm in the sky. He rushed from his office and peered out along the street to see his one remaining Deputy running towards the cloud of dust at the front of the damaged bank, reaching for his gun at the same time.

An extravagantly dressed man of patently Mexican appearance stood off to the side of the building and the Deputy shouted something at him. The Sheriff could not hear the words because at that moment another explosion ripped through the afternoon.

If he had been able to see what was happening Buck Simpson would have witnessed that the rear door of the bank had been destroyed. The timing of the blast was gauged perfectly to inflict casualties as the bank's customers and staff ran from the front of the building to escape through the back. Rattlesnake Joe and his hired guns were ready to shoot any survivors who desperately tried to leave, a turkey shoot would've given the killers a tougher challenge.

On the other side of this carnage the Deputy began to shout again at the Mexican. Simpson could still not hear what he was saying, he never would. Roberto Aguilar seemed only to flick his wrist and the Sheriff lost his last assistant. The bullet from the Mexican's pistol entered through the man's right eye and buried itself in his brain.

Buck Simpson knew he had to try and do something, he couldn't ignore his sense of duty while he still wore a badge. He had to go and get his rifle and his shotgun, and more ammunition. He turned to re-enter his office and found himself looking at the smiling face of Virgo Séptimo, and the pistol pointing at his stomach. Virgo told him to turn around, he did so and the Mexican hit him hard on the back of his head. Everything went black.

When he came round Buck Simpson had one hell of a headache and could sense dried blood matted in his hair. He was tied to the arms and legs of a wooden chair by his wrists and ankles, and he was inside the ruins of the bank. The safe was in front of him, he could see the stick of dynamite placed securely over the lock.

"We couldn't find anyone to open it for us and the keys cannot be found so we have to blow it up." Virgo explained. "I will move you back a little so you don't get killed in the explosion." The Mexican and another man, a scarred man in bowler hat each grabbed a side of the chair and moved him backwards to where the entrance to the bank had been up until a few minutes ago. Virgo stepped to the safe and lit the fuse to the dynamite. Then he and the man in the bowler stepped out of the way and took cover the other side of the wall.

248

The detonation didn't kill Buck Simpson but fragments of hot metal hit him a couple of times in the face and opened up his forehead, the pain was excruciating and he couldn't help but cry out. The door to the safe swung open and Rattlesnake Joe called two of his men over to empty the cash which Virgo had assured them would be undamaged. He was right and allowed himself a smile of satisfaction. He waited until the Rattlesnake and the others had cleared anything of value and then focussed his attention on the injured Sheriff.

"You shouldn't have sent me to jail Sheriff, I told you I would be back for you." He had indeed made that promise and Simpson regretted that he hadn't taken it seriously and retired away from the area sooner. Virgo carefully placed a stick of dynamite in the front of Simpson's belt, leaving half of it visible. He turned the chair around so that it was facing outwards from the shattered building towards the lengthy road leading out of town.

"I will not light the fuse now, I will give you the chance that you never gave me." He told the silent man in the chair. Maybe someone will rescue you before it is too late." He said and walked away to join Aguilar, Rattlesnake Joe and the others. "And maybe they won't." He muttered, smiling to himself.

"You don't have to do this." Buck Simpson grunted through gritted teeth, forcing himself to try and reason with his vengeful captor.

"I know that. Adios Sheriff." Virgo didn't even turn to voice his reply.

He caught up with the rest of the bandits at the end of the street and stopped. He took a rifle from the blanket on his saddle and turned to look back at the scene he'd just left. He raised the rifle to his shoulder and squeezed the trigger. A fourth eruption occurred, this one completely destroyed the chair and it's disinclined occupant, spreading further bits of building, furniture, flesh, blood and bone in all directions. Virgo looked towards Rattlesnake Joe.

"Did I light the fuse okay, Senor?"

Chapter Twenty Four:

Invasion.

They crossed the Rio Grande at dawn, two thousand armed men. The Mexican revolutionary army of Generalissimo Antonio Gomez swept into the settlement at a gallop half an hour later. The young man, José, toiling in the field and his co-workers were cut down in seconds. The gunfire alerted the families living in the half a dozen dwellings a half a mile away and they came rushing out to see what was happening. The raiders kept firing and several of the villagers fell, dead or dying.

The young wife of José found herself running to her children, to try and escape with them. A rope was thrown over her, pinning her arms to her sides as it was pulled tight. Two horsemen dismounted and pulled her to the ground, ripping her clothes from her as she fell. Then they were on top of her, hurting her, violating her, punching her to make her stop fighting and screaming. She saw her children, two boys dragged out of their home calling in a terrified panic to their mother for help. She begged the killers for mercy, to spare her children. She saw them fall, shot to pieces by the rampaging invaders. More men came towards her.

After that she didn't care anymore, she just lay there, letting the men spend themselves inside her until one of them made the fatal mistake of thinking she was unconscious. She grabbed the gun from his holster and shot him in the mouth. Before any of the others could shoot her she aimed the weapon at her own head and pulled the trigger again, and then, mercifully, for her it was over.

Impatience and frustration had dominated the rebel leader's thinking for weeks now. With no word forthcoming from his go-between Rattlesnake Joe or a message from his hoped for ally, Fernando Lopez he had decided to take matters into his own hands and for the first time enter the United States. The General had collected all his forces together, and with a dozen supply wagons fetching up the rear headed north. He would seek out the weapons he so needed or find Lopez himself, and if he'd been betrayed by the Comanche half breed he would take his revenge.

The government forces had been pressuring him northwards for months and that had tipped the balance of his thinking. He really was in desperate need of more weaponry to fight back. He had the cash to pay if he could not steal, but finding the quality of the big guns he required in Mexico was proving impossible.

To feed the men and horses, the forces of General Gomez would descend like a swarm of locusts on any small settlement or ranch in their path. Houses and stores would be ransacked and looted, men would be killed and women raped. Fire and devastation would be left in the wake of the destructive mob. The Mexican Napoleon knew that as long as he could provide such opportunities for rape and pillage, and guarantee regular pay for his men he would have his army.

Gomez had in his entourage a Major Kurt Schmidt, recently of the German army. He was a vicious man who had resigned rather than face charges of corruption and brutality towards his own men. He had worked previously in clandestine operations for the Confederacy under instructions from his superiors to disrupt as far as possible and delay the Union triumph. The German's ruthless methods and willingness to sacrifice his own subordinates eventually led to his recall and he was assigned to a post advising the Mexican Government of the time.

His propensity for sadism and violence led to one investigation too many and he got out before he could be thrown out or charged with anything. He was invited to join up with General Gomez not in spite of his dubious and barbarous ways, but because of them. The German possessed an aptitude for planning and became chief tactical advisor to Antonio Gomez. A small force of American cavalry chased after the marauding army and found themselves outmanoeuvred, ambushed and consequently wiped out. Gomez would use Schmidt's talents to plan and execute the theft of the weapons if Lopez could not, or would not involve himself.

It was in the little town of Santo Juanita that Pancho Garcia and General Gomez would meet. News of the General's move northwards had reached the bandido's ears and now he and his four companions were seated around a table in the saloon. The same saloon where a young Johnny Hawkeye had first encountered Zachariah Smith, over five years previously. The five men had travelled long and hard in their quest to find the General. And now courtesy of his advance guard, two trail weary scouts, they would let him find them. On hearing the two men talking while standing at the bar and the mention of the General's name, Garcia had made himself known and was content to wait until the next day when Gomez was expected, to convey the message sent from Fernando Lopez.

Bert Jackson, Sheriff of Santo Juanita had taken no notice at the presence of Pancho Garcia and his men. He didn't recognise the outlaws and assumed they were just travelling through. When word got to him about the imminent arrival of the Mexican revolutionary and his men he called his Deputies together. He decided to make an example of the two men in the saloon, to send a clear warning to the so called General Gomez and his men to leave his town well alone. Jackson imagined a bunch of perhaps a dozen rag tag bandidos, they would soon go somewhere else, somewhere less well protected. He and his Deputies entered the saloon, two from the front and two through the back entrance. Their guns were already drawn. The Sheriff called out to the scouts who were now seated but still located at the bar.

"I'll take those guns boys." He said and moved closer, his left hand outstretched to take possession of the gun belts.

"No Senor, I don't think......." One of the men began to say. Jackson and the nearest of his Deputies fired and both Mexicans fell. Jackson turned to Pancho Garcia who hadn't moved since the lawmen showed up.

"I'll take your guns Mex." He looked at the four men with him. "Yours too."

"Si Sheriff." Garcia nodded. "You heard the Sheriff." He said to his men. He started to undo his gun belt. One of his men handed his to the nearest Deputy and instead of making sure he'd got a hold of it properly, dropped it to the floor. The second Jackson's eyes flicked over to see what had happened, Garcia launched himself at the Sheriff, knocking him down to the floor. Before anyone else could react his arm had encircled the lawman's throat and a cutthroat razor rested threateningly against his Adam's apple with just enough pressure to draw a small trickle of blood. Jackson and his men were not the first to fall for such a trick.

"I think you had better tell your men to drop their guns, Senor Sheriff." Garcia hissed into Jackson's ear. The Sheriff nodded to his men, carefully avoiding any sudden move that could alarm the Mexican and cause the razor to penetrate further. The Deputies looked at one another and then dropped their weapons. As soon as the last of them had complied with the order Pancho Garcia slit Bert Jackson's throat and the trickle of blood became briefly, a wild, spurting, scarlet river. The Deputies had just enough time to realise they were going to die, and then they did as Garcia's men fired.

By noon the following day the tiny town had been taken over by General Gomez and his forces. Any token resistance had been ruthlessly squashed and his troops were busy plundering supplies, valuables, cash, women and any weapons to be found. Eventually an audience was granted to Pancho Garcia who waited with his men in the saloon, untouched by the violence and carnage erupting all around.

He'd expected to be summoned as if to appear in the presence of royalty but was surprised to see the General enter the saloon. Gomez came to the table and sat facing him, he waved his chubby hand to dismiss Garcia's men. Another regal wave and they were joined by the German, Major Kurt Schmidt.

"So, you bring me a message from Fernando Lopez, what is it? Has he got my guns yet?" The General began.

"He might have them by now, I don't know General. He has told me to let you know he will do what you ask. I left Fernando to find you the day El Serpiente came with your offer."

"But I sent El Serpiente several months ago, why has it taken him so long?" The General was not an understanding man.

"Fernando is a hard man to find, that is how he is." Garcia told him. "The Rattlesnake has many enemies, he is being hunted by lawmen and bounty hunters and cannot rest easy. It takes a lot of time and care for him to move around safely. He does not fit in with the Gringos or the Indians, or even with us."

"Where will Lopez take the guns when he has them?"

"He says for you to meet him here." Garcia pulled a crudely drawn map out of his pocket and placed it on the table. He pointed to a circled area. "This is the town of Apache Bend, it is about half way between here and Fort Boone, and is not far from the border." The General allowed himself a smile."

"That is good." Major Schmidt agreed. We have the men and now we will have the weapons."

"Excellent." General Antonio Gomez said. "We will leave for Apache Bend tomorrow. What happened to my men, the two who should be here waiting for me?" Garcia told him of their fate and that they had been avenged by him and his men.

The next morning the people of Santo Juanita began burying their dead, it would take them a long time.

Chapter Twenty Five:

Casualties.

Marshall Clay McCandless felt better than he had for months. The care and attention given to him by Barton Lee and His wife Nancy was something he would forever be grateful for. Several weeks had passed since the killing of his Deputies and Sheriff Lee had recruited only one replacement, a man called Jake Hawkins. Many were too scared to take a job where the previous badge holders had met such violent deaths.

Barton and Jake along with Rodrigo Lamas found they could manage without too many problems. Barton Lee was taking his usual morning patrol around the busier streets of Apache Bend when he saw Clay McCandless coming towards him. The Marshal walked slowly these last few days, since he'd recovered well enough to venture out of doors. He thought to himself that he was getting stronger and would soon be back to his normal speed. Both looked away from each other, distracted for a moment as a group of four riders passed by them on the way to the store on the opposite side of the street. Mexicans, they didn't appear to pose a threat.

The lawmen greeted each other and Barton Lee asked the Marshal how he felt, having still been asleep when the Sheriff had left the house. McCandless changed direction and they continued the patrol beside each other.

"I feel much better than I did, I think it's about time I got out of your spare room and gave you your house back." McCandless answered him.

"If I let you leave Nancy will never forgive me, she loves having you stay with us, and the boys like you. Besides if I'm not around I know you'll take care of them." Barton Lee knew that a lawman's life was not always a safe one.

"How's the new Deputy, Jake isn't it?" McCandless hadn't met Jake Hawkins yet.

"He'll be okay as soon as he settles in. He was suspicious of Rodrigo at first, he'd never seen a Mexican Deputy before." Jake Hawkins had been very concerned about Rodrigo until Barton explained how he'd come to offer him the job. They walked together towards the cantina, the Sheriff slowed his pace to match that of the recuperating Marshall.

"Let's have a coffee." He suggested and Clay McCandless agreed. The two of them entered and chose a table opposite the entrance. The cantina was quite busy, a mixture of travellers, a few cowboys and two tables together had been commandeered by a group of Mexicans. They were laughing and joking about various women they'd known in a loud and crude manner, the noise subsided to a more acceptable level at the sight of the lawmen's badges.

"A fair few Mexicans in town today." Remarked Barton.

"Yeah, I saw a bunch of them at the livery stable, and some more at the gun shop. Didn't seem like any trouble though, but it pays to be careful."

Jake Hawkins crossed the street from the boarding house where he had a room and strolled towards the Sheriff's office. He noticed a couple of men wearing sombreros cross ahead of him and go into the bank, two more from the same group of eight walked nonchalantly towards the courthouse which also served as the meeting place for the town Mayor and his councillors. The remaining four men tied their horses to the rail outside the saloon, and dismounted. It was nearly noon and the premises would be open any minute. Seeing nothing to cause suspicion or concern Jake made a mental note to mention the influx of an unusually large number of Mexicans.

It was Rodrigo Lamas who recognised the bandido leader. He was due to take over from Jake's shift, patrolling the town, and was just strapping on his gun belt. He happened to look out of the window from his first floor room onto the main thoroughfare and he saw them as they rode into Apache Bend.

Fernando Lopez and his men took up the whole width of the street and were several rows deep. The Bandido leader fearlessly sat tall and proud at the head of the column and did not look to be in any kind of a hurry. Rodrigo recovered from the shock of seeing what he was seeing and finished buckling his belt. He reached for his hat and left the room to go downstairs and find

Barton Lee. He decided to leave by the back door to avoid being seen by Lopez.

A man and woman came out of the bank and crossed the street, having to hurriedly skip out of the way as the Mexican horde proceeded relentlessly on their course.

"Hey Deputy." The man called to the watching Jake Hawkins. "You're the law, are you gonna let these greasers take up the whole street?" He bellowed. Jake didn't have time to reply. Fernando Lopez drew and fired twice. The man fell dead into the street and the horses just carried on, trampling over him as they passed. The woman's scream was cut short as the second shot entered her face, just below her left eye.

Jake automatically reached for his gun and died where he stood. Fernando Lopez fired again, so did several of his men. The bullet riddled Deputy staggered back, it looked like he was struggling pitifully to lift his pistol with unfeeling hands as he collapsed on the sidewalk.

The shots rang out as a signal to the men of Fernando Lopez. The two men inside the bank shot the first of the employees to make a move towards a secreted weapon and a customer who tried to run outside. The manager was forced to come forward and hand over the keys to the huge safe while his staff filled sacks with cash.

The Mayor stood up interrupting his meeting in the courthouse at hearing the sounds of violence and the ensuing commotion and the other men at the table turned to see the two armed Mexicans burst into the hall. The Mayor then began to voice a protest which was soon cut short when the men opened fire killing him instantly and wounding three others.

The owner of the gun shop heard the gun fire and looked suspiciously at the three loitering men in sombreros. He reached under the counter for his own weapon and one of the Mexicans shot him dead before he could lay his hand on it. There were no other customers on the premises and the three men began looting the place, taking guns and ammunition and piling it all together in a heap to be collected or distributed as Lopez saw fit.

The gun shop owner's wife had been upstairs in the living quarters and came down to investigate the shootings. She carried a shotgun in front of her, cocked and ready to fire. She entered by the door at the bottom of the staircase, saw the lifeless body of her husband slumped over the counter and stepped into view of the waiting killers. The one who'd killed her husband snatched the shotgun from her and hit her hard in the face with the stock. Her nose exploded as crimson liquid gushed out, the scream of agony was swiftly obliterated and curtailed as was her life when the shotgun was fired. Both barrels were emptied into the woman's chest which lifted her off her feet and she collapsed, at least what was left of her did, in a heap of blood and bone and torn flesh at the bottom of the stairs. Two of the men carefully navigated the slippery mess to climb the stairs and plunder the private rooms of the deceased couple.

Two men in the cantina rose to leave, drawing their guns as they did so. The abruptly silent group of Mexicans were all prepared and killed them both before they could reach the door. The distraction gave Barton Lee a chance to move, he did. McCandless was ahead of him, they threw themselves on the floor drawing as they fell and firing at the aggressors in sombreros. The Sheriff had time to watch one of them fall before two bullets slammed into him. He suddenly could not move his legs, his hands felt like lead as he struggled to aim again. A third shot and then a fourth hit the Sheriff of Apache Bend but it was the fifth that finally killed him. His head had fallen back and the bullet entered under his chin and drove straight into his brain. The Marshall had a wound to his leg and struggled to roll behind the fallen Sheriff using him as cover. He took hold of Barton Lee's gun in his left hand and made up his mind.

His time was done.

Marshall Clay McCandless painfully forced himself to stand up and faced the five armed Mexicans. He raised the pistols, one in each hand and rushed towards them.

The incredulous sight of an ageing, sick and wounded lawmen coming at them, firing two guns frenziedly in their direction caused the men of Fernando Lopez to pause momentarily in disbelief. The hesitation proved costly, two of them died before they realised his aim was still good enough to hit what he aimed at. The others fired back, hitting the advancing wild man many times. But stubbornly, he still kept coming, gamely shooting with deadly results. Two more of them fell dead or dying, under his lethal onslaught. The final gunman emptied his remaining bullets into the Marshall's chest and fled.

McCandless could tell he was about to fall down one more time than he would get up and took careful aim knowing that he only had one shot left. The last of the six fell dead, still trying to get away. The Marshall arduously turned back to face the carnage all around him and staggered, he held on to the back of a chair to try and steady himself. Through the red haze that blurred his rapidly failing vision, Clay McCandless vaguely recognised the tall man who was suddenly standing in front of him.

"Fernando Lopez." He gasped with his final breath and tried valiantly, but ultimately failed, to raise his empty weapon, one last gesture. Fernando Lopez leisurely brought his own gun to bear and pulled the trigger. Clay McCandless fell, he wouldn't get up again.

"Marshall McCandless." Lopez said.

Rodrigo Lamas followed the sound to the scene of the most intense gunfire but by the time he reached the cantina all was quiet. The town of Apache Bend belonged to Fernando Lopez. Keeping out of sight wherever possible to slip into the premises by the rear door, Rodrigo stepped over the other dead bodies until he found those of the bullet perforated Clay

McCandless and Barton Lee. He had to get word to Clay Milton and James Blue, to warn them of the impressive force Fernando Lopez could, and indeed had wielded against them. He realised with a huge sense of failure that he couldn't protect everyone in town. In fact many of the townspeople didn't trust a Mexican Deputy and would certainly be very suspicious of his loyalties after the events of the day.

Rodrigo had to go and see Nancy Lee, he felt a duty to her and the children of the deceased Sheriff. He dare not venture out into the streets in daylight in case he was recognised by any of his previous acquaintances or by any citizen with an understandable prejudice against him. He would secret himself upstairs in the now deserted cantina until evening and then make his way to the Lee's house. A sombrero wearing figure in the shadows would not attract much attention in the present circumstances.

As soon as Rodrigo judged it was dark enough he collected his horse and rode casually through the streets towards the Sheriff's house. The fancy little fence around the Lee's garden had been smashed and broken, two horses were tied to the remainder of the gate. Not unlike several of the nearby homes, shouting and crying could be heard from within. Rodrigo tethered his horse next to the others and walked boldly but quietly through the open door.

Nancy was around thirty years old, an attractive blonde woman and was fighting off the predatory attentions of two bandidos. Her clothes were torn and hung in tatters from her bare shoulders. She waved a meat cleaver at her laughing tormentors in defiance of their intentions. Her two boys stood trembling in fear on the bottom stair.

The two men did not see Rodrigo enter silently and draw a knife from his belt. He stepped smartly behind the nearest intruder and cut his throat, simultaneously throwing him out of his way as the wound opened up to spray the room with his life's blood. He moved to do the same to his companion but the distraction he'd caused allowed Nancy to strike and before the knife could do its work the meat cleaver buried itself in the man's head. He fell twitching to the floor without a sound.

Wordlessly Rodrigo brought the traumatised woman a coat from the back of a chair and wrapped it around her. He sat her and the children down and told them about the deaths of Barton Lee and Clay McCandless and the day's other events. Nancy and her boys were comprehensibly inconsolable in their grief and shock at the news. Rodrigo knew there was not much time. He had to get them away from town. He was aware Nancy had a sister somewhere not too far away. He would take them there and then set out to find Clay and Bluey, he thought the likeliest place to aim for was Fort Boone. It took too long to get his message through to the bereaved woman and the boys but eventually with a minimum of baggage they set out to Nancy's sister's ranch. It wouldn't be safe to collect

Barton's horse so the two tied outside would have to do. The owners were not in a position to object.

Rodrigo set a swift pace and dawn was still a couple of hours away when Apache Bend had faded from view.

Chapter Twenty Six:

Interlude.

She came to him one night, alone and uninvited, but none the less he didn't refuse her entry. Johnny Hawkeye had been living at Fort Boone for over two weeks now. In exchange for food and lodging he and Bluey had spent a lot of their time scouting around the surrounding countryside. Ostensibly for signs of Indian war parties but always with an eye and an ear alert to the possibility of other threats, Fernando Lopez and his men.

Colonel Jefferson Stard had received them cordially and seemed to have taken the warnings issued by James Blue and previously by Colonel Jack Steele quite seriously. He was certainly more convivial than his Captain, the overbearingly self-opinionated and pompous Bradley Kinross. Plans were made to transport most of the weapons to a secret location nearby, keeping just two strategically positioned cannons and one of the more easily moved Gatling guns inside the fort. Should any attack take place and look as though it may succeed in overrunning the defences, the main arsenal, including two more of the lethal Gatling machine guns could be brought from close at hand to surprise and decimate the aggressors. It sounded simple, too simple to Bluey and Johnny Hawkeye who had not as civilians been informed of the hiding place.

Sally Kinross was fully recovered from her fever and had been as warm and open in her gratitude and friendliness towards the scout as her husband was reticent and hostile in his presence. Surrounding the fort was a small collection of civilian shops and houses, along with a church, a school and a saloon. Sally often visited the various stores with some of the other soldier's wives of which there were few. One afternoon she'd heard one of the wives talking to another woman.

"Oh, he looks like a dangerous man." She said.

"Yes he does, but he is a handsome one. My husband said he used to live with the Indians. Captain Kinross says he's a savage." The other replied. They were looking at the tall figure of Johnny Hawkeye as he strode past the window on his way to the saloon. Sally felt she had to say something.

"That is Johnny Hawkeye, and I can tell you he is no savage. He saved my life and he is a real gentleman." She blurted out.

The women looked embarrassed at the interruption but soon got over it and the second woman carried on.

"Perhaps you wished he hadn't been quite such a gentleman, Mrs. Kinross." At which point Sally had coloured up and walked out of the shop before they could notice, she hoped.

Now her husband was away with his men transporting the weapons from the fort to their temporary new home, and she stood at the door to

269

Johnny Hawkeye's room. He stood bare chested with a razor in his hand as he prepared to shave. He stood aside and let her enter, he put the razor down and turned to face his guest.

"Sally." It was all he had time to say before she launched herself into his welcoming embrace and smothered his mouth with her own. Still locked together he carried her over to his bed and laid her down. Not a word passed between them until the kiss was eventually broken to allow for the necessary act of breathing to take place.

"You knew I'd come." She gasped, Johnny just nodded in a gentle acknowledgement. He took a backward step which allowed her to stand.

"Do you want to go?" He asked her.

"No, do you want me to go?"

"No." He answered. She smiled nervously and began to unbutton her dress, not taking her eyes from him as he watched her. She stepped out of the garment, she kicked off her shoes and slowly removed her lacy underwear. Then, completely naked she laid back down on the bed and waited for him. She could see he wanted her as much as she wanted him.

"It's been a long time." He told her. It had been a long time, several months in fact, since the girl down south, nearer the border. But she'd saved his life. The woman on his bed at this moment could potentially be the cause of his death, her husband hated him already. He undressed and joined Sally Kinross. The made love for what seemed like hours and then lay together exhausted, holding each other.

When she first saw Johnny Hawkeye, the charismatic, tall, and handsome scout, she was immediately attracted to him. Standing at six feet two inches in height with broad shoulders and narrow hips, an easy smile and a charming, gentlemanly manner, Sally knew many women other than herself were smitten by the popular good looking man in buckskins. She snuggled closer to him, her fingers tracing invisible lines on his chest, following the contours of the various scars he's picked up during his eventful past.

"How did you get this?" She asked of the rough jagged two inch ridge along the left hand side of his ribcage, just below the heart.

"I didn't get out of the way fast enough." He laughed as he told her. "Some feller in Texas, down nearer the border didn't like me." He thought again of the woman who'd saved his life. "He thought I was a lawman or a bounty hunter."

"What happened?"

"I went to the Sheriff's Office to try and get some idea if the man I'm hunting was in the area and because I got on well with the Sheriff he didn't like it, thought I was after him or some of his buddies. I wasn't and I told him so. But some people just don't listen and he tried to kill me. He came close, too close."

"Did you kill him?"

"Yes, I had no choice, he ambushed me in a bar, that's how I got this scar. A woman called out to me and

I moved, just not quite fast enough and he shot me. I managed to fire as I fell, I had to stop him getting a second chance. Luckily the bullet only gouged across from the side or I'd be dead, as it was I bled a lot and would have died but the woman helped me. Her father was a Doctor, he patched me up." Johnny kept his explanation as brief as he could. He left out the details of his lengthy recovery and the intense romantic involvement arising from his seven weeks in close proximity with the girl. Dolores she was called, she was lovely, and he could always remember her name.

Sally had to go, she didn't know how long Bradley would be out, he might return before morning all though he hadn't expected to. She got dressed and leaned over to where Johnny remained on the bed, watching her. She kissed him and looked into his eyes, the same eyes that she had found so captivating, so seductively hypnotic upon seeing them for the first time, less than three weeks earlier.

"Johnny, I...." She began to say something.

"I know." He said so serenely and soothingly she believed he did.

When Sally Kinross had left him alone Johnny Hawkeye poured himself a whisky and laid there on the bed where he could still enjoy the scent of her, lingering on the blankets. He thought about her, she was a beautiful woman, very desirable and he had wanted her since he'd offered her his room at the hotel. She and her husband did not strike Johnny as the perfect match. He wondered what circumstances had brought them together, what had led to them being married? He would ask her the next time, he was sure there would be a next time.

And what of Dolores? She had wanted to go with him when he'd recovered from his wound and was ready to move on. He had loved her as much as he'd loved anyone since he'd left the Cheyenne village, but he had had to leave her behind. His was a dangerous path, it would be more so if he had to look out for two people. He didn't want to be responsible for getting her killed. It would not have been fair to either of them, particularly after she had saved his life.

Chapter Twenty Seven:

Red Knife.

"Wild Bear is an old woman, fit only to gather wood for the fire and to sew. He is not a warrior, he is a friend to the white man. I challenge him for the right to lead our people, to be a warrior, a chief who will be spoken of by our children's children's children as a man who would not let our people wither and die under the guns of the white invaders."

Red Knife had brazenly ridden into the centre of the Indian camp unchallenged by the lookouts who now rode at his side. He had supporters amongst the small war party who had taken great exception to Wild Bear's recent perceived leniency towards Johnny Hawkeye, a white man who scouts for the hated cavalry.

Tall Horse came out of his tepee before anyone else to address the interloper.

"Red Knife, you are no longer Comanche, leave us, and do not return." One of the men at Red Knife's side raised his bow and fired an arrow into the massive chest of Tall Horse, who staggered but did not fall down. The wounded man reached for the knife at his side as blood began to flow but he never managed to find it. Red Knife's other recruit shot another arrow into him, this one penetrated his heart and his legs gave way under him. Tall Horse died as Wild Bear emerged from his own tepee. Red Knife looked down from his mount at his father who was suddenly much older than his years. He raised his own bow and without a word let fly an arrow which entered the chief's throat, piercing his larynx to protrude grotesquely from the back of his neck. He watched his father die showing no outward sign of emotion, not even hate. Then he spoke.

"Who is with me?"

The huge barn made a perfect hiding place for the big guns. There were eight of them, supplied in bulk to Fort Boone by the army chiefs back east who hadn't had a clue about how the Red Indian warriors fought. They were intended as preparation for an anticipated attack by the combined forces of all the many native Indian tribes in the vast area of the plains and the mountains surrounding the important, strategically positioned Fort Boone. The attack hadn't happened yet and the threat had largely dissipated due to the ongoing and progressive subduing of the native inhabitants and their ruinous reluctance to band together. As a result the significance of Fort Boone's geographical importance had declined and the population of the adjacent settlement had dwindled to its present low level.

The big guns however had stayed, yet to be relocated to a more essential location. Colonel Jefferson Stard had considered it an honour to be the trustee of such weaponry, but since the end of The War Between the States had not had occasion to use them in conflict. Now he wanted the quantity reduced to a more reasonable level. Even the threat of Lopez and Gomez, he calculated could be dealt with by his well trained professional troops and more conventional fire arms. If indeed the warnings from James Blue and Johnny Hawkeye, could be taken seriously.

He'd done them the courtesy of listening and treating their obvious urgency with respect and coupled with the earlier, similar warning from the Englishman had decided to store the main bulk of the field weapons away from the fort in a secret storage place nearby. Until a year and a half ago he would not have considered such an idea, he would have been in command of enough troops to defend the fort against any force known to man. But with the reassessment of priorities and strategies imposed upon him by Washington his forces were depleted to the point where he had just enough men to deal with the Indian threat. Jefferson Stard was a pragmatist and suspected a concerted insurgency on the scale prophesied by the security forces, was possibly beyond the capabilities of himself and his reduced cavalry, to defend against with any guaranteed degree of success.

A deserted farm with a massive barn and a house close by to enable a permanent guard of six men would be perfect. It was a tactic he'd used very successfully in the past in training, and this would be considered training, an exercise. After all nothing untoward had been reported to him by the scouts causing him to lose sleep over the matter. He had sent Captain Kinross and a small contingency of troopers to transport the artillery the previous evening. The Colonel's thinking was still influenced by scepticism, but he felt the need to show a willingness to be more open to the viewpoint that no matter how implausible the danger of such a strike, it was not beyond the realms of feasibility.

The shooting was sporadic and close. Clay Milton and Shannon pulled up immediately on hearing it and changed direction. They rode towards the sounds of gunfire and as they came closer they could hear shouting and the more dominant whoops and hollers of the Comanche war cries. They could see in front of them that the ground fell away and a fairly steep incline led down to an isolated farm. A small troop of cavalry men defended against the Indians, using horse troughs, a broken down wagon and the farmhouse as cover. Several of their number had retreated inside the extremely large barn and all were surrounded by an attacking band of around fifty Indians. They could do nothing to help from that distance and had to watch helplessly as the marauding war party managed to pull the gates from the makeshift coral allowing most of the horses to escape in their panic.

Clay and Shannon could see half a dozen dead soldiers and a similar amount of dead braves scattered about the yard. Several of the Comanche warriors carried rifles, stolen from cavalry men during this or other confrontations. The descent was difficult and took longer than they would have liked but Clay Milton and

Shannon made it down the tricky slope unscathed and unseen by the otherwise occupied war party.

They rode straight at them from the rear. They were close enough to use pistols by now and did so with more accuracy than could reasonably be expected. The more experienced Shannon killed or wounded four of the attackers and Clay with his more measured aim killed two and unseated another as his bullet missed but killed the man's horse, the man he assumed to be the chief. The suddenness of their unexpected assault caused a gap to appear in the Comanche ranks as the Indians sought to get out of range of the gunmen.

The fallen warrior rolled out of the way of his falling mount and in the same movement threw his knife at Clay. It would have killed him if another brave hadn't chosen that second to jump from his own mount onto the white man's back causing both to fall to the ground. The knife flew harmlessly over the head of its intended victim who landed on top of his assailant, severely winding both of them. Clay recovered first and used his own hastily drawn knife to nullify the threat. The other warrior ran towards Clay as he rose and looked around for his horse which had understandably panicked and galloped away. The bareback unshod Indian mount was closer, Clay leapt onto its back and rushed to catch up with Shannon who had emptied his pistol and now fired rapidly with his rifle to keep the other warriors at bay while he did so.

The few seconds since Clay had been knocked from the saddle had seemed like hours to him but the path through the attacking Indians' circle around the soldiers had not been filled and the two men sped through. They reached the defending troopers without further incident as the Indians retreated to regroup.

"Thanks for waiting." Clay panted. Shannon nodded.

"I am Captain Bradley Kinross." A voice cut in. "Who are you, and what are you doing here?" Shannon looked over to where the voice came from as Kinross emerged from the barn.

"We thought you could use some help." He answered evenly.

"Captain. My name is Clay Milton, my friend here is Shannon, are you from Fort Boone?"

"I am." Kinross snapped. "What of it, I repeat, what are you doing around here?"

"We need to talk to Colonel Stard, a colleague of mine, James Blue should already be there, with another man, Johnny Hawkeye." At the mention of Johnny Hawkeye Clay noticed a distinct grimace, brief but plain as day. The Captain knew, and did not Like, Johnny Hawkeye for some reason. Shannon asked the next question.

"What are you doing out here Captain?"

"That's army business and this is army property. No one else is allowed here without permission." Kinross must have the knack of alienating everyone he met Clay thought.

"You'd better tell them that." Shannon retorted, pointing to the advancing Comanche war party. Bradley

Kinross shouted to his men and turned to re-enter the barn.

"What's in there?" Shannon asked bluntly.

"Army business." He said to the bounty hunter and then raised his voice to his soldiers.

"To your stations. Wait for my order." He turned to Clay and Shannon. "You two help out here." He pointed to a man sporting Sergeant's stripes. "See Sergeant Flynn, he will give you instructions." Then he was running towards the barn. Shannon and Clay watched with undisguised bafflement.

"The man's an idiot." Clay said as Sergeant Flynn came up to them.

"Don't be taking too much notice of the Captain boys, I'd like to thank you both for helping us out. Your friends, Bluey and Hawkeye, they're at the fort. Shannon, that's a good Irish name." He commented and proceeded to make sure they had ammunition and a place of cover. Just then the Indians, who'd resumed their circling and hollering attacked again.

"Who is the chief, that man?" Clay pointed out the warrior he'd clashed with only minutes ago.

"Yes, that's him, Red Knife. He's a bad one, killed his own father to become chief. Since then he's raised a lot of hell and more and more braves are joining up with him. He talks good, they listen."

The battle raged for hours on and off, each attack resulting in more casualties for both sides. The superior numbers of the war party were gaining the upper hand and the acquisition of guns gave them a convincing advantage. They began to overrun the meagre defences of the besieged white men. Including the Captain and Flynn the soldiers were down to eight men, the Comanches still numbered thirty or more.

Shannon had run out of patience with Captain Kinross and decided to see for himself the reason for his secrecy concerning the contents of the barn. He walked inside to be confronted by the sight of several huge field guns, stored on wagons and neatly arranged in rows. All were covered in sheets of tarpaulin apart from two. The two Gatling guns caught the bounty hunter's eye immediately. Kinross noticed him at once and advanced towards him.

"Shannon, what are you……? He did not finish the sentence

"Use the Gatlings, Kinross. Now!" Shannon snarled at the Captain, stopping him in mid vent. "Your men are dying out there."

"I have orders to keep these weapons a secret and that is what I will do." He replied without conviction.

"Kinross, consider this. I can kill you and take the gun and kill the Indians, you could try and kill me and if you do the Indians will kill you. Or, you can show some common sense and let me use it. That way we both get to live and so do your men. Make up your mind now."

"It makes sense Captain, we can't protect the weapons if we're dead." Flynn had followed Shannon into the barn and spoke now to try and force a compromise.

"Okay Sergeant, I take your point." Kinross said realising that any alternative would result in his own death.

"Can you use one of these Shannon?" Flynn wanted to know. Shannon nodded and climbed onto the wagon to load the Gatling gun. Flynn appointed four men to push the wagon while he himself pulled from the front to steer.

The next assault saw the war party finally break through, into the courtyard. Red Knife led by example firing frenziedly at the defenders as his mount cleared the remains of a dilapidated old wagon. Corporal Ryan, using it as cover stood no chance, one of the rear hooves of the horse kicked him in the head as it leapt over him and he fell. The horse lost its balance and also toppled over, throwing Red Knife clear.

The chief scrambled to his feet and looked around to focus on the nearest white man, Clay Milton. He would finish what he'd started earlier. The Comanche war chief discarded his now empty rifle and reached for the tomahawk tied round his waist. Clay saw the look of hate contorting his face and raised his rifle to shoot the advancing Red Knife. And then he did what to any onlooker would have seemed absurd in the extreme.

He lowered the weapon and stood up to meet his adversary face to face. He drew his knife and waited for the inevitable charge. Red Knife was ferocious in his strike, murderous intent showed blatantly in his eyes. He swung the tomahawk viciously to where his practise and experience in hand to hand combat had told him Clay's head would be. It wasn't there.

Before he could turn and attack again he felt a sharp pain in his arm, he couldn't lift it to raise his weapon a second time. He couldn't even hold it and the axe fell into the dirt. He never knew it but the nerves and tendons in his wrist had been severed and his hand permanently disabled. He grabbed his knife with his left hand and frantically lunged at the white man, aiming for his heart.

Again the white man eluded his attack, again he felt a pain. This time his other arm became useless and he dropped the knife. Red knife looked down at his ruined arms, blood was pouring out of them now, soaking the ground at his feet. The rest of his war party hadn't noticed his predicament and were closing in on the barn where three of the soldiers were preparing for a last stand.

"Why don't you kill me white man?" Red Knife shouted at his conqueror, his legs buckled under him and he dropped to his knees.

"I have." Clay answered. Red Knife fell forward, the flow of blood beginning to slow as his heart weakened, he lived just long enough to hear the sound of his men being slaughtered.

"Get down Milton." Bellowed Sergeant Flynn while pulling open the door to the big barn, behind him a wagon was being pushed as fast as the four men behind it could push. Clay could see what was about to happen and ran to the side of the farmhouse to escape, throwing himself down to the ground as he got there. On the wagon was a Gatling gun, behind the Gatling gun was Shannon.

The noise of the deadly weapon was deafening, almost but not quite, obliterating the sound of the Indians' dying screams as it spat out its deathly hail. The battle was over in seconds, any surviving able bodied braves realised this and rode off hastily, soundly and irrevocably defeated. Their numbers depleted to single figures and their chief killed. There would be no further aggression for the foreseeable future.

"Why the hell didn't you use the Gatling earlier?" Clay demanded of Kinross as the casualties were assessed. Kinross ignored him, he seemed to be in a state of shock.

"The Captain said we have to keep the guns here a secret, orders from the Colonel. If it hadn't been for your friend Shannon we'd probably all be dead now." Flynn told him.

"Stupid!" Clay exclaimed angrily. "What happened?" He couldn't believe Kinross would sacrifice his troops in such a way. Flynn related the conversation between Shannon and Kinross. Clay shook his head in disbelief. A groan came from the fallen figure of Corporal Ryan as he came round from being concussed by the hoof of Red Knife's mount. Sergeant Flynn rushed over to help his wounded fellow countryman to his feet.

Clay bent down to retrieve his discarded rifle, he checked to satisfy his own curiosity, it was empty of ammunition. Had he wasted time trying to shoot Red

Knife he would probably have been the one lying dead. Kinross sent the other men out to find and round up as many of the escaped horses as they could find, using their few remaining mounts to do so.

Clay strolled into the barn unchallenged and had a good look around, apart from the big guns, ammunition and the wagons they rested on there was not much of interest. A few old rusty bayonets, a battered old shovel and a hammer with a box of assorted nails.

The Captain made plans to leave Corporal Petty in charge of guarding the guns while he, the wounded Ryan and Sergeant Flynn would return to the fort and report to Colonel Stard. Clay Milton and Shannon believing the Indians were not liable to attack again chose to journey with them to Fort Boone and meet up with Bluey and Johnny. The rest of the surviving soldiers were only suffering from minor wounds or scratches and would remain with Petty. Kinross surmised that if Lopez and his men should show up in the area they would head for the fort where they would expect to find the weapons they searched for.

Chapter Twenty Eight:

Deployment.

The nine riders passed below the unseen watcher as he studied them from his vantage point in the rocky hills above the trail. He'd seen the dust raised by their mounts in the distance and decided it might be best if he was not discovered. He did not want to risk meeting anyone who might be hostile towards him and was especially keen on avoiding the men of Fernando Lopez. It was the right choice, Rodrigo's hand clasped his rifle tightly, just in case, as Rattlesnake Joe, Roberto Aguilar, The Devil's Eagle and seven other men he did not recognise came into view. He waited until the horsemen were out of sight along the trail and descended slowly from his hiding place. He rode away as fast as he dare push his horse, he needed to reach Fort Boone as soon as possible.

A few miles further along Rodrigo came across a fork in the road, one of the signs pointed towards Two Forks Prison. He could see smoke in the distance and paused for a minute to consider. Clay and Shannon had set out for Two Forks, were they still there, in trouble? Fort Boone was under the bigger threat. Bluey and Johnny Hawkeye might have to face the full might of Fernando Lopez and his men and he'd seen how devastatingly dangerous they were. He spurred his mount onwards. Fort Boone it would have to be.

The hotel in Apache Bend, previously used by the stagecoach party had been commandeered by Fernando Lopez as his headquarters. The tables had all been pushed together and he, and all who could be seated comfortably, sat around them. A further thirty or so lounged against the surrounding wall. The hotel staff were left unmolested on the orders of the bandido chief and would stay that way to make sure service was kept as close to normal as possible. Seated on one side of their leader was a freshly arrived Roberto Aguilar and on the other Rattlesnake Joe, next to The Devil's Eagle sat Virgo Séptimo. All present paid attention when Fernando Lopez spoke.

"I have been thinking about what we will do and this is what I have decided." He spoke directly to Aguilar. "Roberto, the Gringo soldier, he is sure that the weapons will be at the fort?"

"Most of the time they are kept in converted barns at the back of the fort. But if they needed to be kept out of the way, there is a farm just a few hours away with a very big barn. It would been used to hide them if the Colonel did not think they were safe at the fort. He doesn't have such a large company of men as he used to, the main threat was from the Indians but most of them are peaceful or dead these days. He says they would not need many soldiers to protect the guns at the barn because no one other than the troopers should know they are there." That was the longest speech from Roberto Aguilar that anyone in the room had ever heard.

"Roberto, you will go with El Serpiente and his men, you will take six of my men and the Gringo soldier. You will find this farm and if the weapons are there, you will take them."

Lopez then turned his attention to Virgo. "I will take the rest of my men to the fort. Virgo, you will come with us, we will see if your skills are as good as Roberto tells me." He looked around to make sure everyone was paying attention. They were. "Wherever the guns are stored we will take them. Wherever the guns are stored we will take the fort. There will be no survivors. We do not want an army chasing us all the way back to Mexico."

The Commanding Officer's office was crowded, present were, apart from the Colonel, Captain Bradley Kinross, Clay Milton, Johnny Hawkeye, James Blue and Shannon.

Hearing of the death of White Bear had disappointed Johnny Hawkeye a little, but not so that of his son, Red Knife. The older chief might have been persuaded to make peace and the destruction of his war party avoided, but it was too late now.

"I'll get straight to it, Gentlemen." Colonel Stard began. "We've all heard what happened at Two Forks. I have to apologise for not taking the warnings from Mister Blue and Colonel Steele as seriously as I should have done. It seems as though we are in considerable danger from this man Lopez and need to take action to prepare for an assault. The first thing I want to do is evacuate all the women and children from the fort. Captain Kinross, you will organise that now. Have them ready to move out by noon. I want one of you civilians to volunteer if you will to accompany Sergeant Flynn and four other men and safeguard the ladies' passage to the town of Lugar, it means place in Spanish. It's a day and a half north of here, it should be safe enough, and the Mexicans will come at us from the south, south east."

"I would suggest Bluey or Johnny, they are the best scouts." Clay suggested.

"This is our mission Colonel, if Johnny doesn't mind, I'll stay here. Johnny?" Bluey looked to Johnny Hawkeye to see his reaction to the suggestions. Johnny thought for a few seconds.

"Okay with me." He agreed, and said to Shannon. "Try to keep Rattlesnake Joe alive long enough for me to deal with him." The bounty hunter nodded.

"I'll do my best."

"That's sorted then." The Colonel continued. "Mister Blue, I would like you and Mister Shannon, if you don't mind to scout around a little further afield, concentrate on the directions I've just mentioned, we need as much notice as we can get. Mister Milton, I would like you to go and warn the townspeople that trouble may be on its way. To leave if they can, and if not move into the fort. If they wish to leave with Sergeant Flynn and the soldiers' wives to be ready at noon. That's all for now. Captain, say your goodbyes and be here as soon as the ladies have gone. You too, Mister Milton, we have further preparations to plan."

"Bluey, I've got an idea." Clay said to the Australian the moment they left the Colonel's office. "Can I talk to you and Shannon before you go?"

Noon came and the wagons left, there were fourteen of them. Along with the women from the fort, several families from the once thriving town of Boone had decided to make the journey to the anticipated safety of Lugar. Zachariah Smith watched as Johnny Hawkeye and Sergeant Flynn led the departure.

"You keep out of trouble for a couple of days eh Old Man?" The scout bid him farewell.

"Don't you get your fool self killed Young Feller." The Mountain Man shouted after him.

Bluey and Shannon had only been away from the fort for an hour when they saw the dust in the distance.

"One rider, coming this way, he's in a hurry." Bluey said to the bounty hunter.

"Yeah, let's get off the trail." Shannon suggested. They rode quickly to a nearby rocky slope and hid the horses out of sight. Taking what little cover was available they waited, weapons at the ready. The rider rode into view and the scouts recognised him at once.

"Rodrigo!" Bluey shouted to him, not yet revealing himself until he was sure the pistolero knew who was hailing him. The young Mexican reined in his mount as he drew level with them.

"Bluey, where are you?" He knew where Bluey had to be but he couldn't see him. Bluey stood up and spoke.

"I'm here Rodrigo, Shannon's with me." The bounty hunter appeared leading the horses. "You're in one hell of a hurry, Son. What's happened?" Rodrigo filled them in as they rode.

"Fernando Lopez, he has taken over Apache Bend, Marshall McCandless and Sheriff Lee, his new Deputy, the Mayor, the Judge and dozens more, killed." He went into further details and the reason for his delay in riding to warn them because of taking Nancy Lee and her children to safety. "And on the way here I saw the Rattlesnake and eight other men, one of them was Aguilar. They were riding towards Apache Bend, I think to meet Lopez."

"They found themselves an explosives man." Shannon explained.

"One of us ought to go back to the fort with him." Bluey said to the bounty hunter. "If they see a man wearing a sombrero they're liable to shoot him first and not bother asking questions afterwards."

"Yeah, you're right, I'll go. You're a better scout than I am anyway. I'll see you back there tonight.

The young pistolero was treated with enormous suspicion at first by the soldiers and remaining civilians at Fort Boone. Kinross was particularly antagonistic in his manner but Colonel Stard accepted the word of Clay Milton and Shannon that he was on their side. He greeted Rodrigo civilly and listened to his tale regarding the fate of Apache Bend.

"How was it you were not killed with the Sheriff and his men?" Kinross had baited Rodrigo.

"Senor, I was off duty in my room when I saw the men come into town. The other Deputy died before I could warn him. When I found the Marshall and the Sheriff they were already dead. I had to make sure the Sheriff's family was safe, some of the bandidos were attacking his wife, and you know what they would have done?"

"Captain, not Senor. What happened to the bandidos, did you just shout at them and frighten them away?" Kinross again.

"Kinross, you're out of line." Clay Milton told him.

"They will not attack anyone else Senor." Rodrigo emphasised "Senor." "I took Senora Lee and her children to her sister's place, they should be safe there."

"Then you ran away to warn us." Kinross uttered one too many insults.

"Senor! I could have gone back into Apache Bend and tried to defeat nearly a hundred men on my own, and I would have been killed instead of coming here to warn you." Rodrigo looked very dangerously at the Captain. "But if you think I should have been killed then I will give you the opportunity to do it." He took out his pistol and removed five bullets. "I will keep only one bullet in my gun, you may have as many as you think you will have time to use. We should settle this outside, in the yard."

"That's enough! No one is shooting anyone, we have enough problems without killing each other." Colonel Stard finally stamped hard on Kinross. "Apologise to the man Kinross, now"

"As the Colonel says we should not fight amongst ourselves. I withdraw my comments." Kinross backed down and left the room, Clay followed him. Rodrigo reloaded his weapon.

"You're an idiot Kinross." Clay was angry with the loud mouthed Captain. "Rodrigo would've killed you before you could move. He killed Fernando Lopez's brother, Juan. Juan already had a gun in his hand and was facing him at the time, are you faster than that?" He left the Captain to consider how close he'd come to dying and went to study the two cannons and the Gatling gun.

Lugar was not a big place, there was only one hotel, not enough for all the people seeking sanctuary from the danger at Fort Boone. Most of them stayed in their wagons, they would sort something out the next day. Johnny Hawkeye had booked the only spare room for Sally Kinross. Sally had graciously offered to share her wagon with the store keeper's wife who gratefully accepted the chance to travel with her and would stay the night with her in the hotel. Johnny would sleep in her wagon and safeguard the few possessions she'd brought with her. The wagons had arrived in town late in the day, they had spent the night before on the trail and he needed a wash, a shave and a hot meal, the latter of which was willingly supplied by the travellers to himself, Sergeant Flynn and the other soldiers. Later, after a few shots of whisky and a short conversation with Flynn he retired to the wagon. He settled down to sleep, trying not to think of Sally Kinross, she would be only a couple of hundred yards away, out of reach, and he knew she would be thinking of him. Her need for discretion would prevent them from meeting this night. He would be leaving early the next day. He closed his eyes and awaited the onset of a much needed sleep. There was a gentle rustling sound as the flap at the rear of the wagon was untied.

James Blue had returned to Fort Boone the previous evening as dusk was upon them. He'd seen no fresh signs of any horsemen on the trail and he'd decided to check on the remote farm to make sure all was well. It was. He spent some time there, inspecting the weapons and the arrangements for security. He didn't expect Lopez and his men to be close for several days. But he knew they would come, and there would be many casualties on both sides. For what? He asked himself. So that a mad man could use the guns against the people of Texas, and then his own people. His job, and that of Clay Milton was to make sure it didn't happen.

Johnny Hawkeye returned to the fort along with three of the troopers. Flynn and one other man had stayed to safeguard the evacuated townspeople and their wagons. They rode silently, each lost in their own thoughts. Johnny's were consumed by the memory of Sally's clandestine visit to disturb his slumber last night. She'd left the storekeeper's wife asleep in the hotel and sneaked out of the back door. She needed to see him more than she feared being missed in the room. She could always think of something to say if the woman woke up and found her gone. The wagon's tail curtain was pulled aside and Sally had crawled inside quietly, she thought he may be sleeping. It was a bright moonlit night but by the time she saw him in the shadowy interior of the wagon he was wide awake. He smiled and put down the gun he held.

"I didn't know who to expect." He laughed almost inaudibly. "I didn't think we'd see each other tonight."

"Joyce, the store keeper's wife, she fell asleep, the snoring kept me awake."

"I will keep you awake." Johnny had promised and moved to hold her. Their lovemaking was sensual, slow and for the most part conducted in a passionate quietness to preserve privacy. Before the dawn broke she had managed to return unnoticed to the hotel room. Joyce slumbered on, her snores the loudest noise Sally had heard all night.

The journey back to Fort Boone hadn't taken as long as the outward trek and it was still morning when they arrived. James Blue and Zachariah Smith, who'd forcibly volunteered himself, were away scouting. Shannon was checking the quality and quantity of the weapons and ammunition available. Rodrigo was assisting the bounty hunter. Kinross was busy drilling the troops, and Clay Milton was with the Colonel discussing tactics, or frustratingly, the lack of them. Johnny went to his room and laid down, he was soon asleep.

He awoke late in the afternoon and made his way to the canteen, he was hungry. Clay, Shannon and Rodrigo were eating together and he joined them. Catch up didn't take long, and he was saddened and angry to hear about the deaths of Clay McCandless and Barton Lee. He listened intently to the relating of Rodrigo's close encounter with Rattlesnake Joe and was somehow relieved to know his nemesis was still alive. No one had yet cheated him out of his revenge.

The following three days revealed no signs of travellers on the trails around the fort or the farm. The soldiers began to let complacency creep in and the awareness of the potential danger was fading. Supplies of food and water were getting low so the Colonel sent a small number of troopers to the river, three miles away to fill up several barrels, Shannon and Clay Milton went with them. The general store was nearly empty of food and so a wagon was sent to a nearby town to replenish stocks. Johnny Hawkeye and James Blue were not available to travel with it as they were out of the fort scouting for any signs of Lopez and his men. The recovered Corporal Ryan and five other troopers were selected to ride with the wagon. Rodrigo had offered his services but Captain Kinross had declined, his distrust of, and blatant prejudice against the Mexican undoubtingly influencing his decision.

Clay and Shannon along with the fully filled water barrels and the troopers were back in the fort by nightfall, the food and other supplies were not expected until the next day or possibly the day after that. Johnny Hawkeye and James Blue had nothing different to report after a long day's searching the area yet again. Zachariah didn't go out with the scouts every day, he was well into his seventies by now, a very advanced age for a Mountain Man. He hated to admit it but he was feeling every one of his years more and more as time went on. He just would not give up in his quest for vengeance against the scalp hunting half breed. Only one of their deaths could make him do that.

Two days later the supply wagon and the accompanying troopers still hadn't returned, Colonel Stard was concerned. Johnny Hawkeye and Rodrigo Lamas rode out to look for them. Zachariah, feeling the need to do something, wanted to help in some way and so he rode out with Bluey on yet another scouting expedition. Bluey explained to Clay that he was going to extend his searching out a little further afield and might not be back by nightfall. If he found anything significant to report he would send Zachariah back with a message.

Chapter Twenty Nine:

Remember The Alamo.

Clay had taken to patrolling around the fort before going to his bed at night, to reassure himself that the sentries were awake. The fear of imminent attack from a mythical Mexican bandit had begun to wane and the alertness of the lookouts was prone to fade with the daylight. Who in their right mind would assault a fort full of soldiers at night? Surely no one was that stupid, were they?

The rear of the fort was taken up with large barns and stables, converted into storage sheds where in normal circumstances the big guns would be kept. Above on specially constructed platforms two cannons pointed outwards at the corners. In the centre pointing forwards into the main courtyard / parade ground of the fort was the recently repositioned Gatling gun, freshly cleaned, oiled and loaded, ready to fire. Opposite, the front gates were an imposing barrier to those looking from the inside or the outside. As you entered the gates, to your right were a group of buildings containing the Officer's quarters and the Office of the Commanding Officer, Colonel Jefferson Stard. To your left you would see the troopers bunk houses, the stables and a canteen with a storage room built onto the side.

The troopers on night duty wandered irregularly around the ramparts supposedly scouring the surrounding area for any signs of unusual activity or sounds. Instead of a solitary stroll as instructed, the sentries tended to patrol in pairs. The conversations consisted mainly of lurid bawdy exploits springing wishfully from their own vivid imaginations, instead of the potential danger that may even at this moment may be lurking perilously in the encompassing darkness.

Not one of the sentries saw or heard anything. The two shadowy figures down below, outside the walls of the fort carried out their task in less than an hour, completely undisturbed, and were gone. The soldiers above continued to reminisce about the girls they'd known in their fantasies.

From the upstairs window of the general store, opposite the front gates of Fort Boone, Fernando Lopez looked out, Virgo Séptimo stood beside him, smiling. The sun was coming up and the view would have made the perfect setting for a painting, if the artist had hurried in his task.

The first explosion took out the main gates, the next within seconds blew apart the left hand wall. The smoke and the screams of injured troopers destroyed the early morning silence. And then they were there, the Mexican hordes, they came from all sides, firing at the soldiers as they staggered, wounded, dazed and blinded out of their quarters to seek cover and salvation. It was not to be, the relentless influx of the attackers decimated the unresisting, in many cases unarmed men.

Clay Milton rushed out, already dressed and armed, he shot two of the invaders as he ran. The third blast demolished the right hand wall and killed many of the surviving troopers who'd run towards it searching for shelter from the death dealing gunfire. Clay heard a cry of pain coming from Colonel Stard's office and being first on the scene he dived straight in through the door, ducking just as a bullet thudded into the remains of the door frame where a second earlier his head had been. The Colonel laid groaning on the floor, blood all over his face and chest, a jagged piece of wood from a damaged picture frame sticking out of his stomach. He died without saying a word. Bradley Kinross entered behind Clay, a look of terror, confusion and pain on his face. His left arm hanging limply at his side, blood pouring from a wound above the elbow.

"Sit down Kinross, I'll bandage that arm." Clay shouted above the noise of gunfire and yelling from outside. He quickly tore a piece of the Colonel's remaining tattered curtain and tied it tightly round the Captain's wounded arm. "Wait there." Leaving Kinross sitting trance like where he sat Clay peered cautiously out of the doorway into the wrecked fort, only the rear part was undamaged. The guns! He looked to where the Gatling gun was about to be put to use. There were no living troopers in sight, the place was swarming with the victorious Mexicans.

Shannon aimed the murderous weapon at the teeming masses below him and seeing Clay waved him out of the way.

"Get out!" He bellowed. "Get to Hawkeye!" And with that he opened fire. Dozens of the bandidos died in volley upon volley of the destructive, malicious barrage of death. Clay ducked back into the ruins of Colonel Stard's office and kicked out the remains of the window, a speedy glance outside told him there were a handful of mounted bandits a few yards to the left of him, he counted five.

"Can you shoot?" He shouted to penetrate the mild consciousness of Kinross. The Captain blinked, regained some of his senses and nodded meekly. Clay drew the Officer's pistol and put it into his good hand. "I'm going out there, we have to go. The fort is gone. Do you understand?" Again a nod. "Follow me." Clay said and climbed out. His first shot killed one of the horsemen, a second wounded another, causing him to fall off his mount. Kinross suddenly found some comprehension of the circumstances and shot one of the other men and a further shot from Clay drove the remaining two Mexicans to retreat from the line of fire to find cover.

He half dragged Kinross along to the dead men's horses, pushed him up into the saddle and slapped the mount's rump, it galloped away, grateful to escape the sounds and smell of death and destruction. Mounting the nearest of the other two animals Clay looked back through the collapsed wall of the once proud fort to see

Shannon still firing at anything that moved. Then the noise ceased. The ammunition belts had been exhausted, Shannon would not have time to go and get any more.

The bandido chief, watching still from the window across the street, had a smoke obscured view of the man using the Gatling gun and took careful aim with his rifle. He squeezed the trigger. A shot rang out to crack the short lived silence and the bounty hunter fell. Clay Milton knew the place would be filled with the enemy in seconds. He jumped off the horse and loosely tied it to a piece of broken window frame. Navigating his way through the murky atmosphere and rubble made his way to where he'd seen Shannon fall. The bounty hunter was barely conscious but had enough presence of mind to realise someone was approaching, he drew his gun and waited.

"Shannon? It's Clay, don't shoot me." Shannon let his arm fall, still holding the pistol. Clay appeared through the haze and looked down at the fallen bounty hunter. Blood ran down his face from a head wound but there didn't seem to be any sign of further injury.

"Can you stand? We have to get out of here." He stooped down to help his wounded colleague. In a sudden movement Shannon pushed him out of the way, sat up in a very fast action and pulled the trigger of his pistol twice, two oncoming Mexican attackers fell.

"Dizzy." The bounty hunter said. Clay dragged him to his feet and guided him back through the wreckage to the hole in the wall where the horses were hopefully still waiting. They were. A glance behind him told him they had to be quick, the yard was crowded with the invading forces, and they would be on them in seconds. Clay helped Shannon to mount up and they sped away from the fragmented remnants of the fort to catch up with Kinross who'd disappeared from sight.

"Remember The Alamo." Clay Milton said to himself out loud when he felt able to stop for a second and look back at the smouldering heap of wood, rubble and death that had been Fort Boone.

Once they were far enough away from the fort Clay looked for tracks hoping to find those of a lone rider, Captain Kinross. He found the tracks of three riders. He remembered the two gunmen who'd run from the scene of their escape and realised they were giving chase to the only known survivor of the battle. Kinross, wounded and confused, was in trouble.

"Shannon, Kinross is out here somewhere, he's wounded and he's got two men after him. I don't like him much but we can't let him die. Will you be okay for a while if I go after him?"

"Yeah! You do that, I'll be okay if I can just shake off this dizzy feeling." Shannon told him to go and he would ride slowly along behind hoping to recover soon.

Two miles further on Clay noticed an old shack, long abandoned and set back half a mile from the trail. The building was hardly worthy of the name and was barely standing, but it was the sort of place an injured man may have stopped to rest. The three sets of horses' tracks led him to take extra care as he rode closer. The two Mexican's mounts were tied to the dilapidated rail of an old coral of which only a solitary gate survived. Clay could make out the sombreros of the men as they crept closer to the broken, incomplete shack.

A pistol poked randomly out of the space where a window would have been and fired wildly in the general direction of the advancing Mexicans. Idiot! Clay thought, not for the first or last time where Kinross was concerned. The burst of gunfire from the ramshackle ruin ceased and a series of metallic clicks could be heard as the hammer fell on empty chambers, Kinross had run out of ammunition.

The two Mexican bandidos, encouraged by the knowledge that their quarry was effectually unarmed closed in on the wounded Captain, not bothering to conceal themselves. Taking his rifle, Clay dismounted and ran to get as close as he could to them before they saw him coming. He was still two hundred yards away when one of them turned and shouted a warning to his associate. If he'd taken cover instead of calling out, he might have lived longer.

Clay shot him before he could do both. The other gunman did seek protection behind the rotting remains of an old horse trough, shooting in the general direction of his attacker. Clay took careful aim at the area of the trough where he estimated the Mexican's chest to be and squeezed the trigger. The bullet went through the rotten wood with ease and the man grunted in pain and surprise. He tried to stand up and another shot hit him in the head, finishing him.

Chapter Thirty:

Fragments Of Despair.

Bradley Kinross was in a bad way, loss of blood, fear, and severe shock had rendered him a shadow of his former blustering, loud, overbearingly opinionated self. His pompous attitude was replaced by a meek, silent obedience. Clay Milton didn't know whether this was an improvement or not. He managed to dress the Captain's wound more efficiently than before, using strips of cloth torn from his shirt as a temporary bandage. Then the two of them set off to meet with Shannon and decide what to do next.

They found the horse Shannon had been riding wandering aimlessly along the trail but no visible sign of the bounty hunter. Backtracking along the route they'd travelled earlier for half a mile they found him lying unconscious where he'd fallen from his mount. Clay held a water canteen to the bounty hunter's lips for him to drink after splashing more of the cool liquid onto his face to bring him round. Eventually and with no help at all from Kinross he helped the wounded man back into the saddle. With two injured men in what was now hostile territory Clay thought the best thing to do would be to try and follow the trail taken by Johnny Hawkeye as Shannon had called out to him in the fort. But first he had to find them somewhere to rest, where he could attempt to patch up the wounds of his companions and rest for the night.

James Blue and Zachariah had come across the tracks of many horses. Bluey estimated a hundred or more, and they had come from the direction of Apache bend. He was puzzled that they appeared to be riding south, away from Fort Boone. The two scouts followed them until dark and on into the night using the clear moonlight to see, it wasn't so hard with the numbers so high. They rested for only a couple of hours and resumed with only Zachariah's less than wonderful coffee inside them. By noon they saw a change of direction and a separation of the riders. The main body of horsemen were now leaving tracks directly to where Bluey had expected them to be headed. Fort Boone. He counted a smaller breakaway group and he knew without any doubt that they were going towards the place where the majority of the guns were stored. Somehow Fernando Lopez had discovered the existence and current usage of the secluded farm and its very large barn.

Warning the old man to be especially careful Bluey sent Zachariah back to warn the fort hoping that one man would travel faster than the large contingent of Lopez's force. The chances were not that good. Bluey estimated that they were too far behind but Zachariah wanted to try. He elected to follow the smaller group of horsemen himself and try to stop them overpowering the soldiers at the farm. Somehow. If he could catch them up.

Rattlesnake Joe had assumed the role of scouting on the journey to the farm. He was better than anyone else at the job and didn't trust the others not to miss something vital. He saw the wagon and six uniformed men, a driver and mate on board and four others riding alongside, from a distance. They were carrying a full load and riding towards Fort Boone. Supplies, he guessed. There was a place five miles ahead where he could wait and ambush the soldiers, a rocky slope just a few yards from the trail. He rode swiftly back to the rest of the party and explained to Roberto Aguilar his plan. He wanted to take six men with him to carry out the raid. It would take them off route and delay them a short while but Roberto Aguilar calculated that to the outlaws the acquisition of a wagon load of supplies and the disposal of six soldiers would be advantageous in the future.

"We don't need six men, we need a driver and two guns, one each side of the trail. I will come with you, you will drive the wagon, yes?" Aguilar smiled, if a smile is what it was. Killing six soldiers would not even cause him to break sweat. The Rattlesnake nodded and grinned, he liked the idea.

"Let's go, Hombré." He said.

Corporal Ryan was the first to die, he was driving the wagon and the first shot hit him in the head, in exactly the same place where Red Knife's horse had kicked him, but this time he wouldn't wake up. Aguilar's second shot killed the driver's mate. Rattlesnake Joe shot the man nearest to his side of the trail, the driver's side, and he leapt out of hiding to jump on the still rolling wagon. He snatched the reins from the dead hands of Corporal Ryan and kicked the body off the seat and onto the road. The nearest soldier tried to draw his pistol but the half breed was faster and shot him before he could reach the holstered weapon. Two more lightning fast shots from Aguilar and all six soldiers were dead. Rattlesnake Joe drove the wagon and they resumed the journey to the farm. His own and the soldiers' horses were tied behind the wagon and taken with them. Roberto Aguilar rode alongside, casually reloading his pistol. Not a hint of sweat was on his body.

Pancho Garcia rode into Apache Bend, alongside him was the German Kurt Schmidt, Major Schmidt, as he preferred to be addressed. Behind them rode the four men who'd accompanied Garcia to find General Gomez, and a handful of the General's troops. Lopez would have based himself in the largest hotel and so that is where they eventually found themselves. The evidence of the bandidos' recent visit was all around them, from the sullen, fear filled faces of the few townspeople on the streets to the closed stores and unnerving silence that permeated the unsettled atmosphere of the once thriving town.

Fernando Lopez and most of his men were absent, carrying out the raid on Fort Boone and would be expected back in a matter of days. To keep the town under control in the meantime, Lopez had left a dozen of his most trusted long serving men. Pancho Garcia would now assume the position of interim leader until Fernando's return.

General Gomez had chosen to make camp in the surrounding countryside and wait until he knew the guns would be his before taking any other action. His forces had left a long scar of destruction and death in their wake, plundering food supplies, weapons, raping and killing for no other reason than because they could. He had sent Major Schmidt and a few of his men into Apache Bend with Garcia to act on his behalf and travel with the expected delivery of the much anticipated weaponry to his waiting army.

The soldiers' bodies had been further savaged after death by the attentions of the buzzards and various animals of the night. The sight of the circling birds alerted Johnny Hawkeye and Rodrigo Lamas, and the discovery of the scattered corpses did not come as a surprise, just a resigned sadness and anger. Rodrigo stayed to cover them with rocks, a protection against further desecration by the carrion creatures until a proper burial could be carried out. Johnny rode ahead leaving easily followed tracks so the pistolero could catch him up. He knew he was hunting at least two men, one driving the wagon, the other riding alongside. Seven riderless horses were with them, presumably tied to the wagon. He felt a stirring deep inside himself, there was something warning him. Beware. The Rattlesnake. This was his kind of move, he could be close. To take on and kill six experienced soldiers the ambushers must be dangerous, and ruthless. But so was he.

James Blue had ridden as hard as he dared without risking the collapse of his horse. He knew the riders were too far ahead for him to catch them before they reached the farm and tried to formulate a plan as he rode. He didn't doubt for one minute that the men he was chasing would overrun the soldiers guarding the guns without too much trouble. Half a dozen unprepared soldiers against fifteen heavily armed aggressors is not good odds. When he added to his thinking the fact that the attack would have been orchestrated by Fernando Lopez, the odds became worse, much worse. Bluey stopped only to rest his mount and snatch a few hours much needed sleep, then chewing beef jerky as he rode, he continued his forlorn chase.

The scout could hear shooting as he came closer to the farm. From the description given by Clay Milton he was in the same position now, as Clay and Shannon had been watching the battle against Red Knife. But this was not a fight against Red Knife, a warrior who would attack face on. This was a different kind of opponent. Two Mexican gunmen were on the roof of the barn shooting inwards and downwards through gaps in the uncared for structure. More surrounded the building on the three sides facing away from the house, also keeping up a barrage of gunfire. Two of the soldiers were lying dead on the ground by the entrance, another tried to run from the house. A fancy dressed Mexican pistolero showed himself briefly from his cover at the side of the dwelling and fired, disappearing from view before the soldier hit the ground. Bluey, watching helplessly in the distance recognised the gunslinger by his appearance, as Roberto Aguilar, The Devil's Eagle. Corporal Petty stepped out of the barn with his hands up in a gesture of surrender, his rifle on the ground in front of him. Rattlesnake Joe followed him out of the door and coldly shot him in the back.

"That's all of them. The guns are ours." He laughed. It had taken them less than five minutes.

"You're one evil bastard, Rattlesnake." Bluey said to himself. "It's no wonder Johnny Hawkeye wants to kill you so bad."

The next three hours went by slowly for James Blue. The soldiers' horses and those used to transport the guns from the fort were gathered from where they grazed, just outside the perimeters of the farm. He watched with a growing feeling of impotence, as the weapons were hauled out of the barn one by one and the horses harnessed to them. He watched in frustration as they left in convoy, eight of them, followed by an army supply wagon that hadn't been noticeable on his last visit. The wagons were escorted by six riders.

Chapter Thirty One:

All Trails Lead To Death.

His head hurt and his mouth was dry, but he was thankful that the dizziness had gone. Shannon woke up to find himself wrapped up in blankets and warm, too warm. He opened his eyes slowly to try and get his bearings. He was in some kind of shack, a fire was blazing in one corner of it and he could smell coffee. He looked around scrutinizing the gloomy room. Someone else was lying a few feet away from him, a light snore coming from their direction. He gingerly touched his wounded head, it was bandaged tightly and he could feel dried blood just above his left ear. His right shoulder and hip pained him greatly. He must've groaned without realising it because he heard someone say.

"You're awake then, how's the head?" He recognised the voice, it belonged to Clay Milton.

"Uugh! It could be better, but I'm okay, what happened, where are we?" He grunted. "Got any coffee?"

"I'll get you some. You're a lucky man, the bullet just grazed you, you'll have a scar but you'll live. You must have a pretty hard head." Clay brought him over a cup of steaming hot coffee. "Has the dizziness gone?"

"Yeah, but I feel kinda weak, and my shoulder and hip hurt."

"You fell off your horse, we found you at the side of the trail and brought you here."

"We?"

"That's Kinross." Clay pointed to the other, still sleeping figure.

"Where's here?"

"It's the shack he was holed up in, it's all we could find close by."

"The Mexicans?"

"Oh, they are still here, they won't be any trouble." Shannon knew what Clay meant and sipped at his drink.

"We have to go after Lopez." His recollections of the killings at the fort flooded back into his mind. "I left my horse behind, Snow. He'll have taken him."

"Snow?" Clay was astonished, the only sliver of sentimentality he'd ever been able to attribute to the hardened bounty hunter. He'd given his horse a name.

"Yes, Snow, he was named for me, by someone I knew a long time ago." Shannon sighed, the pain in his head was distracting him, and he was allowing himself to show signs of humanity. He changed the subject. "Lopez will have the guns, they will slow him down, and he won't be hard to track." He turned to face Clay. "Thanks for getting me out of the fort, I told you to go."

"I didn't hear you." Clay lied. "As soon as you feel up to it we'll move out, Kinross can have a choice, come with us or go it alone." Clay woke the Captain and gave him his choices.

"Looks like they'll be three of us." He informed the bounty hunter.

Shannon forced himself to stand up. His head was still throbbing and the room began to spin, he gritted his teeth held on to a rickety chair but he left the bandage where it was. He splashed himself with water and helped himself to another coffee. His shoulder and hip protested stiffly at his forced effort but it would wear off he hoped once they were mounted and on their way. The first task was to find Johnny Hawkeye and James Blue. Together they would hunt down the Mexican bandido hordes and then work out a plan.

Zachariah Smith stood in what had been the courtyard / parade ground of Fort Boone. He wasn't alone, there were over a hundred other people all around but the only living beings apart from himself were the buzzards, the braver ones pecking at the bodies of the fallen, the others circling above. The gorging birds showed no favouritism or prejudice, they fed on bandido and soldier alike with equal enthusiasm, plucking eyeballs out and tearing at intestines through blood stained shirts. A half a dozen unfortunate horses lay fallen, caught up in the savagery of the battle, they also did not escape the ravenous attentions of the carrion hunters.

Zachariah had been around a long time and seen horrific sights and evidence a plenty of man's inhumanity to man, but the stench and sight of the slaughter before him caused him to vomit, violently ejecting the meagre breakfast he'd allowed himself earlier that morning. He forced himself to search diligently among the dead for his friends, Johnny Hawkeye, Clay Milton, Shannon and Rodrigo Lamas. The old man dreaded what he half expected to discover. He allowed himself a sigh of relief on not finding them before turning his back on the horrors and leaving the buzzards to their feast.

The old Mountain Man had cautiously circled the area before coming to the fort from the north to avoid any possible confrontation with Fernando Lopez and his men. There could only have been one outcome to such a situation, his death.

Now he followed the tracks left by the heavy wagons. He would trail them until he could see signs that the Mexicans were not too far ahead and wait until nightfall before circumnavigating their camp. And then he would ride as fast and hard as he could without killing his mount, or himself, to find Bluey and report the terrible news.

The journey back to Apache Bend would be a slow affair, Fernando Lopez knew it and did not concern himself with the time aspect. The wagons pulling the three big guns would not be able to travel as fast as he would like but there were no soldiers around anymore to pursue them. Roberto Aguilar and El Serpiente should have had little or no trouble in taking the main bulk of the weapons from the poorly guarded farm. As the guns were not present at the fort he had anticipated that they would be there. If they were not, Tyrone Black would have some serious explaining to do. He would meet them on the trail or see their tracks ahead and follow them to the rendezvous point. Lopez would expect Pancho to have made contact with the mad General by now and at the very least be on his way back from meeting him. He would also expect General Antonio Gomez and a contingent of his revolutionary army to be waiting for him when he returned to Apache Bend with the weapons.

He rode toweringly at the head of his men reflecting on the victory he'd achieved. The completeness of which had not been as all-encompassing as planned but never the less, they had eliminated the troops and secured the three guns they now transported with them. It irked the bandit leader that the bounty hunter, he was sure it was Shannon he'd shot at, had somehow managed to turn the Gatling gun on his men, killing at least forty of them. The defenders, both military and the few civilians present, had accounted for a good half dozen more, and two more were missing or buried in the wreckage of the fort. He was mildly disappointed at not finding the body of the bounty hunter among them but didn't give it too much thought, and he could always get more men to replace those he'd lost. The Mexican victors took with them the only spoils of war they could transport easily, weapons and horses, among them a magnificent white stallion.

When Johnny Hawkeye came to the abandoned farm he could see he was too late to prevent the capture of the guns. He saw the tracks of nine loaded wagons and six horsemen leading away, towards Apache Bend. He followed, a little further down the trail he could see another set of tracks. Another tracker was in pursuit of the convoy, a lone horseman, he urged his mount to a canter. Five miles further along the tracks vanished, Johnny knew they'd been obliterated on purpose. The rider had realised that he, the follower was being followed.

"I made it as easy as I could for you, Bluey. What took you so long?" Johnny Hawkeye called out to the rocks on the side of the trail.

"I was playing hard to get." James Blue revealed himself and led his horse out from cover. "Did you come past the farm?"

"Yes, did you see what happened?"

"Yeah, I couldn't do anything about it. I was too far away. It was Rattlesnake Joe and Aguilar, they shot them all and they got the guns." Bluey told him. "They didn't need to kill them, Petty tried to surrender, the half breed shot him in the back."

"They got Ryan and the others too." Johnny Hawkeye's instincts were right when they had warned him, the Rattlesnake was near. "The supplies, they took the wagon."

"I sent Zachariah back to warn the fort, there's around a hundred horsemen headed towards them." He paused. "I hope he made it in time but I think he would've been too late, I was."

"Rodrigo's with me, he'll catch us up by nightfall, we'll have to slow down and wait for him or it will be us two against fifteen, we need a plan." Johnny was trying to come up with a plan, one that didn't include dying.

"If Zachariah didn't get through in time, he'll be coming to find us and let us know what's happened." Bluey and Johnny rode slowly onwards. "We could do with stopping them before they meet up with Lopez and the rest of his men, whatever happens." He added.

"Something's bothering me, Johnny." Bluey had been thinking things over in his mind. "The attack at the farm was not an afterthought. The fifteen men, including the Rattlesnake and Aguilar, left the main body of the Mexicans deliberately to come here, before they could've found out at the fort that the guns weren't there. They knew about the farm. Somebody must have told them."

"It couldn't have been any of the troopers, most of them didn't believe Lopez was even a threat. I'm pretty sure it wasn't any of us, not even by accident." Johnny was also puzzled by the fact. "Somebody on the outside, but who knew?" Neither of them could think of an answer.

As the light began to fade the two trackers could see a thin, spiralling plume of smoke curling skywards a couple of miles or so ahead on the trail. They decided to rest for the night, Rodrigo Lamas caught up with them as they unsaddled their horses and unpacked their bedrolls. They ate only beef jerky and drunk only water, not wanting to risk a fire of their own this close to the Mexicans' camp. The three of them speculated as to what might have happened, and about the fate of their friends at the fort. No conclusions could be drawn but the various potential outcomes were not giving the trackers encouraging thoughts.

"I have an idea." Bluey ended a lengthy silence between the three of them. "That place we stopped overnight, it's on route and it's not far away. The place where you made such friends with Kinross, what was it called?"

"Muddy Creek. Why?" Johnny replied.

"What if we got there before the wagons and waited, we can travel much faster than they can. The Rattlesnake and his men will be wanting to celebrate, they'll be bound to stop there. And where better to meet with Lopez? It's the obvious place this side of Apache Bend."

"It would still be fifteen against three, and two of them are El Serpiente and El Àguila Del Diablo." Rodrigo reminded them.

"If we can split them up somehow fifteen men isn't so many."

"When you say it like that it sounds easy. Say it again." Johnny said. "We'll make an early start, I'll take the first watch."

The farm was just ahead but the stench of death reached them well before they actually saw the dead bodies. The wind was blowing gently towards the three riders and it was not pleasant. They dismounted and looked around at the decaying carrion ravaged corpses of the soldiers. Kinross, still very weak from his loss of blood couldn't prevent himself from vomiting. Clay and Shannon went to look in the barn. The bounty hunter had discarded the bandage and his hair covered most of the wound above his left ear. His head still hurt and his hip and shoulder were stiff but improving every day. As anticipated the guns had gone. They walked back outside to see Captain Bradley Kinross pointing at the rear of the barn. A horse was tethered there, a familiar horse.

"I could've shot you boys without you even knowing I was here." A voice came from the other side of the yard, from within the dilapidated old farm house. The door opened and Zachariah Smith came out carrying his rifle. "Didn't your mamas teach you to be careful when you come to a strange place?"

"You did well at Fort Boone, Virgo, you are an expert with explosives. I will need you again. You can ride with us, be one of my trusted few. The rewards are great and you will soon be a rich man." Fernando Lopez had been impressed with the precision of Virgo's work. They rode together at the head of the convoy, two days from Muddy Creek, and the rendezvous with Aguilar, Rattlesnake Joe and the rest of the weapons.

"Thank you for your praise, Fernando, and I will be pleased to ride with you. But, we both know that you could have blown up the fort without me, you could've done what I did yourself." Virgo was aware that Fernando Lopez had used explosives himself in the past without the need for an expert in the field being required. "I did a far more complicated and clever job at the bank in Mina De Plata, you should have seen that, a work of art. Barrera himself could not have been more precise."

"I know my friend. Roberto told me, even El Serpiente sang your praises and he does not do such things lightly." Lopez told him. "Yes I could have blown up the fort without you. Not so efficiently perhaps, but I would still have had the result I wanted. I have a special task for you, coming up soon. It will need a man more skilled than I am. Virgo, it will need you. No one is to know of this until I am ready to tell them."

The centre of the little town known as Muddy Creek consisted of a dusty square with four streets leading off each of its four corners, similar to nearly every other small settlement in the territory deluding itself into masquerading as a town. Into this tranquil setting rumbled the eight wagons carrying their heavy loads, the army supply wagon and six other riders. Roberto Aguilar appointed two of the Mexicans to stay with the weapons and Rattlesnake Joe sent two of his hired guns to do the same.

Aguilar chose the hotel to be his base while waiting for Lopez to appear. Initially Rattlesnake Joe would have preferred to stay at the saloon but changed his mind and decided to join The Devil's Eagle. The long suffering clerk did not like the look of either guest but fear dictated that he welcomed them to his establishment. The rest of the men, Mexican and Gringo alike opted for the saloon and the attendant whores.

Four of Rattlesnake Joe's men walked into the saloon, with them came the ex-soldier, Tyrone Black. None of them took any notice of the two men sitting in the corner talking to a young Mexican man, and they chose a table in the middle of the large room. The bartender took them a bottle and five glasses. A few minutes later four more men entered and walked directly to the bar, these were Mexicans, Aguilar's party. They ordered the bartender to bring their drinks over to a table they pointed out, situated in the opposite corner from Johnny, Bluey and Rodrigo. They went and sat down, ignoring the presence of the Gringos, El Serpiente's men and the deserter.

The non-integration of the outlaws did not go unnoticed by the watching hunters. One of the Mexicans bellowed for the drinks to be served quickly and requested that some "Senoritas" be sent to the table. The bartender brought the drinks over on a tray and promised to send in some girls. He told them a price and the men paid up willingly, it had been a long time

322

on the trail. Five minutes later four saloon girls were ushered over to the lustful bandits and shortly after that the eight of them vacated the table and vanished up to find rooms on the floor above.

The more the whisky flowed into the five remaining outlaws, the more the volume of noise increased and the more aggressive they became. Girls had been sent for but only four arrived to placate five men. Inevitably trouble erupted. Tyrone Black, the outsider found himself without a woman for the night and was becoming progressively angry at the situation, not helped by the ribald taunting of his companions.

"If it wasn't for me, we wouldn't have found the guns." He slurred drunkenly at the unsympathetic group. Bluey and Johnny looked at each other, now they knew. "If I hadn't told you where they were you'd still be looking for them."

"If you hadn't been a deserter, we'd have been shooting at you." One of the others retorted. Tyrone Black snapped, he had a short temper which is what got him into trouble and sent to jail in the first place. He drew his gun and fired point blank at his tormentor, killing him instantly. The girls screamed as one and ran off to seek cover, they'd seen this type of situation many times and there was always bloodshed. The gunmen all moved to draw their weapons. Black stood back and fired again, another man went down, then a bullet from one of the other guns hit him in the arm and he ran for the door. Shots thudded into the walls and tables around him as he swerved desperately and drunkenly from side to side miraculously managing somehow to stay on his feet. He disappeared from view, the others looked down on their fallen comrades. There was nothing they could do for them, they were both dead.

"I'll get him." Rodrigo said quickly and was on his way out of the door after Tyrone Black.

"Don't, it doesn't matter." Bluey called after the young pistolero, but it was too late.

"Let's go, the Mexicans upstairs will be coming down." Johnny said. "We don't want to get in the middle of them killing each other."

"You ain't goin' nowhere Mister." One of the men called out to Johnny Hawkeye. Bluey shot the man before he could lift his gun and seeing that they were going to have to fight their way out Johnny drew and fired, dropping the last of the assailants. They could hear the Mexicans rushing down the stairs towards them and took cover behind their speedily upturned table.

The four Mexicans burst into the saloon from the stairs, two abreast firing wildly at anything in front of them. They were not as drunk as the Gringos had been and as fast as the rest of the clientele had moved, two of them were cut down in the leaden hail of death that poured from their pistols. The bartender also screamed out and fell to the floor.

Johnny and Bluey opened fire from behind their meagre shelter and the front two men fell. The other two rushed in different directions firing blindly as they did so. Bluey stood up, took aim and shot one of them down. Johnny intended do the same to the remaining man but his gun was empty and he didn't have time to call out or reload. He pulled the trigger and on hearing the click the man showed himself and took deliberate aim at his target. Johnny Hawkeye's knife flew straight into his chest and buried itself up to the hilt.

"Rodrigo." He shouted to Bluey and the two of them chased after the young Mexican.

Rodrigo caught up with Tyrone Black as he reached the front of the hotel. The four Mexicans guarding the big guns took no notice of the man in the sombrero as he came closer.

"Gringo!" Rodrigo called out to the deserter. Tyrone Black turned to face Rodrigo Lamas, his gun was already being raised and his finger tightening on the trigger when the pistolero drew and fired. Tyrone Black staggered back and looked down at his shirt front, it was reddening more with each second as he slid down the wall of the hotel and died. Rodrigo holstered his weapon and touched his hat in greeting to the men watching the guns. Without realising he was not one of their own they reciprocated with a few complimentary comments about the killing of the Gringo.

Another sound, a slow clapping of hands followed by the cold, more of a rasp than a voice congratulating him from the doorway of the hotel.

"Bravo! Pistolero, you are fast, and you are good. But now you die." The Devil's Eagle, Roberto Aguilar stood facing him as he turned to see who'd called out.

Rodrigo Lamas had no choice, he knew Aguilar would shoot him whether he drew or not. His hand moved in a blur to his holstered pistol. He never made it. Aguilar had drawn and fired his gun before the young pistolero could even lift his own, that he managed to touch it at all was a surprise to his killer. Roberto Aguilar gazed unemotionally at the fallen young man lying dead at his feet.

"You were good. Pistolero." He grated. He holstered his gun and walked back into the hotel.

Johnny Hawkeye and James Blue rushing towards the scene could only watch as their friend died. They rounded a bend in the street and saw what was happening just as the killing shot was fired. They got closer and the Mexicans guarding the guns opened fire on them. They retreated out of range and quickly took cover before seeing the figure of Aguilar re-emerge from the hotel and join his men. Watching from the relative safety of an upstairs hotel window Rattlesnake Joe allowed himself a smile on recognising Johnny Hawkeye and reached hurriedly for his rifle.

"Aguilar! I'm going to kill him." Bluey spat out the name. "Rodrigo was just a kid."

"We have to get out of here for tonight, Bluey. Let them think we're running away. There's not so many of them now, we'll come back into town tomorrow night."

Johnny knew they needed time to think, to plan, to mourn.

"There's not so many of us either, we should have sent the boy home weeks ago."

The two hunters crept quietly to their horses and mounted, then they galloped noisily out of town making sure that they could be seen by the Mexicans but were out of range of their guns.

Rattlesnake Joe swore under his breath and put his rifle way.

The following evening the number of men watching the big guns were reduced to two, the other remaining Mexicans taking the day shift. Roberto Aguilar carried out regular checks and patrolled the streets around the centre of the small town on the lookout for any incursion by Johnny Hawkeye, James Blue or other hostile parties. Rattlesnake Joe had spent the day scouting the trail and surrounding country for signs of his hated enemy. He wouldn't find any, he was up against a man who'd learned from the Cheyenne people, how to keep out of sight. He was very fortunate not to have been within range of the hunter's rifle as he searched for him.

Leaving their mounts two miles outside the town limits, Johnny and Bluey slipped inconspicuously through the deserted streets towards the centre square. They stealthily and silently took out one man each and the guns were unguarded. The saloon was the next port of call, the most likely place to find the remaining two bandits and possibly Aguilar or Rattlesnake Joe.

Three out of the four were seated around one of the tables. Roberto Aguilar had stayed in the hotel, closer to the big guns. Bluey entered through the front door of the saloon. The element of surprise and the fact that his gun was already in his hand gave him a second's advantage.

Rattlesnake Joe, his back to the wall saw him first, throwing himself to one side and drawing his pistol as he did so. He was half way to the back exit before the other two grabbed furiously for their own weapons. Bluey shot one of them before he could get out of his seat. Johnny Hawkeye had come in from the rear of the building and the other man didn't see who killed him. Johnny's shot hit him in the head and he too failed to move from his seated position.

Rattlesnake Joe didn't wait to be next, he was already moving fast, he recognised the look of hatred in the eyes of the hunter as they were suddenly face to face. He reacted instinctively, self-preservation, his uppermost priority. He slammed the door hard into Johnny and immediately opened it again. He kicked hard at the hunter who stepped smartly out of the way and hit the half breed full in the face. The Rattlesnake was a hard man, he didn't go down from the blow, and his own simultaneous attack connected, savagely hitting his enemy on the side of the head with his pistol butt. Johnny staggered momentarily and Rattlesnake Joe was gone. Firing haphazardly at Bluey who dived swiftly behind the bar for cover and fired back, the half breed changed direction, and rushed out of the front entrance. Johnny Hawkeye was after him in a second.

"He's mine!" He shouted to Bluey as he vanished in pursuit of his nemesis.

The Australian had felt a pain in his right forearm during the exchange of gunfire with Rattlesnake Joe and could feel the wet warmth as blood ran down towards his hand. It wasn't a serious wound but would need bandaging and would slow him down some. He reloaded his gun and took the weapons from the dead Mexicans. He left the saloon cautiously after wrapping his arm tightly in a cloth provided for him by the bartender, himself sporting a sling on his left arm from the previous evening's shootings. He had reappeared from his hiding place under a table when the gunplay had ceased. Bluey would go after Roberto Aguilar and so he headed for the hotel.

He didn't get far before he saw The Devil's Eagle walking slowly towards him, emerging from the front of the building to investigate the source of gunfire.

"Why did you come back Gringo, only death awaits you here?" Aguilar rasped at him. The Mexican didn't even draw his pistol.

"I could shoot you down now." Bluey told him, he was already pointing his gun at the chest of his target.

"Senor, I can see your hand is not steady, your arm it is bleeding. By the time you can pull the trigger I will have killed you." Aguilar pulled his humourless face into his own peculiar version of a smile.

"I'll take my chances you murdering son of..."

"My arm is not bleeding and my hand is steady." A new voice, a hard, cold voice cut in from behind the Mexican. Roberto Aguilar turned his back on Bluey to face the newcomer.

Shannon stood alone, a spectre in black, his gun pointing directly at the pistolero supreme. The eyes of the bounty hunter were dark, expressionless, and dangerous.

"Shannon!" Aguilar said flatly.

"Bluey get out of the line of fire." Shannon ordered and Bluey, not taking his gun off the Mexican for a second, did so. Shannon replaced his pistol in his holster and stood, ready for the inevitable showdown.

The two gunslingers stood wordlessly facing each other, assessing each other, searching for a sign, a weakness, anything to give them an edge. Eventually the silence was broken.

"You think you are good enough to take me, El Àguila Del Diablo?" Roberto Aguilar seemed almost insulted at the thought.

"I don't think. I know. I know I'm better than you. You are nothing but a cheap Pistolero in fancy clothes." Shannon said evenly. A sudden flash of anger and contempt flashed into Aguilar's normally dead eyes and that told Shannon the waiting was over.

Two shots rang out, if analysed the sound of the second would have been the shortest possible echo of the first. Shannon was falling as he fired and hit the ground, he was holding his left side, blood seeping through his fingers. Roberto Aguilar took two steps towards him and raised his pistol to finish the job, then gasped in astonished bafflement, his gun fell to the street and he followed it down. Bluey ran over to the fallen Mexican and kicked the pistol away from his hand. Clay Milton stepped out of the shadows, holstered his own gun, and went to examine the bounty hunter's wound. Zachariah Smith followed him, rifle primed in case Aguilar should move, Bradley Kinross appeared behind the old Mountain Man.

"You'll live, the bullet went right through you." Clay told Shannon as the wounded man struggled to stand up. "But it needs looking after." He looked to James Blue. "You okay Bluey, your hand?"

"He's dead, bullet went straight to his heart." Bluey told them all referring to El Àguila Del Diablo. "Yes, my arm's okay, just a scratch."

"Where's Johnny?" Zachariah asked Bluey. "And Rodrigo?"

"Johnny's gone after the Rattlesnake, he was here. Rodrigo is dead, Aguilar killed him." Bluey related recent events as the five of them walked slowly to the hotel and checked in. Clay told him about the massacre at Fort Boone and subsequent journey to date.

"I'm glad you got here when you did, I couldn't have beaten Aguilar." Bluey said to the bounty hunter. "I owe you."

"You don't owe me anything. That was going to happen. Him and me, sooner or later. It just happened when it did." Shannon hissed through the pain."

The clerk recognised Bluey and Kinross from their previous stay and had no trouble finding rooms for all this time round. His wife found bandages and cleaned and dressed the wounded Shannon's side, also redressing Bluey's arm.

"Did you know you were better than Aguilar?" Clay asked the bounty hunter as they shared a bottle of whisky between them all.

"No. I had to goad him, I had to try and rile him. I wasn't boasting, I didn't know who was better, I still don't really, but I'm the one who's breathing. I had to make him angry, I needed an edge, and it worked. An angry gunfighter is not so steady, not so focussed, he's too busy with feelings of anger against his enemy to concentrate on the job. It was still too close for comfort."

"Look at that! You took on a man as fast as Aguilar with a shoulder like that?" Bluey was amazed. To allow his wounded side to be attended to Shannon had removed his shirt, exposing a mass of black and blue bruising covering the top of his right arm and shoulder, back and front.

"He fell off his horse." Clay said.

Chapter Thirty Two:

To Rest, To Plan.

Zachariah Smith was sitting in the town square, near the big guns on a chair borrowed from the hotel, with his rifle on his lap when Johnny Hawkeye came back to Muddy Creek in the early hours of the next day. He'd been gone all night on his hunt for Rattlesnake Joe. The half breed's mount was a far superior animal to the one Johnny had commandeered from one of the dead gunmen and he soon left the hunter far behind.

Johnny had tracked the scalp hunter for hours. It was not an easy task, his quarry was a wily, clever man, used to losing people who were hunting him. Even hunters as skilled and practised as a Cheyenne warrior. He eventually found tracks indicating that Rattlesnake Joe had met up with other riders, very many of them. He soon traced those many riders. He kept his distance and was not seen by the group but he could tell at a glance who they were.

Fernando Lopez and his men. He had to get back and warn Bluey. On his journey back to town Johnny did a detour and collected his own mount which he now rode, he led Bluey's along with him.

"Zach, go and find an axe, two if you can, we've got trouble coming." Johnny said to his old friend as soon as greetings had been exchanged and the old man

had explained briefly how he'd met up with Clay, Shannon and Kinross and rode with them to town.
"Where's Bluey, and the others now?"

"They're in the hotel, Boy. It was a busy night. What sort of trouble?"

"The worst kind Old Man. Lopez, we've probably got an hour before a bunch of his men get here. The Rattlesnake's with them. Where's Aguilar?"

"He'd dead, Shannon killed him, I ain't never seen nuthin' like it." Zachariah would've continued but Johnny reminded him.

"The axes, Zach, we'll catch up later." He hurried into the hotel, the clerk greeted him like a long lost friend as he approached the desk.

"James Blue, can you wake him and tell him to get everyone ready to move. And if I was you I'd get yourself and your wife out of town for a while."

"But my hotel, it would get wrecked." The man protested.

"You can repair a building my friend, you cannot repair a corpse." Johnny left the way he'd come in. In a hurry.

When Bluey, Clay, Shannon and Kinross came out of the hotel a few minutes later Zachariah and Johnny had just finished smashing the wagon wheels with the axes the old man had manged to find from somewhere. The big guns were toppled from their sabotaged platforms and were littered unevenly and immovable in an ungainly accumulation of metal in the centre of the square.

"I'll explain on the trail, Lopez is coming, we have to leave. Now." Johnny answered the unspoken question in repose to the confused looks on the faces of the others. The hotel clerk and his wife came out behind Kinross. The wife pushed in front of the Captain and handed something to Johnny Hawkeye. He couldn't see what it was, the item was wrapped tightly in linen and tied.

"For you Mister Hawkeye, my brother sent it to me from back east." She said. "From my husband and myself."

"I thank you Ma'am." He replied taking the gift with good grace and placing it in his saddlebags. "I'll open it later, when we stop for rest. If you're going, go now, it won't be safe here." The couple departed to find their flat boarded wagon and leave the only home they'd known for over twenty years.

Clay nodded to signify everyone was ready. The six of them mounted up and rode out of town at a gallop towards the east, towards Apache Bend.

"Did you catch the Rattlesnake?" Bluey asked Johnny as soon as the town was out of sight of the riders.

Johnny shook his head.

"His horse was too fast for me to catch on the one I borrowed, but I did track him. To Lopez. He's on his way, he'll be there in Muddy Creek this morning. That's why we had to smash up the wagons. We couldn't move the guns and get away with them, there's nowhere to hide them. So I thought it best to stop Lopez being able to shift them, at least until he can get more wagons, I let all the horses go too, that'll take more time, to round them up."

"How many men has he got, Shannon took a lot of them out at the fort?" Clay was trying to think of a plan, he couldn't come up with one yet but needed to fill his head with as much knowledge of the enemy and their strengths and weaknesses as he could.

"It looked to me to be around seventy guns. Give or take a few. He's got three big guns with him two cannons and a Gatling, from the fort."

"We need to rest and plan our next move." Bluey looked around at the others. Shannon was gamely riding alongside him, in pain but uncomplaining, Zachariah looked as if he could sleep for a week. His age worked vigorously against him but the old man refused to quit and would ride until he fell off his horse. Kinross was worse than useless, his mental fragility more of a hindrance than his injured arm which was on the mend. His own arm hurt although the wound would not cause any lasting problems. Only Clay Milton and Johnny Hawkeye were comparably unscathed at present. Bluey thought also of the ones they'd lost, Rodrigo Lamas, only eighteen years old who'd died fighting another man's war, his war. He remembered Marshall Clay McCandless, a man of infinite experience and devotion to duty, and Sheriff Barton Lee who'd died in defence of his town, of his people, against the savage onslaught of the bandido hordes. He remembered Colonel Stard, the soldiers, countless civilians, all gone because of man's incessant inhumanity towards his fellow man.

Yes, they needed to take stock, to rest, to plan.

"One of us has to get close to Gomez, we need to find out where he is. Where the handover of the weapons is to take place, Apache Bend? We need to be sure." Clay had spent the night thinking, unable to sleep, he'd tried to formulate some kind of plan. To move forward somehow in the face of the setbacks they'd incurred so far in their mission. "And I think we need to set the General against Lopez, somehow." The six of them were far enough from Lopez and his men to risk a fire and sat around it now, drinking coffee and finishing off the remains of two wild turkeys, provided courtesy of Johnny Hawkeye's hunting prowess. They'd made camp for the night in a small valley between two grassy hillocks, making sure they were well away from the main trail.

"I've been thinking something similar." Bluey advanced. "How's your Spanish?"

"Okay, but not brilliant, how's yours?" Clay supplied. "I tend to speak it as I was taught, not necessarily as it is spoken. But I do struggle a bit to understand some of it when I hear it."

"Yeah, how about you Johnny?"

"I've picked up quite a bit in the last five years, but I'm not perfect."

"I think we have to rule out Shannon." Bluey glanced over to the bounty hunter, he was not fit enough to risk in action at the moment.

"And Zach and Kinross." Johnny said. "That leaves us three."

"It leaves two of us, Bluey or me, Johnny. You are too well known. We may have to go under cover, Bluey and I have done it all before." Johnny shrugged his shoulders, but he knew the truth of Clay's statement.

"And my Spanish is probably more convincing, I can understand what I'm hearing most of the time, so it's going to have to be me." Bluey stated. No one argued with him.

"One of us will have to go back along the trail and capture one of Lopez's men, we need to know where the meet up is going to take place." Clay said to them. "Bluey you might not be able to handle a gun too well for a few days, your arm. I'll go and take out one of his scouts."

"I'll deal with that, it's what I do, I can move around without being seen easier than most people and I might find the Rattlesnake, he is the best scout Lopez has got." Johnny insisted. Clay and Bluey could see there would be no changing his mind and so they agreed.

"Johnny, take my rifle, the range and accuracy may come in useful. I'm not going to be able to shoot for a while." Bluey told him. Johnny Hawkeye nodded, took the weapon and rode off to hunt. That's what he did.

Fernando Lopez hadn't left Muddy Creek, his men were scouring the town and surrounding area for enough wagons and horses to move the big field weapons. It was taking longer than he wanted, he cursed those responsible. The Rattlesnake had reported to him all the happenings that had taken place before he got there. The killing of Rodrigo Lamas by The Devil's Eagle. And the deaths of all their own men, including, which especially surprised Lopez, the outgunning of Roberto Aguilar himself by the bounty hunter, Shannon. The latter fact supplied to him by one of the locals wishing to ingratiate himself with the invading bandits. The ploy worked, Lopez did not kill him.

The bandido chief took time to absorb the information and decided on his next course of action. He called Virgo Séptimo to come and sit with him at his table in the unmanned hotel.

"Virgo, I want you to send two men out, they don't have to be any good. Send them directly to Apache Bend to report to Gomez, if he is waiting for us yet. If not, my man, Pancho Garcia should be there by now. Tell El Serpiente I want him to take six more men and after an hour follow them."

"You think someone will attack them?"

"It is what I would do, that or track them to wherever they are going."

"Why El Serpiente, Fernando, I feel you don't trust him? Do you think he will betray you?"

"El Serpiente is a very good scout, he can track anything over any type of ground. If our men are attacked, he will find who is responsible, he will trace them to wherever they try and hide." The bandido paused to change the subject. "I trust very few people, Virgo." Lopez looked him in the eye. "And nobody has ever betrayed me twice."

"I will not betray you, Fernando, you have trusted me so far and I have not let you down." Virgo told his leader, calmly returning his studious gaze. Lopez smiled at his relatively new recruit.

"I have a job for you Virgo, you will need to travel alone. Tell no one, but this is what I want you to do." He outlined in detail his idea and Virgo listened with interest. At the end of the briefing he nodded.

"I will leave as soon as I've eaten." He said.

"You will need a stronger horse, take a good one from the ones we have taken from the fort." Lopez added.

Virgo Séptimo chose a good horse, a magnificent white stallion.

Chapter Thirty Three:

To Act.

The rider fell dead from his mount before the sound of the killing shot reached the ears of his companion. From his secluded position on the rocky slope eight hundred yards away Johnny Hawkeye slid Bluey's sharp shooter rifle back into the blanket and took out his knife. He would have to get closer to his next target. The other bandido jumped off his horse, abandoning it along with the rifle tied to his saddle. He scurried behind the nearest rock and drew his pistol, scouring the area for signs of the gunman. He saw nothing, he was still vainly searching when Johnny leapt on him from behind. The man's head smacked against the rock and he passed out. He came to a minute later as water was thrown onto his face. He spluttered, he was bound hand and foot and his head hurt but his biggest fear was the knife he was staring at, inches from his eyes.

"I don't have time to be polite Senor." Johnny said to his prisoner. "Tell me what I want to know and I won't kill you. Don't tell me what I want to know and I will kill you. No other choice. Understand?"

"SI Senor." The terrified man said.

"Lopez, where is he meeting with the General?"

"Senor, I...I."

"I won't ask again." The knife moved closer to the unprotected orb of the man's right eye.

"Apache Bend, Senor, they are meeting in Apache Bend."

"And where is he now?"

"He is stuck in Muddy Creek, he needs more wagons, more horses."

"Thank you Senor." Johnny told him and disappeared from view.

"Senor, aren't you going to untie me, I will die if you leave me here."

"I said I wouldn't kill you, I haven't."

It was nearly an hour later when Rattlesnake Joe and six of Lopez's men found the man lying on the trail, still bound and exhausted by his futile struggles to free himself. The Rattlesnake knew at once who was responsible and dismounted by hastily jumping off his horse, just as the bullet whizzed past his head, taking his left earlobe with it. The Mexican behind him caught the full force of Johnny's shot in the chest and fell to the ground. The other bandidos looked frantically around trying to see where the shot came from.

"Get down, take cover, you'll never see him." Rattlesnake Joe shouted, blood running down his neck and his teeth gritted against the pain of his wounded ear. It took another dead horseman before the message got through and the rest of them found places to hide. Blindly the Mexicans fired in the general direction from which the shots had been fired.

"Save your ammunition, he's too far away to shoot at with a pistol. We need to get closer to him, spread out." The half breed ordered. They did so, taking great care to retain cover, even so Johnny killed another of them as they got closer to his vantage point. He was undecided at first over what to do next. He needed to get back to the others with his information and he wanted to stay in the hope of finally revenging himself on Rattlesnake Joe. He could play cat and mouse for as long as it took without much of a problem being presented by the half breed's bandido associates he was sure.

Eventually it would come down to just the two of them, hunter versus hunted, but how long would it take? Five years and counting already. Defeat was not a consideration but the time factor involved swayed him, his loyalty to Clay, Bluey, Shannon and Zach decided the matter. Captain Bradley Kinross did not feature in his thoughts for one second.

Having pinpointed Johnny Hawkeye's hiding place Rattlesnake Joe and his men gradually managed to surround the position without further losses. On a signal from the half breed they all rushed the position together. No one was there. The hunter had gone, a few shell cases the only evidence of his recent presence to be seen. The Rattlesnake returned to where the bound bandido still lay, where Johnny Hawkeye had left him.

"What did you tell him?" He asked.

"Senor, El Serpiente... I told him nothing."

"Liar." Rattlesnake Joe hissed at the terrified man and shot him.

The others had ridden with him until they'd come close to the huge camp of General Antonio Gomez and his revolutionary army. From then on James Blue rode alone into whatever fate had in store for him. He saw the two sentries before they had a chance to see him but he rode towards them as if he had not noticed them.

"Detener Quién Es Usted? (Halt who are you?) A Qué Te Refieres? (What do you want?)" One of them demanded to know as he stood forward from his position, his rifle raised.

"Inglése por favor." Bluey added the lie. "I do not speak Spanish No Espanol."

"What do you want Gringo?"

"I have come to speak with Generalissimo Antonio Gomez, it is very important. I have news for him, news of Fernando Lopez and the big guns."

"Give me your gun and get down off your horse." It was not a request and Bluey did as he was told.

The mad General raised another glass of wine to his thick rose coloured lips and sipped it all in one movement. He wiped the slight dribble from the side of his mouth with the back of his fat, chubby hand and allowed himself the pleasure of a rumbling burp. He looked down at the overflowing plate on the table in front of him and picked up his knife and fork. He attacked the feast with the excessive enthusiasm of a child let loose in a candy store.

The flap of his command tent opened to let the sentry in.

"Well, what is it?" Gomez hated being interrupted during his dinner. The nervous man garbled something that Bluey, waiting outside with an armed guard couldn't quite make out and then the Australian was being pushed into the tent, into the presence of Generalissimo Antonio Gomez.

"Gringo, what is it you have to tell me. You are lucky today, I usually have Americanos shot on sight."

"General, first, I am Australian, not an Americano and I bring you news of betrayal. Lopez and the Comanche half breed, they have your guns. But they are planning to sell them. Your weapons. To the highest bidder. The Yankees will pay a lot of money to get them back." Gomez, paused mid bite.

"But Lopez is on his way here, I have his man, Garcia, in the town, waiting for him, and the weapons." The General accidently spat out a half chewed portion of beef as he spoke, it landed on his overloaded plate. He took no notice.

"There will be a delay while he tries do a better deal, to try and sell you out. Lopez does not care about the revolution."

"Even if this is true, why are you telling me this, Gringo?" Gomez ceased his eating and drinking altogether to concentrate on this Australian stranger standing at his table.

"I want to see the Confederacy rise again, if losing the guns will hurt the Yankees, then I want the guns to be lost."

"What is your name Gringo, and how do you know this? And how do I know you are telling me the truth?"

"My name is James Blue, you will not know me, and I know what Lopez is planning because I asked two of his men. They were coming to tell you of the delay, they were going to tell you the Americanos were causing them trouble, sabotaging their wagons."

"Where are these men now?"

"Ah, sadly they did not survive the questioning." Bluey explained. "But you will believe me when the guns do not arrive."

"We will go into the town and talk with Garcia, I will know if he is lying to me." The mad General stood up, his fancy table cloth caught in his belt causing the plate and the mountain of food to slip from the table to the floor. He deftly rescued the wine bottle and its severely depleted contents, ignored the mess and walked out of his tent, motioning Bluey to go with him.

The deadly game of cat and mouse had resumed, this time Rattlesnake Joe was determined to be the cat and Johnny Hawkeye was to be the mouse. His left ear was roughly bandaged and caked with dried blood, it gave him a lot of pain. It took the Comanche half breed renegade longer than usual to pick up the trail of his nemesis but find it he did. He and the remainder of his band of bandidos caught up with their quarry five miles outside Apache Bend. He stole noiselessly, alone and on foot, towards the little clearing in a thickly wooded region of the hilly terrain surrounding the southern trail into the town. He could make out three people scattered around the dying embers of a small fire.

He recognised the bounty hunter, Shannon, leaning back against the stump of an old tree, he seemed to be sleeping. He recognised the old Mountain Man pouring himself a cup of coffee. He didn't know the man in the Captain's uniform, but he didn't look to be a threat, his eyes were open but unseeing. Where was Johnny Hawkeye? The man he'd come to kill. And the sharp shooter, or the younger man who'd been with them, where were they?

He could shoot now and probably kill the sleeping bounty hunter which would give him great satisfaction, probably the old man and the army Captain as well before they would even know he was there. But the noise would alert Hawkeye and the others and he would be outnumbered against very formidable opponents. He calculated that the odds were too stacked against him to risk anything alone. He would gather his men and they could attack while he watched and waited for the chance to kill his hated enemy. And with the death of Johnny Hawkeye he would at last end the long saga of the hunter's relentless quest for vengeance against him.

The three Mexicans did not like Rattlesnake Joe, they didn't know anyone who did. But they feared him, which suited him fine, he didn't need friends. With the scalp hunter away from their meagre camp they relaxed. Laughing and discussing how the whores would flock to them in droves after they'd been paid by Lopez for their part in stealing the cannons and Gatling guns for the mad General. No thought was given to posting a lookout, after all they were the hunters not the prey. They bragged to one another about how many soldiers each of them had killed in the slaughter at Fort Boone.

The faint sound of a twig snapping underfoot went unheard by the trio, but not by the soundlessly incoming half breed. He was about to march in on them and castigate the Mexicans for their slackness when he saw Clay Milton emerge into the feeble light supplied by the camp fire, holding his rifle. It was pointed threateningly at the suddenly no longer at ease threesome.

"Senors, do not move." Clay ordered. "Now, slowly, and I mean real slowly, take out your guns and put them on the ground." Slowly, real slowly, they did so. Clay stepped forward and kicked them out of reach. "Now stand up and turn around, slow as before." Slow as before they obeyed. "You." He jabbed one of them hard in the back with the rifle. "Get a rope and tie your friends up together, hands and feet." The chosen one walked slowly over to his horse. Clay kept his rifle aimed at the other two with one hand and drew his pistol with the other, to cover him as the man came back with a rope.

Rattlesnake Joe had raised his rifle to shoot Clay but hesitated, not wishing to give his location away to the, probably, nearby Johnny Hawkeye. The bandido finished tying up his associates and laid down on his stomach as instructed by Clay Milton who lashed him with the same length of rope to the others.

Still the Rattlesnake had not moved, still, he watched and waited for a sign that Hawkeye was near. A night creature streaked past his foot, causing him to move, an involuntary reflex action, the noise he made was almost inaudible. Almost! Taking no chances he flung himself down to the ground, readying his rifle for use in his new position. The knife thudded into the trunk of the tree where a second earlier his head would've been.

Johnny Hawkeye had found him. He fired twice in the general direction from which the knife had been thrown and rolled away, hoping the darkness would hide him. Clay had dropped to the ground the second he heard the knife connect with the tree, and lay, ready to shoot at anything that wasn't Johnny Hawkeye. Nothing moved for what seemed an eternity, then, half a minute later he heard the sound of a horse being ridden at speed away from the camp, away from the hunter who now showed himself. Johnny Hawkeye limped painfully to where Clay waited, rifle primed and ready.

"You're hurt." Clay noticed the limp and blood emanating from the front of Johnny's right thigh.

"He caught me with a lucky shot, I'll be okay. It's just a flesh wound." Johnny said and sat down. "I'll need to clean it and wrap it before I chase after him. Rattlesnake. He should have been a cat, he's had at least nine lives, got to run out of luck soon." Clay went to retrieve Johnny's knife for him, he brought back with him also the half breed's bowler hat.

"He was in a bit of a hurry to go." Johnny said. "I'll take it to him." He cut open the top part of his jeans to inspect the bullet wound closely and called over to Clay. "I need you to take the bullet out, here." He handed Clay his knife and took off his belt. He put a length of it into his mouth and bit down hard as Clay did the cutting, prodding and removal of the bullet. He washed the bleeding gash with water from the pigskin canteen on his saddle and then bandaged it tightly with his neckerchief. He stood up, hobbled about for a minute to prove to himself that he wasn't incapacitated, and sat down again.

"What are we going to do with them?" He jerked a thumb at the three prisoners.

"I thought we might let them go." Clay Milton said. Johnny blinked in disbelief and was going to say something but Clay beckoned him to walk with him out of earshot of the three Mexicans. He followed as bid, a question written unspoken on his face.

"Three bandidos are not going to make much difference to us, or Lopez, considering how many men he has. So letting them go won't be any more dangerous than keeping them prisoner or killing them." Clay began. "But if we send them back to Lopez with a message, he may or may not believe it, but he will think about it." Any doubts we can place in his mind can maybe help us in the long run."

"No wonder you were, are a spy." Johnny told him. The men were scared at the sight of Clay advancing towards them with a knife in his hand.

"We're letting you go because we're not interested in you or your boss. We only want Rattlesnake Joe. Johnny Hawkeye wants Rattlesnake Joe, Lopez will know of this." Clay cut the three men loose and after emptying their guns, gave them back. Johnny brought their horses and displaying a high degree of suspicion the Mexicans mounted up. They rode hurriedly away, fearing that any second they would be shot in the back.

Clay called after them. As an afterthought, or so it seemed to them.

"Tell him also, that the Rattlesnake is not to be trusted, he will do a deal with the General and betray him. We learned this from a pistolero called Aguilar. He was killed by a bounty hunter before he could tell Lopez himself." The Mexicans were soon out of sight.

"You really are good, mixing just enough of the truth with the lies to make them seem possible, even probable." Johnny told Clay. "You should be a full time spy."

"Sometimes it feels like I am." Was the reply.

The two of them made their way back to Shannon and the others, taking great care to scrutinise the dirt track ahead for any clue that Rattlesnake Joe had doubled back and was waiting to ambush them. Johnny Hawkeye knew the only thing predictable about the scalp hunter was his unpredictability. There was no sign of him.

Where would he go? Reporting another failure to Fernando Lopez would not be advisable. The bandido leader had a limited tolerance for incompetence amongst his gang and by now the Rattlesnake must have reached the extent of Lopez's patience. He might cut his losses and run, try and put as much distance as possible between himself and the implacable avenger on his trail. Rattlesnake Joe, Johnny knew was no coward but was a devout pragmatist, his self-interest and devotion to his own survival would always be his overriding priority.

The other consideration would be that he could come after Johnny Hawkeye, to end things between them once and for all. Johnny would welcome a face to face showdown but thought it very unlikely that Rattlesnake Joe would contemplate something so upfront, that would be…Unpredictable!

Shannon's priority was to recover from his wounds and let his battered body heal as far as possible before resuming his task of collecting the rewards on Rattlesnake Joe and Fernando Lopez. Now added to his list was Virgo Séptimo and the recently discovered, increased reward of $5,000 for Roberto Aguilar, although without a body to hand, that one may prove difficult to claim.

Clay's only concern at present was the success of his mission and the safety and progress of James Blue. What to do next, he would have to scout the Mexican revolutionaries' huge camp and see what, if anything he could find out.

Zachariah Smith was as set on vengeance against the scalp hunting Comanche half breed as Johnny Hawkeye but as always, would follow the younger man's lead. Someone had to make sure the young feller didn't go and get himself killed.

Captain Bradley Kinross only spoke occasionally these days and then, only in monosyllabic grunts. His vacant stare into the far horizon was unwavering and could have been unnerving but the others had all seen such behaviour before. Sometimes people came out of it, sometimes they didn't, only time would tell.

Johnny Hawkeye was again struggling with his priorities. His burning, unshakeable desire was to hunt down and kill the Rattlesnake in revenge for the atrocities committed against Morning Cloud, his children, and his people, as he had come to look upon Strong Lance and his tribe. Against this he had to balance the needs of the people he had come to regard as friends. Of the dangers facing them now, in the present. He thought of the people already lost, and the others that would be, if the mission given to James Blue and Clay Milton was to fail. In the end it didn't take him too long to make up his mind.

"I will scout the Mexican camp, you sit here and make a plan." He told Clay.

Chapter Thirty Four:

An Old Enemy.

The young woman crawled battered and bleeding from the bed. Major Kurt Schmidt threw a single coin after her as she hurriedly wrapped her torn clothing around herself and ran sobbing from the room. The German was a beast, a brutal sadist, and had far exceeded the agreed parameters of accepted roughness adhered to by her regular customers. She would take days, perhaps weeks to recover.

The German stubbed out the remains of his cigar on the bedside table and threw off the sheet covering his legs. He got up from the bed, splashed his face with water from a jug and began to dress. He was interrupted by a knock at the door. He answered and was greeted by one of General Gomez's Lieutenants.

"Major Schmidt. The General is here, he says to meet him downstairs with Garcia."

"I will be there as soon as I have finished dressing." He said and shut the door in the other man's face, he reached for his shirt and continued to put on his clothes.

When Schmidt came down the stairs he marched in a straight line towards the group of men sitting around the large table. He saluted the General and stared at the other two men sitting with him. One was the messenger from Lopez, Pancho Garcia, the other was a Gringo. A Gringo he thought looked familiar. Garcia had a look of concern on his face.

"This is a lie." Garcia spluttered in anger. "Fernando would not do such a thing, he hates the Gringos as much as you do General."

"Ah, Major Schmidt." Gomez greeted the German. "Sit." He pointed to a chair and the Major sat. "This is Senor Blue." He pointed to the Gringo. "He has come all this way to warn me that Fernando Lopez and El Serpiente are betraying us."

Bluey and Schmidt made and locked eye contact, mutual recognition was simultaneous. The Major spoke first.

"This man is a spy for the Union, what is he doing here?"

Bluey had to think fast, he did.

Schmidt had worked for the Confederacy during The War Between The States as a spy and intelligence manipulator, a very good one. They'd never met but knew of each other through mutual acquaintances, friends and enemies alike. Bluey had been instrumental in preventing the assassination of a top government security officer, planned by Major Kurt Schmidt.

"Major Schmidt. How nice to finally meet you in person." He stood, smiling and extended his hand to the astonished German who totally ignored the gesture. The Mexicans standing around the room all had their pistols out now, aimed directly at James Blue.

Bluey withdrew his hand and sat back down.

"I tell you this man is not to be trusted. Shoot him." Schmidt was incensed.

"Why should I not shoot you Senor? What did you hope to achieve by lying to me?" Gomez was curious.

"General, I am not lying to you." He lied. "Let me tell you why the Major would tell you I am a spy. I am, or rather I was."

"The fool admits it." Schmidt laughed. "He hangs himself with his own words."

"I admit I was a spy Major, you were working for the south, to obstruct the Union, to weaken it. So was I, I was undercover, working directly for the office of President Jefferson Davis."

"Then tell me why did you prevent the assassination of the Englishman, Colonel Steele?" The German played what he thought was his trump card. "I had planned that attempt for weeks and you killed my most accomplished marksman."

"Two things I can tell you Major. The war was all but over. If you had succeeded in killing Steele, security would have been tightened up all around anyone and anything concerning Lincoln, his plans would have been altered, and so would something I was involved in, I couldn't allow that to happen." Bluey let what he'd just said sink in to the minds of Gomez and Schmidt.

"And what were you involved in that was more important Senor Blue?" Gomez sneered, he was favouring the Major's suspicions.

"Yes, what was more important than removing the security chief of Abraham Lincoln?" Schmidt demanded to know.

"You've just answered your own question. Think about it. What happened on April 14th?"

Gomez had a look of bafflement on his face but Major Schmidt realised immediately what Bluey was saying.

"Lincoln!" He exclaimed. "Lincoln was shot." The General smiled and nodded.

"And what is the second thing you can tell us?" He was beginning to enjoy the interrogation.

"Yes, if you were working for the south as you claim what was the purpose behind the killing of my assassin?" The Major was not convinced by Bluey's story, not by a very long way.

"Self-preservation Major. He told me all about you, if anyone else had asked him questions he would have told them about me. He knew who I was. I had to preserve my cover and remain above suspicion. What would you have done?"

For once the German had nothing to say, scepticism showed in his expression, it would not fade easily. Bluey pushed his case a little harder.

"And why, if I was lying, would I come to you with such a story? It wouldn't make sense for me to risk my neck if I didn't want you to have the weapons."

General Gomez was trying to work out which man he believed, the Gringo's story seemed plausible but Schmidt had proved a clever and useful ally to have around and obviously didn't think it was true. Pancho

Garcia was adamant that Fernando Lopez had not double crossed the mad General. Not that he wouldn't but he hadn't yet. He did not mention the second part of his reasoning. But he did tell the revolutionary Gomez that, Rattlesnake Joe he believed, would betray his own mother if he had one. Something no one in the room who knew of the half breed would take issue with.

"I will not have you shot yet, Gringo. I do not know what the truth of it is, but I will keep you in the jailhouse until I find out. Take him away." Two big men came forward and he went with them quietly.

The Sheriff's office that used to be the domain of Barton Lee had no prisoners. Until now. Bluey was unceremoniously pushed into one of the cells and the door locked securely behind him. The General did not seem convinced of his story but had not been overtly dismissive of it, or he would be dead. He hoped the bandidos would be delayed longer than the few days expected. Why hadn't Pancho Garcia been questioned as forcefully on the subject? A half an hour later Bluey realised he had been, with an equally unsuccessful outcome. Garcia and his men were escorted into the cells and bundled roughly inside. Garcia and another man occupied one cell, the other three, another. That left only one empty.

"Gringo, Fernando will enjoy killing you." Garcia grinned at the Australian and spat a gruesome semi-solid, slimy ball of khaki coloured matter onto the floor.

"I will send some of my men out to find Lopez and see what is going on." General Gomez thought only of making sure the weapons were coming to him. His forces far outnumbered those of Fernando Lopez and any U.S. cavalry troops that might seek to intervene in his plans. But he needed to know what the situation was. Had the Gringo told him the truth? And if not why was he lying. It could only be to set him and Lopez against each other, to what end? No one knew of his plans except a trusted few, very few.

"I will go General." Major Schmidt volunteered. "I will only need one man with me, less to be seen but someone to send back with a message if required."

"Very well Major, take Captain Hernández, he's been with me for several years, since he was a boy, and he can be trusted."

Chapter Thirty Five:

Pieces Of A Puzzle.

From the upper branches of the tree in which he perched, Johnny Hawkeye watched the two riders coming along the trail, one, a middle aged man with a military bearing, emphasised by his uniform, that of a German army officer. The other, a Mexican in a different uniform with a Captain's markings.

The face of the Mexican was known to Johnny, he seemed older now, but he could remember a young soldier, drinking tequila, not so long ago, in a long forgotten town, trying his damnedest to seduce a pretty bar maid and guarding a horse. A black stallion. The stolen mount of Rattlesnake Joe. He allowed them to ride by without taking any action and let them disappear from view before climbing down from his observation point. It would soon be night time and he had things to do.

"Restez tranquille, Senors." The voice whispered. Pancho Garcia could not make out who was moving in the darkness. He could hear the metallic scrape of metal on metal as the adjacent cell door was opened and he could see vaguely that the Gringo was being released. "Here." The voice hissed again and the mysterious figure tossed the keys to the cells through the bars where they landed on the nearest bunk. He turned to pick them up and by the time he was again facing the door, the shadow and the Gringo were gone. He opened the door and that of the other cell holding the rest of his men and they filed out. The two guards lay dead on the floor, one had his neck broken, and the other had been stabbed. No one had heard a thing. Their mounts were liveried close by and they proceeded with extreme caution to find them.

The sound of nearby gunfire woke the sleeping Mexicans. Galvanised into action, hundreds of them grabbed their weapons and rushed outside their tents to find out what was happening. The noise was coming from the direction in which the horses were corralled. The makeshift rope fencing had been cut and the frightened animals were stampeding away from the camp in a panic to escape the closeness and loudness of the repeating gun shots. By the time any of the soldiers reached the scene of the shooting the horses were gone. All of them. The sentries were dead, the first few shots had seen to that. In the distance, just out of range of their weapons some of the revolutionary soldiers could see two horsemen riding away.

Anger was an understatement, totally inadequate, to describe the extreme fury felt by General Gomez when he was awoken from his sleep by the sound of the shooting and given the news. Not only had his prisoners escaped, but his horses had all been stampeded and most were still missing. It would take hours, perhaps days to round them all up.

"This was found in the Gringo's cell, General." One of his Captains showed Gomez the blood stained neckerchief of James Blue.

"Garcia had men in the town. They killed the guards, rescued him and then he let our horses go. They took the Gringo with them. He must have been telling the truth. Lopez has betrayed me." The mad General's face was crimson with rage, he pushed his young bed mate violently onto the floor. "Get out!" He bellowed at her, she didn't need telling twice and left the room, seizing her clothes and covering her bruises with them as she hurried. "Find them." He shouted to the Captain. "Take twenty men, if you can find twenty horses, if not take as many as you can. Find them. I want Garcia alive. Kill the others."

"What about the Gringo, General?"

"I don't care about the Gringo, kill him too. If Garcia hasn't already."

"What did you want my necktie for?" Bluey asked as he and Johnny Hawkeye rode towards the camp where Clay and the others were waiting.

"I left it in your cell, with blood on it, from one of the guards." Johnny explained. "They'll think Garcia attacked you when his men rescued you, and they'll blame him for the horses being run off. That's why I left Garcia the keys. Gomez will think you were telling the

362

truth. You'd better have this back, thanks for the loan."
He returned the Australian's rifle.

"Thanks, how did you know where I was?"

"I borrowed a sombrero from one of Lopez's men
in the town, and took a look around. I was just another
Mexican wandering about the streets. I saw you and
your escort, Garcia was a bonus."

"Did he mind? The sombrero, I mean,"

"He didn't need it anymore. This German Major
you mentioned, the one I saw riding out, who is he?"

"He was a Major, a real one. He worked as an
agitator, a spy for the south in the war. Anything to
weaken the Union. Germany could take advantage
where the French and the Spanish failed. But he was too
extreme by far and after the war they would've forced
him out so he deserted. Now he is the second in
command for Gomez."

"How does he know you?"

"Well you know I worked for the Union, against
him and his kind. We never actually met but our paths
crossed indirectly. We knew who each other was. We
were both surprised to finally see each other face to
face. I would like to meet him again, with a gun in my
hand." Bluey said with conviction.

"You probably will, he was heading towards
Lopez."

Finally Fernando Lopez was at last able to resume
his Journey. His men had assembled enough horses and
wagons to accommodate the transporting of all the big

guns, eight cannons and three Gatling guns. Muddy Creek was fading into the distance behind the party when three of his riders, from the six he'd sent out with Rattlesnake Joe, found him. They told him what had happened to their companions and that El Serpiente had vanished, maybe Hawkeye had found him, they didn't know. Instead of continuing on their journey to find Gomez, they had thought it more important to bring Lopez the message from the other man, the one who'd come to their camp. The part about Clay getting the drop on them and tying them up, they left out.

Fernando Lopez did not doubt for one second that the half breed would think to double cross him. He just couldn't decide whether he believed he actually had. Yet! But forewarned... The bandido chief had barely dismissed the three men when more horses approached the convoy of weapons and their escort.

Pancho Garcia and the four other bandidos rode in. Their story was quickly and breathlessly told and Lopez was left alone to speculate. Would Gomez believe he'd been betrayed? In which case Lopez would adapt his plan, with the same result being accomplished. Apache Bend was only a few days away now and things would soon be resolved. One way or another, and he would deal with whatever transpired in his own way.

Clay Milton had found an abandoned old cabin not far from the place where they had camped out for a couple of days and he, Shannon, Zachariah and Kinross had decided to commandeer it for their own use.

Shannon had spent the last few days practising his fast draw and trying to regain his fitness, his wounded side was beginning to heal and the headaches were fewer and not so severe. He'd made and drunk copious amounts of coffee. He'd come to agree with the others that Zachariah may have talents, but they were not exploited to good effect in the brewing of coffee, he could scorch water. Zachariah, unaffected by the good natured ribbing inflicted by his companions, had busied himself scouting around, and watching out for signs of Rattlesnake Joe.

Bradley Kinross struggled with his inner demons and remained silent most of the time. He ate sparingly, he drank when given a drink, and slept. He did not wash or shave and if his old self could see him now he would be appalled at what he'd become, a shuffling wreck of a human being. Even Johnny Hawkeye felt sorry for him. More so for his wife, Sally.

Johnny and James Blue had easily tracked them to the cabin and sat with Clay on the rickety chairs found around an equally dilapidated table to try and come up with the next plan of action. Clay Milton had come to the conclusion that until Fernando Lopez and General Antonio Gomez had come to together there was nothing much to be done. Unless of course an unforeseen opportunity presented itself soon. Very soon.

"We need to find out how Lopez will react to a visit from Schmidt. He might just kill him if he believes the General is betraying him." Bluey said, Clay nodded in agreement.

"If he lets him leave again it will be to take a message to Gomez. We could do with finding out what it is."

"Two of us ought to scout the trail, we won't be in time to stop him reaching Lopez, but we could get him on his way back. If he comes back." Johnny suggested.

"Schmidt won't talk." Bluey was sure. "He would die first, not out of loyalty to Gomez but his own pride."

"He wouldn't have to, the Captain who rode with him, I've seen him before. He likes tequila and women. He would be persuaded to tell us what we want to know, I'm pretty sure of it." Johnny supplied.

"You and Johnny go looking for Schmidt, I'll take a look around the southern trail in case they come back a different way, if Zach feels up to it, I'll take him with me. Shannon could use a few more days before he's going to be ready to travel." Clay had heard of Schmidt but didn't know him, Bluey had more personal reasons for going after him. Johnny knew the Mexican Captain and so he thought they would be the best people for the job.

The procession of weapons did not stop for rest until nightfall, until the horses and men were about to drop with exhaustion. Fernando Lopez was in a hurry. The German Major and the Mexican Captain had been greeted, listened to and sent back unharmed to General Gomez with a message. The Gringo, James Blue, was

366

lying for what reason he wasn't yet sure. The guns would be the Revolutionary's, but not until payment in full had been received and a face to face meeting had taken place, just the two of them. The bandido supreme and the mad General.

It was the single shot that gave him away. The sound of the rattle had spooked the horse he'd chosen from the selection of mounts Lopez had shown him at Muddy Creek. The majestic white stallion now bucked in fear at the snake poised close to its feet. Without hesitation or thought Virgo drew his pistol and blew the reptile's head from its body before it could strike.

Clay Milton, scouting the hilly terrain was close enough to hear, but not close enough to see, who was doing the shooting, just the one shot. Could be a hunter killing his supper, he changed direction to find out.

Zachariah Smith, a little further away, also heard the shot and steered his mount towards the sound to investigate. Virgo urged the white stallion up towards the top of the slope. He dismounted a few yards before the summit and advanced on foot to scout around. If anyone had heard the shot and was headed his way he should be able to see them.

He should have, but he hadn't.

"Stay still. If you even look at your gun I'll shoot you." Clay advanced from his cover, he held his pistol in his hand. Virgo stood still, he said.

"You were at the fort Senor, you are a very lucky man."

"And you are very lucky that it is me pointing a gun at you, if it had been a friend of mine he would have killed you by now. That's his horse you're riding."

"Ah, you are a friend of Shannon, the bounty hunter. He should thank me, I could have blown up the horses easily with the rest of the fort. The shot you heard, that led you to me. I had to kill a snake, it would have bitten this beautiful creature. If I hadn't done that you wouldn't have found me." Virgo liked to know who he was up against, who he may have to kill.

"Virgo Séptimo, I guess." Clay liked to know his enemies also. "You know the routine, drop your gun belt. Slowly!"

Zachariah emerged, minutes later, from nowhere it seemed, rifle aimed squarely at the Mexican. Virgo was sitting on Shannon's white stallion again now. His hands were tied behind his back and Clay, himself mounted and ready to ride, held the reins.

"I can see you've been busy Young Feller, that there is Shannon's stallion." He said to Clay in greeting, and to Virgo. "He ain't gonna like you much Senor."

Captain Luiz Hernández of General Antonio Gomez's revolutionary army rode alongside the German Major Kurt Schmidt. They travelled in silence, each wrapped up in their own thoughts. Hernandez was favoured by the General and had been loyal to him in the campaign to overthrow what he saw as a corrupt government. Just lately his commitment to the cause had wavered, the audacious plan to reclaim Texas had revealed the increasing insanity of his leader. He became aware that however unlikely, victory in Texas or Mexico, or both, would result in another, much worse dictatorship ruled over by a mad man. Failure in either endeavour would in all probability mean death for himself and most if not all the men who rode with the rebel army. Luiz Hernandez did not approve of Major Schmidt, his ideas or his brutality. He really wanted to forget about wars and violence. He just wanted to go home to his young wife and child, to live in peace.

Major Schmidt did not share the Captain's doubts, with his combat experience and tactical skills he would guide the Mexican fanatic to victory. And, when the time was right, the mad General Antonio Gomez would meet with a fatal accident and be replaced. By himself, as President.

Even if their concentration had been fully employed on the surrounding hillsides they would not have seen Johnny Hawkeye or James Blue.

"Stop!" Bluey called out from his place of concealment behind a convenient grouping of large boulders. "If you run or reach for your weapons you will die." The Major slowly raised his hands, the Captain followed suit. Johnny Hawkeye, gun in hand stepped out from cover on the opposite side of the trail from Bluey and walked towards the mounted men. He removed their weapons and gestured for them to dismount. They did so, Hernández quizzically studying Johnny Hawkeye. The ease of movement, the feather in the hat band, something familiar.

"Luiz, we meet again." Johnny said in greeting, still pointing his gun at the two men.

"You! Senor, Johnny?" Recognition came to the Captain. "The tequilas, the black horse."

"Johnny Hawkeye. Don't make me have to kill you. I wouldn't like that." Johnny meant it, he'd quite liked the young soldier. Bluey showed himself, Schmidt congratulated himself on his instincts.

"I did not believe your lies. I knew you were a spy, Blue." He snarled at his captor. "I will not tell you anything."

"So there is something to tell." Bluey said evenly. "Are you sure you don't want to discuss them, it might save your life? Unlike the people you've tortured and murdered in the name of whatever cause you decided to fight for."

The Major stared James Blue in the eye and spat on the ground.

"I will tell you nothing, Yankee."

"I know you won't, and I'm an Australian." Bluey shot the German. The bullet caught him in the chest and he fell down in a crumpled, lifeless heap at his killer's feet.

"And I thought Shannon was ruthless." Johnny said. "Well, Luiz, let's talk." He looked towards the Captain, the fear was evident on the young man's face.

"If you are going to shoot me anyway, you might as well do it now, Senor." He told them, expecting any second to meet the same fate as Schmidt.

"I don't want to kill you Captain." Bluey tried to reassure the Mexican. "I just need to know what message you are taking to Gomez. You do realise he is quite mad, don't you?"

"Si Senor, I do. He wasn't wrong to fight against the Rurales or the tyrants, but he has become like them. If he gets the big guns from the bandido, many more will die."

"We'll have a sit and talk." Johnny put his pistol away and Luiz Hernandez sighed with a restrained relief.

The three men talked for an hour, Bluey and Johnny asking the questions and Luiz Hernández giving them unforced, clear and honest answers where he could.

"One more question, Luiz. How did you get on with the girl at the bar, the night we met?" Johnny asked with a smile on his lips.

"Oh, Senor, I married her. Her name is Leticia, we have a little boy, Carlos."

"What will you do now?" Bluey wanted to know.

"Well, if you do not shoot me Senor, I will go home. I cannot ride with the General any more. I need to be with my family." He looked from Bluey to Hawkeye, and back to Bluey.

"We're not going to shoot you Luiz, not if you go home." Bluey answered him.

"Thank you Senors, I will go now." And he mounted his horse and rode away, leaving them to their thoughts. Taking Schmidt's horse with them, Johnny and Bluey set off back to the shack.

The twenty men sent after Pancho Garcia and his men returned empty-handed from their mission. Gomez was livid at the failure as he was at each and every setback he'd ever encountered. He would rely on Kurt Schmidt to have delivered his message to Lopez and that he would here from the Major any day soon. The General gave orders that he and his officers with a substantial force would move into the Town of Apache Bend until the business was concluded and the guns were his. He and an elite core of guards would take over the hotel, and it would become their headquarters.

Shannon was elated at the recovery of his mount, he was feeling a lot better in recent days and his wounds were healing fast. Unless he lifted the hair up from his ear, the scar on his head was invisible and the bullet hole in his side no longer required a dressing. His bruised shoulder and hips were yellowing as the black and blue receded.

"What are you going to do with him?" Shannon asked Clay, referring to Virgo Séptimo who was asleep, still bound, on the floor in the corner of the draughty old shack.

"I can't pay you, so when this is over, he's yours, $5,000 I think you said."

"You caught him, you decide what happens to the reward." Shannon was not about to accept something he didn't feel he'd earned from anyone, let alone someone he had come to regard as one of his very few friends.

"Well, if you collect it and give some of it to Barton Lee's family and some to Rodrigo's sister, if we can find her. That would suit me."

"Okay, sounds good to me." The bounty hunter agreed.

"There's someone coming." Zachariah poked his head in the door. "I think it's Johnny, and Bluey. It was. Virgo Séptimo woke at the sound of the intrusion and even the near comatose figure of Bradley Kinross stirred from its inertia. Shannon and Clay went outside with Zachariah to meet the approaching horsemen.

"Kinross, can you watch him?" Clay asked, pointing to Virgo. "I have to talk to the others, outside." The Captain nodded vaguely in the affirmative.

"I'll stay with him, son." Zachariah volunteered and went inside. "I can't understand half what you young fellers say anyhow."

Zachariah poured himself a coffee and sat at the table, glaring with a pronounced hostility at the prisoner. Virgo smiled at the old man, he was fidgeting, trying to get the circulation working in his arms and struggling against his bonds.

"Senor, I would like a cup of coffee if that is not too much to ask." He grinned at the old man. "I cannot give you any trouble, tied up like this, can I?"

"Captain, would you take the Mex a coffee over so I can hold the gun, please." The Mountain Man asked of the Cavalry Officer. On receiving no answer he repeated himself. This time Kinross rose slowly and reluctantly to his feet and did as he was asked.

"You will have to hold it to my mouth, as you can see, my hands are tied." Virgo explained, he also had to repeat himself before Kinross understood. Bradley Kinross leaned over to allow the prisoner to drink.

"Not in the line of fire." Zachariah shouted, but it was too late. Virgo Séptimo swung his right arm round in a vicious arc and hit Kinross hard in his left temple. The Captain would have collapsed across him but his left arm caught him and in a second the Mexican was on his feet. He held the unconscious form of Bradley Kinross between himself and the gun of Zachariah, a rusty six inch nail at the Captain's throat.

"If you do shoot me old man, I promise you I would have enough time to kill this man before I died. Now drop the gun and kick it over to me." Grudgingly Zachariah complied. Running footsteps sounded outside, the others had heard the shout. Without a second's hesitation Virgo picked up the rifle and raising his arms to cover his face he charged straight at the wall behind him. The rotted wood gave way immediately, turning to sawdust and splinters as the Mexican charged through. The horses were tethered nearby, he jumped on the nearest and was gone before the door burst open and Johnny Hawkeye raced in to see Virgo's dust in the distance.

Zachariah Smith explained what had happened as Bluey checked on Kinross.

"It wasn't my fault." Zachariah finished.

"I know, it was mine." Clay pointed to the corner where he'd put the Mexican. See this blood? And the nail. He somehow worked it loose from the wood and worked on the ropes with it, must've taken him hours, it took some of his skin, but I should've seen it."

"Well, he's gone now, we can get after him." Johnny moved to the door.

"Let's give him an hour, then we follow and track him to wherever he's going. If we chase straight after him, he could see us and lead us away from where he's headed" Bluey finished tending to the Captain's badly bruised head and joined in the conversation.

Shannon had gone to make sure Virgo hadn't taken his horse.

"He took the Captain's horse, we'll promote Kinross, and he can ride the Major's."

"What's happening, what the hell's going on...?" Captain Bradley Kinross sat up rubbing his throbbing head. "Will somebody tell me?" He bellowed. The others just looked at each other and laughed in spite of themselves, even Johnny Hawkeye.

"Welcome back Captain." Bluey said the words no one ever thought they'd hear.

Chapter Thirty Six:

The Meeting.

The sun was high in the sky, nearly noon. Finally Apache Bend was in sight. Fernando Lopez had all the guns lined up facing the town. The Gatlings were positioned at the far ends and centre. He had the tarpaulins removed so that the sight of them would be more intimidating to behold. Pancho Garcia volunteered to be the messenger once more, he had a point to prove. He knew Gomez would not imprison him with the mighty weapons aimed in his direction.

Fernando Lopez rode alone to a point midway between his men and the town. It was hot and he'd emptied one of his water canteens before he glimpsed the assembling masses of the revolutionary army in the distance. In front of them riding towards him were three men. One he recognised as Garcia, The portly over decorated man in a General's uniform he assessed must be Antonio Gomez and another man, one of the General's inner circle he presumed.

"General Gomez, at last we meet." Lopez smiled as the two men came face to face for the first time.

"Fernando Lopez, I see you have my guns." Gomez stated. Lopez waved for Garcia to move back, his second in command did so, retreating to ten yards behind his leader. Gomez repeated the instruction to his own man, who did likewise.

"Yes, I do General. As you can see, I have not betrayed you."

"Where is Major Schmidt?" The General expected to see the German alongside the bandido.

"I don't have him. I sent him back to you, with the Captain." Lopez informed him. "I have no reason to lie. Could it be the Gringos caught up with him? Do you have my payment?"

Gomez thought for a few seconds and although not completely convinced gave the bandido the benefit of the doubt. For now.

"$10,000 as promised, yours when my men have the weapons. Where is El Serpiente? I do not see him with you."

"My men will pull back as soon as I give them the signal that I have the money, General, I'm sure you understand my caution." Lopez would not deviate from his insistence on payment before surrendering the big guns to the mad General. "El Serpiente? I sent him to see you, to tell you that because of the Gringos' interference I would be delayed, as you can see, I was."

"It does not matter, He is not a man to be trusted." Something they both would agree on. "Count it." He waved to the officer waiting behind him who now rode forward and dismounted. He unloaded two huge saddle bags, the clinking of many coins was encouraging to the bandido.

"Pancho." He called out and Garcia rode forward and also dismounted, he opened the weighty bags and saw many smaller bags inside, all containing gold pieces. Without a word he spent nearly an hour going through them all and then declared.

"Si Fernando it is right." He struggled to load the saddlebags onto his horse but persevered until he managed to do so.

"Gracias, General. The guns are yours." Lopez smiled and turned his horse around, he raised both hands to the sky and the General noted with pleasure that the bandidos began to leave the guns unattended.

"If you were tempted to shoot me in the back, General, I can assure you that my men would be able to reach the guns and destroy them before you could get to them." He rode slowly away with Pancho Garcia and $10,000. "Adios General." He called out to Antonio Gomez.

That evening the bandido chief distributed $100 to each of his men, $200 to Pancho Garcia and kept the rest for himself. A generous gesture, he thought to himself. But he had greater things to consider.

Chapter Thirty Seven:

The War Chest.

The meeting between Lopez and Gomez had been followed by the withdrawal of all the bandidos and the possession of the big guns by the revolutionary army. Other than the two parties involved in the exchange the process went unwitnessed. Not so the aftermath.

The weapons were covered once more by the huge sheets and transported, not to Apache Bend but to the large encampment in the hills on the other side of the town. Gomez wanted to move out first thing next morning to begin the journey back to his homeland, to his glorious destiny. Several of his less committed followers had been seduced by the freedoms of the American way of life and the easy pickings to be had as a bandido. Desertions were not yet a matter of primary concern for him but the General did not want to allow the trickle to become a flood.

That evening the celebrations were loud, full of drunken soldiers letting off steam and carried on well into the night. Nobody noticed a young soldier as he ventured into the surrounding trees to answer a call of nature, nor the fact that he didn't return. Instead, another man wearing his uniform and carrying a blanket roll wandered around the camp, he appeared to be drunk. He wasn't. Gomez himself ordered two of the unfortunate young women, collected along the way from various ransacked towns, to be brought to his bed.

Watching the festivities from a safe distance, Rattlesnake Joe waited for the right moment. He had seen another furtive movement in the nearby shadows, someone else, maybe two people, were moving in on the mass of armed revellers, but who were they?

Further away but getting closer by the minute were two other interested parties, Johnny Hawkeye and James Blue. Hugging the darker side of the hills to avoid detection by any sentry that may still be sober, they made their way silently to view the proceedings. Unknowingly from an angle of ninety degrees and a distance of less than eight hundred yards from the Rattlesnake.

Of the eight men on duty to protect the war chest of General Gomez, four had been seconded to the southern part of the compound to add extra security for the newly acquired big weapons. Of the four remaining guards two had overindulged in celebratory whisky and slumbered drunkenly against the weeks of the wagon. Virgo had no trouble disposing of the others, his knife flashed twice in the moonlight and the war chest was unguarded. He carried no blanket roll with him now.

He emitted a low whistle and from the darkness emerged Fernando Lopez and Pancho Garcia. They led the eight strong team of horses needed to transport the heavy wagon. The next few minutes were tense for the bandidos, Virgo attached the animals to their waiting load, soothing their nerves by mumbling gently to them as he did so. Then they were ready. Virgo took the reins, Lopez beside him and Garcia inside the back of the wagon and they drove slowly forwards.

Astonishingly the perimeter was in sight before anyone challenged the intruders and their stolen fortune. Two sentries stood in the path of the horses and the guns of Lopez and Virgo. They died before they could raise their weapons, cut down by the double blast from the men on the wagon seat. Virgo cracked the whip and the horses surged forward as fast as the heavy burden would allow.

Behind them the camp lit up and the sound of multiple explosions ripped through the party atmosphere, instilling panic and shock amongst the confused soldiers of General Antonio Gomez. Tents were ablaze and wounded men crying out and shouting in pain and fear. Virgo had been very busy all evening, secretly hiding sticks of dynamite and lighting concealed fuses, timed to go off at the same time. Now. When it was needed as a diversion. The revolutionary army would be concerned about making sure the big guns were not damaged. Only the General would think of his war chest and he did.

Puffing and panting as he struggled to do up his trousers and his uniform jacket, Gomez left the captured women in his bed and half ran, half waddled towards the place where his war chest should have been. Screaming in rage at the top of his vocal range the distraught General finally attracted the attention of a

Captain and physically pulled him away from the bleeding man he was trying to help.

"Get some men together, go after them, they have my safe, my war chest. Go! Go!"

A mile and a half from the rebel army encampment the hilly terrain became more rock than grass. The wagon was driven towards the base of steep incline. Lopez climbed down from his seat and pulled away at various vines and sagebrush, which allowed the moonlight to reveal the opening to a small cave. Virgo drove into the entrance. It was dark inside, he dismounted and struck a match. He located a collection of candles placed inside the cave earlier in the day and lit three of them. Lopez replaced enough of the vegetation to give them cover and he and Garcia set about wiping any visible tracks from the wagon wheels. A better job could be done in the daylight but by then it shouldn't matter.

The three bandidos waited inside the cave for the sound of pursuit, it wasn't long before a large group of horses were heard galloping by outside, they'd missed the cave. Lopez predicted that the troops searching for them would take several hours and probably take alternative routes rather than back track. He and his cohorts would wait until daylight to make the next move and open the safe.

Above all the action below, a solitary figure watched, his scarred face contorting into a smile displaying a wicked intent. He would collect his payment plus a huge bonus from Lopez. The satisfaction of a plan well worked out may have faded with the realisation that following him and getting closer with every passing minute was Johnny Hawkeye.

Bradley Kinross had cleaned himself up, he'd washed and shaved and looked to be more like the Captain he used to be. The knock on the head from Virgo had jogged something inside and his old arrogance and the swagger of conceit returned with a vengeance. He had convinced himself that he was the hero of the situation and circumstances they all found themselves in, and that if it wasn't for him the others would all be dead. The massacre at Fort Boone needed to be avenged and he made up his mind to ride for the town of Lugar, to find his wife and Sergeant Flynn. Then he would contact the nearest army post and report to the highest military authority he could locate, the disasters happening on American soil. He needed to recruit a force large enough and powerful enough to take revenge against Lopez and destroy the threat from Gomez. The reality of which he at last accepted.

He went alone, the rest of the party did not argue with him. They all had other things to do. Johnny and Bluey had left earlier to scout the revolutionary army compound. Clay, Shannon and Zachariah Smith followed later, checking to make sure no one was stalking them from the rear.

Fernando Lopez led the eight horses from the cave, along with his own and Pancho Garcia's. Virgo had

had to leave the one he'd stolen from Kinross at the camp. He and Garcia kept hold of the mounts' reins to steady them when the noise came. A few seconds later the muffled explosion occurred, quieter than expected and muted somewhat more by being enclosed. Lopez thought it would be louder and hoped the charge was powerful enough to have done the job. Virgo stood up from behind the rock where he'd taken cover and waited for the dust inside the cave to settle enough to be able to see. He pulled his necktie over his nose and mouth and went back inside to investigate his latest handiwork.

"This is what I needed you for, Amigo, how is your work?" Lopez called out.

"Come and see for yourself Fernando, I think you will be pleased." Virgo replied with a laugh.

The gigantic safe was still on the wagon, but sloped towards the floor because the rear wheels had been removed. The door was open and the contents displayed unharmed by the explosion. The glitter of hundreds of jewels and gemstones shone and sparkled seductively through the dusty gloom and the many bags of gold and silver coins could not erase or dim the look in the eyes of the Mexican bandits as they salivated in triumph at the unqualified success of their mission.

"The saddlebags are ready, take the money first, we'll take the jewels last." Lopez ordered. They began to work, every time a saddle bag was filled, another was brought in. Virgo would fill the bags, Garcia would carry them outside and Lopez would put the treasure on the horses while watching out for any passing traveller or threat. By the time the coins had all been loaded onto the horses, there were no empty saddle bags to load up with the jewellery. Even the mounts of Lopez and Garcia were weighed down with the haul. The three of them had removed their shirts with a view to filling them and tying them to their saddles when Rattlesnake Joe struck.

Clay, Shannon and Zachariah had caught up with Johnny and Bluey and joined the surveillance of the revolutionaries in their cut short celebrations. In the mayhem that ensued after the explosions had rocked the camp, Johnny and Zachariah had left the point of observation to follow the single horseman whose tracks Johnny had seen earlier, and the wagon seen leaving in a hurry. Clay, Bluey and Shannon stayed, hoping to get a chance at taking down General Gomez. They moved closer to the big tent Bluey had picked out as that of the revolutionary commander and then had to hide quickly when the corpulent figure emerged pulling his clothes on and ranting incoherently to his panicking troops. The noise and the sight of General Gomez screaming at his men would have been funny if he wasn't so dangerous.

The troops sobered up under the barrage of abuse from, and fear of the man who would be a dictator. The watching intruders took note as a Captain and a large posse of men rode out after the vanished wagon, they wondered what could possibly be so valuable, valuable enough to alarm Gomez to such an extent. By now the General was surrounded by his men and was going towards the field weapons to check they were still unharmed. The watchers withdrew and resumed their vigil from a safer distance.

Pancho Garcia was halfway to the entrance of the cave when the first shot from Rattlesnake Joe's rifle caught him. It slammed into the back of his right shoulder, spinning him round as he fell. Fernando Lopez reacted at speed, taking cover behind one of the laden mounts and pulling his pistol from its holster as he did so. Virgo Séptimo dived headfirst behind a nearby rock drawing and firing blindly in his haste towards the sound of the shot. Rattlenake Joe ducked and moved away from his attack position to another vantage point ten yards to his right. The wounded Pancho Garcia took advantage of the respite and struggled to crawl into the cave. Lopez could see him and threw a rifle to his second in command. He retrieved another for himself and scrutinised the surrounding rocks for signs of the attacker or attackers. Virgo glanced over the top of the rock he was using as cover and was immediately rewarded by being shot at. The half breed was disappointed that the bullet only removed the Mexican's sombrero. The bloodied, pain racked, Garcia, saw where the shot came from and caught a glimpse of the shooter.

"El Serpiente!" He called out to Lopez. Garcia could only use his left arm but fired the rifle towards the Rattlesnake's position, chipping a piece of the rock six inches from his target's head. A splinter of the rock struck the half breed in the face, his scar made even more scarlet by the freshly flowing trickle of blood. Angrily the wounded scalp hunter fired off half a dozen swift shots towards the mouth of the cave. They all missed Pancho Garcia but one of them ricocheted into the remaining supply of dynamite.

The explosion could be heard for miles. The cave collapsed into a pile of rocks and dust. Garcia, the wagon and the hundreds of items of jewellery and gems were buried underneath. Fernando Lopez was hit several times by flying pieces of rock, a sharp edged, fist sized fragment glanced off his head, knocking him unconscious and he fell bleeding to the ground. The horses jerked away and fled in panic, the reins were tied together and so they all galloped as one.

Virgo had to risk it, the dust from the explosion he hoped would conceal him from the view of the half breed. He sprinted out from his place of relative safety and leapt onto the saddle of the leading horse as they passed him. No bullet followed him. He and his treasures would have to get away before inquisitive parties came to investigate the massive explosion.

Rattlesnake Joe could just about see the prone figure of Lopez lying below him and squinted through the residue of the falling cave looking for any evidence that Garcia or Virgo posed a threat. Only Garcia's left hand was visible, protruding out from under the debris. Of Virgo, and more importantly, the overloaded horses there was no sign. He took aim to shoot the unmoving bandido chief. He would make sure Fernando Lopez was dead before descending and giving chase to Virgo Séptimo and the treasure. That was his plan but it would not work out that way, not yet, not ever.

Johnny Hawkeye and Zachariah Smith came to the scene too late to intervene in the fire fight.

"Looks to me like the scalp hunter's done some of our work for us." Johnny whispered. "Now we take him." Johnny had circled round to come at Rattlesnake Joe from the front and told Zachariah to distract the half breed with a shot after five minutes. The Comanche half breed stood up to finish off Lopez, and Zachariah thought the opportunity, after all these years, was too good to miss. He stood up himself to get a better aim, and accidently dislodged a small pebble with his foot, he never knew which one. Rattlesnake Joe swung round and downwards as fast as the reptile whose name he shared. He fired in the same movement and the bullet hit the old Mountain Man before he could squeeze his own trigger, embedding itself into his chest, and knocking him down. He was hit an inch to the right of the scar he had from the wound sustained in Mason. Johnny saw Zachariah fall from his new position and cursed loudly.

The Rattlesnake would have recognised the old man and know that he, the hunter, would be nearby. The scalp hunter's priority was escape, as always, Lopez was unimportant now. Keeping low he raced towards where his horse waited and without hesitation mounted and rode away at speed. Rattlesnake Joe had to escape the avenging spirit he knew would be following him.

One day they would have to settle things between them, but he wanted it to be a time and place of his own choosing. The relentless, remorseless Cheyenne warrior only needed a time and place.

Johnny found Zachariah still conscious but bleeding badly and unable to stand.

"Go and get him boy, I'm sorry, I just thought...." Zachariah had tears in his eyes.

"It doesn't matter Zach, you did what you thought was right, that's okay with me. I gotta get you to a Doctor, you need a professional medical man for this. I can't get any Cheyenne herbs in these rocks. I'll bandage you up and take you to Apache Bend, should be almost free of Gomez's people, and Lopez's by now. I Hope Doc. Desmond is okay."

"Don't bother about me boy, I'm an old man, my time is done. I would like to know you got him before I go. Go! Now!" The old man slipped into unconsciousness and Johnny carried him to his mount. He couldn't get him to sit on it without falling and so he put him on his own and sitting behind him held him in place. He cut the old man's horse loose to fend for itself, it wandered aimlessly around while they went. Taking it along with them would slow them down and he didn't have time to waste. They set off for Apache Bend, hoping it would be a safe place to leave Zachariah Smith while he, yet again, resumed his quest for revenge alone.

It was cold and dark when Fernando Lopez finally regained consciousness, the moon was hidden by clouds, they looked dark and ominous but in the daylight they would be white and the sky blue. He could see the outline of a horse standing nearby grazing on the sparse vegetation in the gaps between the rocks. He didn't move, he was listening for sounds to indicate another human presence. Five minutes he lay still, his head throbbing with pain, his throat dry and parched. Eventually he made up his mind and quietly, and casually, he didn't want to spook the horse, he rose to his feet, supressing the urge to be sick with willpower alone. Fernando Lopez reclaimed his shirt and jacket from the dusty ground and approached the abandoned mount. The horse was a docile animal for which the bandido chief was grateful, and it let him come close and hold the reins, apparently without concern.

Lopez kept the reins in his hand and helped himself to the contents of Zachariah's water canteen. The cloud condescended to reveal the moon which in turn allowed the Mexican to survey his surroundings in more detail. There was no sign of Rattlesnake Joe, nor Virgo, and he was not surprised to discover that the horses and the contents of the mad General's mighty war chest had vanished. The jewellery and other valuable stones were buried under tons of rocks along with his loyal acolyte Pancho Garcia, all but his left hand. He set off to find Virgo Séptimo, he had a fair idea where he would be going. He would not need his men, this was personal.

Chapter Thirty Eight:

The Dream Crumbles.

It did not take long for the news to spread around the encampment of the revolutionary army. General Antonio Gomez had the guns but now he had no wealth, no means of paying his soldiers. The bandidos had stolen it all, they'd betrayed the mad General after all. The Captain and his troop sent out by Gomez to track down the thieves had not returned. He sent another larger contingent of his idealist troops out to find and attack the bandido camp, retribution must be swift and seen to be punitive. Some of the more mercenary minded of his recruits deserted, dozens vanished during the twenty four hours following the heist.

The troops that came back from the attack on the bandidos had been severely depleted. The men of Fernando Lopez were not pushovers. Without disclosing the reason, their leader had pre-warned them of the probability that Gomez would send his army to attack them and the revolutionary army rode into an ambush. Out of the one hundred men who ventured forth in the morning, seventeen saw the evening. Twenty of the bandidos had died during the ferocious encounter.

If Fernando Lopez had been there himself the bandidos would have stayed with him and remained the loyal band of outlaws that they'd been in the past. But without a leader, disillusionment quickly set in. The campaign to steal the big weapons for the insane plan of the rebel General had seen their numbers fall from over a hundred men. Taking into consideration the day's events the survivors numbered just twenty nine men. Deciding enough is enough, and with $100 each in their possession, plus whatever they could salvage from their dead comrades and divide, they went their own ways. They drifted off, some alone, some in twos or threes.

The following morning Generalissimo Antonio Gomez awoke from a fretful and intermittent sleep to find that not only had his Captain and the accompanying troops not returned, with or without his war chest, but that during the night his soldiers, his revolutionary force had lost many more men. The mercenary factions had deserted in droves, of the two thousand that had ransacked Santo Juanita, only eight hundred remained, mainly idealistic, radicalised young men, lost until the persuasive rhetoric of the mad General had hypnotized them into believing their search for a purpose in life was over, and at last they had a cause worth dying for.

Seething with anger once more Gomez ordered the remnants of his forces to prepare to move out. He ordered the cannons to be uncovered and primed ready for use, and then turned to face the town of Apache bend. He would test out his fearsome weapons and make a statement that would be heard all the way to Washington. He would claim victory over his enemies and surmount any obstacles on the way to doing so. His troops would soon come back to him, along with thousands more men as soon as word got around, General Antonio Gomez was back! He was unbeatable!

Watching unseen from the outlying ring of tents, all unoccupied due to desertion or duty, Bluey, Clay and Shannon watched. They still waited for the opportunity to reach Gomez himself.

"He's going to attack Apache Bend." Whispered Shannon.

"This could be interesting." Bluey suggested.

General Gomez gave the order to load the cannons and stood to side watching while his men began to carry out the instruction.

"Generalissimo!" A soldier called out to Gomez. "I cannot load the weapon, the barrel is blocked."

"This one is blocked also General." Shouted another, and another.

"These guns have been spiked, and one of them has a cracked barrel, Generalissimo." A Captain of the revolutionary army informed his Commanding Officer. "This will take a long time to fix."

"Time we can't give them." Clay murmured softly through the smile, he wore, along with the other clandestine spectators. While in the barn Bluey had used all and any piece of junk he came across at the farm to jam deep and unseen into the barrels of the big guns, old bayonets, tools, nails, even bits of wood. Clay had done likewise at the fort, although he hadn't had time to get to the Gatling gun before Lopez had attacked. Something he was in retrospect pleased about because Shannon had needed to make use of it.

"Fix them! Get them working!" Gomez screamed at the men and abruptly left them to get on with it. "Ortega!" He called at the Captain, hooked his bloated finger, and marched back into his tent followed by Captain Ortega.

"Now?" Clay to Bluey.

"Now." Came the answer.

"Go, I'll cover you." Shannon readied his rifle and took out his pistol.

Clay and Bluey walked nonchalantly towards the General's tent from the rear, the men working on the guns did not look up as the Gringos stopped at the opposite end to the entrance flap. Bluey drew his knife a let the razor sharp blade slice open the canvas. Clay pulled one side of the newly created opening to the side and stepped into the General's lair.

"Stay still." Clay ordered firmly but not too loudly. Gomez, a startled look on his pudgy face was still, his mouth open as he ceased speaking half way through a vowel. Ortega studied the intruder swiftly, sizing up his chances. He concluded they weren't that good and raised his hands, slowly. His chances became even more remote when James Blue followed Clay into the tent.

"You! Gringo! You lied to me." Gomez let his anger surface yet again as he gazed at James Blue. "I thought you were dead."

"Yeah, I'd put that down to wishful thinking. Sit." Bluey instructed.

"You too, Captain." Clay nodded towards the second chair and Ortega moved slowly to sit down. Clay carefully removed the weapon from the Captain's holster and stood back keeping his gun trained on the seated man while looking around for something to tie him up with. Bluey moved behind the General who now occupied the other chair and took his gun. He walked back around the table to face Gomez. He wasn't prepared for what happened next.

A single shot derringer appeared as if from nowhere in the plump right hand of the Revolutionary. The Australian reacted instantaneously to the threat but was not quite quick enough. He was launching himself at the fat man when Gomez squeezed the trigger. The bullet hit Bluey in the chest but his momentum carried him on and he crashed into the seated Mexican. Antonio Gomez fell backwards from the chair as it collapsed and Bluey landed on top of him, a limp weight bleeding onto the front of the General's uniform. Ortega saw his chance and took it, his right hand streaked down to his boot and came up holding a knife. The Captain almost got to his feet before Clay reached him. He hit the Mexican hard with his gun butt and Ortega fell to the floor. Generalissimo Antonio Gomez was frantically struggling to breathe, the fall had winded him, and trying to push Bluey's inert body off himself caused him to gasp more desperately for each breath. Clay Milton walked over to the wheezing man and pointed his gun into the wet, scarlet face, the sweaty endeavours ceased and fear showed in the revolutionary's eyes.

"Senor…" Antonio Gomez was about to beg for his life, a fat, beaten, weak, and pathetic man whose dream of absolute power had crumbled into dust. Clay Milton pulled the trigger and bits of General Gomez's brains burst out of his skull to shower the tent with blood, bone and gore. Clay bent down and gently pulled James Blue away from the mess. His friend was unconscious, but breathing raggedly and blood had soaked his shirt. Oblivious to sudden bursts of gunfire from outside he carefully lifted Bluey and carried him out of the torn, makeshift entrance, cut into the rear of the tent. Shannon was busy firing at the soldiers who were running to see what was happening, and behind them came more, many more. Clay laid Bluey on the ground and signalled to the bounty hunter that the Australian was wounded. He went back into the tent and threw a cup of water into the dazed Captain's face. Ortega slowly came to.

"Captain. Wake up. Gomez is dead. The revolution is over. My men are here now." Clay told him, covering him with his pistol. Your men are still trying to fight us. I want you to tell them to stop. There's no point in any more killing, you can't win." He added a second lie. "There are too many of us out there."

Ortega looked at the deceased figure of Gomez, at the gun in Clay's hand, said nothing for a few seconds and then nodded.

"If I stop them shooting at you, you will not kill me? You and your people will not attack us on our journey home?"

"You have my word." Clay told him in all sincerity, to prove it he took a chance and lowered his weapon. "But you leave the big guns, they have caused too many people to die."

"Wait here." Ortega said, dusted himself down, straightened his uniform and strode out of the tent. Shannon aimed his rifle to shoot him but Clay appeared again and gestured for him to stop firing. He kept his aim, but did not shoot. Ortega raised both his arms and called to the advancing soldiers.

"Men! Amigos!" He shouted. "The Generalissimo is dead. The war here is over. The Americanos are here. The guns have killed too many of us. Now we go home. Who is with me?" Silence. And then a huge roar of approval. The new Generalissimo. General Pablo Ortega would begin the revolution again, in Mexico. The Gringos could keep their guns, and Texas. He went back to inform Clay Milton of his success. Apart from the corpse of his ex-boss the tent was empty.

Shannon had abandoned his cover and shooting position to help Clay with getting Bluey away from further danger, and together they tied him to his horse, they had to get him to a doctor. Apache Bend seemed the only place for miles where they would be likely to find one, Doc. Desmond, if he was still unscathed by all the violence that had taken place in his town.

Chapter Thirty Nine:

Harbingers.

The most feared outlaw gang in the whole of Mexico and the Border Territories was no more. The erstwhile leader did not concern himself with the proceedings, he didn't need the bandidos anymore. He needed to catch up with Virgo Séptimo and his fortune in gold and silver coins. He was at least a day behind his quarry but he should be able to travel faster with only one horse to consider.

Disaster struck Fernando Lopez two days later, his mount trapped a hoof in a gopher hole and he could hear the snap of bone along with a squeal of pain from the animal. He jumped off before he could be thrown and put the stricken creature out of its misery with a single shot. He carried his saddle and his rifle and walked. A day and a half it took the bandido to stumble upon anything like civilization. A remote cabin with smoke rising from the chimney and nearby, a barn, and a coral with horses.

And less welcoming, a man with a shotgun aimed squarely at him. He was exhausted, thirsty and hungry. He ignored the weapon and carried on towards the unwelcoming homesteader.

"Keep walkin' Mex." The man called aggressively to him. "We don't want your kind here."

"Please Senor, just a drink of water, to fill my canteen." Fernando Lopez appeared almost to beg. He exaggerated the pleading tone in his voice to parodic proportions as he moved closer. "I can pay you, I have dollars." All the time moving closer.

"Ten dollars for water, or vamoose, Greaser." The man growled at him. Closer still.

"I will show you Senor." Lopez reached his left hand slowly to his shirt pocket and took out a roll of dollar bills. Nearly there. He showed them to the homesteader. The man stepped forwards to inspect the money. Close enough. Fernando Lopez dropped the cash to the ground and grasped the barrel of the shotgun, twisting it out of the holder's hands into his own and aimed it directly at the man's stomach.

"I do not like to be insulted or threatened, Gringo." He pulled the trigger and the man died without ever knowing who he had insulted. Lopez picked up the money and walked into the cabin to see a woman cowering away from him in fear.

"Is there anyone else here?" He asked her, showing his gun but leaving it in his holster, the shotgun he'd left outside. The woman shook her head.

"No, just me." She told him, he believed her, fear had a way of encouraging truth to be told. There was a frying pan on the stove.

"Senora, I am hungry." He barked at her. She trembled, expecting to be killed any second but Lopez just pointed to the pan. "Cook." He ordered, she showed him some eggs and a slab of beef. He nodded. "Cook." He repeated and helped himself to a bottle of whisky from the table.

The woman looked about forty but was probably years younger and might have been considered pretty in other circumstances. She showed signs of being beaten and did not seem too upset that her man had been killed. Lopez told her to eat with him and she did, feeling a little safer as the evening wore on. The bandido finished eating and drinking and took a cigar offered to him by his hostess.

"Senora, I need to sleep. Wake me if anyone comes." She nodded, trying to force a smile. She pointed to the only other door in the cabin.

"The bed is through there, Senor." Lopez didn't shoot the woman, he didn't even tie her up. Something told him she would do whatever he said. He was right.

By the next morning she had cleaned herself up tremendously, she was bathed, and wearing a freshly washed dress, her hair was hanging loose and soft around her shoulders and she smelled good. Lopez knew this as soon as he woke up and breathed in, she was lying beside him on the bed. He opened his eyes, she looked ten years younger and certainly was an attractive woman.

"Senor, I will make you breakfast, will you be going today?" She hoped he would say no. Or...

"Yes I am going, but first I will have breakfast Senora."

"Senor, what is your name?" She asked as if in a normal conversation. "My name is Belle."

"Senora Belle, I am Fernando, are you not angry or upset with me for killing your husband?"

"He was a pig. He beat me, I would have killed him myself if I had the courage." She let him know he'd done her a big favour in ridding her of the thuggish brute. She placed a breakfast of bacon and more eggs in front of Lopez and sat opposite him. When he'd finished she moved the plate away and he stood ready to leave.

"I will need to take one of your horses." He told her. She came towards him and looked into his eyes.

"Do you have to go yet?" She undid her dress and put his hands onto her ample breasts, she pushed herself onto him and pulled him towards the bedroom. He smiled at her and followed her inside. Afterwards, as she was getting dressed, she asked him the question.

"Will you take me with you, Fernando?"

"Belle, I cannot take you with me, I have something I have to do." Her face showed the disappointment she felt. "It will not be safe for anyone who travels with me." She came to the door to watch him leave. He chose the strongest looking mount and prepared to go. Before he rode off he reached into his shirt pocket and again removed the roll of bank notes. He threw them all to her.

"For the horse, Senora Belle. Leave this place." He left her in tears, but determined to do what he told her. She would leave, and never look back. The ruthless bandido resumed his chase, he was a long way behind but could travel much faster than his quarry. Mexico would be where he would find Virgo Séptimo and the money. He would catch him and reclaim his prize.

The deserted unnamed township had been abandoned ten years earlier, when the fresh water stream dried up and the nearby mine ran out of silver. Rattlesnake Joe had been hiding there for days, he knew every inch of every building. The half a dozen still standing and the wrecked remains of others. The only street meandered through the centre of town allowing an uninterrupted view of any comings and goings from either end. The roof of the hotel or the bell tower of the church were the highest points from where to look out for approaching riders, positioned as they were at opposite ends of the ghost town. It was to be here the Rattlesnake decided, the last confrontation with the dogged Cheyenne warrior, his nemesis for so many years. Here, in a nameless collection of abandoned buildings, miles from anyone who could mourn him and away from anybody who might wish to help him. There would be just the two of them, a final reckoning. He knew he would come, the white Cheyenne, the trail was not too hard to follow, but not too obviously so deliberately easy.

Doc. Desmond was overworked, with no hospital or lawmen in town and injured casualties in abundance, inflicted during successive occupations by first the bandidos of Fernando Lopez, and subsequently by the revolutionary army of General Antonio Gomez.

Clay Milton and Shannon had instigated the transforming of the Sheriff's Office and the courthouse into makeshift wards for the injured. James Blue and Zachariah Smith were housed in separate cells at the rear of what had served as Barton Lee's office.

Bluey had been seriously wounded, but not fatally so, the doctor was confident that eventually he would make a good recovery, albeit with a damaged lung. A broken rib, although painful in the extreme, was already beginning to mend. The Australian would have to be a patient patient, healing was a long process, months, not days.

Zachariah hadn't fared so well, Doc. Desmond spoke candidly to Clay and Shannon and explained that in his opinion the old man had no right to still be breathing, that an inner strength had kept death at bay so far.

"He's waiting for Johnny Hawkeye to come back." Shannon had told him. "He needs to know something before he goes."

Clay Milton and Shannon hired some of the townspeople to secure and guard the big guns until the army could be contacted to come and reclaim them. Although the remnants of the Mexican revolutionary army had long departed Clay would have to stay until such time as the handover could be dealt with and Shannon stayed with him.

Two further weeks went by, Clay and Shannon had jointly and unofficially taken over the roles of the Sheriff and his Deputies, patrolling, scouting and supervising the security of the big weapons, still standing where Captain (now General) Ortega and his men had left them.

The bounty hunter was undecided on his next move. Rattlesnake Joe he would leave to Johnny as agreed. Lopez, and, since his release from jail, Virgo Séptimo, were on his list but he needed a pointer as to their whereabouts. A large town, such as Apache Bend might be the place where he could pick up a clue, catch an unguarded comment, a careless whisper. He would wait.

One evening Shannon sat on his own at the bar of the hotel where he and Clay had rooms, Captain Kinross, Sergeant Flynn and another soldier entered the building. Flynn beamed at the bounty hunter and walked over to shake his hand.

"Well I'll be pleased to be buying you a drink, Shannon, the Captain tells me you've all been busy." He bellowed. "Drinks for my friend here, my man." He called to the long serving, long suffering bartender.

"Mister Shannon." Kinross said politely in acknowledgment of the man who'd helped make sure he was still alive.

"Kinross." Shannon returned.

"Where are your friends?"

"Well, other than Johnny, the ones who are still breathing are here in town. James Blue's in a bad way, but he'll live. The old man, not so good. Clay's out looking after your guns."

"Hummmph! And Hawkeye, where's he?"

"He's away, some personal business."

"The half breed?"

"That's it."

"What happened, Gomez, Lopez?"

"Lopez, he's vanished, Virgo too. Gomez is dead. The man you thought didn't exist doesn't anymore." Clay Milton walked in at that moment. "And here's the man that killed him for you."

Clay joined them, and the rest of the evening was spent retelling the events that led them all to the situation they were in now.

Not too far to go now, he'd never been to the place he was searching for, but he'd listened to people, Lopez's men, and he learned quickly. The description of the landscape fitted with his expectations, the village hideout of Fernando Lopez would be close, Virgo was certain of that. He didn't know if Lopez had survived the Rattlesnake's treacherous assault or not, but he himself had, and taking advantage of the circumstances was what he did. It was what Lopez would have done had the positions been reversed. The journey had been long and arduous, travelling alone with ten heavily laden horses, keeping out of sight to protect his treasure. The river crossing had been very difficult, he nearly lost two of the overloaded beasts of burden in the attempt, but eventually he managed to enter his homeland undetected and with his complete load intact.

And then he was there, the little settlement revealed itself to Virgo Séptimo from the crest of the slope he was on. He could see a handful of women down below him, going about their daily business, and a few men taking advantage of the shaded porches to rest in the afternoon warmth. He could not detect any signs to tell him that Lopez's band of bandidos were present. Without a leader, he deducted that they would be in disarray and go their separate ways. The next part of his plan might be easier than he thought, but then again...

Chapter Forty:

A Dream Rises.

Sofía sat in front of the mirror combing her long black hair, she wore a simple pink night dress with nothing underneath. A beautiful young woman for sure. She could see the door behind her open in the reflection, and the man enter the room. The angle of the mirror was such that the face of the man was above her line of view.

"Fernando." She called in expectation as she stood up and turned to face him. The look of surprise and fear replaced that of her smiling anticipation as Virgo came into her sight, his pistol pointed at her.

"You must be Sofía, Senorita, the men, they told me you were beautiful, they did not lie." He said with a smile.

"Where is Fernando? He will kill you for this." She retorted, anger at the intrusion giving her the courage to confront him. "Who are you and what do you want?"

"Fernando is dead, I am sorry." He told her in his most sincerely sounding, conciliatory voice. "I have come to tell you this sad news." He put his gun down and smiled. "I did not know how you would react."

"Fernando? Dead? But how? Who?"

"A traitor, one of his men. I came to warn you, he could be coming here. We have to get you away, and the money, Fernando told me he buried it all here. He said you would know where it is." He smiled again, his most sincerely charming smile. Sofía was not wholly convinced by this undeniably attractive man and his words, the shock of hearing of Fernando's death had not sunk in. She could not be rushed. She crossed to the bed and sat down. Virgo watched, drinking in her loveliness and feeling inside a rising desire for her.

"Sofía." He said softly. "Let me take care of you. We will take the money and leave this place. I will take you anywhere you want to go."

"But Fernando, I cannot believe...I"

"You cannot love a dead man, and he is as I told you, very dead."

"I fear you are mistaken, Virgo, my trusted amigo." Fernando Lopez filled the doorway with his frame but all Virgo could see was the gun in his hand.

"Fernando!" Sofía gushed in surprise, the look of joy and relief on her face convinced Lopez and Virgo that she only wanted one man. Fernando Lopez.

"Fernando, I really thought El Serpiente had killed you." Virgo told the man with the gun.

"He tried, but you didn't wait to find out, or come back to check. Believe it or not, I would have done that for you." Lopez showed a look of disappointment on his face that Virgo knew at once was genuine, he'd made a big, possibly fatal mistake.

"Sofía, take his gun." She did as her man ordered. "Fetch the carpet bags, every single one you can find." Without a word she went to obey.

"You wanted to find where I keep my money, Virgo? You will. How did you know about it?"

"I didn't for certain, but the men talked and I know you well enough, you would have to have something, somewhere, and you have been around too long not to have a cache of some value." Virgo answered, pleased at his own deductive reasoning.

Five minutes later Virgo was digging, he dug deep, about four feet, and a hole four feet by three feet was excavated to reveal two huge carpet bags, one on top of the other. One man could not lift either of them alone and Fernando Lopez would not put his gun away to help his former friend with pulling them out of the hole. He sent Sofía to bring a horse from the barn and instructed Virgo to tie the bags one at a time to the saddle of the animal.

One after the other, the heavy loads were dragged out of their hiding place. Sofía led four more horses, attached to a covered wagon around to the burial site and Virgo transferred the contents of the two soil covered containers, thousands upon thousands of gold and silver coins into more manageable sized carpet bags and loaded them into the wagon.

"Are you going to kill me now?" Virgo asked his captor, still puffing and panting with the effort of his labours.

"Of course I am not going to kill you, Amigo, not yet, anyway. You still have to unload your, should I say our saddlebags, did you think I would forget?"

"No, I did not think you would." Virgo admitted. Two hours later the wagon was fully loaded with the contents from, not only the war chest of General Gomez, but the accumulated proceeds of a very prolific twenty years plus of banditry by Fernando Lopez.

Virgo knew the moment of truth was upon them.

"Now, Fernando?" He prepared himself. Lopez pointed the gun at Virgo's head.

"You disappointed me, Amigo, I did not think you would betray me, I am disappointed in myself for believing in you."

"Do I have time for a prayer?"

"A short one, Virgo I have to go." Virgo put his hands together and made to sink to his knees. Instead of actually doing so he leapt forwards towards the gun hand of Lopez and twisted the gun away from himself and towards the holder. The shot rang out, loud and clear. Virgo stood up straight, Lopez turned his gun around again and regained his balance. Virgo turned around, pain etched into his handsome face and fell.

Before losing consciousness he caught a glimpse of the beautiful Sofía, she was holding a smoking gun, his gun. Sofía dropped the weapon as if it was burning her hand and looked towards Lopez.

"Fernando, you are okay?" She was half laughing, half crying to see that he was unharmed.

"You would do that for me?" Lopez didn't quite understand, he was confident he would have won the tussle with Virgo, the girl didn't know that of course.

"Fernando, I could not let him kill you, I... I... love you." The once most feared bandido leader in all of Mexico was humbled by the admission. He had always looked after Sofía and liked her but was unaware that the feelings were reciprocated.

"You would do that, kill for me? After I kidnapped you from your family and friends, took you away, kept you prisoner?" Elements of a humanity lost for decades began to surface in the Mexican outlaw supreme. He was not at all comfortable with it.

"A prisoner? For such a clever man, you just don't understand women, Fernando. You are away so much, I could have left anytime I wanted to. Why would I want to go home? My family were not good to me, I could not run faster than my father, or my brothers, and you must know what that meant for me. You have always treated me well and I would never leave you or let anyone harm you." Sofía had tears in her eyes now as she watched her man climb onto the wagon and take hold of the reins.

"I am leaving." He said to the beautiful young woman. "But I can wait awhile if you want to collect your things before we go.

An hour later they were two miles into their journey to the future. Neither of them were able to see the faint flicker of an eye and the twitch of a finger, made by the bloody, fallen figure of Virgo Séptimo.

Chapter Forty One:

The Reckoning.

It had taken Johnny Hawkeye three weeks to come upon the ghost town but somehow, deep inside he knew this would be it. The final showdown, face to face with his greatest enemy at last. One of them would not leave this godforsaken place alive. The tracks he'd found had not been easy to follow, but they had not been obliterated well enough to make them impossible, it was as if he was meant to see them. Rattlesnake Joe would expect him to enter from a side of the town, avoiding the street, probably at night.

Johnny would spend the day circling the place to get his bearings and would indeed enter from the side and get close during the hours of darkness but would not make a move until daylight, let the Rattlesnake wonder and wait.

A mile to the south of the deserted town his horse was startled by the sound of a rattlesnake, the reptile kind. Johnny steered the frightened animal away from the danger. He dismounted to scout the ground between him and the buildings, he saw no evidence that his enemy had seen or heard anything to cause him alarm. Or even that he was within the boundaries of the ramshackle collection of ruins. He took note of the tall construction at one end of the street and the church at the other, good places to use as lookout positions. But a man alone could only look out from one of them at a time, and the half breed was nothing if not a man alone.

Light streamed through the uncurtained, open window, the noise of a galloping horse penetrated easily and the acute hearing of Rattlesnake Joe alerted him immediately. He looked out of the hotel window to see his horse, riderless, rushing at speed towards the church end of the street. Realising what could happen he pulled back just in time, as the bullet flew past his head to bury itself in the wall behind him. He knew the shot wasn't meant to kill him, but an injury would have given his adversary an advantage in the confrontation to come. The half breed grinned to himself, the final battle had begun. He would take the mount of Johnny Hawkeye as a souvenir of his victory, along with his scalp.

Johnny was already moving along the street away from where he'd taken the shot. The loss of a horse wouldn't trouble the Rattlesnake even a little, nor would a deliberately misplaced shot. Another shot sounded from close by and a bullet slammed into the sign of the deserted shop above Johnny's head. The Comanche half breed knew where he was. He retreated around the back of the building only to re-emerge at the front seconds later, gun primed and ready. Nothing to shoot at. He heard a faint noise like that of something small, a stone perhaps, being dropped, it came from the opposite side of the street.

He was far too experienced to fall for that one, a stone, coin or similar object thrown to misdirect his attention. He stayed still and his eyes scanned the whole town, every inch of it he that could see, anyway, still nothing. Rattlesnake Joe was good, very good. Then he spotted a shadow projected onto the ground in front of him, someone was on the roof above his head. He automatically spun round to shoot but there was no one visible on the roof to aim at.

Rattlesnake Joe had already jumped and was hurtling downwards towards him, his knife blade glinting in his hand. With no time to get out of the way, Johnny twisted his body sideways on, to minimalize the unavoidable contact. He felt an agonising pain in the back of his left arm, above the elbow, and a crushing jolt as the scalp hunter landed on him, pushing the air from his lungs and knocking him to the ground. Winded or not he had to move, with one hand he grasped the wrist of his attacker in an attempt to manoeuvre the knife away from his chest as Rattlesnake Joe pressed home his advantage. The other hand reached for his own knife and he pushed hard as the half breed's other hand gripped his arm to try and stop him. He brought his knee up viciously and the straddling figure of his nemesis grunted in pain as he was struck savagely in the groin. He let go of Johnny and rolled away, Johnny went for his pistol and found an empty holster. The weapon had fallen out as he fell and laid four feet from him. He lunged himself towards it before the Rattlesnake could do the same and whirled round to face him.

His enemy was nowhere to be seen. Johnny stood up and ran into the nearest building, the dilapidated Sheriff's office. The desk was rotten, but still intact and he took cover behind it while he got his breath back. Blood was streaming from the deep gash in his upper left arm. He tied it as tightly as he could using his necktie, and then flexed his arm and fist. The movement caused him a lot of pain but at least he could still function, first blood to Rattlesnake Joe. He would do his best to ensure that last blood was his.

Rattlesnake Joe had vanished from the scene of the first encounter to recover from the debilitating effect of a knee to the groin, the hunter fought well and he respected the fact that he was up against a worthy opponent. He watched from the relative safety of the church tower, nothing moved below, he could see no sign of Johnny Hawkeye, only the faint stain of blood in the dusty street betrayed the fact that any violence had taken place. The hours passed and the sun began to sink in the west. Darkness would have descended on the ghost town but for the light of the full moon. It was cold and the scalp hunter shivered involuntarily in his high vantage point.

Johnny Hawkeye waited motionless in the shadows, he had been there quietly doing nothing for most of the day and evening. He was waging a war of nerves, just letting his enemy consider the options open to him, as he himself was doing. Had there been a working clock in the vicinity the chimes would have sounded twelve when Johnny made his next move.

Rattlesnake Joe had allowed himself the luxury of relaxing a little, He rested, his back against the door to the outside platform which housed the church bell.

Even Johnny Hawkeye could not try and gain access to the walled enclave without disturbing him.

The shot ricocheted off the bell with a monstrously loud clanging sound and flew away into the night air. The half breed jumped up in bewilderment and in doing so saved his life. The next bullet, redirected from the bell itself took a chunk out of the wall where his head had been resting. Two more shots followed in quick succession and one of the ricochets hit him in his left hand, not seriously inhibiting his ability to use it but making it very painful and causing it to bleed profusely none the less. Cursing the hunter, Rattlesnake Joe abandoned his lookout point for the relative safety of the church itself.

With the light came a new strategy, the scalp hunter began at one end of the street, the end nearest the church and systematically searched every building on his left hand side as he came to it. He entered through the rear wherever possible after checking and rechecking to make sure he wasn't falling into a trap set by the Cheyenne avenger. It was while exploring the upstairs floor of what used to be the bank that he happened to glance out of the window into the building opposite, previously a barber's shop. The mirror, facing the street was dust covered but somehow still intact and not too dirty to reflect, albeit without clear definition. In it he saw an opportunity to finish the contest.

Moving inside the building to his left but on the ground floor he saw the discernible reflection of the hated Johnny Hawkeye. He was seemingly doing the same as Rattlesnake Joe, checking out the whole street for his enemy. The Comanche half breed positioned himself at the top of the stairs, Hawkeye would come to the remains of the bank in the next few minutes and he would be waiting, ready to end the long drawn out conflict at last.

Johnny Hawkeye crept silently into the wreckage of the abandoned bank. He slipped in via the front door, he'd seen no sign of Rattlesnake Joe all morning and he moved fast. If he had been noticed he would soon be out again, this time he would use the rear exit. He glanced out of the window, seeking a clue, a slight movement, a noise that didn't fit, anything. He found it. A mirror in the relic of a barber's shop opposite, a slight glint in the dullness, a maybe hint of activity. It came from the building he was inside, from upstairs. He heard the movement on the landing above before he could see anything and blindly fired his pistol in the direction of the rickety staircase above his line of sight.

Johnny heard two grunts of pain, one from above, and one of them from himself as Rattlesnake Joe's hurried shot hit him in the shoulder, above his injured left arm. He fell to the side and the second shot from the half breed missed by yards. He flung himself out of the back door, further aggravating the pain in his arm by landing heavily on it. Stifling further vocal expressions of discomfort the warrior backtracked to the building he'd vacated only minutes before and secreted himself in a darkly, shaded corner, behind the scant shelter of an old stove.

The man with the scarred face and half an ear missing, examined his wounded leg. Many years ago the young He Who Sees As The Hawk had wounded him with an arrow in the same part of his leg, his limp would now be more pronounced. If he survived, which he was fully determined to do. Rattlesnake Joe, very cautiously hobbled out of the building and taking great care crossed the street to the barber's shop. The mirror had evidently worked against him as much as for him. It would not do so again. He smashed the item making as much noise as he could and waited patiently, rifle poised, for the head of Johnny Hawkeye to appear. It did not do so.

Both the combatants had water canteens with them and after two days of one on one conflict, both were running low on the precious liquid, Johnny had used more than he'd wanted to make sure his wounds were clean. Neither of the sworn enemies had supplies of food, both used to dealing with requirements in that department according to opportunity and availability on the trail. The cat and mouse game would have to end, another day of such intensity would weaken both of them and neither wanted to find out who would be the first to succumb to the rigours and oncoming fragility being imposed on them by their various injuries.

Johnny made his way stealthily to the end of the street away from the church tower, towards the hotel. He entered from the side, through a gap in the wall which had once been a large window. He'd had to remove his shirt and wrap it around his wounded shoulder, to stem the bleeding. His wore his buckskin jacket over the top for added insurance against leaving a trail of blood for his enemy to follow. Once inside the long neglected shell of the hotel Johnny stayed still, listening to, watching and concentrating on his surroundings for several minutes before making his way to the stairs. Slowly he climbed, one stair, stop, listen, two stairs, stop, listen, three stairs, crack, fall, as the stair turns to dust under his feet.

As he fell the two stairs below him disintegrated under his weight and he crashed back down to the floor. He landed painfully on his back and intuitively tried to roll away from his vulnerable positon in plain view from the street to find any kind of cover, a fallen desk nearby. He knew the Rattlesnake would have heard the noise and be on his way to investigate. He almost got to the meagre cover of the wrecked reception desk before the half breed found him, but not quite. Rattlesnake Joe showed himself briefly in the doorway and fired.

Johnny was moving away from the scalp hunter's aim but the first shot tore through his buckskin and gouged a vicious furrow across the top half of his back, from just above his waist in a diagonal line up to his wounded shoulder. The second shot ripped through his jeans following a similar trajectory along the back of the hunter's thighs. By the time Johnny reached his hard won shelter and could return fire, the Rattlesnake was nowhere to be seen.

The pain was all engulfing, dulling Johnny's ability to think, and his mobility was threatened. He used a Cheyenne meditation technique, taught to him by Strong Lance. He forced himself to mentally block out the agony from his wounds. He forced himself to concentrate on the problem at hand. He forced himself to be prepared to move fast, whatever the physical limitations he might have to overcome. He realised he had to get out of the building, his enemy knew where he was and that he was somewhat incapacitated. If the situation was reversed what would he do. He would set fire to the place and wait outside, out of sight, and just pick off his adversary as he tried to escape the flames.

And that's what Rattlesnake Joe did. He threw a burning rag into the front of the hotel and disappeared from view. He took cover, rifle poised, behind what had at one time been a store room twenty yards from the rear of the establishment. Johnny was waiting for the flames and smoke to rise up which they did, very swiftly, within seconds, and he moved. He had found an old blanket, filthy and rotting but usable for his purpose. He wrapped himself in it and ignoring his pain, he ran straight through the burning entrance and out into the street.

He discarded the blanket which had caught fire at its first contact with the flames and rolled himself agonisingly over and over on the ground. Primarily to escape any gun fire that may come his way and secondly to extinguish the fire that had threatened to envelop his buckskin jacket. He escaped his predicament without further damage to his ravaged body and slunk away to rest, and think.

Rattlesnake Joe was furious, with himself. He should have anticipated the actions Johnny Hawkeye took. He thought retrospectively, his enemy had done what he would have done in the same circumstances. He should have thought it through more thoroughly. What would he do next? What would he himself do? His own wounds were causing him immense discomfort but he would not, could not give in to the pain. Hawkeye could not have gone far, he would need to rest. The half breed would cross to the other side of the street, away from where he would imagine his enemy to take refuge. The buildings there were in a worse state of repair than the side of the street they were on.

He crossed the street and walked slowly, observing the buildings either side of the burned out hotel. He did not use the barely remaining sidewalk, he did not want to fall through the rotting wood, so he stayed in the dusty street. It was a gamble but he figured the hunter would be slowed by his injuries, his pain and the natural fatigue they both endured. That would give him the edge if he could only get a glimpse of his enemy or his enemy's location. The noise of a falling beam came from the skeletal burnt out shell of what had been the hotel. Rattlesnake Joe paused, ready to react if he saw his adversary.

And that was the moment he gave Johnny Hawkeye his chance. That was the moment He Who

Sees As The Hawk took advantage of the opportunity to strike.

An arm snaked out from under the rotting sidewalk and the blade it was holding slashed viciously at the legs of Rattlesnake Joe, severing the Achilles tendon of his right ankle. The howl of agony and shock went far beyond soprano. Another slash before the half breed could begin to fall inflicted identical damage to his left ankle. Whatever the outcome, Johnny knew the Rattlesnake would never walk again. The Cheyenne avenger rolled out from under his hiding place and kicked his enemy venomously in the head as he fell.

The scalp hunter was a very tough man, he tried to move his incapacitated feet and get to his feet, ignoring the pain, but he couldn't make it. Johnny wrestled his gun away from him and jabbed the butt hard into his throat. Still the Rattlesnake fought, he grabbed desperately for his knife with his other hand, his left. Johnny wrenched it from him, cutting his own hand in the process and held him by the wrist, forcing himself to ignore the agony he felt as the torn muscles carried out his bidding. He bent the trapped arm over his own knee and pushed down relentlessly until he heard a crack, followed by another scream of anguish.

Rattlesnake Joe's arm snapped at the elbow. Incredulously, the Comanche spirit within him still refused to quit. He made an attempt to reach his revolver, Johnny easily intercepted him and without hesitation broke his other arm in the same manner as the first. Rattlesnake Joe was crippled, he couldn't fight without the use of his arms and legs and he waited for Johnny to finish him. The hunter stood over his vanquished opponent and raised his gun.

"Finish it, Cheyenne dog." He spat blood at his conqueror. Johnny said nothing. His eyes were dark, almost black, the devil in him took over. He fired twice, both the Rattlesnake's kneecaps shattered, the agony overcame the half breed and he passed out. Johnny left him lying in the dust and walked unsteadily away. He returned five minutes later carrying his water canteen and leading his horse. He emptied the meagre contents of the canteen onto Rattlesnake Joe's face and watched impassively as his hated opponent came back to a pain wracked consciousness.

"Our business is not complete yet, you scalp hunting bastard." He said calmly. He knelt down behind the scalp hunter and lifted him to a sitting position. Then, using his knee to keep the half breed upright, he took hold of his hair and with his knife he cut, deep, around the hairline leaving a liquid, red perimeter.

"No!" Rattlesnake Joe screamed, finally something terrified him.

"This is for Morning Cloud, for my sons, for my family, for my people. This is for Zachariah, his wife and his daughter. And for all the people you have wronged." Johnny spoke into the Rattlesnake's remaining ear and then tore the hair away from the head of his defeated enemy, exposing a raw, red mass of blood beneath. Rattlesnake Joe screamed again.

Johnny Hawkeye ignored him and walked over to his mount, he came back holding a sack, and inside it something was moving, angrily struggling to get out. Johnny held the sack upside down over the prostrate form of his fallen foe and the rattlesnake, the reptile kind, fell onto his chest, the familiar rattle caused the dying Comanche half breed to force his eyes open. He recoiled in horror and his instinctive struggle to dislodge the creature from him enraged it further. It bit him savagely in the stomach and slithered hurriedly away.

"That was for me." Johnny told him. He sat, detached from his own ruthlessness, unflinchingly watching as the convulsions came and went and his enemy, hated for so many years, Rattlesnake Joe, the scalp hunter, the destroyer of his family, but now finally, irreversibly, broken, breathed his last painful, laboured breath and died.

Chapter Forty Two:

The Aftermath.

It had been a long journey to from Apache Bend to the capital city of The United States. Clay Milton knew the office, he'd been there several times in the past. He didn't know the man, Colonel Henry "Hank" Martin. Jack Steele had returned to London for family reasons after ten years on loan from Queen Victoria's secret service. Colonel Martin was his successor, a good man with similar philosophies to Steele, and had in fact been working for his predecessor during the times Clay himself had done so, but they'd never met before.

He made his report, giving a clear and accurate account of the mission to thwart the plans of General Gomez and prevent the use of the big weapons against the citizens of Texas, recently re-admitted to the United States after the collapse of the Confederacy. He stressed the importance of the assistance received by himself and James Blue from various people, most notably, Shannon, Johnny Hawkeye, Rodrigo Lamas, Zachariah Smith, Marshall Clay McCandless and Sheriff Barton Lee.

Colonel Martin listened studiously as the tale unfolded, interrupting only to clarify a point or ask a specific question. He sat back in contemplation and sucked on his ever present pipe. He remained silent, running things over in his mind, Clay sat in front of the huge desk, studying the new security chief as he thought and sipped slowly at his brandy.

"Obviously, the nation would be immensely proud of you and your friends Mister Milton." He even sounded like Jack Steele, albeit without the English accent, Clay thought. "But equally as obviously, they can never know. It wouldn't be sensible to let the people think we can be invaded by a foreign army. Gomez will be referred to, if at all, as a Mexican bandit, vanquished easily by the lawmen of the towns he raided, a Marshall McCandless and his assistant Sheriff Lee, along with a few assorted volunteers."

"I understand, Colonel." Clay fully understood, politics was not his favourite subject but he did truly comprehend the need for a certain amount of secrecy in the matter. "I would like to be able to make sure Sheriff Lee's family is taken care of, and his those of his deputies if you could arrange something."

"I will see to it."

"Thank you Colonel." Clay believed him.

"What will you do now?" Martin asked him.

"I will travel back to Apache Bend, I left a few things unsettled there, James Blue was still very ill when I left, so was the old man Zachariah Smith. And Johnny Hawkeye was missing, he'd gone after the half breed I told you about, it's personal between them."

"Please express to your friends the gratitude of the nation for their efforts and achievements." Martin said. "I wish it were in my power to pay a huge

426

appreciative reward to you all but of course you were not involved in the matter." This caused Clay to grin broadly, Martin would do. He was more like Jack Steele with every word he spoke, only the American manner of speaking betrayed his individuality.

"You find that funny?" Martin queried. "That I cannot pay you?"

"No Colonel, it's just that I've heard the same things before, from Colonel Steele." This time Hank Martin allowed himself a smile.

"He was a good teacher was Jack Steele, I learned a lot from him. He always spoke highly of you and Mister Blue. If ever you and he feel like working for the government again in the future, get in touch."

"No thank you Colonel, I have to go home, to my family, to our ranch, I'm needed there. But I will pass your message on to Bluey."

"I mean it Clay, we can always use men of the calibre of you and Mister Blue."

"And you Colonel, and you." Clay told him with heartfelt genuineness. Hank Martin changed the subject.

"I have it on good authority that we are going to rebuild Fort Boone. A Colonel Philip Beauregarde, an officer of French descent, a good man, has been allocated the commission of command. He will have the survivors of the massacre, Captain Kinross and his Sergeant, Flynn under him and a full complement of men. They are already on route to survey the situation."

The people of Apache Bend had begun to shake off the fear and effects of the Mexican occupancies and atrocities to rebuild a society they could recognise as their own. With Clay Milton away, Shannon had reluctantly assumed the mantle of Sheriff on his own. But he had stressed unequivocally that it was to be a temporary appointment only, to be relinquished as soon as a suitable candidate could be found. He felt uncomfortable in the role of badge wearing lawman.

James Blue remained very weak and fragile, he was unwell and deeply resented the fact that his body would not react as instructed by his brain. The old man, Zachariah Smith was as critically ill through his injury as he had been when Doc. Desmond first treated him. His age and subsequent frailty worked against him and he spent most of his time asleep and snoring loudly in a jagged, uneven manner. The Doctor was convinced that only God and willpower kept the ancient Mountain Man from his grave. If he was waiting for Johnny Hawkeye to return, the hero had better make an appearance before too many more days went by. Even God would run out of patience sooner or later.

The ship's Captain was adamant.

"I am very sorry Sir, but as I've explained to you, we have no spare cabins and the owner's suite is occupied. His cousin is travelling to Spain on important business for the company."

"Senor, Captain. I am sure that if I could speak to him, he would understand and we could reach an agreement. My wife and I need to travel to Spain on urgent business." The tall, ruggedly good looking, smartly groomed and elegantly dressed Mexican gentleman reached into his waistcoat pocket and took from it a handful of gold coins. "If you would just show me to his cabin, my friend." The gentleman's smile was that of a man who thought he could bribe his way to meet the owner's cousin. The Captain took the money offered and smiled back.

"Of course Sir, come with me, but it will do you no good Sir, he is a stubborn man."

"Wait here Sofía, with the bags." The tall man said to his lovely young wife, and followed the Captain up the steps and onto the ship. The Captain led Fernando Lopez to the door of the most luxurious cabin and knocked on the door.

"I will wait out here for you Sir, to escort you off the ship." The Captain told him and moved away.

The door opened and a short, bald man stood half naked in the doorway, behind him Lopez could see the naked figure of a young woman lying on the huge bed.

"What is it? Who are you?" The flustered man barked. "I'm busy."

"I can see that Senor." Lopez told him and pushed by him to enter the cabin. "I have a proposition for you, I am sure you will accept."

Less than a minute later the man came rushing towards where the Captain waited, expecting to see the Mexican and prepared to escort him from the ship.

"Captain!" He shouted, the fear evident in his voice and his expression. "Have the men collect my things, I'm getting off, I'll take the next ship."

"But Sir?" The Captain couldn't believe what he was hearing.

"Do it! Do it now!" The owner's terrified cousin screamed at him.

"Yes Sir, at once." He looked up in wonder as a grinning Fernando Lopez walked towards him.

"Oh, and Captain. I will go and fetch my wife, can you make sure that my bags are brought on board immediately?" Lopez was not asking. The Captain glanced at the trembling bald man for guidance.

"Yes, yes whatever he says, he is to be my guest, and there will be no fare to pay, understand?"

"Yes Sir, of course Sir." The Captain understood.

"One more thing, Captain." Fernando Lopez said as the woman, now fully clothed came out to join her quivering companion. "Please make sure the bedding is changed."

An hour later the many heavy bags were brought to the cabin and stacked as neatly as possible against a wall. Lopez had declined the usual storage facilities available for luggage to make sure they were all kept within easy reach. No one would dare raid the owner's luxury cabin, the extra locks would be a deterrent, but not as formidable as he himself, Fernando Lopez.

"You called me your wife, Fernando." Sofía said quietly as soon as they were alone.

"You are my wife, Sofía." He answered. "We will make it legal when we reach España."

A knock at the door prevented the continuance of the conversation. Lopez got up from his luxury chair and opened the door. The Captain stood holding a tray, it contained a bottle of champagne and two glasses. He didn't usually perform such menial duties himself but curiosity had influenced his actions in this instance.

"Compliments of the Captain and crew, Sir." He handed the tray to the bandido and turned to go, stopped and turned back again to face Lopez. "Can I ask you something?"

"Ask." Allowed the Mexican.

"What did you offer him, the cousin, to let you have his cabin, his passage to Spain? He has enough money, what would be more important to him?"

"That is easy, Captain. His life."

The sun was at its zenith, the unrelenting heat burned into the wounded man as he rode into Stoney Valley. He pulled his horse up outside the Sheriff's office and dismounted, nearly collapsing to the ground as he did so. He tied his mount, and another horse, carrying a large load wrapped in cloth across its back, to the rail with some supreme effort and steadying himself lurched towards the door. He staggered inside and the Sheriff, a small wiry man got up from behind his desk and reached the stranger as he finally fell. He lowered his semi-conscious visitor to the floor.

"What's your name, Son? What happened to you?" He asked him.

"Doctor Howard, can you call Doctor Howard?" The wounded stranger could not say anymore, he'd passed out.

Doctor Perry Howard looked down at the man's wounds, the two most serious, the savagely slashed arm and the shoulder wound above would need stitches. They would leave noticeable scars but would eventually heal without impairing movement. The various accompanying minor lacerations already showed reparatory signs. He was a very tough man was John, as the Doctor had known his patient.

He remembered the strange young man who'd helped him and his wife with his broken down wagon on the trail so long ago. The sleeping man began to stir at last.

"It's Perry Howard, John. Doctor Howard. You're going to be fine." The Doctor quietly told his patient as Johnny Hawkeye opened his eyes.

"Ah, Doc. It's good to see you, I'm sorry if you were busy, I was just passing through." He made to get out of the bed he found himself in. "Where am I?" He was too weak to get up.

"I had the Sheriff bring you here, you're in my house. Ellie June is cooking you a meal, you can stay with us as our guest until you're fit enough to travel." The Doctor gently eased Johnny into as comfortable a sitting position as possible. "I've patched you up as well as I can, you're going to have some more scars but you'll live."

"I have to get to Apache Bend."

"First you have to rest, or you won't make it any further than the cemetery."

"My horses?"

"They're here, I've had a friend of mine look after them for you. He's wrapped your "freight" in a more substantial covering, the smell was overpowering." He waited for Johnny to offer an explanation, it was not forthcoming. He let the matter drop, some things it was best not to know, such as how the horrific injuries had come to be inflicted on the "freight."

Ellie June entered the room and re-introduced herself to her guest, the conversation veered towards more everyday mundane topics, the mood lightened considerably and the weakened, wounded man ate.

A week later, refreshed and healing, slowly but surely, Johnny Hawkeye, wearing a fresh set of clothes purchased on his behalf by Ellie June, said his farewells. He still felt a degree of weakness but was gaining strength every day. Perry and Ellie June stood and watched as he rode away with his gruesome package. An offer of payment for his treatment, care and board had been soundly refused by the indignant Doctor Howard and his wife.

Johnny Hawkeye had a few more matters to take care of, first and foremost he would keep his word and deliver his cargo to Shannon.

A few hundred miles and several days travel to the south another wounded man was being cared for, and nursed back to health. The women of the village and former hideout of Fernando Lopez found the desperately weak and wounded figure of Virgo Séptimo lying where he'd fallen.

Mistakenly they had assumed he alone was responsible for the disappearance of the bandido chief and all his men and therefore their own subsequent freedom. Over the years the women had gained plenty of experience in the treating of gunshot wounds and unwilling to let their saviour die, they applied all their know how to try and help him survive. At first it looked as though their efforts would be in vain, but Virgo was a strong man and after a few hazardous weeks when his chances were touch and go, his resilience began to pay off. He was lucky the shot was made by Sofía and not Lopez, the bullet missed his spine by a fraction of an inch, cracking a rib and tearing through various other bits of him in the process. Had Lopez fired he would undoubtedly be dead. Recuperation would take a long, long time but Virgo was determined to recover, he had things to do, a fortune to recoup.

Chapter Forty Three:

Separate Ways.

The people of Apache Bend had appointed a new Mayor who now entered the Sheriff's Office to address the acting Sheriff, Shannon.

"Mister Shannon, in the time you've been our Sheriff we have had no trouble, and crime is virtually non-existent since the bandits left town. And we the people of Apache Bend would like you to consider taking on the job full time. What do you say?" The Mayor felt as if he was intruding. "We can offer you a generous monthly rate and you can have as many Deputies as you need." He added, hopeful that his powers of persuasion would prevail. They would not.

Shannon took his eyes away from the studying of wanted posters to answer him.

"No thanks Mayor, as soon as my other business here is done, I'm gone. If you can find someone sooner, I'm gone."

"I'm sorry you feel that way, you've done a good job, and the badge suits you."

"The badge is a target. I'm sorry Mayor but I'm not cut out to be a lawman, you need to find another Barton Lee or Clay McCandless, they were made for the job."

"But look where it got them."

435

"Never forget, they died trying to protect you and your people. That's the kind of men you want, not a wandering bounty hunter." Shannon was adamant, he would not be the Sheriff any longer than necessary.

"Well, thank you for your time, Mister Shannon." The Mayor resigned himself to failure. "And thank you for what you have done for us." He left to search for another candidate.

Shannon walked through to the rear of the building to check on the occupants of the cells, there were two people in residence, no prisoners. James Blue, stronger now but under Doctor's orders to take it easy, he was allowed out of bed for short periods to help with his recovery, and Zachariah Smith. The old man was barely conscious for more than a few minutes at a time and fading fast.

"You should think about it Shannon, you'd make a good Sheriff." Bluey told him.

"I don't want it, why don't you take it, I'll stay until you're strong enough?" Shannon suggested.

"I might just do that, but it'll be a few weeks yet, the Doc won't let me do anything."

The conversation ended right then as the door to the Office was opened, Shannon went to investigate as a familiar voice called out to him.

"Shannon, where are you, I've got something for you." The voice was that of Johnny Hawkeye. Shannon came into view, James Blue, moving more slowly walked behind him.

"Glad to see you upright Bluey, how's Zach?" Johnny enquired.

"Not good, he's out back." Bluey gestured for Johnny to visit the cells.

"Your package is on the packhorse, out front." He said to Shannon as he passed by him to go through the Office to the back. "He's a bit ripe, but who said $5,000 would smell good?" Shannon went to inspect his gift, Bluey and Johnny approached the bedridden old Mountain Man.

"Zach, it's Johnny, he's back." Bluey lightly touched the ancient shoulders of Zachariah Smith to wake him, not to startle him.

"Howdy Old Man, what are you doing, lazing around in bed on a perfectly good drinking day?" Johnny said to him in a forced attempt at humour.

"Johnny, is that you? Did you get him this time?" The voice was little more than a dry croak. Johnny leaned over to let the old man see him.

"I got him Zach, it's over, and your family can rest easy now."

"I'll be with them soon, Boy." Zachariah Smith told him and died, his last breath almost inaudible.

Shannon walked in.

"He's gone." Johnny whispered, his eyes watering involuntarily.

"He was only waiting for you, he had to know you were okay, and that you'd got Rattlesnake Joe. I guess you told him right." Bluey commented.

"He told him right, what the hell did you do to the half breed, Johnny? There's bits of him missing." Shannon had inspected the cargo.

"He put up a fight, he was a tough son of a bitch." Johnny supplied accurately and the conversation ended.

Clay Milton got off the train at Apache Bend three days after the funeral of Zachariah Smith. He was sorry, albeit not surprised, at the death of the old man. At least he lived long enough to know that his family had been avenged and his friend Johnny Hawkeye was safe. Doctor Desmond had given the okay for James Blue to resume a limited amount of mobility and the first thing the Australian did was move into the hotel. The four of them met in the nearest saloon to discuss what each of them planned to do now that the mission was completed.

Shannon had a small bundle of wanted posters and intended to leave town in a couple of days to recommence his career as a bounty hunter. He had relinquished his Sheriff's badge with a feeling of relief not shared by the Mayor or townspeople.

James Blue decided he would take the job as Sheriff, offered to him by the Mayor after Shannon's resignation, provided Clay or Johnny, or hopefully both, would stay on for a while to help, at least until he felt fit enough to be able to do the job properly.

Both agreed to stay in the short term but Clay would leave for home as soon as possible, his father needed him to help run the ranch.

Johnny, likewise had agreed to stay awhile but would have to leave before long to take up the position of chief civilian scout at the new Fort Boone. A job offer conveyed to him via Clay Milton from Colonel Hank Martin on behalf of a Colonel Philip Beauregarde, the new Commander of the fort. He would be closer to fulfilling one final commitment, one last piece of unfinished business while based at Fort Boone.

Shannon was the first to leave, the bounty hunter, dressed all in customary black and mounted on his white stallion bid farewell to the three men he'd come to think of as friends. For the first time in living memory he actually looked back, once, as he rode away.

A fortnight later, with Bluey regaining fitness swiftly although not yet completely, Clay Milton took his leave. He left them with an open invitation to visit him at the Milton Ranch at any time.

Another two weeks went by and then Johnny Hawkeye left on his journey to the new Fort Boone. Towards a probable reunion with Captain Bradley Kinross, and of course, his beautiful wife, Sally.

James Blue watched as the scout disappeared from view and then turned to enter his office. The new Sheriff felt fitter than he had since the encounter with General Gomez. Now he would appoint a couple of Deputies to help share the load. He had a few possibilities in mind. The noise of a scuffle penetrated the afternoon silence, it was coming from a nearby saloon. He we go, he thought, and smiled to himself.

He walked out of his office and headed for the swing doors.

Chapter Forty Four:

Back In The Old Routine.

The salon girl noticed as soon as the tall man entered the place. Dressed completely in black he was hard to miss, a cruel, hard face, but something attracted her to him. He ordered a whisky at the bar and she walked up to him.

"Hello stranger, do you want some company?" She asked him. "I would love for you to buy me a drink."

"Sure." The stranger told her and waved to the bartender who was already pouring the girl a glass of the same whisky.

"Thanks Mister, my names Janie, what's yours?"

"Does it matter?" The man in black replied. "Just do me a favour, take this piece of paper over to a man at the front table, there are three of them, give it to the one with his back to the wall. And then get out of the way for a minute or so." The girl shrugged, downed her drink in one and took the folded sheet of paper from him.

"What is it?" Janie asked him.

"Just do it, meet me back here in half an hour." Was the only reply she received.

She shrugged, walked to the table indicated and put it down in front of the startled recipient.

"The man at the bar, the tall one in black asked me to give this to you." She said and quickly left him to unfold the wanted poster. The man was abruptly shaken by the likeness of the face looking back at him, his own. The legends "Wanted" and "Dead or Alive" were supplemented by the words, For Bank Robbery and Murder, Jed Keel. Reward $2,000. Keel looked to where the man in black stood, giving the impression of a man casually sipping his drink. The wanted man knew at once who he was seeing, Shannon. The description fitted, the delivery of the Wanted poster was all part of the way the notorious bounty hunter worked. His methods served to strike fear into the outlaws he hunted, to unnerve them, to get them to make a mistake or in rare instances, surrender. It was a frequently utilised and successful ploy and this occasion would not prove to be any different. Keel spoke in desperation to his two sidekicks.

"The man at the bar, the one in black, it's Shannon, get him." The three of them all clawed at their weapons, two of them swinging to face the bounty hunter, Keel to launch himself at the swing doors, positioned immediately to his right. Three shots were fired, the fleeing Keel felt something slam into his left shoulder but the doors swung open and he was through them. If he'd taken the time to look back he would have been as dead as his two companions.

Ignoring the onslaught of the pain in his shoulder he climbed onto his waiting horse and savagely lashed it with the reins to urge a speedy escape. The horse bucked wildly and the fugitive suddenly found himself tumbling earthwards to land with excruciating agony on his injured shoulder. Stunned, Keel could only watch helplessly and hopelessly at the looming figure of the man in black advancing from the saloon towards him, gun still in hand.

"I took the precaution of hobbling your horse, Keel." Shannon coldly explained. "The poster says "Dead Or Alive." Your choice."

Half an hour later Shannon came back to the saloon. He was carrying two wanted posters, taken from the Sheriff's Office. One a realistic likeness of Fernando Lopez, the other Virgo Séptimo. He was pleased to note the rewards on both of the fugitives had been doubled to $20,000 and $10,000 respectively. Janie was waiting for him. She looked older than her twenty two years, her looks battered and aged by the demands of her profession. She accepted another drink from the bounty hunter and then led him to the back of the room and to the staircase. The man in black took the bottle from the bar and went with her. The boldly coloured and extravagantly patterned carpet had faded and worn with time and the extensive traffic upon its once luxurious pile, of boots from many, many of the saloon's patrons.

Chapter Forty Five:

The Homecoming.

The huge wrought iron arch that framed the air above the gateway to the ranch proclaimed in large ornate lettering that the weary traveller was at last home. The Milton Ranch seemed to be welcoming the return of its long lost prodigal son. Clay rode a little faster on seeing the ranch house in the distance. A rider came towards him from the direction of the large coral, and drawing closer recognised him.

"Clay, God, it's good to see you boy, Josh will be so pleased you're home at last." Ben Foreman, the Foreman of the Milton ranch greeted him.

"Ben, it's good to be back, it's been too long."

Ben Foreman had been taken in by Josh and Margaret Milton as a child, his parents, and friends of the Miltons had been tragically killed in a train crash. They brought him up as one of the family and he had lived in the spacious house with them ever since.

The evening meal was being served as Clay and Ben entered the house.

"Look who I found on the road, we need another place at the table." Ben announced. Margaret burst into tears, leapt up from the table and rushed over to embrace her son. Lindsey, Clay's sister did likewise. Josh and Johnnie, Clay's younger brother stood grinning as the wanderer hugged the women.

"I can't believe it, the pigtails are gone, and you're looking like a woman." Clay exclaimed to his seventeen year old sister.

"I am a woman, you just haven't been here to notice." She retorted.

"And I'm sixteen Clay, a man." Asserted Johnnie. He was a handsome young man and an eagerness to embrace the adventure of adulthood shone out of him with an abundance of enthusiasm.

"I can see you're getting that way." His big brother allowed, not letting the enforced cynicism brought on by his own experiences of the realities cloud his response.

"Did you really fight a war against the Mexicans? How many did you kill?" Johnnie wanted to know.

"It was just a few bandidos, they're gone now." Clay looked to his father as he answered. He caught the older man's eye. Josh nodded, he would back up whatever story his son told.

"But how many did you kill?" The boy pushed on.

"More than I wanted to."

"That's enough talk about killing." Margaret instructed when she finally released Clay from her welcoming embrace. "The poor boy must be hungry, sit Clay, and eat."

"I'll wash up first, Ma, if that's okay." Clay, thankful for a change of subject took his hat off and moved to leave the room.

"Pa said you met Johnny Hawkeye, he's famous, will you tell us all about him?" Johnnie called after his brother, he was not going to let go of his fascination with the notion of exciting adventure.

Clay spent the next few days resting and catching up with life on the ranch. The initial relentlessness of Johnnie's inquisitiveness had eased somewhat, Clay had played down as much of the violence as he could without telling outright lies and the boy's over active imagination had filled in some of the gaps with his own interpretation of events. Josh was keen to let Clay shoulder the responsibility of administration for the ranch, moving it away from himself, while leaving the day to day hands on running things to Ben. Clay could see that his father was becoming old, weary and tired of the task and he soon adapted with an ease which surprised him to role of ranch boss.

Chapter Forty Six:

Reunions.

Sally Kinross emitted a small squeal of pleasure followed by a gentle, fast receding sigh and leaned up to kiss the lips of her lover as he bore down on, and inside her. He completed the spending of his very life force into her eager and demanding young body with a sigh of his own.

"I do love you, Johnny." She whispered, nibbling at his ear as he moved from above to beside her. She gazed at his long, tanned, firmly muscled, powerful body while he lay there, the panting subsiding now. She inspected again, his many and varied scars bearing witness to too many years spent living on the dangerous side of life. Several were newly acquired during the time they'd been apart. Souvenirs of his deadly duel with Rattlesnake Joe. Not wanting to dwell on her lover's violent past life, Sally tried to focus on more pleasant subjects. She pushed a lock of his long dark hair off his face and tasted the sweat from the hollow beneath his Adam's apple.

"I do love you Johnny Hawkeye." She repeated. The object of her undoubted affections smiled warmly at his devoted lover.

"And I love you too Sally." He told her. "But I have to go soon."

"Yes, I know you do." She watched as he swung his legs over the side of the bed and stood up. He always had to go soon. Sally sighed again, this time in resignation to the fact that tomorrow he would be away from her and she would return to her husband. She didn't hate her husband, but she'd long ago fallen out of love with him and the life of a soldier's wife. Bradley Kinross had changed from a kind, polite, considerate husband into a man who drank too much. He'd become a loud, braggart, crude and boastful beyond her ability to tolerate such behaviour.

The scout doffed his hat to her as he opened the door to leave, taking care not to damage the Eagle's feather tucked into the hat band. He reached for his saddlebags and opened one of the side pouches, making room for a shirt Sally had bought for him as a present. A small wrapped parcel fell out onto the floor. He picked it up and looked at it, he'd forgotten all about the gift from the hotel manager and his wife at Muddy Creek.

"What is that, a present from another Woman?" Sally laughed in mock jealousy.

"It was actually, I'd forgotten all about it, the hotel people from Muddy Creek gave it to me." He opened the parcel and showed her the contents, he couldn't supress a grin.

"Looks like I'm famous." He said. The two dime novels were titled "The Adventures Of Johnny Hawkeye." and "Johnny Hawkeye And The Outlaws." Both were colourfully illustrated by caricature type front covers of a tall man in an action pose with a pistol in his hand and a feather in his hatband. The author was credited as "Close Friend And Confidant, Jonas Gordon.

"Can I read them?" Sally requested.

"You can have them, better not let the Captain see them." A smile and he was gone. If he had asked her to leave Bradley and go with him there would not have been a second's hesitation. Sally Kinross would have gone wherever Johnny Hawkeye would take her.

Unbeknown to Johnny or Sally by this time the man of her desires was a legend of the west at twenty six years old, stories circulated the whole country of his adventures and his exploits were featured in dime novels in the Eastern States. They sold astonishingly well, along with those of Kit Carson, Davy Crockett, Buffalo Bill, Jesse James, Wild Bill Hickok and other heroes and outlaws who helped shape the fledgling nation that was to become mighty, The United States Of America. The truthfulness of the heroic tales could not always be verified of course but what did it matter, the essence of the characters shone through.

The Cheyenne chief gazed with pride as the young boy ran towards his father holding a leather pouch out in front of him.

"What have you found, Brave Hawk, my son?" he saw the pouch and wondered where it could have come from.

"A white man gave it to me. He told me to give it to you." The boy told him.

"A white man, where? A white man could not be close without our scouts knowing." The chief was suddenly wary.

"This one could, Black Eagle, my brother." A voice said and it seemed as if from nowhere that the tall figure of Johnny Hawkeye strode into view. Black Eagle gasped in shock and stood up to face his visitor. A quick appraisal was all it took.

"He Who Sees As The Hawk, my brother." The two men rushed to embrace each other.

"It has been many, many moons." The chief exclaimed. "At times I feared for you."

"I gave my word, open the pouch." Johnny told him. Black Eagle did so. The dried remains of Rattlesnake Joe's scalp were exposed. "Our families have been avenged, the scalp hunter is no more." Fighting to contain his emotions the Cheyenne chief turned to his son.

"My son, Brave Hawk, this is no ordinary white man, this is your uncle, this is He Who Sees As The Hawk, you bear part of his name. He is a great warrior."

"I return this to you, your feather." Johnny took the feather from his hatband and presented to its former owner.

"I would like you to keep it, my brother, I know you will not stay with us, you are John. Johnny Hawkeye, a hero to the red man and the white man. You have work to do, to try and bring a lasting peace between our peoples. Keep the feather, remember where it came from." The cavalry scout replaced the feather into its usual position.

"My necklace, do you still have it?"

"I keep it in my tepee for your return, I will fetch it." Black Eagle was gone a few seconds, Johnny was surrounded now by the curious Cheyenne people, some vaguely recognised him from a distant past or memory, most had heard of the legendary warrior. Black Eagle returned carrying the beaded necklace and handed it to Johnny.

"Come here, Brave Hawk." The returning hero called to the son of the chief. The boy meekly did as he was told and Johnny placed the necklace around the neck of the young boy.

"Wear this with pride as I did, you are Cheyenne, and you will be a brave warrior and a strong chief."

"Come, my brother, you will eat with us, you have many stories to tell." Black Eagle said. He threw the scalp of Rattlesnake Joe onto the fire in contempt. "It is done."

The End?

Author's Notes.

The origins of The Savage Ones dates back as far as the late 1950s when the author as a child received a few Britains' model Cowboys and Indians as a Christmas present. Along with the plethora of cowboy movies and T.V. programs coupled with the comic books of the day it was only natural for the western heroes to inspire a fledgling imagination. Initially the first version of the story was written purely for enjoyment by a 9 year old, as a short story based on characters the author had named in his growing collection of toys. It was influenced heavily by the legendary Shane, Cheyenne, Bronco and many John Wayne films and programs. Over the ensuing decades I have revisited the writings and notes occasionally, every now and then updating, incorporating other influences, such as Sergio Leone, Sam Peckinpah and Terry Harknett, who wrote the Edge series of books under the name George G. Gilman. Hopefully improving and enhancing the contents as time and life rolled on. I have tried to preserve the element of youthful enthusiasm and innocence along with the necessary cynicism and grammar coupled with a certain realism in this final expansion.

I would like to think at last The Savage Ones is ready to be enjoyed or endured by a wider readership.

Time will undoubtedly tell.